Manila Demon

Manila Demon

Manila Demon

Thomas Maul

Library of Congress Control Number: 2012903523
ISBN: Hardcover   978-1-4691-7210-1
                 Softcover   978-1-4691-7209-5
                 Ebook   978-1-4691-7211-8

To order additional copies of this book, contact:
Xlibris Corporation
1-888-795-4274
www.Xlibris.com
Orders@Xlibris.com
112578

CONTENTS

CONTENTS

Dedication

This book is dedicated to the three people without whom it would never have materialized. I first thank my friend and fellow writer, Joren Reysoma. You left early but are not forgotten. I also thank H.C. for helping me learn and grow. Finally, I thank Pleshy Wee for her support, kindness and sincerity. I also thank Pleshy for allowing use of the gorgeous picture that graces this cover.

CHAPTER I
Rocks Off

And sometimes when the night is slow,
The wretched and the meek,
We gather up our hearts and go,
A Thousand Kisses Deep.

"A Thousand Kisses Deep"—Leonard Cohen

was all smiles. She was one-hundred and five pounds of danger, evil, mystery, allure and viciousness. Lily was one of the most fascinating people have had the pleasure and misfortune of making acquaintance. She was also pretty. Asian in blood and Caucasian in expression, her intelligence surpassed my own and the irony of still missing her, after all of the horrendous events I suffered, can be accredited to her diabolical wisdom. assumed that I was steering her in my direction, but had no idea that I was a mere pawn in her chess match against bigger entities in the spheres of politics and commerce in Manila. She also infected me with a dark spirit named Aswang, but we'll get to that in due time. Every gaze out of he institution's wire-reinforced windows brings to mind my family. I still ear her lies on sleepless nights, "I love you. I will take care of you the rest f your life. I'm happier than I've ever been." It's all bullshit, but she's wily nd smooth. Hell, happy people don't stop to tell you how happy they are, hey just are. It would be like you stopping to say as you're reading this, I am breathing!" Luckily, I have been saved by an Angel of Mercy named

Reshi, but more about her later. I've barely escaped with my life and my sanity to tell my strange tale. Everything to follow is true.

Everything prior is false. I first met Lily fifteen years ago. I was a full-time college professor and my marriage was on the outs. I'm still not sure if my penchant for drink, sarcasm and isolation was responsible for the dissolution, or if the squabbling was responsible for my thirst, but it's the old chicken and the egg, yes? I generally managed to keep my drinking to weekends. I would claim the bedroom, with at least two cases of beer as provisions and kept a bottle of vodka under the bed for heavy artillery. Oh, how I looked forward to the weekends. Each Thursday brought joy, knowing that the paradise of oblivion was near. As the relationship became more cantankerous, my alcohol intake increased with renewed self-righteous justification. When the word divorce began rearing its head, it triggered a trip to the doctor to procure a hydrocodone prescription for my feigned back troubles.

It was during this time that I began visiting social networking sites and making friend requests for fetish models, deviants, anarchists, porn stars and pretty much any colorful outcast. My simple criteria, they had to look good and think crazy. I cannot recall which adult film star that Misanthropic Lily was a friend of, since I sent requests by the dozens and hoped to get a few acceptances for my efforts. Everyone used pseudonyms here. It was a shady world of deceit, lust, wild ideologies and freedom; all from the comfort and privacy of the bedroom. What more could a twisted mind ask for? I began to devote an unhealthy amount of time to researching potential perverted and provocative pen-pals.

While scouring the friends of one professional, I saw Misanthropic Lily's profile picture, slender, Asian, silky long black hair, perfect smile and a face of exquisite beauty. I hesitated to add her as a friend for fear that she may not be real. I reasoned that no woman this beautiful would waste her time being the online friend of a porn star. I clicked "add as friend" and hoped for the best. This was the dark ages of MySpace, before Facebook became the trend. I continued my research and continued to drink. This single click would irreparably alter the course of my life and end the lives of others.

The next morning, I rubbed my throbbing temples while checking my e-mail. I saw Lily had added me and I instantly felt less hung-over. I clicked the link to Lily's profile before even getting my morning coffee and painkillers. I was elated! Her writing was flawless, cynical, scathing, brilliant and full of dark-edged humor. Her pictures were sexy and hypnotic. I only wondered, aloud, mumbling to myself, "Is she real?" It seemed too good to be true. A rebellious, tortured, intellectual soul whose pictures were making me slightly aroused; she was everything I dreamed of. I went to brew coffee. I had a job to do. I had to make certain she was legit.

I tried to keep my first message friendly and light. I told her a little bit about myself and asked her a few questions. She was from Manila, a place I'd heard of but had no idea where or even what country it was located in. My cloudy mind conjured up prostitutes, opium dens and Asian gangsters. I associated Manila with ideas of decadence and depravity. Apparently, somewhere in my reading, I had heard things about this city, things that were wickedly delicious. I could not recall just where, but Manila conjured up ideas of an Oriental bohemian paradise.

I sent the message, not sure if she would reply or if she even checked her messages frequently. Someone added me, so I knew there was life at the other end. It was a crapshoot. I also wrote messages to a few models and went about my business of taking pills and turning up the volume of the Rolling Stones as my buzz increased. My bitchy bride went somewhere and was morbidly content in my isolation. It was the way we both liked it.

Later, that very evening, I was thrilled to see a reply from Lily in my in-box. Not only did she answer every question I had asked her, she also asked me some in return. I was ecstatic that the conversation would keep going. She was hot, smart and interested in my life—in my pathetic life! I had plenty of papers to grade and lectures to prepare, but these became completely unimportant. All that mattered to me at that moment was Lily—my Lily—my lovely, caring and dark-humored Asian sensation, Lily.

She was very cordial, matter-of-fact and friendly. She asked me about my preferences in music and books, two of my favorite topics. I smiled, cracked my knuckles, and got down to the task at hand. Somehow, it was easy to open up and be honest with someone I barely knew, particularly when she was living somewhere on the other side of the world. I told her about my work, my education and my tastes in art, music and literature. I also told her about my miserable marriage and the myriad amount of injustices my soon to be ex had incurred against me. I had five paragraphs and finished with a plea of "I hope you really are the person in your pictures and not just some fat pervert typing from his ailing mother's basement in Milwaukee."

After sending the message, a few unmemorable days passed. Work was work and each day when I returned home, I went straight to the computer.

Every day I checked my e-mail. On weekends, it was a few times through the day. An entire week passed and I was worried. I barely knew Lily and was missing her already. I mean, I had some other girls that I was writing to, but their messages were brief, dull and mostly full of awkward grammar. Finally, a reply from Lily came. The other women did not even compare to her high energy, witty phrasing and personable expression. Lily was craftier with American slang than most Americans. She was also hipper to American culture than most Americans. She did not even address my woeful marriage, which showed wisdom and tact. She talked about Bob Dylan and Jim Morrison and *The Omen* and Edgar Allan Poe. She told me how she did not believe in god and how religious hypocrites really got under her skin. She also expressed her view that most wars were due to religious beliefs, and expressed it rationally and logically. She joked about pornography, necrophilia and sodomy. How I was fascinated with the radical ideas of this brilliantly vulgar angel. She felt that " . . . most priests are just molesters in robes . . . carnality will always win over unnatural man-made rules of hypocrisy. It is the way we are and nothing we pretend to do can change it."

And, yes, dear reader, my own carnality was relishing every word. Not that I had a beef against God, but more an indifference, fueled by booze, pills, porn and miscellaneous diversions. Every radical idea she expressed was like cool, clear water to a man dying of thirst. Plus, she assured me that her pictures were her real pictures and that maybe we could talk by webcam when she got to know me better. I had a new friend. I had someone who was more interested in me than my soon to be ex. In thinking, she was as tough as any guy and experienced in the world. She knew things and had done things. Physically, she was graceful, slender, willowy and beautiful.

Eventually we exchanged messenger names and began to occasionally chat in real time. Lily was very computer savvy and knew how to convert files, download files, what programs to use with files, websites that had endless torrents and how to convert and alter pictures. When it came to computer skill, she was light years ahead of me. She was also kind enough to teach me how to do things. I also finally got the pleasure of chatting with her on webcam. She was real. She was gorgeous, intelligent and dark-humored. I was beginning to like her and think about her more and more with each message exchange and webcam session. She claimed to like me.

Over the next few years, we continued to stay in touch. Many changes came about. On my end there was divorce, foreclosure, moving, new jobs and new girlfriends. Sometimes we chatted for a few hours, other times months would pass before we communicated. When either one of us had the time and inclination, we knew the other one would soon make themselves available. It was always easy to get each other up to speed on the goings on of our individual lives. Lily was always a kind and sympathetic listener and offered her insights and support. It felt easy to pour my woes out to her. She became a close friend over the years.

My life took some drastic turns over these years. I gave up drinking and drugging. I resolved to put away all mind altering substances on a New Years Day about nine years ago. This decision came after spending that New Years Eve with the barrel of a loaded shotgun in my mouth. My beagle named Ballsack (yes, I named my dog Ballsack, don't worry about it) licked my leg and I fell to my knees and cried out for God to help me. And I was helped, for awhile.

Life improved for me over the next few years. My finances, relationships and mental health were all moving in a positive direction. I was in a better mood the majority of the time. I was still compulsive enough to enter a relationship with a busty college student during the fall semester of my second year of being sober. Her name was Jan and she was built like a Playboy bunny. She was also an alcoholic. This became apparent when she arrived at my house at ten in the morning and had whiskey on her breath.

"You must have partied hard last night, huh?" I asked.

"Yes, and I had a few this morning too."

"Already?"

"Well, I was nervous about driving over here."

The relationship lasted a mere three weeks. The sex was great, but everything else was chaotic. I poured my woes out to Lily and she was attentive and caring. This was the period of time when the serious consideration of a relationship began to take root. The timing was perfect, as Lily had just ended a long relationship a month prior to a gentleman who refused to commit.

These are the events leading to my own commitment to Lily, which in turn led to my commitment to demonic madness, which led to me committing murders, which in turn led to my commitment at Hoffman Mental Health Center (yes, my dear reader, I am certifiably insane and have the paperwork to prove it). Can you trust my story? Well, I leave you to make your own judgment. Nothing breeds skepticism more than an appeal to one's trustworthiness, at least for discerning minds. I will assure you that my motives for telling my saga are straightforward. It is partly a plea to God for forgiveness. It is partly a confession of crimes against man and nature more grotesque than the rational mind can comprehend. Mainly, I tell my story because it's a release, a catharsis. The demon moves from person to person through intercourse, and not just physical, but ideological as well. Proceed with caution, gentle reader, and be forewarned, ignorance is bliss. If you'd rather not risk being contaminated by evil, then put the book away now. You've been warned fairly.

Lily and I began to talk more frequently that spring. Flowers bloomed as my love for her grew. She was home more on the weekends and I no longer had weekend female guests. Despite being twelve hours ahead of me in time, we began to spend many hours together on webcam and phone each weekend. I was slowly and steadily falling in love with this far away Asian beauty. I knew I had to meet her in person. I had to touch her and feel her and experience the chemistry we shared when we were physically together. I bought my ticket to Manila.

A few days later, I was talking to my friend Pete and he mentioned how he was planning a trip to Cabo San Lucas. I told him of my plans to go to Manila. "I'm going there to visit this chick I've been talking with for a few years, Lily," I stated, proudly showing him a picture of her that I kept on my phone.

"Wow," he uttered, "Does she have any friends or sisters?" This seemed to be the instant question that every male I showed her picture to would ask. I have to confess, it flattered my ego a bit. It's always a fine line between cockiness and confidence, but boys will be boys.

Pete was able to get his ticket on the same flight. He also had a million questions that I had no time, patience or interest for. "I'm just going there to be with Lily. That's my plan." I would answer. This would shut him up for about one hour, when he would call again. I just repeated the plan until he finally realized I did not really care about anything beyond being with Lily. We made reservations at a condominium in Malate, the Mirage. We would be staying in a two-bedroom unit, on the nineteenth floor overlooking Manila Bay. We were both eager and excited to travel.

The night guard reads my notebook on his shift, but more about him later. Perhaps he can better understand how a once well respected professor, an upstanding member of the community, now finds himself in the mental ward. I would behoove you to at least tell me that you are reading it and refrain from being sneaky about it. Sneakiness and deception turn me disdainful. But I am confident

*that my sordid tale is of little interest to most of the workers here.
After all, they have their own lives to be interested in and the mad
scribbling of another loony patient is of minor interest. If you are
reading this and you work here, please call the exterminator and
have a professional kill the legion rats in the walls!*

The twenty-three hour flight to Manila was not so bad. The worst part
f it was the stress of smuggling thirty-six jelly dildos in my suitcase. Why,
ou ask? Well, Lily's friend, Reshi, runs a number of different businesses
nd one of her stores sells sex toys. Apparently, jelly dildos are expensive and
ard to find in Manila, so I was asked by Lily to bring as many "devices"
ith me as I could, and that I would be compensated for more than my
riginal investment. She also told me Reshi was quite hot and proved it
y sending a picture of the two together. Reshi was even hotter than Lily,
hich made it much more thrilling to smuggle and deliver the goods. I
as nervous when imagining the Manila customs agent scolding me in
foreign tongue while waving a dildo in my face, before escorting me
way in handcuffs. I was also worried about explaining to Pete just why
felt it was important to travel with three dozen jelly dildos. There were
o problems coming into Manila, though. The airport was hustling and
ustling with Filipinos and the guards were laissez faire in their inspection
f checked luggage. The uniformed customs lady simply smiled at me and
aid "hello" as I rolled my contraband of cocks through the gate.

The throng of people outside of the airport was a bit unnerving. Horns
lowing, police whistles, people shouting in a foreign language and just
lain crowded. In this sea of people, I instantly spotted Lily. Her smile, her
ilky hair and her graceful movement as she approached me made all of the
oise; the confusion and the mayhem instantly fade away. We embraced.
My heart raced as we hugged. Sure, it sounds lame, but the heart makes
p its own mind, and I was at the mercy of its passion and desire. We
ade our way back to her mini-van where Pete and I fit our luggage into
he back. I sat up front, admiring Lily, as she maneuvered the van into the
haos of the Manila night traffic.

There were cars going in all directions and pedestrians everywhere
eandering through the streets. There were old men on wobbly bicycles
ith baskets of produce working their way through and in between lanes of
raffic. The rundown, ramshackle squalor of boarded buildings and rusty
orrugated metal, with shoeless families squatting around a food kettle on
he ground was a lot to absorb. People were living in holes of concrete walls

and toddlers were sifting through debris on the side of the road. I have traveled throughout the United States, Spain, Japan and even Mexico, but apart from a few areas of Mexico, had never witnessed poverty to such an extent. I mentally questioned our safety in this bizarre city of extremes, the haves and the have-nots, with little apparent middle-class. Lily was among the haves and reassured me of our safety.

"This place is fucking insane," I stated.

"This reminds me of some poor areas when I lived in L.A." added Pete.

"If you are with me, you do not have to worry about anything. Nobody is going to fuck with you," said Lily, in a matter-of-fact tone that enhanced the credibility of her claim.

We continued through the traffic, my eyes glued to the foreign night life. The energy and congestion of the streets made me think it was like New York City on steroids.

"And here is where you will be staying," said Lily, pulling in front of a high-rise building that had a sign over the entrance: The Mirage. Pete and I pulled our luggage from the back and Lily parked the van around the corner. We checked in and took the elevator up to the nineteenth floor.

The room was not bad, not too plush, but furnished, clean and spacious. Pete took his luggage to his room, after some negative critique of the furnishings and a minor tantrum about not getting the larger room. I brought my luggage into my room. Lily entered, closing the door. We hugged and kissed.

"I'm happy to be with you in person, finally" I said, holding her in locked hands behind the small of her petite, yet muscular, back.

"Me too; you're more gorgeous in person than on cam. Did you bring Reshi's things?"

"Yes, three dozen" I laughed, "I never thought I would become an international sex toy smuggler. I was scared as hell coming into Manila. You want to see them?"

"No, she'll pick them up tomorrow." She moved out of my embrace. "I need to leave soon. Have work tomorrow. You are probably tired as hell, aren't you?"

"Not really," I lied, "I just want to be with you for awhile." I gently led her towards the bed, as she laughed and resisted.

"Hold on, I need beer." She stated, before leaving the room, pulling some money from her purse, and heading towards the door. "Do you want anything at the store downstairs?"

"No"

"Okay, I wrote down some rules, do's and don'ts for surviving Manila when I'm not with you. Look these over while I'm gone." She handed me the list. I read the common-sense rules while she was gone:

> *Malls near you:*
>
> *MOA (Mall of Asia): cab fare shouldn't tally more than 100 pesos.*
>
> *RP (Robinson's Place): cab fare shouldn't take more than 75 pesos. Tip cabbies 20-50 depending on attitude.*
>
> *Buy something at convenience store to break big bills; outdoor vendors don't have change.*
>
> *Do not carry big bills when walking on the streets.*
>
> *Do not drink 'weird' drinks, like those ones with stuff floating in them. The water used is unsanitary.*
>
> *Tap water here is not fit for drinking. Get bottled water from the supermarket.*
>
> *Always use metered cabs. If cab does not have meter, look for another one.*
>
> *Absolutely wear no gold jewelry when combing through the streets.*
>
> *Stay away from dark alleys at night.*
>
> *Lastly, do not ever, as in NEVER, drink or eat anything anyone gives you if you don't know them. There's a gang called 'Ativan Gang' here that targets unsuspecting foreigners, robbing them blind after they've passed out.*

She returned fifteen minutes later with a bag full of beer and began placing them inside the refrigerator.

"I hope I don't get mugged by Ativan Gang," I joked.

"You read the rules?" she smiled.

"Yes, thank you for writing them down. You look beautiful, I must say." I approached her and hugged her closely.

"Thank you for saying that, but no sucky fucky tonight," she replied. "I need to be leaving now. I will call you tomorrow, okay?"

"Alright, let me walk you down to the van."

"No; trust me. It's much safer if I just go by myself."

I was puzzled and a bit wounded in my ego. "Why?"

"Because here, nobody dares mess with me; just trust me. Now lock the door and get your handsome ass to sleep."

Later, I would find out the truth. Nobody in Manila would dare to mess with her. I locked the door and watched her walking down the hallway toward the elevator. Her arms swung, business-like, and her body had a slight lean forward. She walked like a tough chick, a badass all one-hundred and five pounds of her. She was bossy, blunt, vulgar and beautiful. I loved how she used the "f" word in all its variations and with such frequency.

Pete and I explored Mabini Street the next morning. We ate breakfast at Jollibee and went to a park and some shops and visited the street vendors. We also visited an internet café to let friends and family know that we arrived safely. This was just a breakfast, scouting run, so we made it back to the Mirage within a few hours. After returning to room 1911, Pete complained of jet-lag and was going to take a nap. I decided to check out the pool on the fifteenth floor.

The pool was large, Olympic sized, and the water was crystal clear. It looked very inviting, and I was the only one there. I took a seat on the edge and allowed my bare feet to dangle in the water. I was relaxed and daydreaming, for a few minutes, when I heard a high-pitched screeching noise. Directly across the pool from where I sat was a small cat-sized, rat. It stopped scurrying and its pink, fleshy tail swirled over the edge of the pool, dipping partially in the water. It turned its head and stared at me with its beady black eyes. The long, white whiskers twitched as it continued to stare directly at me. I wondered how this rat's life was like in Manila, as compared to rats back home. It looked more horrendous than United States' rats, and I could even smell it from across the pool, the mangy wet-dog that rolled around in road kill smell. I sat, transfixed, from the ugliness and continued in the silent stare-down. One side of its mouth lifted, revealing a huge set of sharp teeth. The creature was smirking at me! I felt a darkness upon me that can only be described as a sudden impending black infusion of evil. I broke the gaze and hurried away from the pool, not even bothering to look back. I felt weak; it was like he was telling me to leave before things turn grotesque. I never mentioned the rat to Pete or anyone, until now. In hindsight, this incident was an omen, a warning that I failed to heed or recognize. It was a vile message to get out of there while I still could, but I failed to take it serious, since I was in love. Love conquers all, they say, even common sense, or, in my case, common sanity. I had been given fair warning.

That night we met up in Makati at the Wagon Wheel. The plan was to introduce Pete to the sister of Lily's friend and invite her along for the three day trip to Boracay. Ann was in her twenties and her English was not too great. She served as an underling to her older sister, who married the Australian moneyman behind the restaurant investment. It was a

ypical Manila Cinderella story; farm girl meets rich expatriate and family
uddenly rises in social standing. Only in this case, the family had to keep
he restaurant running. Ann was a manager over her three younger sisters
nd appeared to relish in her limited sphere of power to hide the naïve
nd insecure aspects of her personality. She tried to act and dress the part
f businesswoman/ tycoon, but only a forty-second conversation was
ecessary to gauge the shallowness of her intellect. Pete could have cared
ess. Being in his fifties, there was something about spending three days
1 a tropical paradise with a girl in her mid-twenties that allowed him to
verlook any mental or personality deficiencies. She agreed to meet us at
1e airport the following morning.

Lily called her driver, Sonny, and he was at the Wagon Wheel within
ve minutes to drive us back to the Mirage. When Lily spoke, Sonny
stened attentively, he also referred to her as "boss". Lily explained that he
as worked for her father many years and was one of his most loyal and
rustworthy employees. Lily left with Sonny after dropping us off at the
Mirage. It was late and Pete and I were both exhausted from the long flight.
We agreed a good sleep was in order before boarding the plane the next
1orning to Boracay. Sleep came easy and I was out cold until three in the
1orning when the phone Lily had given me began to ring.

"Hello" I mumbled, barely conscious.

"Hey handsome, wakey, wakey hand off snakey. Reshi's on her way
or the toys," stated Lily. I could barely open one eye to see the clock said
1ree-twenty something.

"She's coming here?"

"Yes, in a few minutes. Get your sweet ass up."

"Okay" I mumbled, hanging up. I threw on some clothes and stumbled
o the suitcase. I pulled the two bags out when there was a knocking at the
oor. I hoped Pete didn't wake up and come out of his room because I did
ot want to have to explain the late night dildo exchange.

I looked through the peep-hole and saw two large, muscular Filipino
1en in tight t-shirts. Then I noticed the gorgeous woman standing
1-between them. If Lily was the Audrey Hepburn of Manila, then Reshi
as the Raquel Welch. She was shorter than Lily, but well-built, chesty,
urvaceous and the energy and charisma to light up a dark room. Where
.ily was good at pretending to have class as occasion called for it, Reshi
as just classy. She was dressed like a fashion model, tight black skirt, black
eels, in a white silk transparent blouse and smelled heavenly. Her smile
as electrically contagious.

"Hi Tim; how are you? It's so nice to finally meet you! I'm Lily's friend, Reshi," she said, extending her hand. To be honest, dear reader, yours truly wanted to kiss her hand, and more. There was an aura of sexuality about Reshi that made me aroused in just the five seconds of meeting her. I wanted to embrace her, but controlled my urge. In terms of raw sensuality, I have met few women that compare to Reshi. Just being near her was arousing.

"Lily said you brought three dozen and paid ten each. I will give you six-hundred," she said with a flirtatious smile. One of her henchmen then extracted a money-clip from his pocket and peeled six one-hundred dollar bills off into my hand. The other guy grabbed the two bags. Reshi giggled, "Aren't my guys hot?"

"I'm not sure about that," I answered, a bit shocked by her brazenness.

"I am, but don't you worry, Tim, I think you're kind of hot, too, in an American sort of way."

"Do you? Here I thought it was just the dildos."

"Those helped, but your blue eyes help more."

"Do you want to stay for awhile? There's some beer in the fridge."

"I really can't, this time, Tim. Anyway, sorry about waking you up; I was in the area. We will be leaving. I look forward to seeing you next week when you guys get back from Boracay. Don't do anything there I wouldn't do!"

"Okay, I won't; and it was great to meet you, Reshi, bye for now!" I watched them walk down the hall. I went back to bed aroused as I fell back to sleep. The sensual aura of Reshi was a tough mental image to let go of. Her vivacious beauty was intoxicating. "Screw going to Boracay, I thought, "I want to spend more time with Reshi." Men are simple creatures, a fact both Reshi and Lily were well aware of.

Chapter II

Loving Cup

Did you ever wake up to find
A day that broke up your mind
Destroyed your notion of circular time
It's just that demon life has got you in its sway

"Sway"—The Rolling Stones

Lily arrived the following morning and we ordered a breakfast of adobo from the Aristocrat. After breakfast, we caught a cab to the airport. Ann was to meet us there before we checked in with Cebu Pacific. Pete was scouring the crowd of people for his young angel. "There she is," he announced happily, walking to meet her. She was wearing an olive green business suit, which seemed kind of an odd choice for a weekend getaway to the beach. We got in line and boarded.

Our plane was unable to land at Caticlan due to weather, so it landed at a smaller airport further south, Kalibo. We had to ride a bus back to get to the ferry to take us to Boracay. The bus careened around narrow jungle-like terrain and steep cliffs without guardrails. I kept my attention on Lily, sitting next to me, and stole glances of her legs. She was no Reshi, but she wasn't bad.

After a short boat ride, we arrived at the tricycle taxi (motorbikes with a welded passenger seat attached) area. These motorbikes were the common means of transportation on Boracay. We bumpily rode our way down the main tourist strip, past shops, restaurants, hotels and finally came to our destination, a cozy series of cottages on the beach called Sea Winds Resort.

Lily and I entered our room while Pete and Ann went to theirs around the corner. The rooms were homey, spacious, all hard-wood floors and the best feature—not one clock in the place. We could see the blue beach from our room and the aqua water was only a short walk down the powdery white sand. The Sea Winds had a plush buffet, so we ate there and, after dinner, Lily and I walked on the beach as the sun went down.

The Boracay sunset is a splendid sight, and we watched it together, hugging, kissing and laughing. The soft sand, gentle, warm breeze, orange sunset, neon blue water all worked together for the benefit of our romance. I showed off a little for Lily by walking on my hands. She called a peddler over and bought fish chips, pork rinds and balut. "If you eat balut, I will eat balut," she challenged. It was on. I was somewhat leery about eating partially evolved duck embryo, but I wanted to see Lily eat it. Part of what made it tough for me was seeing the grubby cooler it came out of with the word "baloot" sloppily misspelled on the side.

I peeled the innocent looking brown egg and began to eat the murky, slime covered ball inside. Not only was it gamey, but the yolk never seemed to end in my mouth, every chew made it grow. There were also some unexpected culinary speed-bumps in the way of tiny feathers and the crunchiness of a tiny beak near the last bite. When I finished, I pounded on my chest with a fist in order to help keep it down. With watery eyes, I said, "Okay, a bet is a bet, your turn, dear."

"Okay," she agreed, smiling. She quickly peeled the egg, then popped the entire embryo ball into her mouth and swallowed it in its entirety with little fanfare. Then she chased it with a swill of beer. "I don't fuck around when it comes to nasty stuff." I was amazed, and completely seduced by her intensity.

When we returned to our room, we made love for the first time. I did not want to close my eyes while kissing her, or while being intimate with her. We proceeded to have some fantastic physical fun. Being with Lily ranks way up there in my personal highlights reel, though my thoughts drifted towards Reshi occasionally. It was a splendid Boracay free-for-all fuckfest.

Afterwards, we lay next to each other and talked. I asked her about the tattoo of Chinese letters on her shoulder. "It stands for one who kills others," she replied, before taking a sip of beer. I chuckled, amused at her seriousness.

"Like a killer?"

"Exactly"

"Isn't that kind of weird when Chinese people see it?" I asked.

"There's a reason behind it," she began, "you may find out or you may ot. Let's just enjoy Boracay for now."

Judging by her serious tone, I figured best not to bring it up again, hough I was still curious. "I like you, Lily."

"I like you, too, Tim. And I never say things like that. Let's go to sleep ow. Your ass is going to walk the beach with me in the morning."

I buried my face into Lily's long, black silky hair and slept peacefully nd content there all night long. Lily was up before any sliver of sunlight 1ade an appearance. "Let's go walk," she stated, while taking a bunch of ifferent vitamins with swigs of bottled water. The night before, I watched his petite beauty down at least twenty beers, and here she was at 5 A.M. ompletely unaffected, appearing like a model in Ms. Health and Fitness 1agazine. I loved the chameleon ways about her, the ability to vacillate etween extremes. She could change roles at any time and play all to erfection. Her versatility matched the contrast of her city, Manila. She was, fter all, a product of her city. I would come to despise this broad-ranged amut quality of hers, but for now it was endearing and for the city it emains so.

This walk was no romantic stroll on the beach to admire the sunrise. ↴o, not at all; this walk was a marathon of endurance and speed. The first 1ile or so, I enjoyed with no trouble. I could keep up with her pace. The 1n rose a bit higher, and it seemed, so did her pace. Her arms swung like ›ng pendulums, eyes fixed forward and body leaning slightly forward to eep her momentum steadily brisk. As her pace increased, so, too, did the ›rward lean of her body. I continued to fall behind, usually pretending that found an interesting shell or some other trinket, then catching my breath nd running to catch back up with her. For her, this was mere exercise, for 1e, it was a death march. Luckily, she stopped somewhere between about x and eight miles; she had to, since the beach ended and the wall of a cliff ⁻ould not allow passage. We took some memorable pictures, me happily lowning in the aqua water, her with the seascape in the background. On 1e return walk, the sun was higher, and hotter. Her pace remained the ame, relentless. I was dying. The girl was hardcore.

We enjoyed a breakfast buffet back at the hotel. After breakfast, I egan the "process". Pete wanted to go scuba diving, jet skiing and every ther expensive tourist trap diversion that the island had to offer. I just ⁻anted left alone to work on my process: step one being to simply float nd swim in the aqua blue water, which was remarkable even while one was swimming in it. After forty-five minutes on step one, it was on to step two of the process: walk up the beach to the pool of the Sea Winds and float in there for about 45 minutes. Step three was simply to walk to the room and get hugs and kisses from my Asian companion, then have coffee and a snack, if needed, and then repeat the cycle. This rotation was continued throughout the day. Lily, not wanting her skin to be exposed to the sun, stuck to her own process: drink beer and stay in the shade.

That evening, after Pete and Ann returned and the four of us had the dinner buffet, we all walked down the beach in search of a club. Lily was on a mission to get Ann hammered. So far, it was successful since she couldn't find her sandals to walk down the beach, only after a few glasses of wine. The night scene on the beach was lively. People were dancing, juggling and vendors were hawking their goods. I saw stairs leading up to a place with techno music blaring and lots of lights flashing, so I motioned everyone to come up the stairs with me. We managed to elbow our way through the crowd and find a small table in the back of the place. I'm not sure when it dawned on me that this was a gay club, but it might have been when I saw two guys dancing at the stripper pole in the middle of the dance floor.

"You brought us to a gay bar," shouted Pete.

"Yeah Tim, why?" added Lily, just to bust my chops a bit more.

"I had no idea what kind of bar it was," I countered, "Just remember, what happens in Boracay, stays in Boracay."

"Sounds like you'll be sleeping with someone else tonight. Just sayin'" added Lily, while lighting a cigarette.

The next morning, our final morning there, Lily was up well before the dawn. I found it amazing that she only needed four hours of sleep to function on. I heard her wake up and was secretly praying that I would not have to endure another death march. I was relieved when she suggested just going down to the beach to watch the sunrise. It was still dark and it was only the two of us. We took pictures and made out. This morning of us being together, alone on the beach, was as good as it would ever get. There was an ominous darkness on the horizon. Regardless of the ugliness and horrific events that eventually put my sanity over the precipice, I do cherish the memory of this innocent morning in Boracay with Lily. Afterwards, it was all uphill, upside-down and sideways.

"I should not have told you the things I told you last night," she stated looking directly into my eyes.

"It's fine, Lily; I can hold my dirt. Nobody will ever hear a word about from me." I replied. She continued to stare into my eyes. There was a ong, awkward moment of silence.

"You got that right," was her reply, in a serious, emotionless tone that vas chilling. I sensed a cooler breeze and had a premonition that things vould never quite be the same between us again. The knowledge of her vil apple and my curiosity in asking for details had caused a fall in the elationship, which was now tainted. To be honest, I took the things she ad told me the night before with a grain of salt, placing them in the nental category of tall tales a drunk person makes up to create awe in the stener. Now, I wasn't so sure. She seemed so serious. I tried to recollect etails of her inebriated confession the night before.

It started when we returned to the room after the gay bar. Lily opened vhat must have been at least her twentieth beer of the evening. I was not rinking, but I was looking forward to more rounds of thrilling romps in ne sack with her.

"Can I trust you?" she asked.

"Of course," I replied.

"I've done some bad things," she began.

"Haven't we all?" I replied, taking my shirt off.

"No, listen, I mean really bad things. Things I've not shared with nyone, things that if I tell you, you must promise to never share with nyone, not Pete, not your brother . . . not anyone."

"No problem," I answered, used to these kinds of drunken theatrics :om years of growing up with an alcoholic grandmother around.

"You may not want to be with me in a relationship after hearing these nings. I'm cool with that, but I would rather you know how I really am."

"Okay, let's hear it," I replied.

"The tattoo I have is true. I am one who kills others."

"You have killed people?" I asked. This was becoming interesting, specially while looking at the hundred-five pound, willowy, lithe, and etite Asian beauty with pouty lips in front of me.

"This was years ago, I worked with people in the Arroyo administration nd many of the local politicians in Manila. This administration had people ney needed terminated. I hired people to kill people," she stated, not miling or blinking an eye. Her earnestness in tone made the confession onvincing.

I considered what she was telling me. It was years ago, it was in a place n the other side of the world from where I was from and she wasn't the one pulling the trigger. "Well, if it was a while ago and you're not doing it anymore, then it's all good. Hell, Lily, we've all done things that we regret, right?" I tried to console her, but the ulterior motive running through my mind was simply the selfish hope of continuing the awesome vacation with her.

"Children were killed. Things went wrong. I was responsible for innocent kids being murdered, along with intended targets. I had to get away from the business after that," she stated, before taking a long pull of beer.

"Like, the guys you hired just killed everyone in the house?"

"Yes, sort of."

Now it was sounding worse, but she did not tell them to kill whole households. "Well, that's more on them than you. You didn't tell them to kill everyone."

She released a deep sigh, "I also tortured, kidnapped, maimed, pimped, bribed and blackmailed."

I'm not sure I even wanted to know or believe what I was hearing. I did not know what to say, "Well, you just hired people to do these things, right?"

"It's all the same, Tim. Manila is one messed up place in some ways. The politicians are just gangsters in suits. All of them have their hands dirty in drugs, murder, prostitution, bribery, payoffs, loan-sharking, extortion and bribes. They are simply criminals with immunity. To survive well here requires getting your hands dirty."

She did not mention any specific names, outside of the Arroyo administration, and my general knowledge of Manila politics was sparse. I was intrigued, but more immediately interested in how Lily looked in her black panties. It seemed like she was being sincere, even if she had lots to drink. Lily had a higher tolerance than most large men. She was even able to function normal in the mornings, appearing happy, sensible and healthy, regardless of how she may have felt. I had to accept the fact that, somewhere in the past, Lily ran in a circle of corrupt politicians and men who did crimes, like murder, for money. I accepted it, and chose to disregard it.

At least, these shady days were behind her. After all, dear reader, she would not have felt compelled to confess these things if they were not part of her past and were troubling to her conscience, right? With Lily, however, things often had a way of being more complex than they appear, partly because her mind runs like a computer chess program, two moves ahead of whoever she is paired with. I would later learn, at great price, she was also a master of deception.

We left Boracay in the morning, after one more outstanding pork
ocino breakfast at the Sea Winds. Other than seeing policeman at the small
irport drinking beer on the job, the flight back to Manila was uneventful.
Our taxi back to the Mirage took much time and many turns through
rowded streets in order to drop Ann off at her home. We got back to the
Mirage and ordered pig knuckle and golden noodles. Pete went for a walk
own Mabini Street after we ate. I used the time alone with Lily to try to
auge how she felt about me.

"Do you like me as much as I like you?" I asked.

"Yes, Tim, I do, and, frankly, it scares me."

"How come; is it because you're not used to it?" I asked her, while
etting a little lost in her fascinating eyes.

"No, because, well, forget it." I wasn't sure what her response meant,
ut as she kissed me, it took away some confusion.

For the next three days, we had a great time in Manila, though things
egan to get strange. We shopped at Robinson's Mall in Malate, Mall of
sia in Makati and Lily's sister, Jenna, met up with us at Green Hills to
elp with getting a good price on pearls. My plan was to buy a bunch of
earl necklaces and take them back to the U.S. with me to resell at a profit
n internet auctions.

Jenna was very pretty in her own right and a bit more outgoing and
ess complicated than Lily. She was congenial and open, but it was her
ift for negotiating that was truly amazing. She took me to the booths of
he pearl merchants and gave me a crash course in size, appearance, luster
nd value differences between the hundreds of different pearls and bright
orals on display. It was much to learn in a short time, but Jenna explained
he important aspects with the precision and clarity of a seasoned college
nstructor.

"Here's how we do it," she coached, "you look around and let me know
vhat you want, then keep far enough away so the seller does not know we
re together. If they think I am with an American, it will be hard to get the
est price."

I looked around at the merchandise of a few booths and, despite Jenna's
etailed lecture on different aspects of pearls, it was taxing to choose from
mong thousands of strands. "I want to get ten white and ten pink medium
ized for long necklaces."

She nodded and went straight to work with nearest vendor, an elderly
Muslim lady. I watched from a safe distance and saw that when the lady gave
he initial price, Jenna frowned and dramatically made a loud, disappointed

clucking noise. She then turned and began to walk away from the lady, until the lady called her back. She returned and held eye contact while arguing in Tagalog. Then she used humor and made the lady laugh. Her technique involved a skillful balance of fierce negotiation with lively humor. She also constantly made a lower counter-offer to any offer the woman gave. I was witnessing a master haggler at work. After nearly forty-five minutes of persuasion, cajoling, manipulation and laughter, the price had dropped from 3000 pesos to 800 pesos per necklace. Jenna motioned me over once the bargaining dust had settled. The old Muslim lady smiled, shaking her finger at me, "You are very smart to bring her here. I'm not making any profit from this!" I liked Jenna.

Later that night at the Mirage came the beginning of the end. I cooked spaghetti and Pete asked if it was okay if he invited a girl over for dinner. He knew her from some dating site and she was visiting Manila from Subic Bay. Lucy was in her mid-forties, Japanese in appearance. While her body was decent, and she seemed nice enough, there was one feature about her that was hard to ignore. She had a slight mustache. Lily and I stole smirking glances at each other, trying not to laugh, and knowing exactly what the other was thinking.

After dinner, we listened to music and drinks were flowing for Lily and Lucy. They appeared to get along well and spent hours talking on the balcony, smoking and drinking. Pete joined them for an occasional smoke while I strummed a guitar I scored from Mall of Asia earlier in the day. It was a pleasant evening and everyone had a good time, until later. Lucy was spending the night with Pete and Lily and I were on the verge of sleeping when we heard screams, shouts and thuds.

"You're a crazy drunk. Get the hell out of here!" shouted Pete, before locking her out of his room.

"Tim," whispered Lily, "go see what's wrong." I threw on some shorts and went out to the living room. Lucy was sitting at the dining room table, sobbing, with her face buried in her hands. I approached her and tried to console her. I placed a hand on her shoulder. "There, there, it'll be okay," I said.

Suddenly, she reached up and grasped my hand, tightly, with both of her hands. I was shocked by her strength and more disturbed when she began a low growl, with a man-like voice. Her head turned to face me and she was now smiling, but her eyes were missing. They were completely white, glazed over and vacant. I yanked my hand back in shock, but her grip was supernaturally strong. I could feel a vile coldness and a smell like ourn sulfur coming from her mouth. Something strange had momentarily ransformed her, then it faded. Her eyes were no longer all white and she vas no longer growling. "I guess I had too much to drink," she said, softly, "Pete was angry at me. I need to sleep."

"Look, I don't know what the hell is going on or what just happened, out you can sleep on the couch. There are some pillows in the closet," I old her, before turning away and going back to the bedroom, where I tried o regain my composure while locking the door. A wave of anger suddenly overtook me, as I could hear her, through the closed door, getting positioned on the couch. In the brief flash of rage, I imagined myself strangling her. It vas odd for me to have such a violent flash. I was feeling and thinking in new ways, and not all for the better. I turned and got into bed beside Lily, vho lay sleeping peacefully.

"Everything okay out there?" asked Lily, groggily.

"Yes, she's sleeping on the couch. I guess she drank too much."

"Goodnight" she offered, before repositioning her body and drifting oack to sleep. I lay there, admiring her back, her bony shoulders and her olack silky hair. I was also looking at the features on her Chinese symbol attoo, when I noticed a small hole in the far wall of the room. I could oarely make out the legs of a large, menacing spider as it slowly made an appearance out of the hole. I was not concerned or even startled. In fact, I hoped that it was ambitious, full of venom, carnivorous and angry. I drifted into sleep.

I began to dream that I went out to the couch and placed my hands around Lucy's throat and strangled her. I realized that I needed to get rid of her body. I picked her up, and balanced her over my right shoulder while holding her legs against my chest with my right arm. I carried her out the door of our apartment and down the hallway to the stairs. I then trotted down nineteen flights of stairs, getting a rhythm going that made it nearly effortless, though I was breathing hard when I carried her out the back door to the nearest dumpster. I put her on the ground in order to lift the lid open. I hoisted her up onto the trash that nearly filled the vessel. I then slowly lowered the lid. While riding the elevator back up the nineteen floors, I whistled "I'm so Lonesome I Could Cry" until reaching my floor.

I got back to the room and washed my hands in the sink. I turned and noticed her large black purse on the dining room table. "Crap" I muttered, then put the purse inside a plastic grocery bag and left for the stairs again. I made it back to the dumpster, and lifted the lid with my free hand. There was the smell of wet dog and I could see fur. It was a rat, crouched on her neck, with its head burrowed into her mouth. The rodent was busily gnawing on the pink flesh of her tongue, as blood dribbled down her cheeks from the overflow of the pool of red that filled the mouth of her lifeless body.

The rat turned its head with a strand of human tongue flesh still dangling from its mouth. It stared into my eyes. I recognized it as the rat that was at the pool. I'm sure it was the same one because of the way he also stared into my eyes. I threw the bag containing her purse at him, but he deftly climbed over the edge of the dumpster, still holding the tongue flesh as some morbid trophy, and scurried out of sight. The sound made by the lid as I lowered it caused me to wake up, in a sweat and with shortness of breath.

Lily lay beside me, the Chinese lettering now highlighted by a strand of moonlight that fell through the window. Had I actually murdered Lucy? I was unsure. The sights, sounds and details all seemed so vivid, so real. I rose out of bed and quietly opened the door a crack, relieved to see Lucy there, curled up and sleeping peacefully. "What the hell is wrong with me lately?" I asked myself. Things were fine in Hamlet's Denmark, but something was rotten in my head. In the morning, Lucy was gone.

The following day Pete and I met up with Lily and her mother in China Town. The factor of feeling like a foreigner was ten-fold here. The environment was more Asian. The streets were narrower than the rest of Manila and there was an efficient economy of space, with a shop or vendor tucked away in every nook and cranny.

Lily's mother needed her regular visit to the Chinese doctor. She has been going to this same doctor, once a week, for the past thirty years and she was in good health. We entered a building and walked down a long hallway to the waiting room. The doctor wore glasses and looked to be in his mid-sixties. His manner was very curt, gruff and to the point. Personality wise, he was the opposite of Lily's mom, who was soft spoken, gentle and very kind. The doctor motioned her over to his desk. He took her pulse, shined a small flashlight into her mouth, before scribbling a prescription down in Chinese characters. We took the prescription around the corner to the pharmacy, which was more of an herb shop. The glass cases on both sides of the shop held every kind of root, plant, leaf, claw, insect and herb that one could imagine. Four workers were continuously busy mixing, grinding and measuring an assortment of pills, potions and powders. I wondered if maybe I should have had the doctor shine his light in my mouth to prescribe something for the new sulfur taste that would not go

way and for the horrendous nightmare episodes. We got the medicine and
went to have lunch at an authentic Chinese eatery. I enjoyed the company
f Lily's mother. She was kind and sweet.

That evening, Lily invited some friends to the Mirage for dinner. There
was Berto, Sherry, Norb and Jolen. I had heard much from Lily about Berto
nd Jolen, as they were close friends of hers from back in her college days.
Norb and Sherry were friends of Jolen. Everybody was friends with Jolen.
He had a charm about him. He was short, muscular, friendly, sensitive and
uick-witted. I liked him immediately, just the kind of person you know
ou can trust. He and Norb were homosexuals, but not together. Jolen had
he rare gift of being a great listener. He could get sincerely interested in
he life of whoever he happened to be listening to and just focus on them.
Berto was also very cool; friendly, outgoing and a laid-back sense of humor.
Lily cooked fried fish and mushrooms and the meal was tremendously
asty. We all gathered to mingle and laugh after dinner. Pete pursued Sherry
while the rest of us simply enjoyed each other's company for a few hours.
As everyone said goodbyes, Lily turned to me, "I have to work tomorrow.
will call you in the morning."

Pete and I said farewell to the others. Jolen and Berto were the last ones
t the door. "You guys will see us again," said Berto, with a smile.

"Cool" I replied.

Jolen pulled me aside and whispered into my ear, "You must always
trust Lily. No matter what; trust her, my friend."

"Okay, sure," I agreed, not really sure what he meant, though it would
ll become clear soon.

Just before drifting off to dreamland that night, I had an odd idea of
etting out of the bed, climbing over the balcony and leaping into the Manila
ight from nineteen floors up. In the morning I had seen kids swimming in a
reen cesspool down below. I felt sorry for them swimming in the unsanitary
water, but who am I? I'm just an arrogant guy with no personality, outside of
what I can beg, borrow or steal from those around me who happen to have
more on the ball. I thought of the irony involved when the kids find my
plattered body on the pavement, my fractured skull, seeping out dull gray
rain matter like spoiled cottage cheese. My sprawled body, splattered blood,
uts and bone exposed to the Manila Bay sunrise. A rodent or two might be
scurrying away with bits of trophy flesh in their mouths as the kids approach.
Maybe they would feel sorry for me, the confused American tourist from
he nineteenth floor who outsmarted himself in an international one-way
ove quest. Or maybe, they would just see what was in my wallet; another

expatriate with money to waste, except this one is out of commission. Such hopeless thinking was out of character for me and I questioned where it had come from before I finally went to sleep.

At four in the morning, Pete and I were both awakened by loud, constant knocking on the apartment door. Pete was already in the living room when I came out of my room. "Who the hell keeps pounding on our door?" I asked.

"Shhh, holy shit, it sounds like the cops!" he answered.

"What the hell?" I walked to the locked door as the knocking continued unabated. "Who is it and what do you want at this hour?" I shouted.

The knocking stopped, finally, and from the other side was, "This is the Manila police. Open your door, sir, so we will not have to break it down."

Pete peered through the peep hole. "Dude, it's the freaking cops; I'm going to open it." He unlocked the door and swung it open.

There were three uniformed men standing there, armed. The one up front said, "We need both of you to come with us. We have questions to ask you."

"Questions? Questions about what?" asked Pete.

"We have evidence that at least one of you was involved in smuggling illegal contraband into the Philippines. Now you can come with us voluntarily or we can arrest you and bring you with us. It's up to you."

It dawned on me suddenly that I recognized the cop behind the one speaking. He was one of the men with Reshi the night she showed up at three in the morning. He was the one who grabbed the bags of dildos while the other one paid me.

"Wait a minute. We didn't smuggle anything!" yelled Pete. I didn't have the temerity to inform him, at that moment, that I brought a dickload of dildos into Manila. It wasn't that I minded him knowing I was crazy, but I didn't want him thinking I was a freak.

"Look," I persuaded, "let's just go with them, answer their questions and be done with it."

Pete was not having any of it. He began throwing a minor tantrum, kicking a wall and demanding his rights. One of the officers drew a gun, while another had us put our hands behind our backs and cuffed us. "I demand to know what we are being arrested for!" continued Pete.

"For being a stubborn asshole," said the officer. I could not help but to laugh.

"This situation isn't funny! You guys will be sorry when I tell the U.S. Embassy about this!" he shouted as we were led to the elevator.

We were taken to a white van parked in front of the Mirage. As the van went down Mabini Street, I began to regret bringing the suitcase full of toys. I also wondered just why in the hell the police would be so vigilant about monitoring dildo trafficking. In a few days they would have the inauguration of a new president, Benigno Aquino III, with the ceremony right in Malate. There were also two people killed at a cockfight in Makati the day before. Weren't these items of more interest for the security and safety of the Manila citizens? Why all this uproar over a few dozen jelly dildos? What the hell was wrong with the cops here?

As the van turned on to Taft Avenue and the three officers were joking and talking in Tagalog, I figured I should come clean with Pete. "Hey, listen," I whispered, "I brought some things in my suitcase that you didn't know about. I never dreamed it would be such a big deal." Pete looked at me with Napoleonic fury in his eyes.

"What the hell, you brought drugs with you?" he asked. A joke or two crossed my mind involving ecstasy and dildos, but I could tell he wasn't in the mood for humor. It's funny how some people lose their sense of humor as soon as things do not go their way.

"No man, I brought a bunch of dildos," I confessed, "They are tough to get here, so I made a profit."

"Shut the hell up back there!" barked the officer driving. So we did. As he continued to beep and nudge the van through the Manila traffic, Pete silently mouthed "dildos" with a puzzled expression in his eyes and raising his hands upwards while shrugging his shoulders. I had to chuckle, nodding my head affirmative. We bounced along in the van for another twenty minutes, when the guy who was with Reshi, whose name I did not know, came back to where we were sitting.

"Listen, I have to blindfold you guys the rest of the way." He said, calmly.

"Just what kind of keystone cops are you guys anyways?" began Pete, with another tantrum, "This is ridiculous!"

"You need to just shut up," he returned, "We're not the police. We have more power than the police. You guys don't know anything about Manila. We're not going to hurt you, unless you piss us off too much. Now hold still and let me cover your eyes." He put a wide, black stretchy cloth band over my head. I couldn't see, but I could hear Pete.

"Can you at least tell us how far we have to go? I have to piss," pressed Pete.

"We'll be in Caloocan City in ten minutes. Now shut up." He said, before covering our heads.

The van slowed down, stopped, and the driver exchanged words in Tagalog with someone, then we slowly rolled down an unpaved road for about another quarter-mile.

We were led from the van through what sounded like a metal door of some sort, then down a hallway and made a right turn and another right turn before a short left turn into what seemed like a room. "Just sit here and wait," one of our captors said, before pulling off the blindfolds. "Now, I'm going to remove the handcuffs. This will be your only warning, if you try anything stupid when the cuffs are off, you will be shot in the head." I hoped Pete had heard him as clearly as I did. "There's a toilet across the hall if you still need to piss."

Pete walked to the bathroom in the hallway. I stood, awkwardly silent, while the cop began text messaging. I wasn't sure where the other two were and was wondering who these guys worked for, since the one told us that they weren't the police. Maybe they were some kind of military police force? They seemed well trained and knew how to get things done in a no-nonsense kind of way. I could hear voices further down the hallway and then the guard's phone rang. He listened, spoke briefly and hung up. Pete returned and I was relieved that he didn't try to make a run for it. Hell, where would we run to? It's not like we had a clue where we were. Caloocan City might as well have been on the moon for all we knew of Manila geography.

We proceeded down the hall and entered another room. At a large table with a single light hanging above it from the ceiling sat Berto, Jolen, Sonny, Reshi and Lily. Lily sat at the head of the table, in a denim skirt and sleeveless, tight black top. She looked skinny and sexy.

"Lily, what's going on?" I asked, as Jolen, who sat beside her, put a finger up to his lips and shook his head no, signaling that I should not ask her.

"Just sit down, Tim and Pete," she began. "Pete, you kind of got caught up in this by accident, but your lame little tantrums haven't done you any favors. Tim, look me in the eyes so this comes through clear as a bell. I know how you are, but listen to me well. It is over. We are through. There is no more relationship. We had some fun together, and that was that. As of here and now, it is officially over. And don't beg, please." I did not really want to believe what I was hearing. This woman who I was considering possible future with was ending it all with complete indifference. How ould she feign affection with such sincerity and then turn off her heart like switch? I wanted to beg; I wanted to plead, but I didn't want to look like he sad cat that I was inside. It was a bit crushing, but my ego hurt more han my heart. I still hoped it was another strange dream.

"So what's the bottom line here? You're going to kill us or kidnap us to ry to get a ransom or what?" asked Pete. Everyone at the table, except Pete nd I, began to chuckle.

"This one is so uptight," observed Reshi, "Maybe he wants to sit next o me and loosen up?"

"And get a handjob," added Jolen, before they all began to laugh even arder. The sad part was that Reshi looked so movie-star sultry with her erfect body, stylish make-up and silk black dress with a slit up the side o show lots of leg, that I knew Pete had to want to sit next to her. Hell, ny man wanted to sit next to her. Her striking beauty made me forget all bout being taken hostage.

"Tim, you already know kind of why you are here," began Lily. "I was runk and you kept asking too many questions; sucks for you. Instead of ıst killing you, both of you, I'm going to give you a chance to do some ⁄ork for us. If the work meets our expectations, you will get back your assport and a plane ticket."

I could not even focus on what she was saying, still puzzled from being nanghaied and dumped. "Lily, you really don't feel anything for me?"

"No," she said, coldly, "but if you keep on asking stupid questions and mbarrassing yourself, I will feel hatred. If I feel hatred, I will kill you. I ope you got the hint."

"What kind of work do we have to do?" asked Pete.

Lily soon made it clear, "We are a syndicate. The syndicate controls 1ost of what happens here, as far as Manila business and political circles re concerned. There are other cells, like us, but only the leader of each cell an meet with other cell leaders."

"This is crazy," I said, "like fantasy Matrix stuff."

"Welcome to Manila" replied Lily. "You are stuck here and life is very heap here. Deal with it."

"So we have to kill people?" asked Pete.

"Yes"

"I don't think I can do that," stated Pete, as if he had a choice.

"Well, you either can or you can't. If you can, you will live. If you an't, you will die. Tomorrow morning you will go to Baguio and kill a man. Berto will be with you and Sonny will drive. It may take you ten minutes or it may take you ten days, but you must accomplish the task. Finishing the job is non-negotiable." She advised. "Berto will fill you in on more of the details. Go wait for him in the bunk room down the hall. That will be all."

CHAPTER III
Ventilator Blues

I will put enmities between thee and the woman,
and thy seed and her seed: she shall crush thy head,
and thou shalt lie in wait for her heel.

Genesis 3:15

Berto informed us of our target, Larry Coker, a professor at The University of the Philippines who had risen through the ranks in criticizing the Arroyo administration. He appeared on television and was interviewed in newspapers grinding his axe against certain politicians and turning the public opinion sour against the Arroyo political structure.

"Won't they know something suspicious is going on when this Coker guy just gets murdered after saying negative things against the president?" I asked.

Berto chuckled, "Of course, and that is why we're doing it. See, once they see what happened to him, any other mouthpieces in waiting will think twice before running to the newspapers. They will know it is a bit unhealthy," he smiled. "It's how things work here. Welcome to Manila, my friend."

Next, we studied a detailed map of Baguio and photos of Coker, his house, his favorite bar and his office. Some different logistical plans were made according to his daily routine and the number of potential witnesses at different locations. The syndicate warehouse also had an area for shooting guns. Pete and I were both given M1911 .45 caliber pistols to practice shooting at targets. Berto told us that he trusted us, but just in case, Sonny had a scope on us and one wrong move would result in a kill shot to our head. I was on board, and hoped Pete heard him well enough not to try any kind of heroic Rambo stunt. We had an endless supply of ammunition and practiced shooting and improving our target scores over the next few hours.

Our sleeping room contained two cots and a sink. The bathroom down the hall contained a toilet and a small shower head with a drain in the floor. Another room served as the kitchen and had a small stove, some shelves with provisions, a refrigerator, sink and a counter. I was also relieved to see a large, industrial coffee brewer. For lunch, Sonny cooked rice and sardines. Later for dinner, he brought back a huge container of pancit from somewhere, which, after spending the day training to be an assassin, we were grateful to eat heartily. The plan was for us to leave early the next morning for the five hour trip to Baguio.

> *Dear reader, I feel the demon. I am slipping into the mindset of darkness. I fight it and resist it, but it is futile. Now, I just accept it as normal and allow the dark spirit to have control of me. I know it is coming when anger, sorrow and despair begin seeping into my mind, making me demented. I will meditate in the blackness. The demon wants me dead, but seems content with keeping me miserable. The good thing I can say about these episodes of is that they give me temporary relief from missing my syndicate family in Manila. I suppose it's really no better than swapping a toothache for an earache, but sometimes I'd rather let the demon have me and escape my woe of being homesick. Funny how being forced against your will to be a part of something can result in a sense of vital belonging to the something you once resisted. Stockholm syndrome be damned, I miss my family. I miss Manila.*

The warehouse bunkroom was not the easiest of places to sleep, at least not the first night. For starters, Pete would not stop going on and on about how it was my fault that he was in this whole messed up situation. I let him rant all he wished. There was no sense in pointing out to him that his petty tantrums were also partially responsible for his current predicament. When a person is angry and believes that their anger is justified, what can you do? No amount of reasoning, evidence, logic or proof will change their mind. The only hope, possibly, is the passage of time. Time changes nearly everything.

"Why the hell would you smuggle dildos into Manila?" he asked, angrily.
"It was just a way to make a little money, to recoup some of the trip
xpenses. I didn't think it would be a big deal." I replied.
"Who did you sell them to?"
"Reshi"
"The smoking hot chick?"
"Yes," I continued, growing tired of the third-degree, "Listen, we should
et some sleep. We got a big day ahead. We have to get up and kill a guy."
"That chick had some nice tits! You gave her dildos? Damn! You must
ave been excited! Where was I?"
"Asleep, she came by at like three in the morning at the Mirage.
peaking of sleep, we should get some now." I suggested.
"Well, I guess it makes more sense now. Hell, smuggling sex toys for a
ot chick like that is kind of hard to resist. Did you hit on her?"
"Well, sort of, I know she is smoking hot and everything, but I didn't
ant to piss off Lily, plus they're friends. I like Reshi more, though, but
1at's just between us."
"Yeah, but it seems like that ain't happening now. We're just like
risoners, worse even since we have to do the jobs they don't want to."
"Yeah, and thanks for reminding me." I replied, perturbed.
Before drifting off to sleep, my mind was changing, though. I began to
1ink how good it was going to feel the next day to actually kill someone.
 romanticized the notion that, maybe, if I became a good enough killer,
.eshi might feel attracted to me and Lily would allow me more freedom.
:illing was no problem; I was someone different now. Something changed
1e since my arrival to Manila. There was no conscience. I'd do anything
 win over Reshi.
I heard scurrying sounds all through the warehouse. There were also
cratching sounds and tiny shrieks everywhere. In the walls, on the roof,
own the hallway, in the warehouse and, yes, even in our bunkroom, they
ame alive. I knew what they were without even turning the light on. Rats
row restless at night. I heard one scampering along the wall, right under
1y bed. I was getting used to sleeping with rats, whether in my dreams or
1 reality. I felt a certain kinship with the pied piper. My dreams and reality
ere pretty much becoming interchangeable anyway. It dawned on me
1at real life was exceeding my dream life in terms of the bizarre, and this
ealization made me want to kill one of these rats, just for the sport of it.
I had seen an old mop down near the kitchen area. When I flipped the
ghts on, I saw at least six rats scurrying in our room. As I went to get the

mop, I saw three more scurrying down the hallway. I grabbed the handle
and unclamped the mop part. The handle itself, made of hard wood, would
make an effective rat killer. I might not be able to kill them all, but I knew
I could get one. It would feel great to just kill one of these pests. Plus, it
might send a message to the rest of them, this guy doesn't screw around, so
stay out of his bunkroom or he'll kill you.

I went back to our bunkroom. Pete was sleeping soundly, even with the
light on. I knew the rodents were still in here somewhere. I crouched and
peeked under my bed; voila! There huddled against the wall was a large
rat. His pink, fleshy tail moved slowly across the concrete floor like a thin
serpent. He turned, and his beady black eyes met my blue ones. It was the
same kind of stare that I had with the rat at the pool. It was also the same
stare I got with the rat from the dumpster dream. I had to kill this one.
These stare-downs were getting old.

I clutched the handle as firm as I could, then brought it forward, toward
the creature's head, with as much force and speed as I could muster. The rat
simply dipped his head backwards as the end of the handle smashed into
the base of the wall. When I brought it back to try another strike, he ran
from under the bed towards the doorway. I went after him with fury and
brought the handle down from overhead with all my might, but he was
too quick. The loud smash of the handle banging off the floor cause Pete
to jump awake.

"What the hell are you doing?" he asked.

"Trying to kill this rat; he's too fast." I replied.

"Well, I'm trying to sleep. Can we go hunting some other time?"

"Alright, alright" I resolved, propping my infertile rat killer weapon
against the wall near my bed.

Berto woke us up early the next morning. "Hey guys; rise and shine!"
he greeted us, while turning the light switch on and off. "You got about
twenty minutes to get ready. I'm going to brew some Filipino jet fuel down
in the kitchen, just meet me there."

"What if we refuse to do any of this crap?" asked Pete, not a happy
camper this morning.

"Well, Lily said to kill you if you don't cooperate," he replied, smiling
and patting the pistol concealed in the side pocket of his cargo shorts.
"Look man, I'm just trying to get this job done, and I will get it done,
whether you're with me or not."

Luckily, there were some large Styrofoam cups in the kitchen to fill
up with some travel coffee. I had pretty much sworn off booze, dope and

igarettes, but coffee was a vice I could never let go of, *though this watered
down brew we have here at Hoffman may not even have caffeine in it; I still
like drinking it for the placebo effect. It helps to keep me writing this tale, dear
reader; well, the coffee and the pain of missing my family.*

After filling our cups up, we followed Berto to the white mini-van
outside of the warehouse. "Look, I'm not going to blindfold you guys. Just
don't pull any stupid stunts. You guys are smart enough to go along with
what needs done and get your plane ticket to get out of here, right?"

"Yeah, let's do it," I answered. "I had no idea Lily was involved in all
his mafia/ spy lifestyle, but it's cool." I replied.

"Back when I lived in Los Angeles we used to do things like this all the
time, but that was when I was young and dumb. I just hope Lily is true to
her word that once we finish this, we get the on that plane back home. I do
not like this, not at all," said Pete.

"One of you will sit shotgun up front with Sonny, I will sit in the
back," instructed Berto, as we approached the van. Sonny had it idling and
nodded to us with a smile as we got in. He was burly, strong and reliable.
As he pulled out of the warehouse area and onto paved roads, Berto began
looking at a map. "We have about two-hundred kilometers to go, which
will probably be about five hours. Baguio is a cool place, though, known to
have some of the best lechon in the Philippines!"

"Pork is god," I replied, before everyone in the van, including Sonny, slowly
nodded their heads in agreement. There was finally one thing that all of us
could agree on. After an hour or so of stop/ start traffic getting out of Manila,
I decided to break the awkward silence. "So, Berto," I began, hoping to gain
some insight into our situation and trying to pass the time with conversation.
How come you guys want to use a couple of clueless Americans to do dirty
work for you? Isn't there a better chance of getting away with murder, so to
speak, if you don't have two foreign, amateur newbies doing it? I'm not trying
to argue or anything, but just curious. Is it okay if I ask?"

"No, it's cool to ask questions. Hell, I would have questions too if I
was you. The truth is that it's not too uncommon for syndicates to use
expats and foreigners to do risky jobs. I guess a few of the reasons are that
nobody expects an American to be making a hit, since most of the time
they are only here for fun, drinking and getting laid. Plus, to Filipinos, all
Americans kind of look alike, any witnesses would have a more difficult
time giving a detailed description beyond saying they were white."

"What if they get caught?" I continued, "Isn't there some sort of
problem with them telling the police who they were working for?"

"Well," he chuckled, "usually, if something goes wrong, they end up dead, even in police custody. Most syndicates have police cooperation to some degree. Life is cheap in Manila and pretty much anything can get done with the right amount of pesos."

"Just freaking great," interjected Pete, "we're about to go kill someone and our chances of getting home alive are slim to none. This is just dandy!"

"Oh, not really," countered Berto, "you just need to focus on getting done what needs to get done, then, it'll all work out."

"How long have you been with the syndicate? Is this like your full-time job?" I asked.

"Oh no, Lily works with her family's business, I work as a graphic artist, Reshi is a businesswoman involved in stocks, retail, internet marketing and also works as a model and actress. Jolen is an artist and a writer. We all have our own lives, but belonging to a syndicate is an honor. The syndicate is like our second family, for some of us, like Sonny here, the syndicate is his family. It also helps with social networking and business opportunities, but usually syndicate business is different from what we do in our day to day jobs. The thing about Manila is that, to get ahead, it's not really about how hard you work, but more about who you know and how well you can get along with people."

"Is there someone in charge of all the syndicates?" I asked.

"Not really, but politicians have a crazy amount of power here and when you combine that with the abuse of corruption, it makes for a lot of politicians keeping their own teams in play in order to gain, or at least maintain, the positions of power they hold." He answered.

"So how long have you been doing this?" asked Pete, now more interested.

"Well, I guess we started back in college, like sixteen years ago. Jolen, Lily and I were in college together, and Lily has known Reshi since high school. In college, we got to know and become friends with some politically connected people. There were kids of politicians in school with us and also kids who would gain political appointments after graduation." He replied.

"How can you find time to do syndicate work when you all have your own jobs?" I asked.

"It's not like we're busy all the time. I mean, we just all get together and meet when things need done. Sometimes, months will go by where we don't even see each other. And other times we're together for days r weeks, it just depends. But when something comes up, we all work ogether on it."

"How did Lily get to be the leader?"

"Well, in addition to being smart and business savvy, as you know, he also has a knack of not letting emotions cloud her judgment," Burton ontinued, "In the Philippines, it is not too difficult for a woman with ntelligence and ambition to obtain a position of leadership. Lily has the nind of a man when it comes to syndicate business. Hell, she is more of man than most men. She can be friendlier than friendly or she can be itterly vicious, depending on which Lily any given situation calls for. She's wolf in sheep's clothing, but prettier than a sheep!" he laughed.

"Well, she sure dumped my sorry ass quick." I confessed.

He laughed again, "Yes, join the club; I once asked her to marry me ack in college. There's just something about her. I mean, I got over it nd we're very close friends. Some girls just aren't meant for romantic elationships, I guess."

"There's not many like her, thank god!" I laughed, "I talked with her or years but never knew she was Miss Mafia Kingpin. Her and Jolen are lose, huh?"

"Jolen is kind of lucky because he is gay," began Berto, "It makes it easy o just be friends, I guess. Those two together are inseparable. He has been ke her guardian angel."

"He seems very cool, friendly, witty and caring."

"Yes, and the more you get to know him, the more you're going to like im. He's a writer."

As we arrived in Baguio, the landscape and scenery began to change, nore open country here and lush hills and flowers growing all over the place. It did not seem as likely of a place to commit a murder as Manila id, since it was scenic and tranquil. Berto called somebody and spoke n Tagalong, as Sonny parked the van next to a two-story building. A vell-dressed man was waiting across the street in a parking lot and Berto old us to wait while he went to greet him. After talking a bit, the man gave im a key and left. Berto used the key to open the door to an apartment in he building, and then motioned for us to come inside.

The apartment was up a flight of stairs. It was small, but tidy. There vere two couches, a bedroom, a bathroom, a small kitchenette and a dining oom table with chairs. "It's not the Hilton, but it will do. One of you will ave to sleep on the floor, there's a sleeping bag in the van along with the xtra clothes. Let's rest for an hour, get settled in, and then we'll scout

out the University and follow Coker on his afternoon weekday routine," advised Berto.

Pete and I brought the stuff in from the van, while Sonny rested on a couch and Berto rested in the bedroom. "You know," began Pete, "We could make our escape to freedom right now. If we use our heads, they will never find us. We can get to the U.S. Embassy and explain our messed up predicament. They are probably just going to kill us anyways. We know too much, they will never just let us go."

He had a valid point. I could understand his desire to make a run for it. Hell, under normal circumstances I would have made a run for it, but I couldn't go anywhere. Dear reader, I kind of liked this syndicate life; killing someone now sounded like fun, even more fun than running away to freedom and safety. I was enjoying the sense of belonging to a group, a family. I wasn't going anywhere. My new lust for adventure superseded my logic. Since the strange spirit entered me, I've been itching to kill someone. For me, being a hostage with a murderous syndicate was a win-win situation.

"No, I can't do it. I'm going to trust Lily to follow through." I resolved.

"Come on, it's better to make a break for it with two of us. This is like life or death, now or never. We may not have another chance to get away like this," he pressed.

"I can't. I won't. I'm going to trust Lily to follow through." I repeated, firmly.

"This is pathetic. We might as well just walk in front of a jeepney and end our lives now," he pouted.

For lunch we ate at the Aristocrat and shared a few plates of crispy pata. We then began what would become our routine for the next two days, following Coker and scouting his home and workplace. The surveillance got boring from the beginning, since Coker did not have a varied routine. His home was ten blocks from the University, where he would drive each morning to arrive by eight. From eight until five, he taught four classes that were each an hour long. The other five hours he spent secluded in his small office. While there was shrubbery around his home, there were too many eyes and ears around, including his own family. Berto decided by day two that his office at the college was ideal, particularly in the late afternoon. There were few people around, no windows and only one long hallway to keep watch over.

The night before the planned hit, Berto gave us specific instructions. Pete, you are going to kill Coker. Tim and I will stand guard outside of his office door."

"How come I have to be the shooter?" he asked.

"That's how Lily wants it." He replied, "I guess she wants to be sure that you are on our team."

"That's messed up." He said.

I kept a gun in the waistband of my cargo shorts, concealed by a short-sleeve, untucked button shirt. In addition to the pistol, we carried 'akal knives in sheaths on the opposite side of our shorts. These knives were razor sharp and designed specifically as close combat daggers. Pete also carried a book-bag, which is where his gun was kept. The plan was for him to enter Coker's office and ask for his assistance to review a grant proposal. No tenured professor could resist being involved in writing grants. Grants equaled prestige and money. Pete would then place the book-bag on his desk, reach inside, and fire the gun into Coker's torso and fire a follow-up to the head to seal the deal. Berto and Sonny emphasized over and over that this hit had to result in Coker's death.

Berto and I walked down the hallway at 4:30 in the afternoon. We each discreetly took a post on opposite sides of Coker's door. Coker's door was open and he was hunched over at a computer typing, oblivious to the hallway traffic. Pete entered the building last and strolled down the hall, while Sonny had the van parked near the doorway, idling. Prior to leaving, we loaded the van back up with all of our belongings and filled up the gas tank. We were ready to get straight back to Manila after business was done.

Pete entered Coker's office. "Excuse me, Professor Coker?"

"Yes"

"I have a question about a grant proposal I am writing and I was told that you might be able to help me," stated Pete.

"Well, possibly," he returned, as Pete put the book-bag on his desk and pretended to look for papers in the non-existent contents.

"I assume you are a graduate student at the university?" asked Coker, leaning forward with both elbows on the desk and clasping his hands together before resting his chin on them.

"Uhm, you know what? I left the proposal in the car," he stammered, while zipping the book-bag closed. "I'll go get it. I'm very sorry."

Berto looked at me, angrily whispering, "What the hell is he doing?"

Pete entered the hallway and I took his arm, "Guard this door" I told him, pulling my Pakal blade from its sheath. I whispered to Berto, "I got this," and entered his office, closing the door behind me. There was something inside me that was hungry for the sight, smell and feel of blood. I was actually relieved that Pete chickened out. I hid the blade behind my back and extended my right hand, grinning, "Professor Coker, hello; my name is Lucifer."

His partially extended hand was quickly retracted when he heard my name. I made a quick upswing with the blade and plunged it under his chin area, near the throat. Warm, red blood began to flow down the knife handle, over my hand and down my forearm. Coker began to scream as his arms flailed frantically.

I pulled the knife downwards, out of his throat, thrusting it directly into the center of his neck, piercing the wind-pipe. "Please to meet you," I half growled, half sang, "hope you guess my name" while twisting the handle to make a larger hole with the blade. His eyes began to bulge outwards like a squeeze toy. Blood poured from his neck, splashing onto the floor. As he attempted to scream, the dark, red liquid oozed and bubbled from the gaping holes. I pulled the blade out again and sliced across his throat, with the blade halfway deep into his neck. His body collapsed and he tried to crawl towards the door, but soon fell flat against the floor. The pool of blood surrounding him expanded outwards. Dear reader, it was a beautiful, scintillating sight. I felt powerful, like god. I wanted to re-kill him again and again. There would be others. I knew there would be others.

"Holy Christ," observed Berto, cracking the door for a peek, "we need to go."

I wiped the bloody blade of the knife on Coker's back and closed the office door before leaving. My sneakers left footprints of red down the length of the hallway. We exited the building and Sonny had the side-door of the van already open for us. "Let's go!" ordered Berto. Turning back in the passenger seat, he said, "Pete, I don't know why you pussed out, but you are lucky to have a friend who covered you." We continued, in mostly silence, for the next 30 minutes. I was lost in a daydream, mentally reenacting the feel of the knife as it cut through the tendons and cartilage of Coker's throat. It was as if his life being drained had made mine more full. Pete's voice broke me out of my pleasant reverie.

"So, will we be able to get our passports and get the hell out of here now?" he asked.

"You haven't done anything yet," returned Berto, "Those decisions are up to Lily."

"Will we be able to kill some more?" I asked, smiling.

Berto began to chuckle, "You really liked that hit, didn't you?"

"Oh yeah," I replied, seeing Sonny smiling with approval in the rear-view mirror.

It was late when we finally returned to the warehouse in Caloocan. There were no blindfolds put on us coming in this time. "Get a shower and meet the other members back at the meeting room in about thirty minutes."

After showering and putting on different clothes, I found Pete pacing the hallway, looking nervous. "I'm worried" he stated.

"Why? We got the job done. It's all good."

"They might just kill us now that they got their use out of us," he reasoned.

"I doubt it. I trust Lily. Let's go down there," I said before walking down to the meeting room. Pete gave in and followed.

Lily sat at the head of the table. She wore a short, tight fitting white dress and black boots. She looked good, stylish, graceful and elegant. Reshi, however, was so stunning that I could not take my eyes off of her. She was wearing a chic, silky blue dress that came to a V and showed ample cleavage. There were also slight protrusions made by her nipples. Her heels were also blue, sleek and four inches high. The smell of her perfume was pleasantly intoxicating.

Berto and the two officers who brought us in the first night were also at the table. Pete and I took seats. They were talking in Tagalog and as we waited for the conversation to turn into English, Sonny entered the room. He approached Pete from behind and clamped his forearm across his throat then braced the other one on his head. As he secured the choke-hold, the two officers rose from the table, one with a coil of clothesline and the other with a roll of duct tape. "Hold still!" Sonny barked. As the officers pulled Pete's arms behind the chair and tied his wrists together.

"No! Please! Help! Tim, help!" Pete gasped the loudest he could with being choked. As one officer tied each of Pete's ankles to a leg of the chair, the other officer wound duct-tape around his head, covering his mouth to contain his screams. They also wound rope around his torso to bind him to the chair. I wanted to help him. I felt like we were betrayed. I looked at Lily, then at Jolen. Jolen gave me a signal with his hands and a nod of his head to chill out. For an instant the thought crossed my mind that at least they weren't tying me up too, but then I was angry at myself for being so selfish. I feared this would not end well for Pete, but, fuck it, he should have done what he was supposed to do.

"The deal was that you were supposed to follow orders and if you did not, you would be killed," said Lily, coldly. "What part of that could you not understand?" she asked, now rising from her chair. Pete's eyes grew wide and he began to vehemently shake his head in protest. "There is no forgiveness. There are no second chances. I don't do forgiveness; never have, never will," she stated, before taking a swig of San Miguel. She rose up from her chair, walked over to Pete, and stood looking at him, her hands resting on her slender hips. Her white dress clung to her body as she stood over him, glowering. Suddenly, she brought one of her skinny legs up, putting the bottom of her boot against his chest, and shoved him backwards. The chair tilted back and teetered in slow motion before falling. The back of Pete's head ricocheted off of the concrete floor upon impact. He began squirming on the ground.

Lily walked up towards his head, placing a black boot on each side of the chair's back. Her crotch was directly above Pete's head, as she taunted, "Do you like what you see?" She looked at the others as they laughed. Apparently, maybe Pete did because he was now squirming less. "Typical male dog, about to die and all you care about is seeing up a skirt. Well now, at least you can't say that I didn't make your final moment alive an unpleasant one, can you little Petey?"

She quickly brought her right leg up directly over his face and stomped down, hard. The heel of her boot smashed directly into his face. Pete began to squirm frantically and one of the officers held his bound feet to keep him from rocking the chair to its side. She lifted her boot again and furiously brought it down into his face again and again and again for a rapid succession of six times. "Yeah baby, you like that shit don't you?"

Blood was streaming from his disfigured nose and purple eye socket. One eye was sunken into his skull and blood oozed from his lips, causing the duct-tape to slide from his mouth. He could be heard pleading through a gurgle of blood, "Please, please, for the love of god!"

"My boots are your god, you chickenshit! Now, look at them!" shouted Lily, as her boots straddled each side of his head. "You still like looking up my skirt, don't you? Take a good long look. It will be the last beautiful thing you ever see." Pete began whimpering, half in painful agony, and half in defeat. The blood was now forming a pool around his head. "Okay, break is over. Let's do some more of that kinky stuff, baby."

She brought the heel of the boot down savagely with all of the force
er hundred and five pounds could muster, again, and again, and again,
nd again. Pete's nose was completely unrecognizable and both eyes were
ow buried into the cavities of his skull. When his head turned left, she
tomped the right side, and when it turned right, she gouged the left. Blood
pread across the room and was now splashing on her boots as she stomped.
fter another countless round of vicious, barbaric stomps, his head was
ompletely deformed into a ball of bloody flesh. The facial features were
ow non-existent. He no longer squirmed, or even twitched. It appeared
ke every drop of blood in his body had been spilled onto the floor. Lily
topped, spit on what was once a face and splashed through the blood,
valking back to her chair at the head of the table.

"Tim, you are going to clean this mess up, make it spotless. Then you
vill bury the body. You're the one who brought the little pussy here in the
irst place. Sonny will show you where to bury him."

"Okay Lily" I replied, still digesting the brutality of seeing my friend
nurdered.

"Get the body outside, mop up the floor and then you can clean my
oots. Once my boots are clean, you can go and bury the body. Now drag
im outside and go get the mop." She ordered, while seductively crossing
er slender legs. My anger and shock melted away with the thought of I'd
etter do as she asked.

I untied the feet from the chair while Sonny cut the ropes binding his
orso to the chair. I grabbed the lifeless ankles of my dead friend and began
ragging the body out of the room and down the hallway, following Sonny.
he blood left a red smear the length of the hallway while dragging the
ody, like making a surreal painting with a corpse. Sonny held the door
pen as I continued dragging Pete out under the night sky. Sonny pointed
o a burn barrel in the middle of a field, "You can leave the body next to
he barrel for now and later just bury it right underneath. I left the shovel
n the side of the building there," he said, pointing towards it.

I was about to thank him, but for what; for showing me where to bury
ny murdered friend? The whole situation had me confused. There was lots
f death in a short time. I savagely killed a complete stranger and my best
riend was brutally killed. Normally, I wouldn't be too complacent about
o much death in my day, but the new dark spirit in my head relished
:. Sometimes he controlled my whole range of thinking, sometimes he
vas just in there, closely watching but letting a few of my own thoughts
hrough too. I was changing into a new person, but was thinking that just

because something is new it does not mean it is better. I was conflicted and unsteady, wavering between darkness and light. I dragged the body through the field and looked down at my former friend. His face was grotesquely disfigured, like a mound of hamburger with blood poured over it. It was not even human looking.

When I returned the group was at the table, drinking San Miguel beer, laughing and talking loudly in Tagalog. I brought the mop and bucket and began trying to soak up the blood that was all over the floor. The water in the bucket turned as red as the floor in a short time, and I had to make about ten trips down the hall to pour out the bloody water and refill it with fresh. On the last trip to dump the bucket, I scanned the field for Pete's body, with the help of the moonlight. I saw an arm move, or I thought I did. "What if he is still alive?" I asked myself, before putting the idea out of my head. The thrill of possibly seeing Reshi's shapely legs up-close and those electric blue heels she wore crossed my mind. I hurried back to finish the mop job.

As I continued sopping up the blood, Jolen was telling the group an entertaining story. They were all laughing hard as he animatedly waved his arms and speaking in crazy voices. Berto was almost on the floor laughing and Reshi had laughter tears in her eyes that were smearing her make-up. I finished with the floor and took the bucket down the hall to dump it for the last time. When I returned, I took a seat at the table. Jolen was through telling his hilarious story and the conversation was back to normal. Lily looked at me, "My boots," she barked, before taking a long swill of beer. There were at least ten empty bottles on the table in front of her. I debated telling her to "piss off" but there was something inside me, the demon spirit that had me in its sway. I would kill anybody and enjoy it, but Lily and the syndicate were different. They were family now. Besides, she was sitting next to Reshi, which would put me in close proximity to ogle her delicious legs.

I grabbed the spray cleaner and paper towels and approached her. I wondered what the group might think of me, but they just continued their conversation. My eyes scanned Reshi's silky black hair and the elegance of her flawless Asian face. She crossed her slender, shapely legs and took a pull of San Miguel, her plump, pouty lips seductively enclosing the bottle-neck, before speaking to the group in Tagalog. I knelt in front of Lily, trying not to get caught sneaking glances at Reshi. I misted both upper sides of the leather boot from the spray-bottle. I braced the sole of the boot with my free hand and began wiping the black leather in small circles. She continued to alk and sipped beer while listening to others. The heel and lower back of he boot was where the majority of dried blood was. The paper-towel was oon dark red with my friend's blood. I did not care. It was too arousing ust being so close to Reshi and seeing her legs near me as I cleaned Lily's oots. I wanted to caress Reshi's golden calf and kiss it while fondling her recious feet in the blue heels, but I knew it would be a death sentence. I vould take what I could get, furtive glances.

"Come to the other side so you can clean the right one. You're kind of king this shit aren't you, you little pervert?"

I just smiled at her, while moving to where she adjusted the chair and ow had her right leg crossed over the top of her left. I knelt in front of he shiny black boot and began to clean it like the first one, from the top own. I was now able to move even closer to Reshi's crossed legs and smell er sweet perfume. I took my time while the group continued talking and rinking beer. When I was finishing the bottom and the heel, Lily popped he cap off a fresh beer and began to put the sole of the boot against my ace.

"Lick it," she ordered. I put out my tongue and ran it from the center lowly up to the tip. "Keep licking, you like that." The group was chuckling. .eshi made a comment in Tagalog and they all began laughing harder. I idn't care. The demon inside had me in its sway. "Put the toe part in your nouth. See how much you can fit in there. And don't you scratch it with our teeth!" Everyone laughed at my expense. The demon who loved to kill nd maim was submissively obedient to Lily. She bounced the toe of the oot in and out of my open mouth.

She continued in discussion with the others and drinking beer. I spent t least thirty minutes licking and cleaning each of her boots while she sat ith her legs crossed, changing legs at half-time. I had no pride, no ego nd no shame. It's just the demon life that had me in its sway. For an hour, ear reader, I was a boot licker, but I would have preferred they were on .eshi's feet. "Okay, clean up these bottles and crap. We're done here for the ight. Then go bury your dead friend. He has to go in the ground before unrise," she ordered.

"Okay Lily," I answered, telling myself I had to do what I had to do 1 order to get by in the situation I was in. The reality, though, was that I ked being a part of the group, my new family.

"Good," she said, in a tone more civil than mean. Her single word ?sponse, spoken with a hint of niceness, made me feel better. As everyone ?ft and said their goodbyes to each other, I put the empty bottles, of which there were many, into trash bags and emptied the ash trays. Reshi approached me and said goodbye, and gave me a hug. When I felt her ample breasts against my body, I had an instant reaction. I could smell her delicious scent, I felt the silkiness of her hair against my face and did not want to let go, but I had to. Once the bags were filled, I sprayed down and wiped the table clean. I carried the clinking trash bags down the hall and outside to the dumpster. I then proceeded to grab the shovel and walk to the field.

As I approached the body, under the light of the moon, I saw three rats burrowing in to areas of what was once Pete's face. They were feasting on the raw, bloody flesh. I began to run towards the body and two of the vermin scurried off into the field. The third lifted his head and turned towards me. He held a tiny strand of bloody flesh that dangled from his tiny mouth. His mouth worked at the flesh as his tiny eyes stared into mine. His black eyes were beady and defiant.

"You rotten little fuck!" I screamed, rearing back with the shovel. The rodent trotted down the side of the head right before the impact of the shovel blade made a splat sound upon impact of what was once a face. He scurried off into the higher grass with the piece of bloody flesh still dangling from his mouth. I knew it couldn't be, but the rat with the flesh looked just like the one by the pool I had seen upon first arriving to Manila, the same rat in my dream that was gnawing on Japanese mustache girl in the dumpster. Impossible, I know, but the feeling I had with the stare down of each was identical, searing into the depths of my mind, penetrating my soul, if I have one, and connecting with the demon that sways inside me.

My friend was brutally murdered tonight and I did absolutely nothing to save him. I splattered what was once his face with the blade of a shovel. I painted the hallway red with his blood while dragging him out to a field, to be gnawed at by rodents. I even licked his blood from the boots that had killed him. What kind of a treacherous friend was I? What kind of a man am I? And now, here I stood, sweating under the moonlight, hiding the evidence of this heinous crime. The ground was firm, dry and digging a grave sized hole was no easy task.

"Need a hand?" asked Jolen, startling me. He was standing nearby watching for I don't know how long. My body, mind and emotions were exhausted. His offer to help was like the sound of water to a man dying of thirst.

"Sure, I would really appreciate it. I'm beat," I answered, before he took the shovel from me and began digging with double the efficiency hat I could. With Jolen's help, we had Pete's body deep in the ground and overed back up in a short matter of time. "How come you're still here?"

"Well, I'm moving in here for awhile," he replied.

"Cool, but you should know that there are rats running around all over he place in there at night," I warned.

"That's very good," he answered, smiling, "they will match the crazy houghts running through my dreams."

I liked the way Jolen looked at things. I was happy for his company.

CHAPTER IV

Let it Loose

I went down to the crossroads, fell down on my knees.
I went down to the crossroads, fell down on my knees.
Asked the Lord above for mercy, "Save me if you please."

"Crossroads"—Robert Johnson

I don't remember any of it. They tell me I lost it, though. The night guard, Kinsey, told me that I tried to strangle Dan. What the hell? I thought he was an evil bird who was attacking me. Kinsey is pissed, but he still reads my notebook; I guess that shows just how boring the night shift is here at Hoffman. He said he knows I am possessed by a demon and that sometimes the demon completely takes over. I said; tell me something I don't know. And while you're at it, Kinsley, since you're probably reading this, screw you. Exposure to knowledge of the demonic opens one up to receive Aswang, either that or it can transfer via sexual intercourse. But don't get your hopes up, because I wouldn't touch you even with Mac's dick. My mind is bent on destruction. Soon your mind might also be bent on destruction, Kinsey. The only thing that brings me joy in life is to make death. I need the syndicate. Only my Manila family can pacify the restless Lucifer living inside of me. Without them, I am a time bomb, a mad-brained bear and a midnight rambler.

They doped me up and moved me to isolation in a solitary room. When I am by myself, I am in bad company, but at least nobody gets hurt, yet. Oh well, now I can write free of distractions.

I wonder, will ever be released from the Hoffman Mental Health Center? I really don't think I belong here in the first place, after all. Most of the time I have all my marbles, it's just the dark spirit takes away my lucidity by degrees. When he completely takes the reins, I don't remember anything. Maybe it's just the longing and despair of missing Manila that distorts my reality. I could probably function and blend in with society if I could control when the demon takes over, but it's out of my hands. The burden of guilt and remorse for the things I've done weighs me down, too. There ain't no easy way out. The irony is that those I've tortured and killed are probably better off than I am. I see life through the eyes of a rat. Read on, Kinsey, my good man on the night shift, read on.

Berto arrived in the morning with beef tapas and longaneeza from Jollibees. I was happy to see his smiling face, especially when there was food below it. Killing people and burying friends can really work up an appetite.

"Breakfast is served, gentlemen," he announced. Jolen and I looked at him from our respective cots.

"What time is it?" Jolen asked.

Berto held his watch up in front of his eyes, "Either it's 9:15 or Mickey has a hard-on," he said, "Rise and shine sunshine."

I shuffled down to the meeting room, the room that flowed with blood just ten hours before. I had a seat right near where my friend had his face stomped in. We began to eat in silence. "Alright, Lily called me this morning," he began, "Jolen, she wants you to meet her at SM in Greenbelt at noon."

"S&M, sounds kinky," I quipped.

"Kind of, it's Shoe Mart; lucky gay boy gets to go shoe shopping with her," chided Berto. "Tim and I, on the other hand, we have to work."

"Shoe shopping with Lily can be work, too," Jolen affirmed.

"Yeah, right;" returned Berto.

"Do we get to kill someone?" I asked, ever hopeful.

"Well, not exactly, but maybe. Lily has a friend, Annie, whose brother is the assistant director to the Department of Labor and Employment in the fifth district. Annie and her brother are involved in dealing with shabu and cocaine."

"So Annie is politically connected?" I asked, "What is shabu?" I wanted to learn as much as I could to be valuable to the syndicate. Not so much for survival, but more for the idea that the group would like me more if I was valuable. They were my family now.

"Shabu is what you would call meth, I think, and, yes, she is connected politically with her brother. It seems someone was arrested, a petty dealer, and he leaked Robert Caldo's name to a corrupt cop. We need to pick up the dealer and torture him until he tells us where he got his information," explained Berto.

"Sounds fun, so we're kind of keeping the disconnected from being connected?"

"In Manila," began Berto, "there are three groups of people; the connected, either politically or financially or often both; the poor and the working class. The working class is just above the poor, but the gap between the connected and the poor is immense. It is a city of contrast, where life is cheap. The connected have ways of staying connected, by hiring syndicates to insulate them."

We finished eating and Sonny soon arrived with the minivan. Berto and I said our farewells to Jolen, kidding him to go easy on the S&M with Lily, and went out to the van. We were soon deep into the busy traffic on our way into Makati. The horns were all beeping with cars everywhere and movement was start and stop.

"Okay, apparently this dealer, Carlito Perillo, runs with a group of young socialites known as the Gucci Gang. I got a lead on his whereabouts once I visit somebody at J.J.'s off Burgos."

Berto's cell phone rang and he had a five minute conversation in Tagalog as Sonny worked the van through the heavier traffic of Makati. He hung up and announced, "We have to stop at Ayala. I need to pick up a few things at Ace Hardware. We have to swing by my house so I can get a spare birdcage too. Tim, my man, judging by what you did to Coker yesterday, you're going to love what we do to Perillo today. Lily is getting very creative, that's all I'm going to say."

After visiting Ace, where we picked up a box-trap and a heat lamp, we arrived at J.J.'s. It was a typical Makati watering hole, expats looking for love and young Filipinas looking for their money. The three of us went inside and sat at the bar. Berto and Sonny were on their second San Miguel when a cab driver came in, sat next to us, and Berto ordered him a beer. "Tim, I want you to meet Juvi, the best damn cab driver in Manila. He's also a friend of the syndicate," said Berto, as I shook hands with the smiling, young Filipino. Juvi proceeded to give a rundown of all the places frequented by Perillo, including nightclubs, girlfriend's apartments and even his parent's address. Before leaving, Juvi also wrote down his phone number and gave it to me. "If you ever need a cab, day or night, just call

1im," advised Berto, while patting Juvi on the shoulder and giving him a
folded wad of peso bills.

We drove to Berto's home so he could get a birdcage, then we were off
to Mckinley Road where Perillo's girlfriend had an apartment. "What the
hell are we going to do with a birdcage?" I asked.

"I'm telling you," smiled Berto, "just wait; you're going to love it."

Luckily, Perillo's silver Corolla was parked on the side of the street
near her apartment. It was now a waiting game; and a warm waiting game
under the sizzling sun. We had a basic, rudimentary plan. I was going to
grab him and get him to the van and Berto would stick the gun in his face
to hopefully settle him down. After sitting in the van for three long, hot
hours, it was no problem to grab this guy. I felt like strangling him on the
spot for keeping us in such discomfort. When Perillo finally came trotting
out to his car, looking like a gangbanger wannabe, I quickly got out of the
van, leaving the side door open. I approached him asking for directions
and, when close enough, yanked his arm down and snatched him in a
headlock. Being on a wrestling team in grade school had some practical,
real-life, application. Old Coach Sinnot would have been proud. As it
was, Berto and Sonny were proud. In fact, Berto didn't need to show his
gun in public, since I was able to drag Perillo right into the back of the
van. The instant his feet left the pavement, Sonny began rolling the van
down Mckinley. I kept a tight hold on Perillo, who was now putting up
some resistance. Burton slid the door closed and pulled his gun, pointing
it at Perillo's face.

"Settle down or I'll blow your fuckin' head off!" he yelled.

"Fuck you!" shouted Perillo, defiantly. I had to admire his chutzpa,
but I adjusted my forearm and squeezed the choke-hold tighter. I wanted
to reinforce the notion that settling down and cooperating might be in his
best interest.

"We're not going to harm you if you just chill out," assured Berto. "It's
up to you."

"What do you guys want?" he asked, fearful eyed.

"We know you told the cops about Robert Caldo, we need to know
how you knew about him being involved with coke and shabu," stated
Berto.

"I never told the cops a thing!" he exclaimed.

"The fact is established. You were just trying to save your ass. Now,
who told you about Robert Calado? Who did you first hear his name from?
You can save yourself much time and misery."

"Fuck you," he repeated, back in defiant mode.

"Okay; suit yourself, tough guy," returned Berto, while gathering a coil of rope and a roll of duct-tape. "Let's get him flat and tie his wrists, then I'll duct-tape his mouth if he can't shut the up."

Perillo took the hint and, for the most part, managed to keep his mouth shut on the drive back to the Caloocan warehouse. I knew when we arrived without blindfolding him that his time as a living person was soon to end. I was excited to know that I would have a hand in sealing his fate. It felt like winning a prize.

Sonny kept an eye on Perillo in the meeting room, while Berto and I set up the box-trap near the dumpster in the back of the warehouse. We used a piece of longaniza left over from breakfast as the bait. I wasn't sure why we were trying to catch a rat, but I was all for it. Had I been a Native American, the rat would have been my totem-animal. We had a human to kill and we were going to catch a rat, life was good, dear reader. Once the trap was set, we brought the birdcage, duct-tape, rope and heat-lamp into the meeting room.

Berto addressed Perillo. "Okay, final offer, are you going to tell us where you heard information about Robert Caldo?"

"I have no idea who you're talking about," he pleaded.

Sonny went to pick up our dinner, Ebi tempuras and Pancit Canton. Berto and I tied Perillo flat on his back on a narrow table. We wound the rope tightly around his chest, torso, hips, thighs and calves, going around both him and the table. We left a twelve-inch gap at his abdomen and left his neck free so that he could raise his head to peer down at his body. Perillo was rendered immobile.

Berto removed the plastic tray from the bottom of the birdcage and placed the cage on top of Perillo's stomach area. We threaded rope through the cage and wound it around the bottom of the table to secure the cage to his stomach. Perillo complained that it was digging into his skin, until we clamped it even tighter. We then secured the heat-lamp to the top of the birdcage, facing down towards his stomach, with the duct-tape. Finally, we carried the entire table near the wall where there was an electrical outlet so that we could plug in the heat-lamp.

"Now we need just one more small, but necessary, ingredient" announced Berto, "Let's go check the trap."

The door on the cracker-box size trap had been sprung closed. I first saw the tail of the rat as it twitched outside of the mesh caging. "Got one!" shouted Berto, "That was fast!"

"Well, there's a ton of them around here," I replied, "You should see he warehouse at night. If Japanese were rats, then it would be Tokyo in here every night."

The rat was medium-sized and very active. He was scurrying back and orth the length of the trap, frantically searching for a way out. I picked up he trap by its carrying handle and carried it back inside. As we returned o the meeting room, Berto said, "Just set the trap on his chest for now. Maybe it will make him think about giving up his source."

Soon, Sonny arrived with the food and not long after came Lily and olen. "Well, well, well, looks like we're just in time for dinner and a how," said Lily, as she went to the refrigerator for a San Miguel. She wore pen-toe, strappy black heels, olive capris, white blouse and a gold, orange lass leaf pendant on a thin chain of white gold. She certainly had style. he opened her beer and took her seat at the head of the table. "Any trouble nding dirtbag?" she asked.

"No, we had to wait outside his girlfriend's place for about three hours, ut once he came out, Tim here snatched him up quickly," said Berto.

"Tim does pretty good work," added Sonny, smiling, "for a white guy." veryone, except Perillo, laughed.

"Well, let's eat, drink, watch the show and be merry. Maybe dumbledickfuck vill decide to share with us how he heard about Robert Caldo."

Berto and I matched up the doors of the box-trap and the birdcage. The rat was leery to make the move. "Wait a second, pull the trap away," aid Lily, "We need to prime the pump." She removed her leaf pendant nd, holding it firmly, gracefully put her arm through the door of the irdcage. She smiled up at Perillo and scratched a line across his stomach, leep enough to draw blood. She then made another line, intersecting to orm an "X", as Perillo winced in pain. "Now let's introduce our furry little riend to the crossroads," she teased.

We lined up the cage doors and I shook the trap to get the reluctant odent onto Perillo's stomach. The rat ran a fast circle around the perimeter f the birdcage. Berto plugged in the heat lamp. We washed up and sat at the able eating. "So did you guys have fun shopping for shoes?" asked Berto.

"Yes, I had to get two pairs of heels, one red and one black," said Lily.

"Those sound pretty hot. I can't wait to see them on you," I said. Lily vas one tough nut to crack, and always difficult to gauge her reactions, but he unpredictability helped to make her a competent leader.

"Well, Jolen had me trying on nearly every damn shoe in the place," she egan, "It's good and bad to take him shoe shopping with me. Good because he has an eye for fashion, but bad because he wants me to try on a thousand different shoes. It got to a point where he was more interested in shopping than I was. Maybe next time I will bring you with me, Tim." Jolen made a frowning face and I wasn't sure how to respond, so I just smiled. "You, too, of course, Jolen, darling," she added, and his frown turned to a wide grin. Jolen's grin was contagious and made all of us, except Perillo, grin with him.

"I brought you guys a case of Nong Shim Shin Korean ramen," she said, as we looked at the red box on the table. "Tim, take them down to the pantry and get me another beer on the way back." I carried the box away, Perillo began to scream in agony. His body struggled violently against the ropes that bound him.

"Well, well, well," teased Lily, "looks like somebody isn't having much fun."

When I returned with her cold beer, she was standing over Perillo, munching on a fried shrimp. The rat was focused on one small area of Perillo's stomach. It continued to claw frantically, dipping its head into the blood-filled hole, before going back to clawing. Perillo was now screaming in sheer torment. I handed Lily her beer. "Thank you, honey," she said, before dropping the tail of a shrimp directly into Perillo's open mouth. He promptly spit it out and spit towards her.

"Motherfucker; let me out!" he shouted.

"Oh, my," cooed Lily, elegantly sipping from the beer bottle with a pinky extended. "Somebody has a potty mouth. Maybe potty mouth wants to save himself a tummy ache by giving us some information."

The rat continued to digging, the center of the "X" carved by Lily, the crossroads. Blood flowed steadily over both sides of his hips, dripping onto the white floor. The rat now had his head burrowed into the stomach, attempting to go deeper into the bloody hole in order to escape the fiery rays of the heat lamp.

"Please, for the love of God, stop!" screamed Perillo.

"I don't believe in any god," stated Lily, "well; bacon, I like bacon as my god."

"Please, I beg you," he pleaded.

"Just give us a name, dumbass. Who told you about Robert Caldo being involved in drugs?" she asked.

"Giselle, Giselle Binez; she works at M Café; now please, let me free!" he confessed, shouting.

"Gentlemen, go get Giselle; we need to find out if dumbledipfuck is telling the truth."

"I am! I am! It was Giselle! Please let me free!" he screamed, as the rat was now burrowed halfway into his stomach.

Sonny, Berto and I went to the van. We had to go back to Makati. "Okay, my guess is that Giselle is probably a bar girl on the prowl for expats. Tim, you're going to go in like you are alone and just chill at the bar. Sonny and I will scout around from a table in the back," advised Berto.

"Should I ask for Giselle by name?" I asked.

Berto considered it before replying, "No, she probably goes by a bar name. I need to call Juvi and try to get some lowdown." He dialed his cell and had a five-minute discussion in Tagalog.

M Club was off of Makati Avenue. The crowd here was a bit upscale, artsy-fartsy and wannabe socialites. There was a mix of college students, expats and fashion-conscious yuppies. I entered and took a seat at the corner of the bar, ordering a soda while perusing the menu. I saw Juvi show up within fifteen minutes, entering with Berto and Sonny. Sonny got change and pretended to pay Juvi, as if for cab fare. Juvi and Berto talked for a bit and Juvi left. Berto approached a table of well dressed men and women and began talking to one of the girls who wore a short blue dress. She was in her mid-twenties, petite and very easy on the eyes. She was also dressed for seduction, the dress showing lots of soft skin, the neckline lots of cleavage and the length was between her knees and waist, revealing lots of leg. Berto managed to coax her outside of the entrance door and Sonny followed. I drained the remnants of soda, left a bill on the bar and headed out. The dark spirit in me was feeding off of the excitement from capturing a new victim, and a very pretty one at that.

Once out of the door, Berto clamped her in his arm and held a gun on her while leading her to the van. He did it in such a way that the casual observer would merely assume they were a loving couple out for a night on the town. Sonny opened the door of the van and she was lifted in without drawing any unnecessary attention. Once she was on board, we began to drive back to Caloocan.

"What's this about?" she asked, "Are you guys going to rape me?"

"Don't flatter yourself, sweetheart," said Sonny, "though it's not because you're ugly. I'm a married man and these two are homos." Berto and I laughed.

"We just need to ask you some questions" said Berto. The demon inside my head wanted to add 'and torture and kill you' but I resisted saying it out loud. Inside, though, I could not wait to torture and kill her. I was feeling the itch. Perillo and his rat had stirred up a fever in me; like an appetizer to this main course. I wanted to make more pain; create more death. I wasn't who I used to be.

"Where are you taking me?" she asked, growing more restless and fearful as the van crawled through a sea of honking horns. Her eyes were darting around the van, looking for a way out. "What is it you want to know? Just ask me here and let me out!"

Shut the hell up or I'll cut your tongue out and eat it myself! I barked, the demon now driving my brain. She began to cry and sob. We ignored her. I was delighted when we reached the Caloocan warehouse and no blindfold was put on her. This was a promising sign.

We took her by the arms into the warehouse. Jolen and Lily were chatting at a table and there was a massive pool of blood drained onto the floor from Perillo's hollowed out abdomen. His head was turned sideways and his tongue hung from the corner of his mouth. It was a sweet view of death.

"Hey, that didn't take long," said Lily, "Any trouble finding the chatty bar slut?"

"Nope, offered her shabu and she came right with me," replied Berto. The only real trouble we had was that Sonny kept trying to bang her on the way here, and while he was driving" he teased, Sonny scoffed and gave him a flapper with his hand. "So rat boy is down for the count; couldn't even hang in there long enough to welcome us back?"

"No" answered Jolen, "Lily forced his head up so he had to watch the rat eat all the way inside of his stomach. It was awesome; but I'm afraid the poor boy lacked the intestinal fortitude to appreciate it."

Giselle began to scream when she realized what fate had come to Perillo. She turned away, sobbing, asking through sobs "There's a rat inside of him?"

"Yes honey, a rat bigger than Sonny's cock," said Lily, "but we're not going to use a rat or Sonny on you, so don't worry your pretty little head. But, that's only if you share with us how you knew information about Robert Caldo. We need to know honey . . . or else."

"What information? I barely know Robert." She replied.

"How did you know of his involvement with shabu and coke? It's vitally important you tell me, dear."

"I partied with him one night and he gave me some and sold some to other people while I was with him."

Where did you meet him?" Lily pressed.

"Okay, he picked me up at the bar; seemed nice and had money. We went to A Venue and got a room and drank and did dope and we, well, had sex a few times. That's the entire story. In the morning, we went our separate ways and I don't even think he took my phone number or anything. That's all, and it's the truth," she said, no longer crying and sounding sincere.

"Did you know he was a politician?"

"Not really, lots of men make themselves out to be big-shots, so I never really believe what they say. He was handsome, fun, had money and dope; that was what attracted me."

"Take her to the warehouse and wait by the garment rack," Lily told Sonny, "Berto, Tim, come with me." We followed her out to her car. In the back seat was a six-foot long, two-person saw. The two-person bucksaw had very large teeth to it, one-half of an inch deep. It was the kind of saw usually depicted in pictures with two burly lumberjacks pushing and pulling their way through the base of a thick tree.

"Holy crap," exclaimed Berto, "What do you got planned with this thing?"

"You and Tim," answered Lily, "Are going to perform a magic act, sawing a woman in half."

Sweet! I blurted out, happy to maim and kill and happier that Lily chose me for the task.

"Oh man," chuckled Berto, "I don't mind doing some sick things, but this is kind of pushing it. I mean, can't we just shoot her? Besides, all she did was screw some horny politician."

"No, I want a magic show. And it isn't the screwing, it's the blabbing her mouth that sealed her fate. Robert is a friend of the syndicate. She needs to go, in style," said Lily, firmly. Berto and I carried the saw into the warehouse.

We removed the wheels from the sturdy base of the industrial garment rack. We then tied Giselle upside-down by her ankles from corner to corner, so her legs were spread. Her screams grew louder and louder, so we taped up her mouth. Once suspended, we tied her wrists from corner to corner at the base, forming an "X" with her body. The demon in me delighted to be at the crossroads again. First, the lines scratched by Lily's precious hand on Perillo's stomach, and now legs and arms spread. Just as the rat burrowed where the lines intersected, so, too, would we begin the saw at the intersection, right at the base of her cunt-bone. My mind also whirled at a crossroads between sanity and insanity. I was joyous inside at the thought of sawing her in half. I went down to the crossroads and was no longer the same.

Berto held the opposite handle of the long bucksaw as I passed it to him through her upside-down, fully spread legs. Lily, Jolen and Sonny stood off to the side, drinking beer and watching the show. It was a unique feeling to rest the teeth of the saw blade right on the flesh between her legs. I shoved the blade forcefully towards Berto, as her body rippled in contorted, agonizing pain. The blood began to flow quickly down her body from the initial incision of the half-inch teeth. It poured down her chest and back, going into her hair before oozing onto the concrete floor.

Berto pushed the blade back towards me as I pulled. Now blood was spurting from her, arcing up into the air and splattering all over the floor. Her body was now electrified with pain, convulsing violently. Her eyes, dear reader, were a beautiful sight. They were wide-open and pleading in appearance, as blood flowed around them and over them, gushing like a river from her crotch. They would blink through the blood and become fully wide-open again. I looked at Lily and she was smiling, as if we both knew what the other were thinking, that this was a beautiful act of disturbing magic.

I shoved the saw back towards Berto. We were now cutting through bone and the grind of the teeth over the hard calcium felt satisfying as it sent vibrations through my forearms. White chips of cunt-bone flew through the air. I pulled the blade back towards me, maniacally. Berto's face was pale and he did not push from his side. He released the handle of the saw and doubled-over with his hands on his knees. He began vomiting bile and beer onto the floor, where it splashed into the blood. Lily and Jolen began to laugh hysterically, pointing at him and leaning on each other in laughter. With his head still turned downwards, he managed to raise and arm, giving them the finger.

"I'll take over from here, out of the way, girlie man," teased Sonny. Berto backed up and began to dry heave.

Sonny pushed the blade, and we began to saw with renewed vigor. Blood squirted and bone chips flew through the air as we continued to saw. I grinned at Sonny and he grinned right back. Blood was splattered all over our faces, arms and chests. Bits of white bone were flaked in with the blood, giving it a glittery effect. Dear reader, Sonny and I were Mclovin' it. He was as insane as I was, but more skillful as a driver.

By the time the blade had cut through to her belly, sawing through tailbone and spine, we were both sweating and soaked with blood. Even

ur legs were painted red, with white flecks of calcium. I wanted to saw
all the way down, splitting her skull. I believe Sonny was game for it, too,
but Lily said, "Enough, you need to clean all this blood up and bury these
bodies."

"Okay Lily" I agreed, releasing my grip on the saw and wiping away the
sweaty blood from my forehead.

"This place is like a slaughterhouse, so get busy. I'll see you guys
omorrow afternoon. Jolen will fill you in on the details," said Lily, before
eaving.

There was blood everywhere. I knew it was going to take hours just to
get the blood up off the floor with a mop. "I'm going to go dig the graves
before I haul the bodies out there, otherwise the rats will be gnawing away
at them."

"Okay, I'll start mopping in here," said Jolen.

"You're going to help?"

"Sure, you're my friend," he said, smiling. For someone who was
enjoying killing and torturing so much lately, I felt truly happy to hear
him call me his friend. I suppose, dear reader, even the most vile and evil
among us need friendship. I belonged to the family.

I went outside and began to dig. The moon was nearly full, making
the Manila night fairly visible in the open field. I dug a grave on each side
of where Pete was buried the night before. About every fifteen minutes,
I could see Jolen opening the warehouse door to change the bloody mop
water. Killing and torturing was easier than the cleaning up afterwards.

I went back inside once both graves were dug. I cut the rope from
Giselle's wrists and her arms dangled straight down, soaking in a pool of
blood. When I cut the rope from her ankles, her body hit the hard floor
with a thud, like a sack of rice. The huge incision from the saw was gaping
ed with bloody flesh and bone. I grabbed her ankles and pulled, walking
backwards to the exit door. A trail of smeared blood followed the corpse. I
dragged her to the hole and covered it with dirt. About the fifth shovel full
of dirt, I thought I saw her arm move. Perhaps the light of the moon was
playing tricks upon me. I somehow felt horrible to bury her alive, yet no
emorse at viciously sawing her in half. Wouldn't a sane person choose the
ormer over the latter? I felt compelled to make certain she was dead before
urial, so I rammed the spade of the shovel forcefully through her throat,
evering her head. Her mouth opened and her eyes stared at me, growing
vider as the shovel went through her neck, as if thanking me for the favor.
I filled in the grave with dirt.

I went back in the warehouse to get Perillo. Jolen had mopped up the majority of the blood on the floor. I took the knife and began to cut the blood soaked ropes binding his body to the table. I then unplugged the heat lamp and removed it, before hacking at the ropes going through the birdcage. After cutting the ropes on one side, I lifted the cage to cut the ropes on the opposite side. While reaching across, the bloody knife accidentally slipped from my hand, landing in the open cavity of Perillo's hollowed stomach. Without thinking, I reached into the bloody cesspool to grab the knife. A searing pain traveled from the tip of my finger, up my spine, reverberating signals of agony into my brain. "Ouch, damn!" I screamed. The rat had sunk its razor sharp teeth into the tip of my index finger.

In a rage, I grabbed the knife and aimed for the rat, catching his hind leg. He squealed, turned and bit the wrist of my knife hand. "Bastard!" I shouted again. The rat hopped off of the body and wobbled quickly out of the room. I looked down at my throbbing hand. It would be a miracle if the bites were not infected, considering the mix of Perillo's blood, the rat's blood and my own blood. The pain pulsated with an immense intensity. The cuts were deep, due to the rat's long incisors. The bleeding would not stop.

"Who's the bastard?" asked Jolen, who came to see what I was shouting about, as I wrapped a rag around my wrist and held it there with duct-tape.

"That fucking rat bit me, twice," I replied, showing him my duct-taped hand.

"Ouch; that sucks; you're going to need to put something on that to avoid infection. I'll run to the store."

"Thank you; I'll be out back burying Perillo. I appreciate all of your help, Jolen."

"No problem, besides, you're crazy enough already without getting rabies into the mix," he said, laughing.

I had to laugh as well. As I drug Perillo outside I thought about rabies. I'd always heard if you got bit by a rat, you would get rabies. I wondered if I would get rabies. Jolen was joking, but he had a point, with the dark spirit swimming around in my mind, how would I even know if I was rabid? I pushed the thoughts away. Crazy or rabid or both, they made no difference to me. I buried Perillo.

Jolen returned after I was finished. "You'll need to soak the bites, and then wrap everything with this clean gauze." He handed me a bottle of eroxide and a box of gauze. "I'll finish up mopping this room and the allway. You go clean those bites."

That night, as I lay on my cot exhausted from another long day of idnapping, torture and murder, I wondered to myself about who I had ecome. What kind of person was I now? Who would I be in the future? What kind of future could I look forward to? The throbbing pain of my vrist and finger would not allow me to sleep. Then came the what ifs; what f Perillo had aids? What if the rat carried bubonic plague? What if the eroxide was too little, too late? The pain shot up my arm and I imagined he disease of rabies traveling with it, spreading itself in the blood that raveled the circuits of my body. Just when all of my thoughts darkened bout the hopelessness of how my entire situation would end, I thought f my new family. I thought of Reshi. Nothing else mattered, really. My ommitment to the syndicate was unconditional and absolute, even if it vas not always reciprocated. Like the old blues singer, Robert Johnson, I old my soul, at the crossroads of the world, to the criminal underworld of Manila. I was Lily's killing machine. I am a machine of the syndicate. Since wasn't in Stockholm, I had Manila Syndrome.

I somehow fell asleep that night and dreamed that I was on a beach vith Lily. We were walking together, side by side. But my footing somehow ecame slippery, as it often does in nightmares of being chased. I could ot catch up to the pace of her death march. I tried to speed up, but the ap between us remained consistent. She turned back and looked at me, he sun reflected off of her beautiful, elegant Asian face, her black silky air blowing in the sea-breeze, and smiled at me. I wanted to catch up o her. I doubled my effort to catch up to her with renewed vigor and letermination, but, alas, it was no use. After giving me a smile, she turned nd walked straight into the ocean. I followed her. She walked until it vas to her delicate neck, turned and smiled once more, and then walked nder, the water being deeper than her head. I followed her, walking under he water. It became impossible to breathe. I was near death. My body uddenly bolted upright in my cot, gasping for air. Between the throbbing n my hand and the nightmares in my head, I did not sleep well that night; still do not sleep well. I have been plagued with dreams involving death nd separation from the syndicate, which, to me, are one and the same.

The next day Jolen and I talked about all things which we both are assionate about. He's a writer, sensitive and perceptive. We talked about oetry, theology and psychology. We also talked about Lily and Reshi. olen was as passionate about Lily as I was about Reshi, though without the sexual attraction. He loved her like his sister. We were both in love with their minds. Lily is full of imagination, logic and has a rapier wit to an extent that her mind is unique in its versatility. Reshi thinks creatively and one can never predict what she is thinking or what she might say. She is also kind and generous, yet perceptive and able to read anyone like a book. I have no idea of their IQ scores, but my guess is that they are both out of the ballpark. Lily can also shift from caring and compassionate to cold blooded killer and back again within the blink of an eye. For Jolen and me, our emotions often cloud our logic which is something we discussed in great detail. For Lily and Reshi, their logic and emotions are disciplined. They can exclude one from the other at will, or use any combination or measurement of each as the specific occasion might call for. It was clear that Lily was Jolen's best friend and it was also clear that his love for her will always run deep.

I was at ease with Jolen, since he was a good listener, and shared with him how I felt about Reshi. He was supportive but warned me that Lily was still my boss and to be discreet. I also told him about my new passenger, the dark spirit that took over the reins of my brain at times. I told him that I haven't felt the same since Boracay. How, since it entered me, I have been hungry to kill, maim and torture people that I do not even know. Jolen empathized because he also felt compelled to hate anyone who Lily hated, though he wasn't keen on the violence. He also related to having a demon, but his dark spirit caused him to punish himself. I did not press for details, since I could sense he preferred not to discuss it in detail. We saw ourselves as two sensitive souls trying to survive in an often insensitive world. We loved beautiful things and beautiful people. We both worked for the most the most vicious syndicate vixen in Asia.

CHAPTER V
All Down the Line

I mean, they call it Stockholm Syndrome and post traumatic stress disorder. And, you know, I had no free will. I had virtually no free will until I was separated from them for about two weeks.

—Patty Hearst

The next night, Jolen and I met Reshi and Lily at a club in Malate, the Bed Club. On the way there, I asked him, "So, what's this Bed Club like?"

"Oh, it's cool; it's a gay bar, but nobody will bother you if you just tell them you're not gay."

"Uhm, okay, how come Reshi and Lily go there?"

"Gay bars are the best. They're treated like divas and the drunks aren't hitting on them the whole time. Sometimes Reshi turns a gay guy temporarily straight," he revealed, laughing.

"I can believe that. Who the hell wouldn't want to screw Reshi?" I asked.

"Me" answered Jolen, as we both laughed. "And Lily, well, she just has fun hanging out with gays, like a true fag hag."

"This should be interesting," I replied, as we entered the club. Surprisingly, there were a lot of women here, good looking women. "What's the deal," I asked Jolen, "Are all these hot chicks Lesbos?"

"Well, my friend, nothing is cut and dry, especially here in Manila. Usually, the only thing separating a straight chick from a dyke is about a bottle and a half of wine," he joked, laughing.

Reshi and Lily were both dressed to kill; Reshi looking not just beautiful, but movie-star beautiful. Lily wore a silky black dress, with black strappy heels and black jewelry. Her elegant cheekbones gave her an aura of royalty and her graceful movement added to the majesty of her appearance. Reshi had her hair pulled up and pinned, Geisha style. She wore a tight black skirt that showed the shape and curvature of her fine ass. Her waist was cinched tight with a double-studded black belt that was three-inches wide. She wore a red silk blouse, unbuttoned nearly halfway down her chest with no bra; evidenced by the way her nipples subtly protruded from the loose, breezy material. Her cleavage accentuated the size and shape of her ample breasts. With blue eye shadow and light blue blush and ruby lipstick, her face gave the appearance of the most alluring China-doll to ever come to life. Her black, five-inch stilettos not only made her taller, but she knew just how to walk in them. Her hips swayed with each short step, one heel landing directly in front of the other. Reshi's bubbly, outgoing, flirtatious personality that made the package complete.

She rose from our table, the outline of her nipples pressed teasingly against the red, bright, loose silk. "I'm going to find a couple of boy toys," she announced, laughing. Lily and Jolen laughed and cheered her on to do her thing. I wasn't completely ignorant to fetishes and kinkiness, but since this was new, I had to ask, "If these guys are all gay, why does she want to pick them up?"

Jolen chuckled, "You Westerners want everything in neat categories, like no behavior, preference or taste shall ever cross or blend into another self-imposed category."

Playing devil's advocate, I returned, "But you're gay; you wouldn't want to have a girl trying to pick you up, would you?"

Jolen and Lily laughed, "I might pick him up and poke him with a big strap-on," stated Lily.

"Oooh, I like the sound of that," returned Jolen, "Do I get dinner and a movie first?" We all laughed.

Reshi approached two Filipino men in their late twenties who were dancing together. One wore a tight, white, v-cut, t-shirt with tight jeans. The other wore a loose black dress shirt and jeans. Reshi began rubbing both of their backs in a slow circular motion, in time to the trance music, smiling at them as they danced facing each other.

"Reshi has exquisite taste," observed Jolen, licking his lips.

"She wears a ring, is she married?" I asked, still confused by the lack of sexual inhibitions.

Lily and Jolen both laughed, "Tim, just put away your rule book and et people be themselves, accept them as they are. Don't be a judgmental rick," said Lily.

"Okay, I got this," I replied, "Live and let live."

"Yes" answered Lily.

"Unless," I joked, "Lily says otherwise."

"Damn straight," answered Jolen, before pointing towards the bar. 'That guy at the end is kind of cute. I'm going in. Wish me luck." He left he table to approach the bar.

"Good luck, Homeo," teased Lily. Jolen turned back and winked at her n route to the bar.

Reshi came back to our table with her two new friends. "Tim, Lily, I'd ike you to meet Pablo and Thadeus. Pablo, Thadeus, meet Tim and Lily." We traded handshakes and Pablo held Lily's hand and kissed it.

Lily made certain to keep the drinks flowing while the two men sat on each side of Reshi, discussing music and fashion. Reshi flirted coquettishly vith both of them, laughing and rubbing their chests and gently stroking heir arms. Pablo mentioned that he liked her shoes and Reshi replied with, 'Maybe if you play your cards right you can wear them later, honey."

"Oh yeah" Pablo grinned, giving a high-five to Thadeus.

As the three of them laughed, drank and got to know each other better, Lily shared stories with me about when she was growing up in Manila. I heard tales about her and Reshi getting in trouble as rebellious teenagers, and expelled from school, to adventures in downloading and reselling pirated movies. It was clear that her youth was not just as wild as mine, but nore so. The opportunities to get into trouble for a gorgeous, rebellious, teenage girl in Manila were endless.

Jolen came back to our table, "I'm going to go out with my new friend, Orlon" he told Lily, "I'll see you tomorrow."

"Okay, honey, have fun," she replied.

A few drinks later, Reshi suggested we go to a nearby hotel so she could have playtime with her new boy toys. We went out into the night and walked a few blocks, turning up Mabini Street to the Thai-themed Dusit Thani Hotel. Reshi paid the clerk for the largest two-bedroom suite available. The room was clean, spacious and had plenty of mirrors. Lily ent me on a mission to get more beer, saying it might be a long night.

I walked up to the nearest convenience store and got a case of San Miguel. By the time I returned, things had begun to get very interesting. The first thing I noticed was that Pablo and Thadeus were completely naked. Apparently, Reshi had them remove their clothes while I was out. I put the beer in the refrigerator, opened one and handed it to Lily.

"Thank you, hon; have a seat, things are about to get interesting," she said, then louder to Reshi, "Have these guys kiss like in a romantic fairy-tale."

Reshi, smiled, sitting across the room, and began to laugh, "Okay, you guys heard the boss; hold each other tight and kiss."

I felt kind of awkward seeing two naked guys making out, but I was happy just to sit next to Lily and enjoy her company. Reshi rose from her seat and approached them, rubbing their backs before moving her hands downward, slowly.

"I think Tim and I are going to go in the room and leave you guys and gal in peace," said Lily, before going to the refrigerator and carrying out six bottles of beer. Our room had a queen-sized bed, mirrors, red curtains, a small balcony and its own small bathroom.

"That was kind of weird," I said to Lily.

She laughed, "Oh, I'm sure it's about to get way more surreal. Reshi's kinky, and she likes what she likes. What about you?"

"What about me?" I asked, puzzled.

"Do you want to do me?" asked Lily, smiling.

"Hell, yes" I replied, enthusiastically.

"You can, let's go on the balcony. I want to finish my beer," she replied, matter-of-factly. We went out on the balcony, looking out at the city view of Makati. We talked about Bob Dylan, John Keats, hypnosis, death, perversion, truth and beauty. Discussing ideas with Lily was always fascinating because she saw sides of things from many angles, her perception and interpretations were always multi-dimensional. I loved her mind and body. We also discussed "Stockholm syndrome" and the fun and freedom I had found since being "kidnapped".

"Hasn't it crossed your mind to escape or run off to the Embassy and tell them your situation?" she asked.

"Not really; though Pete wanted to."

"Fuck Pete" she said, taking a swig of beer.

"I like being with the syndicate. It's like family to me." I confessed.

"Oh Christ, Tim, surely you have family back in the states."

"And what if I like this one more?" I asked.

"Well, it's great for us, I guess."

"Are we still going to fuck tonight?" I asked.

"Oh yeah"

"Well, that's great for me, then," I smiled.

And we did it, dear reader. It began out on the balcony. It was animalistic, he demon in my head connected to Lily in passion. Her flexibility gave ntercourse a whole variety of dimensions, and allowed for positions I never knew existed. My eyes were locked into her eyes and the steady rhythm of our bodies made sweat drip from both. I wanted it to last forever. It went on and on, until something flickered and I screamed as she moaned. The breeze from the open balcony door blew the red curtain towards us and ecstasy filled the air with most intense release. We rested and did it all over again, a lion and lioness living like animals all through the Manila night.

A few days went by before I saw her again. I passed the time helping Sonny run errands around the city. Sonny worked as a driver for an automotive parts company and no two work days were ever the same. Sonny had a wife and children and his family meant the world to him. I just tagged along as he made his rounds.

I could not distinguish between the aching in the tip of my finger and he constant throb from the bite on my wrist. My entire hand throbbed and, at times, was on fire. I kept clean gauze taped around the bites. What worried me was wondering if simply rinsing the bites in peroxide was good enough to keep away infection. The whole hand was swollen. I banked on he great physician of time to heal it.

Sleep was also a rare commodity. The pain was more intense at night and, combined with the continuous scurrying of rats through the warehouse, made it difficult to finally fall asleep. Even worse, when I could fall asleep, I was plagued with nightmares. Once I got back to the warehouse, after Lily dropped me off, I had an unforgettable one.

I dreamed there was an angel standing at the foot of my bed. Her face was radiant, peaceful and smiling. She stood five-foot, with silvery wings and luminescent beauty. She whispered to me, "come" and I followed her as she glided down the hallway, illuminating a path for me. "Sit, I will comfort you, and you will know peace," she smiled.

"I could use some peace," I told her.

Her body gave of an aura of white light. I could hear her wings gently rustle as she leaned forward and kissed me on the head. Her lips sent a gentle warmth down my spine and through my body. She smiled, "eat he fruit, child" and a bowl of plump grapes appeared directly in front of me. I began to eat, slowly savoring the sweetness of the fruit. The grapes were like no grapes I had ever tasted before, the texture of their skin, once broken, was like miniature water balloons bursting with sweetness.

The angel stood and backed up towards the outer-darkness. Her smile slightly changed to a grin, an evil grin. The shift was subtle, but very frightening. As her grin widened, I noticed fangs at each side of her mouth. She quickly lurched forward, her face directly in front of my own. Her wings hunched high, towering over me. Her face turned wrinkled, ancient and distorted. The eyes tinted green and her breath smelled of sulfur. She began to laugh in a deep growl that was menacing and genderless. I pushed myself backwards, but was trapped against the wall. I screamed in terror and was suddenly aware of being awake. I was not in my cot, though. I was in the darkness of the warehouse. I had something in my mouth, but it was not the sweetness of grapes. There was something in my hands and I brought them up to my face to see the half-eaten bloody carcass of a rat. Guts were hanging from its stomach and there was blood smeared all over my clothes. I screamed, realizing I had been eating a dead rat and not sweet grapes.

I spit out the vile fur, bloody tubes and rodent organs onto the floor. "What the hell you doing out here?" asked Jolen, who was awakened by my screams.

"Uh, something weird happened," I said, still spitting fur. Jolen turned the light on and was taken aback by my late-night snack. I looked closely at the carcass and could see a puncture wound in its hind leg. I grinned with joy to know that I was eating the rat that had bit my hand a day before.

"You're eating a rat and smiling about it?" asked Jolen, puzzled.

"It's the rat that bit me. I dreamed I was eating grapes with an angel, but it was a rat."

Jolen laughed, "Okay buddy, whatever floats your boat. I'm going back to sleep. You do your thing."

Dear reader, I was going insane and enjoying it. It was as if Lily had transferred something to me during our time of together. I was not the same. I was turning into a stranger, one who lived to kill. *Insanity saves.* I took the bloody rodent to the back door and threw the carcass outside. I went to the sink and washed my hands and rinsed out my mouth before returning to my cot to try to sleep again.

Lily, Sonny, Reshi, Berto and Jolen were all at the meeting table the next morning. They were having another breakfast from Jollibee. "You want some?" asked Sonny.

"No thanks, I'm not too hungry," I replied.

"Why the do you have blood all over you?" asked Lily. I was not sure what to say, but I was too tired to make up a creative alibi.

"I thought I was eating grapes and when I woke up it was actually a rat." Everyone in the room began to laugh, hard, to the point of slapping knees.

"He was reading John Steinbeck, Grapes of Rat" added Jolen, and they all laughed harder. Realizing it was hopeless, I began to laugh too.

"Well, damn, go get cleaned up," said Lily, "That shit's nasty."

I left the room to shower and could still hear them all laughing from the hallway. After showering and putting on clean clothes and wrapping my hand with fresh gauze, I sat down, rejoining the group at the table.

"Okay, listen up," began Lily, "There's a dyke who owns an upscale restaurant, Je Suis Gormand, and she has been a close friend of the syndicate for a long time. Her former business partner, Sheryl Andrada, is trying to file a lawsuit against her, claiming that she is half-owner. What I need is for you guys to find Sheryl, bring her here and we need to make her tell us where all of her legal and business documents are located. Once we have those, we can make her vanish."

"So, we get to torture her first?" I asked.

"That is correct, rat boy. And I'm thinking of using my personal favorite torturing device, the iron maiden, baby!" said Lily. We began to chuckle at her enthusiasm.

"Where will we get one of those?" asked Reshi, "The name has a delightful ring to it."

"Well, Jolen and Berto can make one while Sonny and Ratatouille go get Sheryl. She lives in an apartment in Bonafacio. Sonny, you can call Juvi for the location" said Lily, adding "Our iron maiden will be more of a contemporary design. We will use a crate large enough to hold a person when it stands on end. The spikes will be five-inch nails pounded through on all sides except the bottom where she will stand. The nails should be long enough to just puncture her skin when the front is closed tight."

That sounds awesome! I exclaimed.

"Oh, yeah," replied Lily, "Sonny, call me once you have Sheryl."

"You got it" said Sonny, before we left in the van. The traffic jams made us lose time and we spent more than a few ten-minute periods at a complete standstill, but such is life in Manila. Sonny called Juvi during one of the traffic gridlocks. We finally met up with him where his cab was parked around the circle at Market Market. He gave us Sheryl's address and also cautioned us that there were security guards there.

Scoping out her apartment, we realized it would be next to impossible to abduct her. Not only was there a guard monitoring traffic in and out, but we also saw security cameras at the entrance to parking. We parked the van two blocks away and entered on foot, under the guise that we were looking at an apartment to rent. We walked to the parking area and located the spot reserved for Sheryl, where a gray Nissan was parked. We went back to our van and pulled around to the street meeting the entrance and parked and waited. It was only a matter of fifteen minutes before Sheryl's car pulled out of the gate. Sonny got right behind the Nissan and two blocks later, at the first traffic light we came to, clipped the rear bumper of her car with the front of the van. Sonny immediately got out of the van, putting on an Oscar performance by acting apologetic. He pointed to the side of the road where she could pull over. Sonny then pulled the van behind the Nissan, leaving a four-foot gap between vehicles.

Sheryl got out of her car. She was dressed professionally and, while she was not the most attractive woman, her breasts were huge. She surveyed the damage to her car, kneeling down in a tight skirt for closer inspection of the bumper, while Sonny and I inspected her bumper. There was a bit of structural damage and a dent made where the van's bumper was higher.

"I'm very sorry, miss. For some reason the brakes just weren't working. May I borrow your phone? I need to call my boss. We might be able to take care of this very quickly."

"Of course," she responded, handing her phone to Sonny. I stood with Sheryl while he called somebody, or pretended to. While on the phone, Sonny went back to our van and began rummaging through the glove box, getting the gun, duct-tape and rope ready. I noticed badminton equipment inside of her car, so we talked about the sport. From there, our conversation drifted to ping-pong.

"Excuse me, mam," Sonny interrupted our conversation, "My boss would like to talk with you," he said, holding her phone out in his extended arm. He remained standing beside the open side door of the van.

"Of course," said Sheryl, walking to get the phone. Before she could say hello, Sonny forcefully shoved her into our van, where she began screaming and punching at the door as he closed it.

"Let's go," he yelled, running to the driver's side. I jumped in the passenger seat, realizing she still had her phone, "What about the phone?"

Sonny started the van and, smiling, held the phone battery up for display. "Get her tied up and tape her damn mouth shut. She's a loud one; you might want to give those titties a good squeeze too, while you're at it."

I grabbed the rope and moved towards her. Apparently badminton kept her in good shape because tying her up was easier said than done. She ounched me in the side of the head. My initial reaction was to stab her in the throat with the knife I held in one hand, but I remembered that we still needed to get information from her. She began clawing at my face, shouting and raising her knees up sharply as I tried my best to subdue her. I finally got a tight grip on her long hair and began violently shaking her head until her eyes became disoriented. Then I jammed her face flat into the seat and put my weight on her back.

I pried her arms back and managed to get her wrists tied together, in spite of her resisting with all she had every step of the way. I was covered in sweat, breathing hard and the gauze on my bitten hand came off in the struggle. Of all the syndicate targets so far, Sheryl put up the most fight. As much of a nuisance as it was, I liked her for it. Putting up a fight shows strong character.

I wrapped her mouth with duct-tape to stop her wailing and then tied her ankles together, after getting kicked about six times with her flailing legs. Sonny called Lily to tell her we were on our way. As we approached the Caloocan warehouse, I felt some concern over Sheryl's future. Whether the demon in my head was on a vacation or because of talking about badminton and ping-pong, I did not feel right about killing Sheryl. It seemed my conscience was acting up for the first time since I landed in Manila. I calmly explained to her the importance of cooperating if she wanted to stay alive. She attempted to head-butt me and kneed me with both knees for my compassion.

Sonny and I carried Sheryl into the meeting room. They were eating crispy pata and drinking beer. "Any trouble finding the bitch?" asked Lily.

"No, not finding her" said Sonny, "but getting her to cooperate was a bit difficult."

"Oh, a fighter" quipped Jolen, "and with big tits."

"Yeah," said Lily, "That's kind of hot."

"Should we put her in the iron maiden?" asked Berto.

"Damn" said Reshi, "Someone is very proud of their little torture chamber. Can a girl finish eating first?"

"Maybe she will just tell us where the papers are," I suggested. Lily looked at me with a raised eyebrow.

"Maybe someone wants to fuck this bitch," she returned.

"How romantic, the honeymoon with honeydews," offered Reshi, giggling.

We continued to eat and talk, leaving Sheryl on the floor to squirm and grunt. "Pull that tape from her mouth," instructed Lily, "Now listen, bitch,

I know you think you are entitled to be half-owner of Je Suis Gormand, and that you have a lawsuit filed. I'm here to tell you that you are not and nor will you ever be half-owner. In other words, let go, give it up and move on. You let me have all of your legal and business papers related to the restaurant and we will let you go and call it a day." I finished getting the tape off her mouth so she could respond.

"Fuck you!" she shouted from the floor. "Screw all of you and I hope you all burn in Hell!"

"I don't believe in Hell, sweetie," replied Lily, calmly, "but if that's your thing then I will help you get there, soon. Maybe you can get sodomized by Hitler. Take her to the maiden, oh yeah!" exclaimed Lily.

"Let go of me! Help, no!" she screamed before Berto grabbed her legs and I the upper-half. We took her to the warehouse.

"That looks badass," I commented on the box standing on the floor. With the door opened, the inside brought to mind Hellraiser, with hundreds of sharp nails all facing inwards. There were hinges on the door and a clasp handle. "How long did it take you guys to build it?"

"Just a few hours; Jolen has some carpentry skills. How'd your face get all scratched up?"

"Well, miss kitty cat here put up one hell of a fight. Plus, with those tits it was hard to fight back with a woody" I replied, as Berto laughed.

"Let's get her in," he said. We cut the ropes and forcefully held her in the box. We could feel the tips of the nails just piercing her skin as we closed the door.

The rest of the group was now in the warehouse and Lily walked up to the door and asked, "So, where can we find the legal papers?"

"Fuck you, skinny bitch!" screamed Sheryl from behind the closed door.

"Okay, honey, enjoy your stay at the Maiden Inn," Lily opened the door quickly and slammed it hard and we heard Sheryl scream from the movement. "That ought to take some of the wind out of her tits," she said, smiling, "Let's go drink some beer while she gets settled in to her new lodging."

We all sat at the table and the case of beer was gone in nearly an hour. Since I was the only one not drinking, they elected me to be the beer runner. Sonny looked at Lily and asked, "Aren't you worried he might drive off with the van? He is a hostage after all."

"Nah, he wants to fuck me again. He'll be back with the beer," she answered, as they all laughed. I didn't really laugh because I wanted to bang Reshi.

When I returned with the beer, Lily told us to go and carry the maiden back to the meeting room. As Berto, Sonny, Jolen and I lifted it, we could hear Sheryl screaming as the movement caused the nails to pierce her flesh deeper. We finally got it down the hall and into the meeting room. We set it down beside the table and everyone went back to drinking beer.

"Are you ready to tell me where the papers are, bitch?"

"Fuck you!" shouted the defiant voice from inside the box.

Lily stood up, walked to the door, pulled it open and slammed it shut. Then she repeated it, again and again and again and again. Each time the door opened, I could see Sheryl, full of puncture wounds, bleeding from hundreds of holes in her body. She cried and screamed louder with each vicious slam of the door. It was as if watching an old black and white film that flickered a scene of streams of blood as they ran down her body.

"You feel like telling yet? We'll let you free," yelled Lily, before taking a long pull of beer from her bottle on the table.

"Okay, okay," conceded Sheryl, "the papers are in the trunk of my car, in a black briefcase."

"Good honey," Lily replied, "Sonny, if you're okay to drive, I need you to go and get those papers. Call me as soon as you locate them and bring them back."

"No problem," answered Sonny, while pulling the Nissan keys from his pocket to make sure he had them.

The beer drinking continued. Reshi told some stories about her trip to Canada and how cold it was there and about different guys that hit on her. Then Jolen told a story about back in college when Lily was completely drunk and starting a fight in a bar and he had to get her out of there before she was killed. During a tragic story about one of his exotic birds that died, Berto was interrupted by Lily's phone.

"The briefcase is there? The papers inside talk about Je Suis Gormand? Okay, great, just bring it all back with you."

"Are we going to let her go?" I asked.

Lily raised an eyebrow, "Oh, we're going to let her go all right," she said, raising her leg up and putting her black boot against the door of the box, "Let her go to Hell!" She pushed her leg sending the iron maiden box teetering backwards. It balanced on edge as her boot extended its toe forward. The box fell backwards with a force that sent a chilling gust of wind through the room, slamming onto the ground. Blood began to seep out of the sides. "Go bury the bitch in her coffin," said Lily, now laughing.

For some reason, I felt bad about this one. I felt part of something that I didn't fully agree with. The irony was that just a few days before I had no qualms about sawing a girl in half. Why the sudden change? I have no idea. I only know that sometimes I am somebody else; someone who relishes blood-lust and murder, someone capable of carving their mother's heart out of her chest and eating it raw. Right now, though, I wasn't feeling it. "Okay Lily" I replied, before Jolen helped me lift the box and carry it out to the burial field.

I got the shovel and began to dig. The hole had to be wider and deeper this time to accommodate the box. The lack of rain also didn't help, making the ground harder to unearth. It took at least two hours to make a big enough hole.

"Please, please" echoed a soft whimper from inside of the blood-soaked box. Apparently, the hard fall on the nails did not kill her yet. I was already feeling mixed emotions, now this coupe de grace. "Don't let me die, please" said the soft, shaky, frightened voice.

I mentally debated burying her while she was still alive. I felt trapped in a Poe story and wondered what it would be like to be buried while still alive. I tried to put myself in her shoes, the sound that the dirt would make as each shovel full landed on top of the box, steadily, until completely covered. I tried to imagine the darkness, the lack of oxygen and the shadowy time between life and one's final breath. Who's to say where one ends and the other begins? I was melancholy and saddened.

Then I thought of Lily and the syndicate. What must be done, will be done. I recalled Jolen's words from the first night that I met him, when he said, "You must always trust Lily." There was a fine line between trust and agreement. I loved being with the syndicate. I just wished Reshi was the leader because she was a Goddess with a kinder heart. I trusted Lily, to some degree, but she was heartless. I agreed to agree with Lily and proceeded to "bury the bitch".

I struggled to shove the bloody-box into the hole. Eventually, it slid in and I positioned the other end in for a perfect fit. I began scooping dirt over the top, over and over. "Please, God, no" came the voice from inside, now the pleading growing louder and more desperate.

"It is Lily's will" I resolved, before pitching another shovel full of dirt over the box. I repeated the process of scooping dirt, over and over, until there was no more pleading or whimpering heard. It was a relief to add the scoops of soil that drowned out her muffled protests. When it was all filled in, I patted down the dirt with the back of the shovel-head. Then I walked all over it to make it compact.

I walked back to the warehouse exhausted. I washed the dirt off my arms and hit my cot. I was physically drained, but there was no peace. My mind was racing, gushing like a faucet turned on full blast. I tried to adjust my position, lying on my back, on my stomach, and on my side. Just as I was about to enter the sleep mode, I heard a squeaky voice. I listened closely, completely still, and heard, "please, please, God no." It was Sheryl's voice. I wondered how she could have escaped the box and crawled from the grave to make it in here. I heard her again, she was under my cot! I leaned over the edge, peering into the darkness underneath. Two beady eyes stared back at me from under the cot. He squeaked, backed up to the wall, and scurried away.

CHAPTER VI
Turd on the Run

Di'mond rings, vaseline, you gave me disease,
Well, I lost a lot of love over you. Oww oh play it yeah
Boozin' in the bar rooms, cruisin' in the dark;
Tie your hands, tie your feet, throw you to the shark.
Make you sweat, make you scream, make you wish you'd never been,
I lost a lot of love over you.

"Turd on the Run"—Rolling Stones

I am gone, precious reader. I am god. I am a machine of chaos.
I am the master of shit storms. I don't remember choking Dan. I was
screaming in my sleep and he was just checking on me and I attacked
him. I liked Dan. He was witty, had a vulgar but amusing sense of
humor, though most of his jokes involved some aspect of pooping.
He was weird, yes, but he was still my buddy. Most of the time, he
was downright friendly. Luckily, Kinsey, the night guard, did damage
control on my behalf. He saved my insane, demon possessed ass. He
told them that the attack was not malicious, that I meant it to be
playing around but got too rough. The blue, bruised neck and stitches
looked like more than 'playing around' but Kinsey insisted I meant
no harm. He put his job at stake for me and I have to respect that.

Not only was I spared from going to jail, but now he still brings
me my notebook and pen, even in the solitary isolation ward. I have
minimal furnishings here, bed, sink toilet is about it. I'm allowed
into the main recreation room on a trial basis for a few hours a day,

between lunch and dinner, when they day staff is at its fullest. I hate
the invasion of privacy and resent Kinsey reading my notebook every
night, but he did go to bat for me. What can I do? Kinsey says he is
enjoying reading my story and asks if it's all true. I just smile and say
"don't worry about it." He hasn't ratted me out to any of the counselors
or doctors here, so maybe I can trust him, maybe. If you're reading
this now, and I'm pretty sure you are, Kinsey, thank you very much.
The demon may reward your reading. Careful what you read.

It has been nearly a year since I've talked to Lily or Reshi. I
wonder where they are, what they are doing, who they are with,
what Reshi is wearing, how she looks, what she is saying, what she
is thinking, what is making her angry, sad, happy and what makes
her laugh. I feel like an infant, a toddler, suddenly separated from
the mother he cherishes and adores; now helpless, hopeless, sad and
lost. The only thing saving me is writing. Pouring the memories onto
the page is therapeutic, like vomiting up my sorrows. It also keeps
the hope alive of seeing or hearing from them once more. I miss all
of them Juvi, Jolen, Berto and Sonny. They became like family in
the short time I knew them. Now I am an orphan and have only
loneliness. My demon relieves me of my loneliness, but at what a
price! Ironically, I find peace when the demon steals my mind away,
but I kill even friends during this tranquility. Such is my sadcat
story, gentle reader, now let me get back to how things were when I
was a lion, in the concrete jungle of Manila.

Pete and I paid to have our room for an entire month at the Mirage,
but now that Pete was in the ground and I was living at the Caloocan
warehouse, Reshi took over our room there. Being an entrepreneur, it
became a business location for her to do photo shoots, since she was a
model. She also dabbled in domination with a few wealthy submissive
businessmen who craved a spanking and whatnot from a beautiful woman.
Jolen shared with me some of the juicy details of ways that Reshi made the
most of her beauty and creativity by having some wealthy perverts who
paid for things like worshipping her feet, dressing up in her clothes, verbal
humiliation and one who just liked to be locked in a cage and ignored for
a few hours. Jolen explained how most of the men were married and they
paid top dollar for Reshi to help them with the kinky, forbidden pleasures
they dare not try at home. With Reshi, they had a gorgeous woman they
could trust and one who understood fetish, even better than they did.

"The guard at the Mirage royally pissed me off," said Reshi, as we sat at a table in a restaurant in China Town. I was happy to hear she was pissed at someone because the demon in me wanted blood. In fact, I felt like Major Payne when he said, "it's been two whole weeks since I killed me a man, and I got the itch." I no longer felt remorse about burying Sheryl alive. I was back in the death-horse saddle again. And to kill for precious Reshi, the Goddess of gorgeous Goddesses, made the idea even sweeter.

"How come, he hit on you in a rude way?" asked Lily, delicately turning a dimsum at the end of her chopsticks.

"No, the slimeball had a petty scam with a locksmith. On Sundays the manager is gone and he's the only guard on duty. While I went clothes shopping with a client, the jerk locked the deadbolt on the door that I don't have a key for. Then he pretended like nobody had a key for it and offered to call a locksmith, who happened to be his age, young kids. We had to wait in the hot musty hallway for an hour and then pay 800 pesos to get the door opened. I was so pissed!"

"What a petty scam," I said, taking a bite of some unidentifiable green vegetable.

"I know," replied Reshi, "I would have been happy to tip the pathetic moron one or two thousand just to be nice and helpful."

"Let's punish these pricks," said Lily, "I have no respect for smalltime crooks going after nickels and dimes. They're fucking worthless."

"Should we get them both?" asked Jolen.

"Oh yeah," said Lily, smiling. I knew that look on her face. It was the look that made my demon come alive. I could not wait to torture these guys now. That look could have persuaded me to kill anyone, even myself.

"The guard couldn't take his eyes off me. I could get him to go anywhere," stated Reshi, with unabashed confidence. In the guard's defense, I thought how it would be difficult for any man to not keep his eyes on Reshi. Lily was a looker, but Reshi was undeniably hypnotizing.

"We can just get the guard to the warehouse, and then make him call his buddy to come there," said Jolen.

"This has potential to be fun, let's get kinky with them," said Lily, giggling.

"We can film them doing naughty things to each other, then they will never tell a soul, if they survive," said Reshi.

"I doubt they will; these pricks messed with the wrong girl," said Lily. "We can stop by to ensnare the guard on our way back. Make him think he was a hot date with you tomorrow night," she added, while delicately biting into the dim-sum that was releasing steam at the end of her chopsticks.

"This will be fun," giggled Reshi, "I'm going to bring some goodies."

Lily arrived the following afternoon, announcing for us to carry in the three cases of Red Horse beer from her car. She carried two bottles of Johnny Walker Black in her arms. This was going to be a hell of a night. Lily wore jeans and a seductively transparent white top with strappy black heels.

"Reshi is on her way with the guard. Have your guns ready, gentlemen," she stated, as we brought the beer to the refrigerator.

The Filipino guard had no idea he was being set up, human nature being to accept things that seem too good to be true. He was all smiles, laughing and joking while walking with Reshi into the warehouse. Reshi wore a tight, stretchy, white mini-skirt, black tank top and heels that were clear. As she seductively sashayed into the meeting room, Sonny stood by the entrance and put his gun to the guard's head. "Okay, Einstein, one wrong move and I will blow your fucking head off" he warned.

The guard looked shocked and began to back away in fear. Lily fired her gun from where she sat, with a deafening blast that caused all of us to flinch for cover. The bullet went through the wall merely inches above the guards head. "Move again and the next one will be lower," she yelled. "Now call your locksmith butt-buddy and tell him to meet you at Jantzen Incorporated's Caloocan warehouse. You mess up this call in any way shape or form, you're dead."

It took only thirty minutes for the locksmith to arrive. Sonny greeted him out front, put a gun in his face and took the keys to his vehicle, before escorting him to the meeting room where the party was underway.

"Well, well, well, looks like we can let the games begin now that your girlfriend finally got here. I think he wants to pop your lock with his lollipop," said Lily, turning to Reshi, "Do you have something more comfortable for these girls to slip into?" she asked, giggling, before taking a long pull of Red Horse.

Reshi unzipped the travel bag on the table. "Hmmm, let's see what nice things we have here. Oh, some cute nighties! And what's this? Wigs!" she exclaimed, giggling.

"What have we done?" How come we were brought here?" the locksmith asked, nervous and wide-eyed.

"Don't play innocent you greedy little petty thief fucktard. You locked a deadbolt on the wrong door and split the money with your fuck-buddy here. You shouldn't have done that."

"He's not my fuck-buddy and," began the guard, before Reshi interrupted him.

"Oh, he will be" she said, "Now, shut up, take off your clothes and put this on. No more arguing, sweetie," she held up a pink nightgown, the hem at the bottom just touching the concrete floor. She smiled and held it forward.

"I'm not putting that on," he protested.

"Listen, dipshit, you can either put it on or I can shoot you in the foot and then you can put it on. I'd rather shoot you in the foot, but it's your call," resolved Lily.

"You guys should be very happy," reasoned Reshi, "Lots of guys pay big money to do things like this with two beautiful women."

He began to strip down, begrudgingly, as we began laughing and Jolen whistled. He pulled the nightgown on, awkwardly. Reshi approached him, smiling seductively and standing close enough that her protruding nipples in the tank top grazed his chest. "Oh honey," she began, "I think you look hot in pink. Doesn't the soft material feel good against your skin?" She moved her face closer to his, and then stepped backwards. The outline of his semi-erectness revealed itself through the soft material.

"Well, well, well, somebody is enjoying being a little slut," observed Lily, teasingly. "Okay, Goldilocks, you put on the red one." Reshi handed the locksmith the red nightgown.

"This is stupid," he complained, while taking his pants off.

"I'll blow your stupid head off," snapped Lily, "Now join on in the reinqueer games and stop being negative Nancy."

"Oh, fabulous," exclaimed Reshi, "Now you can help each other get your pretty wigs on." She threw the red one to the guard and the blonde one to the locksmith.

"Primp and preen those wigs just right, girls. I want you both to look good. I also want Red to do something naughty to Blondie, oh yeah!" said Lily, before tilting up a bottle of Red Horse and sliding her mouth up and down the neck as she winked at them.

"I'm not doing that," protested Red.

"Fine," said Lily, "Since you want to be a party-pooper," she lowered her .38 directly at him.

"Uh, wait," he cussed under his breath, and then went to his knees in front of Blondie, who lifted his nightgown for easier access. Then he did what he said he would not do.

"Ooooh, that's hot," purred Reshi, now standing beside Blondie and twirling the synthetic hair on the wig. "That's it, don't stop. See, you girls have fun when you work together, don't you?"

Reshi and Lily had them perform a whole array of depraved acts on one another for the next hour, as they drank beer and cheered them on in their forced debaucheries. Lily approached me and whispered in my ear, "I have an idea. Go find a small plastic bottle with the cap and fill it with gasoline."

"Okay," I agreed, before going down to the warehouse and rummaging around to find an empty iced-tea bottle in the trash. I took it out to Sonny's van and filled it up with the gas can he kept in the back. I brought the bottle to Lily.

"Perfect, let's have some fun now. You guys hold Goldilocks down over that stool," she said, smiling. "Reshi, dear, can you be a sweetie and lube up my gun?" She held the .38 forward in her extended arm.

"Why, of course, honey," Reshi replied, before coating the barrel of the gun with lubricant. Lily sat back in the chair, spread her legs, and held the gun in both hands, pointing it up from her crotch as if it were a penis.

"Okay, Little Red Riding Hood, come and ride the Big Bad Wolf," she ordered. The guard protested until she aimed the barrel at him, then he obediently walked over to where she sat, turned and lifted his nightgown. He slowly lowered himself onto the gun, working the tip of the .38 into an area where the air quality was questionable. "That's a good girl," she laughed, "Look at you, so eager! Now, I want you to ride it, up and down and up and down. That's it, baby; bounce!"

"I think Blondie feels neglected," Reshi said, picking up the plastic bottle and coating it with lubricant. "Blondie gets a big one; I bet she is very happy, aren't you?" She approached him, still sprawled over the stool, from behind and worked the cap end of the bottle into his body. He contorted in pain as she continued to force it in, not stopping until half the bottle was lodged. "Blondie is tight, aren't you honey?" she said, patting him gently on the butt cheek.

"Ride me Red Riding Hood! That's it! Bounce you slut!" shouted Lily, as Red continued to bounce up and down in her lap. "Tim, you need a smoke break," she suggested, smiling.

"Oh yeah," I replied. She had given me the smile. The smile I craved; the smile that endorsed me to commit pain and murder; the smile that makes my demon come alive and smile with her. I wasn't a smoker, but I knew what her smile suggested, something deliciously evil.

I fished a cigarette from the open box on the table and lit it. I then took a puff and motioned for Reshi to back way up. I put the ember end of the cigarette against the plastic bottle and held it until it melted a hole through the plastic. I then pushed it inside, where the gasoline ignited in an internal combustion. His scream was deafening, nearly louder than the gun blast of Lily's .38. She yelled "I'm cumming!" before firing the gun into Little Red Riding Hood's inner-sanctum, the bullet leaving his body through his throat.

Blondie frantically scrambled around the room, with a bluish orange flame burning from his hindquarters. The unsavory smell of burnt flesh, burnt plastic and gunpowder smoke weighed heavy on our breathing. Blondie continued to scream in sheer third-degree agony, while Red lay on the floor, apparently dead, with smoke and blood leaving his orifices.

The nonstop screams of Blondie, gripping his smoldering ass with burnt fingers, became too loud to endure. Lily lowered the .38 and shot him in the face out of mercy. Blood, bone and flesh flew against the wall behind him. "Oh well," observed Jolen after the deafening blast when silence returned, "At least they got to pleasure each other good before they died. I think it is how their families would have wanted it." We all began to laugh.

"Tim, come," called Lily, once the laughter finally subsided. "Kiss me," she said, and I did. "Now, take care of this mess and the bodies. Reshi and I are going out tonight. Just bury them in their wigs and gowns." I did not mind the kiss from Lily, but deep down I wished it were Reshi's lips I was kissing. Her plump, perfectly shaped lips would have been pure ecstasy. I wanted so bad to tell Reshi how much I adored her, but it was dangerous. Lily was the boss and her friend. If I pissed off Lily, it was a death sentence. Of course, this complication and obstacle made my fire of desire for sweet Reshi burn below the surface with even greater passion.

They all went out together as a group; Reshi, Lily, Sonny, Jolen and Berto. I was alone, but not in my head. I had a bat in the belfry, whatever a belfry is. The bloody silence was deafening, with the walls and floor splattered red and two horrendously disfigured bodies on the floor. I suppose being shot in the face is an improvement when your ass is truly on fire. I opted to head out to the field and get the hard part over with, digging the hole. I liked the idea of one big hole for both bodies since it involved a little less digging than making two holes. I got the shovel and walked outside under the Manila moonlight.

Digging the hole was tough duty, between the dry, hard earth and the increasing soreness of the bites on my finger and wrist. The gauze unfurled from my fingertip within minutes of digging. The tip was swollen and yellowish, which might not be a good sign, so I figured the fresh night air might do it some good. What was getting me, though, was how it throbbed with every strike of the shovel. It began at the fingertip, picked up reinforcement at my wrist and traveled up the arm, through the shoulder and neck to make a direct throb of pain in my brain. A throbbing head is hard to ignore (Kinsey, please don't say 'that's what she said' when you're reading this). While I did not know how to summon the demon to take full control of my mind, I certainly was open to the idea. After all, the dark angel could use my body to dig, bury, mop and clean the walls without me feeling any more pain. The pain was unnoticeable by the time the hole was fully dug, so the demon may have been doing the dirty work. Being possessed by an angel of darkness is a bit like being a fish watching itself in an aquarium, only you're the one in the aquarium.

The lights were off when I went back inside to drag the bodies out. I had to feel my way along the walls to try different light switches, but none worked. In the darkness, I could hear the scurrying of rats all around me. There was a multitude tonight and they sounded more active than usual, maybe because of the darkness or due to the dead bodies and blood and guts all over the meating room (a pun, Kinsey). I clambered along the hallway wall, groping in the dark, trying to locate the breaker box. I finally found it and got the metal door open and peered closely to try to see if any of the switches were out of position. I had to run my hand down them on both sides, like a blind electrician.

I felt something, but not with my hand. It was down at my ankle, now stuck inside the pant-leg of my jeans and crawling upwards, a rat! "Get away!" I shouted, kicking my leg as hard as possible, but not before feeling a searing painful sensation shooting up the side of my calf. The little fucker bit me! He squealed, mocking me, before dropping to the floor and running away into the outer darkness. I resolved to just drag them out to the field in the dark. Maybe the electric would be on by the time I got the hole filled in. I felt my way in the dark towards the meeting room, ignoring the pain that was like having a railroad spike driven into my ankle. I could still hear rats squeaking and running in all directions, so

I tucked my pant-legs into my socks. I was covered in dirt and drenched in sweat and no doubt dehydrated. Screw it, I told myself, *killers don't worry about stupid shit like Gatorade and replacing electrolytes, they just get shit done and ignore pain until it goes away.* It worked. It always worked.

I patted my hands through puddles of blood and flesh and finally latched onto a pair of ankles. I lifted them and began pulling the body out and down the dark hallway. I didn't know if I had Red or Blondie. It didn't matter, really. The bigger question I toiled with was whether to position them in a spooning position, or sixty-nine, decisions, decisions. It was much easier to see once I got outside and was dragging him under the light of the glowing moon. I had me Red, *Got me dirty Red!* I yelled, to nobody in particular. During the fracas of being dragged, she somehow lost her wig and the nightgown was now soaked with blood and dragging behind the body, covering the head. I pulled the body through the field and to the freshly dug hole, sliding it to the opening before kicking it in.

I went back in to find Blondie, groping my way down the wall of the dark hallway. I found the meeting room and fumbled around with my hands on the table, finding a pack of matches among the empty Red Horse bottles. I struck a match to shed some light on Blondie's location. Holding the match forward, I approached the nearly headless corpse on the floor. As I located the ankles, I saw movement. The tell-tale sign of a pink, fleshy twirl gently moved back and forth around Blondie's char broiled ass. "Get away!" I screamed, kicking the body. The rat turned, a strand of roasted flesh from Blondie's butt roast was clenched tightly in its teeth. He held the meat, staring his beady eyes into mine. The match went out and I kicked the body again. I grabbed Blondie's ankles in the darkness and began to drag his chewed corpse down the hall, to the field and into the hole.

There was a black dog sniffing around the corpse and he backed up when I arrived with the new body. He sat, solemnly, watching me in the moonlight. I kind of liked his company. Just for entertainment, I kicked Blondie into the grave upside-down with Red. Then I adjusted them a little. I looked over at the black dog and asked, "What do you think, Blackie, is there life after death?" He returned my question with a low bark, just one. "Well, these two can live happily ever after in an eternal sixty-nine." He barked once more.

I began to fill the grave, scoop by scoop. Blackie sat watching me, like a noble Sphinx. He seemed like a calm dog, mellow but serious, and was a trouble-free companion. I liked him and could tell he was low-maintenance.

The fresh rat bite on my ankle burned like hell and gave the troubling pain
n my finger a run for its money. At least filling the graves in was not as
strenuous as digging the hole. My arms and legs were cramping, covered
n sweat. I was also very light-headed and felt like I had a high fever. The
est is kind of a blackout. I mean, the last thing I can recall was telling
Blackie how I hoped that I didn't contract rabies from the rat bites. Blackie
answered with a solitary bark, and I went into a dream.

I was with Lily in a cottage. The cottage was set in the woods. It was a
cozy place and the sunlight pouring through the open windows shined on
the varnished bare wood floor and walls. A breeze blew through the open
windows and light, white curtains gently fluttered in the warm spring
wind. Lily sat in a corner, behind an easel, painting. In this dream, we had
been a couple for some time and I was always elated when she painted.
Her artwork struck me as remarkable, though she insisted on referring to
her works as the labor of a mere hobbyist. I learned the hard way that it
was hopeless to try to encourage her to paint more, as her brushes only
moved when the spirit moved her. How I loved when the spirit moved
her! Not only because I enjoyed the beauty of her scintillating paintings,
but also because it was easy for me to write when she painted. It allowed
me the freedom to write and dream about my ideas. The chemistry of our
history together all felt perfectly natural within the context of the dream.

I asked her, "Can I see what you are working on?"

"No, it's horrible" she stated, while continuing to focus on the tip of
her brush against the stretched canvas.

"I'm sure it's good. I can't wait to see it once you're finished."

"Maybe, maybe not; I might just trash it. It's not good. Please stop
bothering me now."

It wasn't until later, as she lay sleeping and I woke up to piss, I tip-toed
into the room where her easel was. I stepped around the easel and sat on
her stool, directly in front of the painting. It was a close-up portrait and
the devil was in the details. While it could have been taken for an intense
looking elderly man with a ruddy complexion, the yellowish eyes gazing as
f looking into my soul were a dead giveaway. This was Lucifer.

As I stared at it a bit longer, I noticed the slight horns from the
upper-forehead and the shimmering, Van Gogh like affect of breathing.
The cheeks and nostrils seemed to gently respire. The eyes turned menacing
as I gazed into them. *Hello Tim* he spoke, in a calm, refined voice.

I looked over the easel, behind me and all around the room, but there
was nobody. Surely, the painting was not talking to me, it was an absurd

notion, but, dear reader, I heard it speak! I decided against my better judgment to just go along with the prank or whatever it was.

"Hi, I'm kind of surprised that a painting can talk," I replied. There was silence, a long, uncomfortable silence. I supposed that I had just been hearing things. Then it spoke again, just as my guard was down.

Well, this painting is unique, one of a kind, you might say. An infusion of art and spirit, a surreal blend of what you refer to as the supernatural.

"Like a ghost or something inside a painting?" I asked.

No, what you call ghosts are just spirits without hosts. This painting is my host. Your body is also a host, a very promising one, I might add. Anyone reading this once you write it for me might also be a host.

"Okay," I answered, realizing that what was happening could not actually be happening. I was also worried what the hell Lily might think if she woke up to see me talking to her painting that she did not want me to look at in the first place. "What was wrong with me?" I thought to myself, a question I was asking a lot lately.

There's nothing wrong with you. You just have more sensitivity to your awareness than most. Just roll with it. Maybe nothing is wrong with you; it could be that the majority are deceived with their temporal diversions, distractions and constant pursuits of selfish pleasures.

"Are you the devil?" I could not help but to ask.

You people give me different names; Beelzebub, Tenderfoot, Necromon, Mammon, Antichrist, Satan, Lucifer, blah, blah, blah. He replied, suddenly his face shifted and his smile became terrifying. *Know this; I am your worst fucking nightmare. Your petty god cannot help you now!* He growled, in a low, guttural voice. I was paralyzed with fear, completely petrified.

In desperation I shouted, "Jesus Christ is my savior!"

The devil smiled, saying *Jesus shmeezus. He can blow me and swallow the seed. Behold, I come quickly,* he laughed and the smell of sulfur came from his breath. The laughter reverberated and echoed in my head. I had to escape the vile, vulgar and profane presence, but I was paralyzed. There was constriction in my throat and I could not breathe, while the laughter continued echoing in my head. I was losing consciousness and fading fast when something snapped my head. I had no idea where I was or even who I was.

My eyes opened through the slight crust that had them stuck shut. The dream was over. The brightness of the sun was stinging my eyes. I could faintly hear someone shouting as I shielded my eyes with my calloused, dirty and swollen hand.

"Tim, what the fuck are you doing?" demanded Sonny. I could see trucks on the nearby road entering and leaving the factories. I could also hear the beeping sound of a forklift in the distance.

"Where am I?" I asked, looking in front of me. I was in shock to see Sheryl's three-day old, bluish, bloated and foul smelling corpse directly in front of me. One of my arms was pinned under her side. Mounds of fresh dirt were behind her, as was the iron maiden box with its door opened.

"Get up!" screamed Sonny, "Why in fuck's sake did you dig her back up? You're going to get us all busted!"

"I don't know what happened," I replied, while sliding my arm out from under her.

"I don't either, but it looks like your twisted mind was trying to screw a corpse! Get in the warehouse; you never cleaned up the blood and mess in there, either!"

As I struggled, wobbly, getting to my feet, Jolen approached, helping me steady myself by grabbing my arm. "Tim, maybe the bites are infected or something. You might need to see a doctor."

"Yeah, a brain surgeon," chimed Sonny, unsmiling.

"I swear to you, I don't know what happened."

"I don't either, but you've dug up a corpse and right now it is broad daylight. We got to get this dead body reburied before we all go to jail," added Sonny.

"Just go inside. Get cleaned up and rest. I'll take care of things out here and the blood inside," said Jolen, as he helped Sonny put her corpse back into the iron maiden.

I was grateful to have a friend who was willing to help save my ass. Sonny, however, looked like he wanted to strangle me. I noticed Blackie at the edge of the field, sitting stoutly. He appeared to have something in his mouth. I wondered if it was a human body part from one of the bodies. It was difficult to tell from the distance.

"Blackie, come here boy!" I yelled.

"Who are you yelling at?" asked Sonny, now lifting one end of the wooden box to put back in the hole.

"The black dog over there; he's got something in his mouth," I answered, pointing.

Jolen and Sonny lowered the box into the hole and both scoured the direction I pointed in. "There's nothing there, my friend. Go inside and get cleaned up."

"He's right there!" I protested, calling him again, Blackie, come here, boy!"

"There's no dog there, dipshit; just go inside!" scolded Sonny.

As I walked towards the warehouse, Blackie also trotted in the same direction. I continued walking, wondering why they could not see him. I stopped at the door of the warehouse and Blackie stopped, about twenty feet away. He dropped a bloody rat on the ground, before sitting and staring at me. I saw Sonny and Jolen shoveling dirt back over the box. I thought of telling them about the rat, but decided best to leave a sleeping dog lie. I wasn't sure what to think. Why had I decided to dig the box up with Sheryl in it? Even worse, why did I pull her rotten corpse from the box and sleep beside it? I could smell the stench of the road-kill scent. It made me nauseous to the point of gagging. No wonder Jolen kept repeating to get cleaned up. I entered the warehouse reeking of foul decay.

The most troubling thing, however, was how they could not see Blackie. This meant that either I was hallucinating and having visions of things that did not exist, or that they were playing some kind of prank. Sonny, for one, seemed like he was in no mood for pranks. Why couldn't they see Blackie? Maybe the bites were infected and influencing my perception in a skewed manner. I stopped in the hallway, did an about-face, and walked back to the door. I opened it and poked my head out. I saw Sonny and Jolen patting down the dirt. I also saw Blackie, sitting still and staring right back at me. I went back inside to get a much needed shower.

I could hear the rhythmic squeaking of the mop bucket wheels as I slept on the cot. I had no idea what time it was, what day it was, or even where exactly I was. All I knew was that Jolen kindly said he would mop up the blood, and that made it easier to go back to sleep. I'm not too sure how long I was out until Lily tapped my shoulder, "Tim, get up; we need to talk."

I rubbed my groggy eyes and stumbled out of the cot. My bit ankle throbbed like hell as I hobbled down to the meeting room where Lily sat, alone, dressed neatly in business slacks and a blouse.

"How are you feeling? You look like shit," she observed.

"Well, I'm a little hungry, but I'll be okay," I answered.

"Well, what the hell is going on? You're all bit up by rats, you ate a dead rat, you are seeing dogs that don't exist and you're digging up bodies that are dead for days. You could have got us in deep water here. You're good at killing and a useful soldier, but lately you're becoming a problem for us. I'm a fixer. I fix problems, if you know what I'm saying. Are you okay?"

"I know this will sound weird, but I have something inside me, like a bad spirit or something. It gives me nightmares and takes over my thinking sometimes and I don't remember doing things."

"Well, work with it better; hell, I have a demon, too. Jolen has one as well. We just accept it and deal with it. Demons can sometimes steer us into compulsive, often destructive or risky decisions, but only if we are willing. You need to get some backbone and control that shit. You need to learn that no matter how messed up things get in your head, to play it cool on the outside. It's all about appearances, and your appearances have been pretty shitty lately."

"I don't even remember what I do. It's like I go into a blackout," I reasoned.

"Just channel the energy, redirect it in a useful way," she said. "We can't afford any more surprises. If Jolen and Sonny didn't like you, you'd be gone by now. Get your act together and quit fucking up."

"Okay, I got the message," I said, knowing full well the demon had a mind of its own.

CHAPTER VII
Stop Breaking Down

The boundaries which divide Life from Death are at best shadowy and vague. Who shall say where the one ends, and where the other begins?

—Edgar Allan Poe

Kinsey brings me my notebook before he leaves in the morning. We have a good system. He drops it off so I can pour my demented memories onto the page during the day and at night he gets to read the scribbled madness. His constant question is "did this stuff really happen?" I just smile at him. How am I supposed to answer him? Does he want me to incriminate myself so he can squeal and get a promotion or a trophy or something? He sees the scars from the rat bites. He saw me try to kill Dan. If it looks like a duck and writes like a duck and acts like a duck, isn't it a duck?

Kinsey also claims he is my defender here. According to him, the big cheese here at Hoffman Mental is Dr. Taylor, some young ambitious upstart. Kinsey says Taylor views me as an inconvenient time-bomb, a potential media and public relations disaster just waiting to happen. He claims Taylor wants me transferred to a jail for criminally insane offenders. Then he assures me that he went to bat for me and saved me. He supposedly told Dr. Taylor that my attack on Dan was just a friendly tussle that accidentally got out of hand. I think Kinsey is just tooting his own horn, blowing smoke up my ass. In his mind, he's shrewder than me, but who's fooling who? I won't be manipulated into feeling obligated to keep writing for him. I could give a shit; I have nothing,

zero to lose. Without Reshi or the family, the building I'm stuck in or
the food I eat or the people I put up with mean absolutely nothing,
zero. Hang me, burn me, shoot me, drown me; I'm down. I just write
for me. I know the demon would not write through me. Surely, that
can't be the case. Whoever heard of a demon being crafty, deceptive
or manipulative? I am not a mere scribe for an evil spirit, or am I?
Whether the demon moves my pen or not isn't important. Writing keeps
me sane with the bit of sanity I have left. So, read on, gentle reader, or
don't. There's nothing to fear but yourself, choose wisely.

The syndicate had lots of pokers in many different fires. There was a
political situation that trickled down to a car theft ring. The car thieves
were untouchable for over a decade because they had a few prominent
politicians in their corner. The Domingo group in North Luzon was
responsible for nearly twenty-thousand car thefts in Manila in a period
of ten years. Domingo was married to an actress and rubbed elbows with
politicians. It was Senator Juan Ercito who coddled Domingo to become
an untouchable. Ercito was also a part-time actor. He became friends with
the syndicate through Reshi, who was friends with Domingo's wife, Paula
Katarin, the actresses meeting while on the same set.

Ercito was being fingered by fellow politician and congressman, Tommy
Ramena. Ramena was recently quoted in the press as saying "Domingo has
been allowed to steal cars with impunity for a decade because he enjoys the
favor of a certain senator who has been in office a decade."

Reshi explained all of these background details although they were
difficult to follow because of the silky blue dress she wore that showed
abundant mouth-watering cleavage. "So, what are chances of Ramena
backing down if we send him a message?" asked Berto, as we sat at the
meeting table three days after killing Blondie and Red.

"I think Tommy has a personal beef with Juan. I don't know how far back
it goes, but I heard it was a while ago," said Reshi, "It was over some young
fashion model. I doubt any message is going to make him shut his mouth."

"So, we'll just get rid of him," resolved Lily.

"Ding, ding, ding!" yelled Reshi, "We have a winner!" She pulled a
folder out from her purse that was a portfolio of Tommy Ramena, including
pictures of him and his home.

"Wow, someone really did their homework," I said.

"Quiet, Tim," said Lily, "You don't know anything. The syndicate, well,
Reshi, runs a small but exclusive escort business for politicians. It's pretty much

just introducing young actresses to politicians. She keeps files on her clients so the girls can be more familiar with the men before they even meet them."

"It's a good business," added Sonny, "Like an expensive dating service."

"And we kind of provide protection for the girls and for the big boys?"

"You got it. Now, getting to Ramena might be difficult. He's flashy and a socialite, and he's hardly ever by himself. This guy is one of those people who cannot stand to just be with themselves."

"Is he married?" asked Jolen.

"Why, you got the hots for him, Jo?" asked Lily.

"Shhh, Sonny might get jealous," he returned.

"All these greedy, horny, power hungry big-shots are married. This hit will bring down some heat. We need to plan this out thoroughly," said Lily, before turning towards me, "We can't afford to have any fuck-ups."

After much discussion, we decided to make the hit on Ramena in his home. He was too well known and too much of a flashy social butterfly to risk getting a clean hit on in public. We needed a layout of the inside of his house and a key to avoid the noise of forced entry. Sonny saved all of the tools from the locksmith's van. When Ramena wasn't there, Berto would pick the lock under the guise of being a mail courier and get pictures of the inside layout. Ideally, the hit would be made on a late Saturday night so his absence would go unnoticed until Monday.

"Can I be the one to do it?" I asked the group, but focused on Lily. I had more than a single motive. I wanted to make up for the fiasco with Sheryl's corpse and other dumb blunders like eating a rat. Mainly though, I had the thirst for blood. I wanted the feel of blade in skin.

"How you plan to do it? A gun will draw instant attention with noise," said Lily.

I'm going to slit his fuckin' throat.

"That sounds hot," said Reshi, as the group laughed. I was pleased knowing she liked it.

"You might slit his throat and then crawl into bed with him. I'm not sure we can count on you," said Lily.

"That's exactly why I want to do it, to show I can still be counted on."

"Okay, he's yours. But don't fuck this up," cautioned Lily.

On Thursday, Berto had visited Ramena's house and was able to pick the lock to get inside, after waiting three hours for the housemaid to leave. He took some pictures, located the bedroom, and, most importantly, unlocked the first-floor bedroom window. The chances of Ramena noticing his window was unlocked before Saturday night were very slim.

Two factors were in my favor late Saturday night, as I waited for Ramena to return home. The window was still unlocked and Ramena got dropped off, stumbling to the door. His inebriation caused him to struggle for nearly five minutes with his keys before opening the door. I saw the bedroom light turn on and off, and then I sat under the window and waited, until he was in a deep drunken sleep. As I lifted the window, I could hear him snoring like a vacuum cleaner. If my demon was there, he was keeping my head clear. I wanted to kill, but quickly, silently and efficiently. Like a cat, I stealthily climbed my way through the open bedroom window. I waited, still, for three minutes, allowing my eyes time to adjust to the darkness inside the room.

I tip-toed my way towards the snoring, chubby man's two lips. I held the knife handle with both hands, blade down, on the far side of his neck. I pulled it towards me, keeping it straight the entire slice. His throat was slit like a fresh loaf of bread, deep and instant. I could feel some cartilage through the wind pipe and Adam's apple, but the sharp blade slid right through. Ramena never had a chance to even wake up before blood simply gushed from the deep slice and filled the mattress. It was the easiest murder I had committed, painless, noiseless and easy access.

I wiped the blood from the blade and made a smooth exit out of the window. I hit the ground in a running crouch, and got into the van where Sonny sat behind the wheel. "That fast?" he asked, surprised.

"Don't worry about it; and I must add, it felt delightful!" We both grinned as Sonny drove back to Caloocan. There wasn't as much traffic this time of night. The trade off was that the cars that were out were all over the road because most of the drivers this late were drunk. The only real window for easy driving through Manila was between five and six in the morning. For that sole hour, most of the city has a brief cat-nap. The other twenty-three, however, it's New York City on steroids.

Making the hit in a quick and effective manner helped bring some of my credibility back and reestablish some value with the syndicate. I was learning to live with the demonic possession. In some ways, it's the perfect thing to have if you're supposed to be a killer because it not only removes guilt and remorse, but also makes taking lives very enjoyable. The key to controlling the demon wasn't in trying to tame it, which made things only worse, but to just stay alone in isolation when I felt complete possession was imminent. Finding a hiding place and putting all responsibilities on hold was the best solution. I usually glued myself into my cot until it passed and nothing seemed to go very wrong. It also helped that the bites on my hand were less painful, nearly only scars. I never did go to the doctor, who needs that shit?

The bad part about the Tommy Ramena hit was the publicity. The crime became the buzz of Manila. Filipinos love gossip and if the gossip involves someone popular, it becomes even more vital to the gossip fodder. The Tuesday after the kill, every newspaper and news station was running the story around the clock. It became the primary topic of conversation all through Manila, from the elite country clubs, to the shabbiest titty bar in Malate. It became such a story that Lily chose for the syndicate not to meet in Caloocan for awhile. There was also a freeze on murders. All of the publicity generated by Ramena's murder was rolling downhill and even the police were actually showing interest in a murder.

I started helping Lily and Reshi with their many weekend and night-time enterprises, including, but not limited to, imports and exports on goods for restaurants, Reemall online shopping, organizing poker events, arranging cockfights, providing construction workers to mining jobs and providing girls to work in a few bars. These weren't the typical girlie bars of Burgos Street, but quieter places frequented by financially stable expats, like Heckle & Jeckles, Conways, The Brewery and The Giraffe. Because Heckle & Jeckles and the Giraffe stayed open all night, I was spending more and more time at both in order to help the syndicate keep an eye on the girls and the clients.

The Manila night scene and the girls in the bars were not the sordid, seedy traditional operation of pimps and prostitutes. Most of the girls working with Lily and Reshi were friends and relatives of friends. Many were in college and used the money earned to ease the burden of their families. It is worth noting that the girls worked with Lily and Reshi and not so much for them. It was more of a partnership that everyone benefited from. Reshi and Lily had connections, experience and business acumen to help the girls maximize their profits and the bar owners and managers benefited from increased business, syndicate protection and discount booze from Lily's syndicate connections at Clark Air Base.

The expats were like putty in the hands of the girls, once Reshi explained how they need to control all relationships. They gave the foreigners just enough attention to keep them hooked, but nothing more until pesos were invested, with the process repeated over and over. Most of the expats were in their fifties and sixties, and were married or had girlfriends, so their main concern was to find a young, pretty girl they could trust. The relationship also appealed to them because they had more freedom to explore with their forbidden sexual fantasies than they could with their partners. They wanted a pretty young girl to hang out with, drink with and have sex with without any of the petty annoyances brought on in the long-term relationships that they were trapped in. They wanted someone pretty and trustworthy to indulge their most secret fetishes and fantasies. And of course, they paid for the privilege.

Reshi gave the girls an overview of how to lump the men into three categories: the vanillas, the fetish freaks and the pain puppies. The vanillas just stayed in the realm of straight sex. The fetish freaks were the most diverse, including role-play, body worship, foot fanatics, toy play, costume play, leather and whatever kinky scenarios their imaginations concocted. The fetish freaks also generally engaged in vanilla at some point during their freaky explorations. The pain puppies were the hardest to adjust to, including things like whips, restraints and power exchange scenarios involving masochism and sadomasochism. Generally the pain puppies included aspects of fetish and vanilla, as well. Reshi made sure the girls understood the "do's and don'ts" and, more importantly, that the expat clients understood the "don'ts". Reshi or Lily, or both made brief appearances at most of the bars each night, or checked on things by phone.

I learned a lot about Lily while hanging out in the bars. Mostly from talking with Jolen and Berto, since one or the other usually hung out with me each night for a few hours. Berto lived near the Giraffe, so he usually stopped by and hung out many nights. Berto's laid-back demeanor and sense of humor made him a very likable companion. We also had similar tastes in music and enjoyed listening to lots of blues guitarists and eighties and nineties bands.

One late night, as we sat with Raina and Fay, two of the bar girls, Berto asked me, "So, Tim, is it kind of weird to go from being Lily's lover to just being one of her worker bees?"

The question stung, but I knew it was valid and I kept my ego in check. Hell, the romantic feelings for Lily were long gone, but I didn't want to tell him about my Reshi crush just yet. I could not stop thinking about Reshi, mostly in inappropriate ways. "I don't really want to talk about that," I replied.

Fueled by boredom or beer or both, Berto persisted, "Well, suit yourself, but sometimes it feels good to talk about stuff that's maybe eating at your head and heart, isn't that right girls?" They both moved their heads up and down, agreeing wholeheartedly. "Besides, anything you say here stays here and will not be told to anyone, even Lily."

"We're going to mix and mingle at the bar," said Raina. I had to give her credit, she was wise beyond her years and smart enough to know when to make an exit. Berto and I mindlessly stared at their young, firm asses as they wriggled from the booth and made their way to the bar.

"I know exactly what you're going through," said Berto, "Hell, I once proposed to her."

"Do you still love her?" I asked, taking a sip of my diet coke.

"Yes," he confessed, "though not in the same way. I love her as a friend, though I still think she is hot as hell and fun to be with. Besides, I have a great girlfriend, young, built, smart and I am very happy with her for all of my romance needs." We both chuckled at the way he emphasized 'romance needs'.

"I see," I replied, "that makes sense. I just feel loyalty for her and Reshi. It's such a powerful feeling that it's beyond my control, like a sense of loyalty. I mean, if the best I can hope for is to spend the rest of my life just working for them, then I'm down with that. Plus, I cannot stop thinking about Reshi. At least I get to be close to them. Why the hell are we talking about this anyway? Real men just keep their emotions to themselves, yes?"

Berto laughed, "Well, I suppose that's how we're supposed to be, but with Lily, it's easy for real men to become unreal. There's not many women like her, is there?" The clinking of glasses, billiard balls knocking, music, conversations and laughter all fell silent as he asked the last question. It was as if it was the only thing I could hear. He already knew my answer to it, but I was grateful because it gave me an opportunity to discuss what made her unique among women.

"No, there really isn't," I began, "In many ways, inside at least, she is more like a man. Somehow she can always mask her emotions like a true stoic. Not many women are able to pull that off."

"Yeah, she does have a certain mental toughness that is unreal," agreed Berto. "I really don't think of her as a girl, I mean, it's like she's a tough buddy or tough sister to me."

"She is a paradox of beauty and inner-toughness, that's for sure," I added.

"You know, in spite of her narcissism, Lily is the best friend a person could have, but if she is your enemy, look out."

"Hey, who's the guy talking to Raina?" I asked, looking towards the bar, where a tall, fairly built, balding man in his mid-fifties was loudly animating a story.

"That's Paul Scheper, he does some kind of import stuff with Lily. If she refers to "the German" that's who she means. He's a pudknuckle, always acting like a big-shot, a complete alcoholic and rough with the girls sometimes. His money is the only thing that makes him tolerable."

"Looks like Raina is going to get some of that money out of him."

Berto laughed, "I think all of the girls have profited from his drunken stupidity. You want to come to the cockfight Sunday?"

"Sounds kinky, count me in," I replied, smiling.

Raina approached from the bar, "I'm taking off with dipshit Paul. Hopefully, he'll just pass out, again. Did I hear something about cocks fighting?" she laughed.

"You sure did, sunshine, we're going to the cockfight with Lily on Sunday."

Raina smiled, "Ooooh, sounds kinky. I'll see you guys later," she said, before walking back to the bar. Scheper acted like he was in a hurry, leading her by the arm out the door.

"The German was hammered. I hope he's not driving," I said.

"He always drives; has to show off his car like a big-shot needing to mask his insecurity."

"Well he looked a bit too drunk to be behind the wheel."

"Welcome to Manila; where drunk driving is a favorite pastime."

Early Sunday afternoon, Berto and I rode with Lily to the cockfight at the Caloocan cockpit on Cabiga Street. Lily had a rooster in a portable box in the back of the van. I looked at the bird, and he didn't look too friendly. "So you're going to fight this rooster today?" I asked.

"Oh yeah," she replied, "You're going to love my cock," she teased, smiling. "Hold onto this while we're there, just in case," she said, handing me her .38 pistol. I tucked the gun into the waistband of my shorts and pulled my shirt over to conceal it.

As we entered the arena, there were people everywhere, many carrying roosters and waving peso bills. The crowd was at least two-thousand, and as noisy as a crowd at a rock concert. The majority of spectators were men, and the smell of beer and cigarette smoke filled the stale air. "I'm going to my booth. You guys stay down by the kristo and I'll text you my bets to place," said Lily.

Bets were being shouted all around, as Filipinos of all classes stood elbow to elbow. Peasant and politician seemed one and the same; the cockfight was the great equalizer, though, the politicians placed more substantial bets.

"Man, this place is crazy," I observed, looking around at the noisy, colorful crowd. We maneuvered, veered, side-stepped and jostled our way to the pit. The smell of beer, piss and cigarette smoke filled the air. Everybody was shouting. "How in the hell can they keep track of bets?" I asked Berto.

The kristos are very skilled at what they do," he explained, "Nothing is written down. Their special gift is to remember every face, every bet and at what odds. See him?" he asked, pointing to a skinny Filipino with a ball-cap and a cigarette dangling from the corner of his mouth. He was continuously accepting peso bills from people and giving bills in change, like a machine, left and right.

"How do you know the odds?"

"Both birds are displayed and the llamado gets higher odds, while the dejado gets lower."

"What's with the hand signs?" I asked, feeling like a fledgling student in cockfighting 101 class.

"When it gets too loud, the kristo takes bets through hand gestures."

"Damn, there's a hell of a lot of pesos changing hands here."

"Oh yes, my friend, cockfighting raises millions of pesos here in the underground economy."

We watched as two roosters ran towards each other, both blazing angry. The plumage around their necks was fully extended, making them look not only larger but more menacing than they actually were. There were also razor sharp blades tied to each leg of the birds, midway on the leg. The closer it got to each fight, the louder the noise grew around the cockpit. When the noise level was nearly unbearable, hand signals could be seen being flashed to the kristo. It was like watching someone take one-hundred phone calls at once, with a jackhammer making noise behind them, and they remember every message. The kristo was an incredible and vital component of the cockfights.

The referee held both birds up for display and then they were set apart. The crowd noise grew unbearably loud when the birds were up for display. At this point, all bets were locked in. The fighting style of the birds varied. Every fight was unique. Some birds were flyers, rising above their opponents to make quick, sewing-machine like strikes. Other birds were grounders, just waiting and capitalizing on their firm, stable base to make a powerful, knock-out blow. The flyers were more entertaining to watch, but it appeared that the grounders won the majority of the fights.

We watched fight after fight and each one unique. Some lasted a few minutes, while others only fifteen seconds. In between fights was a noisy frenzy of peso bills being bandied about and exchanged with the bets. Some fights were very violent and bloody while others ended quickly with a well-aimed strike at the throat. The most exciting, longest lasting fights seemed to be when two flyers went at it with pecking and leg strikes by the dozen, with none quite powerful enough to make a final, conclusive blow.

Lily's cock was a flyer and extremely fast and aggressive. He won his fight, but was bleeding from two gash wounds on his body. His opponent, now dead, was given to Lily after her bird delivered the required, customary two pecks from the winner. She came down to the cockpit to retrieve her wounded fighter and to also receive the lifeless losing rooster. "Here," she said, handing me the dead bird, upside-down by its feet, "I want you to eat my cock." The men within earshot began laughing.

"I can't wait to eat your cock," I replied with a smile, "but I'm not sure how to cook it."

"Well, you could eat it raw, but have Jolen help you. He knows what to do with cocks and how to make them tasty."

I returned to the Caloocan warehouse that night with the dead bird. Jolen seemed familiar with seeing dead roosters, "Lily's cock won again!" he announced, smiling as he looked at it.

I laughed, "Yeah, she said you would know what to do with it."

"Oh yeah, we need to pluck it, chop it up and marinate it in brine for about three days. It's different than chicken, so if you don't soak it, it will be tough as hell."

"Sounds like a plan, I'll take your word for it."

"I've been eating Lily's cocks for a long time," he smiled, "we can make a stew with garlic, black pepper, tomatoes, onions, soy sauce and serve it over rice."

"Sounds fantastic."

"Want to play some ping-pong?" he asked.

"Sure, where at?"

"I made a table in the warehouse with some scrap wood."

Jolen and I played game after game of ping pong. He was good at it and I was getting a little better with each game he beat me.

As we neared sleep that night, in our cots, I asked him, "Do you believe in God, Jolen?" I had to ask because of everyone in the syndicate, he actually was caring and interested in other people, in a way that seemed spiritual. In his own way, he was a very spiritual person.

"Well, I am not an atheist. I mean, I don't deny the existence of a force or a divine energy that spun everything into motion. I just don't see this force being involved in our day to day affairs. I suppose I'm agnostic," he replied, in the darkness. "Of course, I could be wrong." I could hear rats scurrying, making their night-time rounds.

"I guess everything has to start with something. I feel like an evil spirit takes control of me sometimes."

"It's all part of the inner-struggle, my friend. Just don't think of it as evil," replied Jolen, "we all have our demons we fight against."

"Well, I never thought of myself as a murderer, but now I get in a certain mood, or a mood overtakes me, and I enjoy killing and hurting people. Later, like the next day or something, it scares me. I don't really like what I become."

"I can kind of relate to that, but I punish myself more than anyone else. When I think of how old the Earth is and look up at the stars and how far away they are and think about all of the people and how brief their lives are, it just makes me feel humble. We seem kind of insignificant in the big scheme of things."

"Yeah, that's true; I just wish I didn't lose control of myself," I replied, "It can be some scary shit."

"Well, when you lose control, just do what is good for the syndicate. It's just a matter of perspective. You can be as crazy as you want, as long as you're doing what Lily and Reshi want."

"Yeah, I just hope my demon stays on Lily's side."

"Seems to be that way so far, doesn't it? I mean, except for the little late night necro action with the corpse," he added, as we both chuckled. "If you get too crazy, I will let you know."

"Thanks Jolen, you're like the coolest friend I got."

It was a few nights later, after we ate some cock stew, that Berto and I went to hang out in the Giraffe and keep an eye on the girls. We also used this time discussing various strategies on how to beat Jolen at ping pong, since Berto couldn't beat him either.

"Hey, how come Raina isn't saying hi to us? And why is she wearing sunglasses?" he asked. I looked towards the bar and saw her talking with two of the other girls. Berto was right, there was something was unusual about her not greeting us.

We walked towards her and when she noticed us coming, she made a quick exit for the door.

"Raina, hey, wait!" yelled Berto. We rushed outside and caught up with her on the sidewalk. The traffic crawled and beeped around us. She stopped but she still would not face us.

"What's going on?" I asked, now noticing her purple, swollen lower lip.

"Paul hit you?" asked Berto.

"He was drunk and started punching and yelling," she confessed. I could see anger on Berto's face. I could also feel a vengeful rage beginning to boil through my veins.

"When?"

"Two nights ago, I hit him back and got out of there," she revealed, lifting her sunglasses to show us her swollen, purple raccoon eye. She turned away and put her glasses back on, "It's no big deal. He was drunk. I took care of it. The other girls know."

"Drunk or not, I'm going to talk to Paul," said Berto.

"No, just drop it. He's into kinky rough play. It just went a little overboard."

Berto and I went back inside and sat down. "Listen," I began, "I don't know what it's like here, but where I come from a man who hits a woman is like the lowest form of life. I really, really want to beat the shit out of this slime-ball."

"Well, it's the same way here, but we can't just go hunt the guy down. We have to talk to Lily about it."

"Hey," I added, "if he's into kinky, rough play then he will really get a hard-on out of being slowly choked unconscious."

"We can't touch him until Lily gives us the okay, even if he waltzes in here. That's just how we have to do things in the syndicate. You start doing your own thing and bad shit happens."

"Well, I'm sure she will give us a green light on roughing up this prick. Where does he live?"

"I don't know, but just wait to get a go ahead. We have to wait."

"Juvi probably knows. He knows where everyone lives."

"Look, Tim, I understand your anger. I'm pissed, too. But with all of the publicity Ramena brought, now just is not the time to play vigilante cowboy."

"Okay, but when she says it's a go, I want in on the action. Raina is young and wild, but she's a good kid. She doesn't deserve that crap no matter how much money he gives her."

Berto took a swig of his beer and changed the subject, "How come you don't drink?"

"It's just not good for me."

"Maybe it would help relieve stress, like how you talk about being possessed by demons and go into a fury when you're killing someone, the booze might help to blow-off some of that pent up steam."

I smiled, taking a sip of my coke, "It just quit working for me. It was my solution for many problems for many years, but it quit working. Lots of people can use it to just blow off steam, but I'm no longer one of them. For me, it became a great dissolver. It dissolved my marriages, friendships, jobs, bank account and sanity."

Berto smiled, "I'll drink to that; cheers!" He held up his bottle and I tapped it with my soda glass.

"Cheers," I said, raising my Coke, "Besides, I'm crazier now than I ever was drinking. I don't want booze clouding up my insanity"

Jolen was not at the warehouse when I returned and I was missing playing some ping pong. I also had trouble falling asleep, maybe from all the Cokes I drank at the Giraffe. An ominous restlessness grew upon me and I became increasingly fidgety. As I laid in the cot, changing position for about the tenth time, I heard a scratching sound at the back door of the warehouse. It sounded like an animal and though I ignored it, it was persistent enough to finally force me up. I had to investigate the source of the noise. It was much louder than the sound any rat could make. Living with them every night, I was certain this was no rat. I walked down the hall and through the warehouse. The scratching erupted again in the warehouse and I realized it was coming from the back door.

I pushed the door open and looked around. There sat Blackie, sitting with his back straight and breathing a bit hard, but with a slight canine smile on his face. "Blackie," I said, "where have you been boy?" He returned a single bark that left ringing in my ears. I told him to come and he followed me back into the warehouse. "Since you're good at catching rats, you can keep them out of my room tonight."

I got back in my cot and left Blackie free to roam the place, but he just sat, like a statue, back straight, staring at me from five-feet away. "Blackie, keep them rats away so we can sleep in peace," I said, from my pillow.

He returned one bark and I went into a dream. I was in a cottage on the ocean. It sat on stilts above the dunes of sand. Lily and I lived together here, happily. Tranquility and peacefulness were the primary moods, as we were both successful artists. I was earning my living as a writer and Lily was a world renowned painter of beautiful pictures. The warm ocean breeze blew gently through the screened doors and windows.

Lily sat with her back to the window, painting a scene on the stretched canvas at an easel. The sunlight shone on the painting, which was near completion. The scene was of a white two-story house on a grassy hill. There were four symmetrical windows placed evenly, two on each side of the door. Wooden steps led up to the door and a woman was approaching the steps, hunched over and carrying a package. I continued to stare at the painting and something clicked in the area where my spine turns into my neck, actually it made a cracking noise, then I found myself next to the woman in the painting. I thought little of the sudden transition, since paintings are a dream of reality and to dream of a painting makes a sort of limitless reality.

The woman was struggling as she approached the stairs, "Here, let me get that box for you," I offered. I took the box from her hands and it did not feel nearly as heavy as she made it appear. She slowly opened the door. The weather changed as the door opened. The sun faded and it became cooler. The sky was now grey and it was windier.

"You can just put the box on the table," she said. I set the box on the varnished, wood dining table. It suddenly dawned on me a vague recollection of the absurdity of finding myself within a painting but before I could follow the thought through, she said, "Please sit down. Let me get you some tea." I was not thirsty, but sitting down and having tea seemed to be the polite thing to do. I figured that she didn't really need help with the box in the first place. She just was lonely and craved some attention. She set some glasses on the table and filled them with dark golden tea from a glass pitcher. She sat at the corner of the table. I thanked her and drank half of the glass out of courtesy.

"So what's in the box?" I asked, before taking another gulp of the sweet-tea.

"Oh, just a few knick-knacks," she said, smiling. "What brings you to these parts?" Her question triggered a vague notion involving a painting, but the connection was tenuous. I had the feeling of not quite being able to recall something, even though I knew I knew it.

"I'm not sure, exactly," I answered, struggling now to remember anything.

"Guess what?" she asked, excitedly. I was not sure what was wrong with me, but my hands began to feel very heavy.

"What?" I asked, playing along.

Your god cannot help you now, she said, as her pleasant smile shifted into a grin, a knowing, evil grin. The light in the room dimmed as her face shifted slightly to take on a Japanese pallor. I had a feeling I knew her from somewhere. She now looked so familiar. Then it dawned on me, it was Lucy, the crazy Japanese woman! The giveaway was her mustache. No sooner had I recognized her when her eyes rolled up into their sockets.

They appeared as two whitish, yellowish sideways ovals. With zombie-eyes she said, *Pleased to meet you, hope you guess my name* in a teasing tone.

My body grew more heavy and numb. I knew there had to be more than tea in the tea. I was reminded of things I had read about henbane, jimson weed and mandrake root; sedatives that paralyzed the body while leaving the mind active. My mind was fully alert, but I could not move. I could not even turn my head away from her.

Maybe you want a little snack? she asked, rising and going to the cupboard to get a jar of peanut butter. She turned and faced me, holding the jar in front of her stomach in both hands. With her white glazed eyes, it was like a horrid peanut-butter commercial from Hell.

I tried desperately to move, to rise up out of my chair, but my utmost effort was rewarded with collapsing onto the hard-wood floor. Despite being unable to use my body, I still felt a sharp pain from the impact of my head against the floor. I laid on the floor, on my side, my body limp and my head at a downward angle. I could see the baseboards of the kitchen and Lucy's dirt sneakers. *Oh my,* she said, walking towards me. She placed the jar of peanut butter on the floor, in front of my face and unscrewed the lid. She dipped her finger in it, saying, *just a little snack, to boost your energy.* She smeared the peanut butter down the bridge of my nose and across my lips. Had I been able to move at all, I would have bitten the finger off of the zombie-eyed Japanese bitch. She then playfully put a dab on each of my eyelids. I tried to scream, but hardly any sound was audible. Whatever she put into the iced-tea had me completely paralyzed.

What's the matter? she asked, after twisting the lid back onto the jar. She replaced the jar in the cupboard and wiped her finger off on a towel. Then she took the box from the table and poked a slit in one end with a knife, she slid the end with the slit close in front of my face. The slit began to move and pulsate. I could see small, sharp teeth and chunks of the box being removed. *Rat got your tongue?* She began to laugh in a low growl, demonically with her white, glazed eyes.

She then sat in a chair ten feet away, just watching. Grey whiskers appeared at the hole, twitching and the elongated snout of a rat poked through. His nose moved upwards as he sniffed the air and burrowed his head further out of the box. As he came through the hole, a second rat followed behind him, then a third. The rats appeared to be starving, since they went straight towards the peanut butter on my lips and nose. I could see the beady eyes directly in front of my own eyes, and feel the nibble on my nose. The sensation was awkward, but tolerable. Perhaps, more intolerable was the feel of the whiskers tickling my skin. The nibbling soon ended.

Lucy giggled with vicious delight when the first rat sunk his razor teeth into the bridge of my nose. I could feel a piercing pain and see blood spurting out of the incision. I wanted to move, to scream in pain, but I was completely paralyzed. His incisors were stuck in my flesh and he began twisting his head to tear flesh away from the bridge of my nose.

The rat at my lip followed up by sinking his teeth into my bottom lip. The pain was excruciating and I could only endure it with open eyes. Whatever had paralyzed my body had no affect over my senses. I could feel everything, all of the intense, burning pain, but was completely immobile. The third rat was at my eyes. I could not close them and I knew he was after the dab of peanut butter on each of the lids. His whiskers rubbed into my pupils, causing my eyes to burn and water from the irritation. I was unable to close them.

While the other two rats continued to bite my lip and nose, it was the bite through my eyelid that brought the searing pain, pain unlike any I have felt in my entire life. The level of pain was such that I would have given away my life, my soul, my family in order to make it cease. His teeth pierced the eyelid and crushed in my upper-eye as if it were a fragile eggshell being broken. Lucy continued her manic laughter as all three of the furry, beady-eyed rodents continued to devour my face. I could no longer see, since the bites through my eyes had taken away my vision, but I could feel it all and hear the sounds of their aggressive biting and Lucy's laughter in the background.

The rats continued chewing out my face, and just at the point when I felt life slipping, when it was no longer bearable, when death was a mere sigh away, I sat up in my cot, soaked with sweat. I thanked God it was only a nightmare, a Manila nightmare. It had all seemed too real. The cottage, Lily's painting, Lucy and her mustache, the rats, the biting and every detail was just as vivid as real life.

I saw Blackie still sitting, staring at me. I tried to return to sleep, but was fearful of having anymore night terrors. At some point during the night, I must have dozed off because it was morning and Blackie was gone. I walked through the entire building calling for him, but he was nowhere to be found. My ankle was still a bit swollen, but at least my face was intact. It was time to brew coffee and begin a new day.

CHAPTER VIII
Torn & Frayed

God is cruel. Sometimes he makes you live.

—Stephen King

Kinsey keeps acting like he's my savior. He must have picked up his degree at some community college. That's probably why they put his put him on the night-shift. He tries to act like some compassionate Greenpeace save the nuts from themselves kind of samaritan. He just gets off on reading my story, living the wild life in safety, vicariously, by just reading someone else's escapades. "Is this stuff true? Did this really happen?" Blah blah, blah. I just write. I write, I die, I don't write. Maybe I should just kill him, but not today, but sometime, maybe, he dies. Like Kerouac said, "we're all gonna die". Sometime we all die. Then what? What does it matter what we do here when we're all going to die? It's just a matter of when. When I create someone's untimely death, I'm like a god. I determine when they go, how much they suffer. I'm god. You clear on this, Kinsey? I haven't slept well in five years. The pills and meds they give me don't really count as sleep. I need real sleep, deep sleep. The Manila nightmares, the rats, the longing, Lily, Reshi have kept away any hope of peaceful slumber. Oh well, I will sleep when I am dead. I want to get back to Manila. I need to see Reshi again. If she sees me in person, she will love me. Reshi loves me, this I know. For my demon tells me so. Little ones to her belong. I am weak but she is strong. I miss ping-pong. I miss Jolen. I need to get back to Manila. Bend over, gentle reader, and I'll drive you to Manila.

I began to obsess about killing the German. Well, not just killing, but killing in a slow, painful way, like repeatedly slowly choking him unconscious, over and over, maybe a period of six hours or so. The repeated lack of oxygen to his brain would make him dumber than he already was; turn him into more of a slobbering, blathering idiot. I could make that happen for him. Having twenty or so years under my belt as a solid Pennsylvania wrestler through high school and college, I could make it happen. Raina is such a good kid. I like her. He had no business hurting her. If pain is what floats his boat then I was really going to thrill him, though he will be on the receiving end for a change. I bided my time at the Giraffe and every weekend I wished and hoped to see the German come sauntering through the doors. I knew some Friday or Saturday night, he would appear. So, I waited.

"Lily said to leave the German alone if he shows up here," advised Berto, as we sat at the bar together. I could not believe what I was hearing. I could not fathom just why she wanted to protect this alcoholic, arrogant dirt-bag asshole who hit women. If it were coming down from anyone else, I would not have even listened, but with Lily, it was different. She was my boss.

"Come on, man, the worm beat up one of our smartest, nicest girls. How can we just let him slide?"

"I'm telling you what I was told," said Berto. "Lily said she would handle it. She said she made a phone call."

"That really sucks. I wanted to kill him, slowly and painfully. When are we meeting again? It's been weeks."

"Well, that's the other thing," he stated, before taking a long pull of Red Horse, "We're going to get together this Sunday night. There's a few things to cover but I think for us, the main item is that we'll be going after some Japanese guy."

"Cool," I replied, "I can't say I ever killed a Jap before. It will be nice to expand my portfolio. What's his story?"

"I guess he's been involved in recruiting Filipino brides for Japanese nationals, so they can work as entertainers in Japan, mainly, the island of Okinawa. There's a seedy area there outside of Kadena Air Base called B.C. Street and he supposedly recruits the girls under the guise of being entertainers, but most of them are kept doped up on liquid opium and end up working as hookers to support their habit. This guy is pretty much solely responsible for the majority of hookers on B.C. Street."

"B.C. sounds kind of weird for a Japanese street," I replied.

"Well, it's what the servicemen call it there; stands for banana connection. Many of the bars have the girls entertain by going up on stage, putting a banana up their pussies and then squeezing it out in inch-sized pieces, often while squatting over an open-mouthed, drunk serviceman."

"Now that's what I call wholesome family entertainment," I said, as we chuckled.

"Well, apparently, this guy has been refusing to pay tribute to our syndicates here, so Lily wants to send a message."

"This sounds like someone I can't wait to meet, or slice in to meat," I replied, before noticing a folder Berto had placed on the bar. "What's in the folder, info about Jap man?"

"Oh man, yeah, I forgot; you are going to like this, my friend," he said, beaming a wide grin. "I have some glossies from one of Reshi's recent photo shoots."

"Oh yeah" I replied, "She's sizzling!"

"Wait till you feast your eyes on these, then," he said, handing the thick folder to me.

"Hey, does Lily ever do modeling?"

"No, she's not as flamboyant and voluptuous as Reshi."

"Yeah, Lily could use some meat on her bones."

"I have some meat for her bones, and a bone for her to meet," said Berto, as we laughed.

I looked at the pictures, eight by tens, and my jaw was nearly on the floor. Reshi and the camera had an intimate relationship. They were meant for each other. The photos were completely captivating and I began to get aroused the more I studied them. Just when I thought the one that I was currently looking at was my favorite, I flipped to the next picture only to find a new favorite. There was red lipstick, pouty lips, silk, lace, thick eyelashes, blue eye shadow, reds, blues, pinks, long flowing hair, short page-boy hair, blonde wigs, fairy tale costumes, geisha girl outfits, leather, policewoman outfits and more. There were at least fifty photos and all of them looked sensational. After flipping through them, I still had one important question.

"How is Reshi is so beautiful? I mean, it's almost intoxicating."

"Well," began Burton, "She has been modeling for awhile. I also have a pic series on my computer where she posed as Alice in Wonderland."

"That sounds pretty hot; much better than Albert in Wonderland."

"What I remember most about the Alice pictures is her amazing eyes."

"Berto, if you could get me copies of those pictures, I will suck yo dick," I joked, adding, "My room at the Caloocan Hilton could use some beautification. Could you print them?"

"Yes, I'll even use photo paper and you don't have to blow me for them," he laughed, "I'll bring them Sunday."

"Sweet" I replied.

As we sat at the bar discussing which photos we liked and why, the German came in with a friend. He was loud and boisterous, slurring through a story in his native tongue. Apparently his friend also spoke German, or he was too drunk to care. "Just keep it cool," said Berto, seeing the fire glowing in my eyes as I stared at the sloppy drunken German. "Let's go check out Conways. We haven't been there in awhile."

I knew I had to go along with Lily's orders and it would be much easier to ignore the obnoxious Kraut if I didn't have to look at him. I followed Berto out the door. "That jackass doesn't even realize how lucky he is; doesn't even have a clue" I said, as we made our way across the street. "If he shows up at Conways, I can't make any promises!"

On Sunday night the whole gang arrived at the warehouse. It was fun to see everyone again. I realized these tightly-knit Asians were becoming my family. Lily was wearing a silk red dress with black heels. She looked good. "How'd you like eating my cock, Tim?" she asked, smiling at me. For as awkward as the question was, I liked seeing her smile while saying my name. I enjoyed the company of this dangerous woman.

"He thought it was saltier than mine," replied Jolen, as the group laughed.

"Well, well, well," began Lily, "I see we have a genuine connoisseur in our midst, a connoisseur of cocks" she punned, patting me on the head.

"You mean besides Reshi?" asked Berto.

"Apples and oranges, my dear, apples and oranges; my cocks are way out of Tim's league" replied Reshi, laughing.

The joking went back and forth for another thirty minutes as we all enjoyed each other's company again. It was a pleasant reunion and everyone was drinking the San Miguel. Finally, Lily said, "Okay guys, listen up," and the chatter around the table ceased. "Alright, the cops and the reporters are still having a field day with Ramena, so we probably won't be meeting like this again at least for a few more weeks. First things first, I need Berto, Sonny and Tim to fetch me a Jap. His name is Yoshimi Fuji and he stays in the Fort. I need you guys to bring him here, alive, sometime within the next three days, preferably at night. Bring him in blindfolded and restrained. Juvi can fill you guys in on his location."

"How old is this guy?" asked Berto.

"In his forties, I think, but one important detail, he was some kind of ju-jitsu champion back in Japan."

"Sweet" I replied.

Lily smiled at me, "Tim, weren't you some kind of wrestling champion back in your school days?"

"Yeah," I replied, "Hopefully he'll start something so I can see what he's got."

"Good, just make sure he comes back alive. Only kill him if there is no other way, but I want him alive, clear?"

"As a bell," I answered.

"What are those doing here?" asked Reshi, looking at her pictures, the ones Berto printed for me. I happened to have them lying in front of me on the table. My face blushed. I looked towards Berto for assistance. He was smiling.

"Tim asked me to print some pictures of you so he could hang them up near his cot," he said. Although I was embarrassed, I was also relieved that he spoke up for me.

"Awwwhhh, that's sweet," said Reshi, causing my heart to beat faster.

"Yes," added Berto, "He even offered to blow me for them, doesn't get much sweeter than that."

"Wow," said Lily, "Quite a compliment, the pinnacle." She smiled. "You bring back Yoshimi this week and maybe Reshi will give you a real treat," she said, as Reshi smiled at me, licking her lips.

"Lily, how come we can't straighten out the German? I don't like that loudmouth at all," I asked. "He keeps coming around the Giraffe after he beat up Raina, acting all pompous and proud."

Lily looked me in the eyes, "Because I said not to and that is that." I knew not to press the issue any further.

The following morning we met Juvi at a Dunkin' Donuts and got the address for Yoshimi. He kept an apartment off of the eighteenth-floor of the Penhurst building. While we could keep potential witnesses at a minimum, there would be some security to watch out for, particularly in the lobby with guards and cameras. Berto and Sonny already figured Yoshimi was not going to come easy because, being Japanese, they felt he would be proud, defiant and stubborn. I felt he might not cooperate simply because of his ju-jitsu background. As it turned out, all three of us were correct.

We got to the Penhurst around noon and parked the van in the back, near a loading ramp behind the kitchen. We wore hats and sunglasses to minimize witness recognition. We first planned to just do some scouting and surveillance, coming back during the night to abduct him. After seeing the layout of the building, however, we felt we should just get him right then and there. We got knives, rope, tape, a folded tarp and Sonny had a .45 pistol. Since we were supposed to bring him back alive, we thought one pistol would be sufficient.

His room was 1812 and Berto knocked on the door, putting his sunglass wearing face right in front of the peep-hole. "What?" asked Yoshimi, through the closed door.

"Maintenance sir" answered Berto.

"I have not called maintenance" he replied from behind the door.

"We're inspecting all of the units."

"I will call the office then to verify."

Sonny cleared Berto out of the way and charged the door, ramming it hard with his shoulder. The impact made some cracking noise but did not bust the door open. Sonny backed up, took a deep breath and charged it again. Just before hitting the door, Yoshimi opened it and Sonny's momentum sent him sprawling into room 1812.

Yoshimi pounced on him immediately, kneeling on one of his arms, his other knee on Sonny's throat and his hands extended across to stretch Sonny's other arm out. It was a good hold and he locked it up quick. Berto and I entered the room, knowing we had to get to Sonny's .45 before Yoshimi did. Sonny was grunting and gasping for air, but Yoshimi held him tight.

"What do you want? I will crush his neck if you come any closer."

"We need you to come with us" said Berto, "If you just come along, we can resolve this. Someone just wants to ask you a few questions."

"I'm not going anywhere. Now get the hell out of my apartment!"

I vaulted from behind Berto and sprung onto Yoshimi like a wildcat. He rolled backwards and I rolled with him. When he instantly sprung to his feet and crouched in a fighter's stance, I knew this was going to be no easy tussle. I lowered my level and quickly shot in for a double-leg takedown, the way I had thousands of times in my youth of wrestling. I was in deep and used my neck and head to drive him sideways in the opposite direction. His feet left the ground and I kept charging sideways with him in the air until I drove him into the wall. He hit the wall hard and I drove all of my body weight through my shoulder into his ribs. I heard him grunt in pain before collapsing to the ground, but he quickly locked up my sore ankle in his arms with some kind of funky ju-jitsu hold. He began to torque pressure on it and I had to roll to the ground with it or risk him breaking my leg. I rolled towards the pressure and caught his head by locking my hands around his neck and through an armpit. I tried to squeeze off his air but he rolled out of my lock. We continued to tango like two cats, breaking furniture, appliances, knick-knacks and anything else in our way. My shirt was ripped and Yoshimi had blood coming from his ear.

"Alright, stop the crazy fight or I will shoot!" screamed Sonny. By now the cacophony of noise coming from room 1812 could most likely be heard by every tenant in the Penhurst building, even deaf ones.

Yoshimi attempted to strike my throat and I caught him with a foot-sweep, kicking his legs out from under him just as Sonny fired a bullet that went into the wall behind us. On the ground, I managed to cinch up a headlock and just choke the crap out of him until he turned purple.

"We got to get out of here fast!" yelled Berto, trying to tie Yoshimi's wrists together as I continued squeezing his neck. Finally, Sonny approached from behind and bashed him in the head four times with the handle of the .45, allowing us to get him tied up. We rolled him up in the tarp and carried him down eighteen flights of stairs. By the time we managed to get him into the back of the van, we were all completely out of breath.

"Holy Christ!" exclaimed Sonny, "That little guy has a lot of spunk in him!"

It took another few minutes for Sonny to catch his breath enough to manage driving. We were in the stop and go traffic on Buendia Avenue going through Makati. Berto was in the middle of a hilarious story about one of his pet birds that kept escaping from his cage. Sonny's shoulders were shaking in laughter as he drove and I kept laughing with each new detail Berto shared. Then we all heard it, the sound of the tarp moving in the back. Yoshimi was upright, staring at us with blood still dripping off his ear and a wide grin on his face. We were all shocked. I wondered if Yoshimi was grinning because of overhearing the funny story or because he was just plain nuts. I heard Berto say, "Oh no, not again," as he sighed in disappointment. Yoshimi got to his feet, free of the ropes and came at us, still with his crazy smile.

Sonny looked to his rear-view mirror, saying "What the fuck is this guy, the Japanese Houdini?" Berto and I struggled with Yoshimi, again. The cramped area, combined with the seat and armrests made it difficult to fight well. Sonny pulled the van over to the side of the road, put it in park and then came back and joined in the melee.

Although Yoshimi gave us a challenge, it proved impossible for him to overcome all three of us at once, coming at him from different angles.

Sonny pulled the .45 out and pressed it against Yoshimi's head, "Keep struggling and I swear I will blow your fucking head off!"

Yoshimi calmly, yet quickly, reached up and took the gun from Sonny's hand. The sudden transfer of the gun caused all of us to begin punching, gouging and choking him with renewed interest. Sonny was able to get the gun back with no shots being fired. This time we used the entire fifty-foot coil of clothesline to tie his hands and feet and then connected the tied hands and feet to the armrests of the backseat for more insurance. Yoshimi was beaten, bruised and battered, but we did keep him alive, as Lily wanted. Once again, we were all out of breath by the time we were able to get back on the road. Sonny called Lily to let her know that we had Yoshimi in custody. She agreed to meet us at the warehouse later that night.

Once arriving to the Caloocan warehouse, we carried the tied-up captive into the meeting room and secured him with more rope there, just in case. Lily arrived later that night. She wore jeans, black strappy heels and a nearly transparent white blouse.

"Hello handsome," she said to me, smiling. She carried two bags in and handed the clinking one with beer bottles to me, "put these in the fridge for me, sexy."

"Sure thing, Lily" I replied, taking the heavy bag.

"Are Berto and Sonny still here?"

"No, just Jolen," I answered, making room in the fridge for the fresh soldiers. "He's in the shower."

"You know," she began, smiling in her deliciously wicked way, "we could save on water if you two took showers together."

"Hmmm," I returned, "only if you join us."

Lily now grinned, "That scenario could be very hot. I'll think it over, maybe, sometime." My imagination launched into an instant fantasy involving Lily, suds and warm water. Then I substituted Reshi in Lily's place. "So Yoshimi put up a little bit of a fight?"

I began to laugh while stacking the beer. "That's an understatement. The little guy fought, escaped, was shot at, pistol whipped and came back for another round in the van, even getting the gun for a bit while we were on Buendia."

"Those Japanese, stubborn, crazy, misogynistic, tiny-peckered pests," she replied, as I opened a beer and handed it to her.

"So what are we going to do with him?" I asked.

"Well, he's either going to give me money or we are going to have fun with him. If he's smart, he will pay. If not, he will pay in pain. It's essentially his choice, life or slow, painful death."

"I choose shower, with you," I said, smiling.

"Maybe, just keep being a good boy and don't try to fuck anymore corpses, you sicko," she quipped, before putting her lips around the tip of the beer bottle.

Yoshimi began to grunt and squirm from his position on the floor, cursing in Japanese. Jolen and I sat at the table, while Lily pulled a chair up to Yoshimi.

"Okay," she began, sitting in front of him as he lay struggling on the floor, "you're nothing but a slave trader, a con artist talent scout involved in human trafficking. Even worse, most of the girls you so deviously trick and deceive end up hooked on dope and working as whores and having to please tiny dicked Japs. Frankly, I just want to kill you. And I really don't give a flying fuck about whatever Japanese syndicate you belong to. You're on my turf, dumbass. However, if you pay twenty million pesos, a paltry amount considering what you actually owe to us, you can live. We've been telling you to pay for far too long. You seem to think you can just ignore us. I got news for you, tic-tac dick, you can't."

"I will pay nothing," said Yoshimi, in a defiant tone. He rolled on the floor, squirming quickly and caught a leg of Lily's chair with his tied feet. He then rolled like a log, attempting to tip the chair. Jolen quickly jumped from the table and kicked him in the stomach.

"That's it, crotch stain, you almost made me spill some of my beer" said Lily, now standing, before she pushed the chair across the room with a sweep of her leg. "Tim, run out to my car and get my work boots" she said, "It's time to get serious with this stubborn Japanese con artist pimp."

Lily's work boots were the same black leather boots she wore when stomping Pete's face to a pulp. I felt a bit of a thrill just feeling them in my hands and the scent of the leather. Maybe it was having the knowledge that they were used to kill and once splattered with blood or maybe it was the intoxication of licking them clean under Lily's orders while recalling the view of Reshi's legs from beside her or some combination. Lily was sitting at the table when I returned with them. "You want to help me put these on, don't you?" she teased. Actually, I wasn't thinking of it, but since she mentioned it, it seemed like a good idea. "Go ahead, but get me a beer first and this can't take all day."

I returned with her opened beer and she crossed one of her muscular, petite and shapely legs over the other. "Start with this one and be careful with the little buckles on the straps of the shoes."

"He's like a lion when it comes to fighting and killing, but with you he's like a lamb," observed Jolen. I didn't care what he said about me, her legs looked pretty good and I was in close proximity.

"Yes" agreed Lily, "he makes a good pet, loyal and tender, but vicious when I need him to be."

"Like an attack pet?" asked Jolen.

"Exactly, and he always comes when I call him" she said, as they laughed.

I took my time removing the heel from Lily's foot. It is embarrassing to confess, but I was fantasizing the entire time. Reshi completely occupied my heart and mind. Her exquisite, refined beauty made simple pleasures with Lily become monumental. There was a quality to Reshi that grew and grew in my fantasy world of imagination. I could appear to be devoted to Lily on the outside and go through the motions, but inside, dear reader, my heart, soul, mind and cock were chained and pointed completely towards Reshi.

Lily continued talking with Jolen, allowing me to take my luxurious time removing her shoe. I held her calf in my hand, imagining it was the golden calf of Reshi, while sliding the shiny leather boot over her foot. After one boot was on, she slowly crossed her other leg on top of the other and I moved to the other side to begin the second-half. I was in erotic Heaven changing her footwear only because I was able to imagining she was Reshi, the truly dangerous, sultry Asian beauty. After taking my time pulling the zipper up, as if in slow-motion, Lily put her empty bottle on the table with a loud clunk. "Okay, well done, Tim. Let's get this kamikaze clown to the warehouse. I want him suspended, upside-down, blindfolded, with his head about six-inches above the floor. Hang him from one of the eye hooks in the ceiling."

Jolen and I quickly went to work, carrying Yoshimi, who needed a few stiff elbows to the head to quell his squirming, to the warehouse. Jolen nimbly climbed a stack of pallets and sewed one end of the rope through the eye hook in the ceiling. The other end was tied to the rope that bound Yoshimi's ankles together. We both heaved and hoed the rope to suspend him upside-down. Once his head dangled about six inches above the floor, we tied the loose end back around his ankles. We covered his eyes with a wide black headband. Yoshimi began sounding less defiant now as he swung, blindfolded, lightly to and fro, now sounding like he was pleading for mercy in Japanese.

Lily entered the warehouse, sipping a beer and moving lithe and gracefully, "Looks perfect gentlemen, a lovely Japanese piñata filled with shrimp-dick trinkets and baubles. Tim, be a darling and go get me a chair. This could take awhile. I want Japman to get his money's worth."

She positioned her chair about three-feet away from Yoshimi. "I need to soften him up a bit first, some anesthetic." She stood on the chair, leaned sideways and roundhouse kicked him, the toe of her boot going directly into his crotch. "Yeah baby," she said, as Yoshimi moaned in pain. "I think I got him in his raisins."

Lily then sat in the chair and began with a few quick, precise kicks directly into Yoshimi's face with the toe of her boot. "Okay, now for the Nagasaki," she said, rising to her feet. She reared her leg back and brought it forward with vicious force. The toe of the boot went through Yoshimi's mouth, busting his teeth out. "How's that feel, you fucking toothless, penny pinching Jap?" she yelled, enraged. Yoshimi screamed and made crying noises while spitting forth teeth, blood and pieces of teeth. Lily got her beer and sat back down, crossing her legs and taking a long pull. She extended her leg, putting the bottom of her boot on Yoshimi's chest and giving him a gentle push. He swung like a pendulum and when he came back towards her, she kicked his face with the hard toe of her boot.

Lily continued to push and kick, over and over, while Yoshimi screamed in pain. Jolen and I began a game of ping pong while she continued with kicks that were not as full-force as the one that had knocked his teeth out. These were sharp enough to stop each return swing, but not lethal. Lily continued to push and kick, over and over, while finishing a few beers and watching us play ping pong. After I lost best out of five games to Jolen, Lily decided to try something new. Yoshimi dripped blood from his nose, mouth and ears and a pool of blood formed under where he hung. Blood spilled heavily from his mouth. "I have a new game for you guys, if you're done playing ping pong with your ding dongs."

Jolen smiled, "I once played ping pong with King Kong in Hong Kong with my ding dong."

"I'm sure you both enjoyed that," said Lily, "but how about some bowling, Japanese bowling?"

"Sounds fun," I replied, "how do we play?"

"Well, you pull him back and swing him towards me. If his head directly hits my heel, like solidly, you earn a strike."

"Sounds fun!" exclaimed Jolen, "may I go first?"

He pulled Yoshimi backwards as Lily straightened her leg and braced herself in the chair by gripping both sides of the seat. Jolen released the body and it swung in an arc until impacting against the bottom of Lily's boot heel. "Was that a strike?" asked Jolen.

"No, a spare; Tim, you're up." I pulled Yoshimi back. He groaned in pain as I held him upwards, "On three, one, two, three" counted Lily; instead of just releasing him, I gave him an extra push at the end, increasing the speed and the impact his face made against the boot heel. "Whoa! Steeerike!" shouted Lily as Jolen celebrated by giving me a high-five. Yoshimi moaned, pleading for it all to stop.

"How come you're celebrating?" I asked Jolen, "now I'm ahead of you."

"Now I know your technique" he replied.

"Okay," said Lily, with her leg fully extended, "on three, one, two . . . three" Jolen pushed the body hard and it swung with fast momentum into Lily's boot, where her heel punctured his eyeball, pushing it far back into the eye socket. The sound made was similar to pushing down the foil seal on an aspirin bottle with one's thumb, followed by an ear piercing, deafening scream. The heel pushed right through the blindfold and was stuck inside the eye socket so deep that Lily had to shake her leg for the heel to slide out. There were now two new features to Japanese bowling; Yoshimi's blood curdling, incessant screaming and the blood that poured out of the eye socket. "Now that was a game winning steeeerike!" yelled Lily, as she laughed venomously. "Let's call it a game and go back to the meeting room. Tim, I have something for you."

"Should we just leave him here?"

"Yes" said Lily, "his Godzilla loving ass can bleed to death here."

In the meeting room Lily went to the other bag that she came in with. She pulled out a painting and handed it to me. It was red and black, abstract, with red circles resembling pac-man shapes, though some had antennas, making them kind of look like lady-bugs. "It's just a lousy painting I made. I call it 'Rampage'".

"Very cool, kind of reminds me of blood. Thank you, Lily."

"You are welcome. I have to leave now, so you know the routine, get shrimpdick buried and clean up inside, okay?"

"You got it. And thanks again for the painting. You are a talented artist."

"I'm a fucking hobbyist. Oh, I almost forgot, my boots are bloody, do you want to help me get back into my heels?"

"Yes"

"I knew it, perv" she laughed and sat down, slowly crossing her legs. "I don't have much time, so get my heels back on by the time I finish this beer. I'll just leave the boots and you can clean them later, if you want."

"I want," I said, quickly sliding her heels onto her feet and fastening the tiny buckles on the straps. Once again, I imagined Reshi.

"Good."

After Lily left, Jolen and I went back to the warehouse. Yoshimi hung, lifeless. The pool of blood beneath his inverted body made a wide circle that glistened under the fluorescent lights of the warehouse. "You want the body or the blood?" asked Jolen.

"Tough choice; I'll take the body," I replied.

"Good call; once I get the blood up, I'll be out to help you."

"Thanks" I replied, before cutting the ropes. Yoshimi's head hit the floor, followed by his body, which made a splash in the red pool of blood. I grabbed him by his ankles, around the blood soaked socks, and dragged him out the back door of the warehouse. It was another Manila moon illuminated night. I dragged him out to the burial field and went back for the shovel. The ground was hard and, as I worked the shovel, I looked at Yoshimi's pale, blood drained body. As I looked at him, I had a nostalgic memory from childhood. It was my mother singing "ashes, ashes, we all fall down." The sing-song phrase resonated in my head as I continued to shovel. I even began to sing it out loud to myself.

I had the grave dug three-quarters of the way when Jolen came out. I was relieved to have his help.

"What song was that?" he asked, reaching for the shovel.

I laughed, "It was just some silly nursery rhyme my mom used to sing to me. It came back while I was digging and looking at Yoshimi 'ashes ashes, we all fall down.'"

"That's kind of a morbid song for kids, isn't it?" asked Jolen, laughing, "no wonder you're so fucked up."

"Yeah, and to be singing it as an adult, means I'm beyond repair," I said, noticing Blackie trotting at the edge of the field. "Blackie!" I shouted, "Come here, boy!"

Jolen stopped shoveling and looked around the field. "There's nothing out there, Tim," he said.

"He's right there," I insisted, pointing at him.

"No, he isn't. Your eyes are playing tricks on you, amigo."

"Okay, if you say so," I replied, looking right at Blackie, as he sat stoutly, staring right back at me. I didn't care to argue with Jolen. If Jolen didn't see him, that was none of my business.

Later that night, I hung Lily's painting on the wall above my cot. I also set her boots beside my cot and before drifting off to sleep, asked Jolen, "Does it ever bother you, killing so many people?"

"Nah, if it did, I wouldn't do it. Besides, doing it with Lily makes it fun. Does it bother you?"

I laughed, "It sometimes bothers me that I like doing it so much. I didn't used to be like this. Now it bothers me if I go too long without killing."

"Well if you like killing, you are in the right place."

"Yeah, I think you're right. Lily makes killing fun. Even her painting makes me feel like killing. To be honest, though, and just between us, I can't stop thinking about Reshi."

"Well, I know; but just remember that Lily is the Queen Bee of our little outfit." said Jolen.

"I know, but in my head, Reshi is the Queen of all Queens," I confessed.

I stared at Lily's boots as I drifted off to sleep. The scurrying of the rats did not bother me at all. It was commonplace now. I was desensitized. As I drifted into sleep, I could hear music and screams. The music was of a horse carousel, with its cheesy, repetitive organ refrain. The screams were far off, like coming from people on an amusement ride. The smell of onions and funnel cakes wafted through my nostrils. It all seemed so familiar, the sights, sounds and smells. I had arrived. I was at the fair.

"Step right up, everyone's a winner, old, young and in-between; feast your eyes upon the prize!" announced the man at the nearest game booth. It was the simplest game of fairs everywhere; pop a colored balloon with a dart, to win whatever prize was tagged on the paper behind it, usually something small, with the promise of cashing in small ones for a bigger one.

"This is like a kid's game," I taunted, "I need more action than pop-a-balloon."

"No, no, no; things are never as simple as they appear, kind sir," he began, "everyone's a winner here. Kid or adult; the adult prizes are best. Come on, you've got nothing to lose and everything to gain."

"I'll lose my dignity playing this shitty game," I continued.

"Nonsense, mere nonsense; when something is lost, something is gained and nothing remains to remain unchanged," he answered, as I saw a rat scurrying quickly through his tent along the back wall. "Pay your money and pop your prize. Everyone's a winner!"

I aimed at the red balloon in the center of the large square of balloons. Just as my arm was in motion to release the dart, I saw another rat scurrying across the back wall of the tent. My dart veered to the left as I wondered where these rats were going. It struck a black balloon. Smoke rose from the balloon when it was punctured. "Bingo black balloon, we have a winner!" he shouted, "A triumphant victory, a smashing success, the toast of the town! Let's see what the prize is," he said, pulling a slip of paper off of the wall that was pinned behind the balloon. "Okay, it says," he strained his eyes to read, "black balloon, black dog, toast of the town, ashes ashes, we all fall down!"

I had a moment of déjà-vu, "it really says that?"

"Not the last part, I added that for flourish," he said, while reaching up to pull down a black dog that was hanging high on the wall. "Ashes are black, corpses are blue, a lovely black dog is the prize for you!" he grinned, handing me the stuffed dog. The dog looked very familiar and I tried to recall where I'd seen him before. The succession of déjà-vu was mildly confusing. "Everyone goes home a winner!"

I thanked the carnie and tucked the small black dog under one arm before taking a stroll around the fairgrounds. The people walking around and playing the games and waiting in lines for the rides all shared a common feature, their eyes were missing. Not entirely, but they were glazed, white and had no pupils or irises, just filmy white orbs. Even small children with their parents had zombie eyes. The only exceptions were the carnies, their eyes were all normal. I began to wonder if my eyes were also white when I was accosted by a well dressed, eloquent carnie.

"Step right this way, sir," he said, looking tall and thin in an oversized suit-jacket and wearing a top-hat and a bowtie. "Are you prepared for a phenomenal, monumental and extravagant experience that will leave you astounded and redesigned for eternity?" he asked. I stepped back and away from him, leery and considering the maxim that if something sounds too good to be true, then it probably is untrue.

"Oh, I assure you it is true," he answered. I wanted to ask him just how he read my mind, but he continued, "True as ashes and dust; the verity of my vernacular is utmost and upright, I assure you."

"What kind of ride are we talking about?" I asked.

"Not a mere ride, my friend, but an experience. A funhouse in appellation but it is a catalyst of awareness in experience. Step right up, good sir, and begin the journey to broaden your experience. Life is short, it's a merry-go-round, ashes, ashes; we all fall down."

Maybe I sung it out loud? Was I humming it?

"Come along; what have you to lose? Come and see what all the Razzle Hazzle Diazzle is all about; you will find your horizons broadened and your dreams fulfilled."

"Sounds to me like your mouth is writing checks that your crusty funhouse can't cash," I replied.

"Ashes to ashes, dust to dust, come into my funhouse, come in you must!"

"Okay, Dr. Seuss," I said, before giving a deep sigh, "let me check out this little shoe-box you're promoting."

"Very well, very well; a wise choice indeed, sir; right this way!" he exclaimed, leading me by the arm.

The outside of the funhouse was painted with a nighttime scene, a full-moon emanating an eerie glow over an old cemetery. A woman with flowing hair and a torn blouse looked upwards, wide-eyed and in shock, screaming, while on the ground, at the base of a tombstone, was a rat. The painting resembled a horror movie poster from the sixties. The carnie gave me a firm pat on the back as I entered the dark doorway. The sign painted above the doorway read "ENTERNITY".

"Smells like mothballs and piss in here," I complained as I walked in to the complete dark passageway. I tried to feel my way ahead in the darkness for fear of walking into something. There were no buzzers, ghosts or recorded screams, only darkness. I began to walk sideways, utilizing short steps, in anticipation of something about to jump out just ahead. These cheap fair funhouses always have the board you step on to make a ghost or demon pop up. I stopped momentarily, to allow my eyes time to adjust to the heavy darkness. I heard scurrying at my feet. There was nothing phony about it, the rats were real. I could tell not only by the sound but by the way they also bumped my feet. There were at least four of them running around down there. I shuffled both of my feet to warn them out of the way and continued forward. The walls of the passageway grew narrower and eventually formed a tight space just wide enough for my body. There were still no buzzers, blasts of air or fake screams, just blackness. Finally I could see a sliver of light and continued towards it.

I entered a small, square room with a projector screen covering one of the walls. I stood in front of the screen as it came to life with black and white, silent, grainy footage. The scene looked vaguely familiar. It was Professor Coker and he was in his office. Then I saw myself enter the scene. The film flickered. I brandished a knife and viciously plunged it upwards underneath Coker's chin. Blood spurted out like paint as I twisted the blade. I turned and smiled into the camera. Then everything went dark. I fumbled through the darkness to find another passageway at the opposite end of the room, after trying to locate the passage that brought me into the room. It was now sealed, making the funhouse one-way only. I slid through the space that was barely wide enough to allow passage. I was again accompanied by the scurrying at my fee and the squeaks of rodents in the darkness. I was relieved they seemed to be in too much of a hurry to bite, I just wondered where they were running to.

Soon, a small ray of light appeared and I continued forward, to another square room with another projector screen covering one wall. The film began to roll. There was Perillo, tied down with a birdcage on his stomach, screaming in agony as a rat burrowed into his stomach. Then the footage flickered and it showed Giselle, hanging upside-down with legs spread wide apart. I could see Burton and me working the long saw, pushing and pulling as her mouth formed a large "O", screaming in immense agony. I turned towards the camera with blood specks on my face and grinned, evilly. It was not a look I had ever seen in myself, as if someone or something else had taken the reigns. The film cut off and I was in blackness again.

I again groped my way through the dark and located an opening on the opposite side of the room. So far, this funhouse was not too scary, just weird. The scariest thing was the self-knowledge of seeing me in a way that was unfamiliar. The objective view of my hideous deeds was deeply unsettling because it was something or someone else in my head during the scenes. I had little idea of the brutality inflicted, until it was shown in the film footage. I also wondered who made these movie clips. I continued through the narrow passageway and was now desensitized to the rat traffic at my feet. They had their places to go and I was just trying to get through this uncanny cinematographic maze. I worked my way through the passage into a third square room with a projector screen. The footage began of Lily, placing her boot against the door of the iron maiden and pushing it backwards. She was laughing as the blood seeped out of the seams and formed a pool on the floor. The film flickered and showed Lily viciously stomping on Pete's face with her boot heels. Pete's face became more and more disfigured as the footage flickered and faded out.

Next there came a scene of Red in nightie, sitting on Lily's lap. Even in slow-motion, his face contorted to instant shock as blood suddenly spilled forth from his mouth and smoke rose from behind him. There was more flickering, and then came Blondie crawling past the camera on all fours, howling in agony as fire burned from his ass. A bit more flickering and I saw Ramena, sleeping peacefully, as I slit his throat and blood flowed outwards onto the white mattress. Then the screen went black. I began my search for a passageway out of the room.

As I stumbled around in the blackness, the projector screen flickered a few times. An image of Reshi, smiling, appeared. She held up a small sign that said "Kiss Me" on it. Joy instantly flooded my heart. Even in the grainy, flickering black and white footage, Reshi looked astounding. I began to think that the carnie outside of the funhouse really wasn't lying. This place showed the two components of life, when you boil it all down to bare essentials: love and death. All human actions are motivated by one or the other; take your pick, dear reader. And choose wisely. Reshi motioned for me to come closer to the screen. I approached it and she smiled at me, pointing at the sign. She puckered her lips and leaned forward and I puckered mine and leaned towards the screen.

I kissed the screen with my eyes wide open, to take in all of her enchanting beauty. The instant my lips met the surface of the projector screen, however, she vanished. In her place were small circles of different sizes, orbiting around each other in an abstract pattern. Then her flawless face reappeared. I somehow knew it was merely a celluloid image of her face, I did not care. I continued to kiss away. As Mick and Keith once sang, "I tell you love, sister, it's just a kiss away. It's just a kiss away. Kiss away. Kiss away." The screen went black.

I groped along the wall blindly, eventually finding another passageway. I walked down it, but it led to a dead end. I retraced my steps to where I had entered and it was now sealed by a wall. I was trapped in a rectangular corridor as rats swarmed over my feet. The corridor was sealed at both ends, but somehow rats kept coming in. It became difficult to move as the rat population grew to a point where they were up to my knees, and getting higher. They ran on top of each other like a moving mass of brown, furry liquid. I began to scream and kick my legs violently. Then music was pumped in; just the same repetitive phrase over and over, sung by a children's choir, "ashes, ashes; we all, fall, down . . . "

"Get me out of here!" I screamed as loud as I possibly could, but there was no answer, save "ashes, ashes, we all, fall, down . . . " The volume of the children's choir increased as the level of rats also increased. I tried to move, but it was as if I were wearing fishing waders that had filled with water. The rats burrowed and scurried over one another and were now up to my waist. "Ashes, ashes, we all, fall, down . . . " over and over and over. I clutched the stuffed black dog I had won and felt the warm, fleshy tail of a rat graze my arm as it clung to the stuffed animal. I screamed and shook the rat away and screamed until I could not vocalize a sound. I felt a piercing pain on my inner-thigh. One had bit me and it opened the floodgates. A herd of rats began biting simultaneously. I felt sharp, horrendous incisions all over my legs, rising up to my tender regions where the pain became more than I could bear. I screamed my final desperate scream only to hear, as if mocking me, "ashes, ashes, we all, fall, down . . . "

I bolted upwards in my cot.

"You okay man?" asked Jolen, "You were screaming like crazy." I wanted to answer him, but I was not sure. The dream had been so vivid, so real. I felt my legs, patting them down. They were soaked with perspiration, but not blood. I looked around the room, trying to regain my bearings.

"These nightmares are beyond fucked-up," I replied.

"Welcome to Manila," answered Jolen.

I stared at the wall, fixing my eyes upon the "Rampage" painting through the darkness. The circles began to orbit and move until they formed the beautiful image of Reshi's flawless face.

CHAPTER IX

Casino Boogie

No good, can't speak, wound up, no sleep.
Sky diver insider her, skip rope, stunt flyer.
Wounded lover, got no time on hand.
One last cycle, thrill freak Uncle Sam.
Pause for bus'ness, hope you'll understand.
Judge and jury walk out hand in hand.
Dietrich movies, close up boogies,
Kissing cunt in Cannes.

Grotesque music, million dollar sad.
Got no tactics, got no time on hand.
Left shoe shuffle, right shoe muffle,
Sinking in the sand.
Fade out freedom, steaming heat on,
Watch that hat in black.
Finger twitching, got no time on hand.

Casino Boogie—Rolling Stones

Kinsey the blowman; was a happy jolly soul, thumpity thump thump, thumpity thum thump look at Kinsey go. Thumpity thum thump, thumpity thump thump I'm going to kill him slow. Thumpity thum thump, thumpity thump thump stab him in the throat. Thumpity thum thump, thumpity thump thump, my sacrificial goat.

Fucking Kinsey, acting like a kid I knew in elementary school, Rusty Jones. Kid loved nothing more than to know information you didn't and then dangle it over your head as long as he could. Shit. Kinsey tells me I only have ten more days in solitary. I think to myself, "Self, ten days is nothing, piece of cake." That was forty-eight days ago. I know because I keep daily marks and I'm not telling where I keep my marks. I know you love passing your time on the night shift by reading this shit I scribble, but damn. Kinsey, I could write a hell of a lot more if I was allowed to roam free on the range with the other nuts. Me only with myself for too long is not a good mix. We both know what happened before was just an accident. I didn't attack anyone, we were just horsing around. You even told Dr. Taylor the same. And why the hell is he coming around all buddy-buddy to talk to me every few days? What the fuck is that all about?

Dr. Taylor makes bad shit go on in my head. He asked me to pray with him and I had to fight the urge to tell him to go hang himself. I envisioned strangling him the entire time he rambled on about his loving fairy tale super-hero. I also thought about scooping out one of his eyeballs with a teaspoon, then rolling it around in my mouth like a jaw-breaker, before crunching down on it while he watched me with his one good eye. Then the pompous prick has the nerve to leave me with a Bible? I can't have paper, pencils, crayons, magazines or books, but it's okay for me to have a Bible? I've got Lucifer swimming around in my head; a Bible, what the hell? Oh well, I'm glad he left it. I take turns starting at Genesis and going back from Revelations. I plan to finish somewhere in the middle. For my daily devotions I rip out a few pages to wipe my ass with and the pages in Genesis? Well, you don't really want to know, Kinsey. I will just say there is a reason the pages are all stuck together up to chapter four or so. Don't worry about it. Eve has been quite a fantasy figure for many men greater than I, so what? What the hell do you expect from a nutcase in solitary left alone with those smooth, tender and titillating pages?

Anyway, I hope you can read in-between the lines here, Kinsey. Nothing that follows is true and I'm not going to kill you soon if you do not get me out of solitary somehow. Use your head because two negatives make a positive. Use those math skills, Kinsey, you're a smart guy. I need to be with my people. The people need me. Make it happen, Kinsey. It would be a shame and bad press to have the ambulance here again and all that shit. You won't avoid it by keeping me alone; you'll only make it happen, so make it happen. I could double my output of

writing if I was just another Bozo on the bus to the funny farm. It's a
win-win. Everyone's a winner. Step right up and on with the show.

Yoshimi must have been our good luck charm because things started
getting back to normal after we buried him. Well, at least as far as syndicate
business was concerned. It was like the police and the press forgot all about
Ramena and moved on to the new flavor of the month.

"You know, nobody seems to be talking much about Ramena anymore,"
I shared with Berto, as we sat at the bar in the Giraffe.

"Yeah," returned Berto, "The people here aren't really concerned with
justice as much as gossip. If the gossip involves someone well known, it's all
the better. In Manila, people choose style over substance."

"Like, you mean it's better to look good than to actually be good?" I asked.

""Yes, as long as the outside of the cup is shiny, it's fit for drinking out of.
I mean, think about it from the perspective of the police here. As long as the
chief showed concern initially and vowed to bring the perpetrators to justice,
they did their part. No sense in actually following through and finding who
is responsible. There's too much time and work and no publicity in that."

"Is it the same principle in operation that makes so many people here
pretend to be wealthy when everyone knows they really aren't?"

Berto nodded his head, "Style over substance, baby, and gossip, gossip,
gossip."

"Hey, I'm going to head around the corner and get a real cup of coffee.
You want me to pick you up anything?"

"No, I'm good," he said.

I walked down Burgos and up a few blocks on Makati Avenue. I walked
into the coffee shop, savoring the smell of the roasted beans brewing. After
getting the largest cup of black coffee they had, I went back out on Makati
Avenue. I stopped, took the lid off the cup, and began blowing on it to cool
it down enough for a sip. I noticed a small kid, maybe seven or eight years
old, shiny black hair, dark skin and his t-shirt was all stretched out and a bit
too big for him. The shirt had stains and he looked kind of grubby. Maybe
it was the steam rising from the cup at my lips, but I could have sworn the
kid's eyes appeared all white for an instant.

"Hey mister, you want to buy a poker chip?" he asked me, holding a
blue chip in the air.

"Sorry, kid, gambling isn't my thing," I replied, seeing disappointment
cross his face. I took a sip of coffee and asked, "How much you selling that
gem for anyways?"

The kid looked downwards and lowered the chip and rubbed one of his dirty sandal clad fee against the other one, before looking back up. "Well, this is a lucky chip, mister. It makes you win."

I chuckled, "Is that right? I have two questions, if it's so lucky, why do you want to sell it? The second question, how much are you selling it for? You never told me." I looked at the kid and began to feel pity for him. No kid this young should have to be out this late walking around the city trying to sell a lousy bingo chip. He was probably just trying to get enough to help his family have rice and sardines the next day. People on the street tried selling everything from flowers to snacks to sunglasses but all this poor kid had to offer was a crappy bingo chip he probably found somewhere.

The kid's eyes drifted again from being all white, to having pupils. Maybe he was just tired from walking around all night. Or maybe the steam from the coffee was playing tricks with my own eyes. The kid replied, "I have more lucky ones, but this one only costs one-hundred pesos."

"Dang, kid, that's a pricey piece of plastic. I'll tell you what, though, it's kind of late for you to be out walking around. How about you walk home and once we get where you live, I'll give you the money for the lucky chip, deal? You live around here, right?"

"Yes, this way," he began walking with a short little stride. It made me feel good to see him smile when I told him that I would buy his lucky chip. I felt like I was somehow making amends for all of the bad shit and crazy misdeeds I had enjoyed since being in Manila. It was refreshing to finally help someone just for the hell of it and do something good for a change. I walked beside the little tyke, who had to take two steps to every one of mine, down Kalayaan Avenue, occasionally stopping so I could get a sip of coffee without spilling it.

"Hey kid, how do you know the chip is lucky? And what's your name?"

"Seven"

"Not your age, kid, your name," I repeated.

"It's really Seven, mister. Everyone calls me Seven, even my parents."

"That's kind of a weird name, no offense," I began to chuckle, "Do you have six brothers and sisters?"

"No, just a sister," he replied, smiling.

"Well, are you really seven?"

"No, I'm nine, but I've always been Seven," he answered, wiping his nose with his dirty forearm.

We continued to walk and walk, block after block. My coffee was almost gone. "Say there, Seven, you walked a long ways to sell a bingo chip; how much further do we have to go?"

"Oh, not far," he answered, looking up at me with two small white ovals that were zombie-like, then they shimmered and his pupils appeared. Either Seven had eye trouble or I had vision trouble. Somebody's eyes weren't quite right. I considered asking him if he was doing some kind of trick with his eyes, but I didn't want to make him feel bad if it were some kind of genetic or medical problem. We were approaching a large sign that read "MANILA SOUTH CEMETERY".

"Uh, Seven," I said, "This looks like a cemetery. I don't think we're allowed to cut through here."

"It's where I live, mister. It's okay," he reassured. I followed Seven around the perimeter where there was a small path. A bit further up the path, after turning the corner, there was a small hole cut into the fence. We both crossed through the hole and entered the cemetery. It was another glowing Manila moon and its beams shed a luminous radiance over the tombstones, statues, mausoleums, above ground tombs and shrines. As we continued deeper into the cemetery, following the path along the edge, I could see rows of shanties and hear families talking and see small fires used for cooking, with the smells of onions and chicken in the air. I began to feel a bit nervous and edgy, since this seemed like the wrong neighborhood for a person with white skin. I really didn't belong here. I could also see further ahead, a group of Filipino men in a circle, holding bills, smoking and drinking. It looked like they were involved in some kind of gambling game. I decided that I brought Seven close enough to his home.

"Hey, Seven, you're close to home now. Here's a hundred peso bill and make sure you share it with your mom and dad, okay?"

"Thank you, mister," he said, fumbling the sticky blue poker chip out of his pocket. He looked up at me while handing me the chip and I was completely taken aback; his eyes were completely white, "I'm Seven but I'm nine," he said.

"You sure are, and that's awesome," I answered nervously. I turned to leave, "Bye, Seven, it was nice meeting you." I began to follow the path back to the hole in the fence. As I continued walking, I couldn't help but wonder what the hell was wrong with Seven's eyes. Sometimes they looked fine and other times, usually for a fleeting moment, they were just white and scary as hell. To my left I suddenly saw a hooded black shape moving towards me. It was not walking, but sort of gliding.

"What the hell?" I said out loud, stopping to try for a better view. It crouched and quickly concealed itself behind a statue of an angel. I then saw another fleeting black cloaked figure moving from further behind where the angel statue was, before it crouched behind a tombstone. I turned and looked down the path, then turned back and saw three more figures lower themselves behind tombstones. Maybe the moon and darkness were playing tricks on my eyes, maybe. I was suddenly filled with terror. I turned and began sprinting down the path.

As I ran at top speed, I could see from the corner of my eye, off to my left, figures moving parallel in the same direction I was running. They were darting and weaving from structure to structure. I continued to sprint as fast as I could, jumping over trash, bottles and debris. I could sense that the dark shrouded entities were gaining on me, getting closer and closer. I was nearly out of breath and relieved to see the gap in the fence where we entered the cemetery. I sprinted with everything I had and crouched low, shooting out of the hole in the fence like a cannonball. I continued to jog until I made it back to Kalayaan Avenue. I had to stop for awhile to catch my breath. I felt safer amongst the blowing horns, traffic and people getting on and off jeepneys. As I walked, I felt a little better and less afraid. I wasn't sure what happened in the cemetery, but I was in one piece and everything was okay.

When I got back to the Giraffe, Berto was sitting at the bar, "Damn, dude, where'd you go for coffee, to Colombia?"

"Almost," I replied, "I had to do a rare good deed."

"You fucked a nun?"

"I didn't realize your mom was a nun," I shot back, "Did I miss anything exciting here?"

"Nothing, a couple girls left with some big spenders from England and the crusty Australian guy at the other end of the bar blew a nasty fart." As Berto was telling me these things, I saw something odd. Seven was back, standing outside of the glass door, looking in at me and motioning with his hand for me to come outside.

"How in the hell did he get back here so fast?" I asked no one in particular, completely bewildered.

"Who?" asked Berto.

"Seven, that kid standing outside the door," I replied, signaling with my index finger for him to wait one second.

"Uhm, Tim, there is no kid at the door," said Berto, squinting and leaning forward to see the door better.

"Dammit, let me see what he wants" I resolved, heading back outside. I went outside and looked down at Seven. He smiled, looking up at me.

"Seven, buddy, you were supposed to stay home. That was part of our deal. Why are you back here and how did you know where I was?"

"It's my parents; they wanted me to find you. They want to thank you. They told me to come and get you. My mom has something for you," he pleaded, giving me his best sad-eyed treatment, until the headlights of a turning car shone on them and made them turn momentarily white. There was nothing appealing about the idea of going back to that damn cemetery.

"Seven, I'm sorry, but I don't want to go all the way back to that cemetery."

"Neither do I; but they will be mad at me if you don't come back, please mister. They don't believe someone bought the poker chip. If you don't come back with me, they will think I stole it somewhere and I will get punished. Please mister."

After having the scare of my life being chased out of the cemetery, I had very little inclination at wanting to go back. In fact, that damn cemetery was the last place on Earth I wanted to go to, but it was hard to say no to Seven. "Oh crap, you little punk," I complained, "I will go back there, but I'm buying another damn coffee on the way. You have to promise me this time you will stay home, damn, kid, you're freakin' killin' me!"

I stopped back at the coffee shop and we made our way back on Kalayaan Avenue. It was like a cycle of déjà vu and even though I was greatly perturbed at having to go back to the cemetery, I kept in mind the old saying, no good deed goes unpunished. Seven and I made small talk along the way, since it was our only option.

"Where are you from mister?"

"I'm from way across the ocean, a place called the United States of America. Have you heard about it?"

"Sure, that's where basketball comes from and where they make movies."

We continued to talk about movies, school and what school was like for me when I was his age. I told him about my third-grade teacher and how her breath always smelled like garbage. I also told him about some of the games we used to play that he never heard of, like freeze-tag and to the wall. Finally, we arrived at the hole in the fence leading into the cemetery. I thought how just an hour ago I was running for fear of my life through this gap and here I was, back again.

"Hey, Seven, do you ever hear strange noises or see weird things in this graveyard?"

"Sometimes," he answered, "like at night. I hear things. I'm Seven, but I'm nine."

"Yes, and I'm pretty certain we have already established that your name and your age are both different numbers," I answered, with a tone of sarcasm. He smiled mischievously, like he had a sadistic streak that found humor in my frustration. I chuckled because his sense of humor was like mine when I was his age and would giggle when my dad was upset over something. The little tyke was alright.

"So, what kind of weird stuff have you seen here at night?" I asked, as we walked up the path along the edge of the cemetery.

"Sometimes people say they see or hear weird things," he answered, as we continued walking the path.

"Well, that makes sense I guess, since it's a place for dead people. How much further till we get to your house?" I asked, as we got closer towards the group of men who were gambling.

"Not far, mister, and the dead people don't scare me as much as the living ones."

"That's deep thinking for a nine-year old, Seven." We continued walking towards the group of men drinking beer, smoking and playing cards.

"Hi" one of the men said. There were candles and oil lamps sitting on the stone slab of a crypt, covered with a gaming tablecloth, or tapete, and the men sat on crates and folding chairs around the crypt, using it as their card table.

"Hi, you guys playing some poker?" I asked, trying to be friendly and avoid any conflict, as the entire group surveyed me with their eyes. I noticed that the cards they held were different than traditional playing cards, looking more like Tarot cards, with ancient symbols of swords and coins and men on horseback brandishing swords.

"No, we're playing sakla. You want to try your luck? We can deal you in this round," he offered.

"No thanks," I replied, "I appreciate your offer though."

"That's kind of weird seeing people gambling in a graveyard," I said to Seven, as we continued walking.

"I think they use the money to help people pay for getting buried here," he answered, matter-of-factly.

"I guess it's good then, just kind of a weird place to gamble, but who am I to judge; how much further until your house, Seven?"

"It's right there, mister," he said, pointing to the next shanty up the path. There were chickens in the space next to the shack and some laundry hung by the doorway. "Go ahead, mister. Tell my mom I brought you here so she'll believe me."

I approached the small shack that was topped with corrugated metal. I could hear talking inside. I knocked on the frame of the open doorway. "Hello, is anybody home?" I asked, loudly enough to be heard. A woman was talking in Tagalog to someone. She approached the door. She was in her thirties, dark skinned, pretty, but with a suspicious approach.

"Yes?" she asked.

"Hi mam, Seven brought me here because he said you didn't believe him and that you wanted me to come so you could thank me," I said, looking for Seven who was mysteriously gone now. Her eyes grew wide and she began to gasp for air.

"Is this some kind of sick joke?" she demanded, getting very emotional.

"No mam, he brought me here because he said you wanted me to come. You are his mom, yes?" I asked, as she balled her fists up and began to swing at my head. She was now screaming and crying. "Seven, tell her, tell her dammit!" I shouted. Seven appeared behind me, smiling, looking up at me with white, zombie eyes.

The lady shouted at me, "My son died exactly two years ago on this very night. He was seven! What kind of sick joke is this?" she screamed in a rage, still swinging at me with fury. A man came out of the shanty, hearing all the commotion. He was brandishing a metal pipe. My brain scrambled to think of how the kid tricked me, how Berto could not see him, how, possibly, nobody but me saw him. The man came at me with the pipe and I turned and sprinted.

The sakla players were coming up the path, so I ran straight into the graveyard before the man could get a clean swing at me with his pipe. I could still hear the woman screaming and crying as I began to hurdle jump the tombstones. The man continued to chase after me, yelling in Tagalog. I sprinted as fast as I could, leaping over crypts, dodging statues and zig-zagging around more than one mausoleum. I sprinted a ways before turning back to see if the man was still in pursuit. I didn't see the guy with the pipe, but I continued to run. When a man is after you with a pipe, it is best not to take any chances. I approached a tombstone and high-jumped over it, when I flailed my arms in the air before crash landing into an excavated hole on the other side. I hit the ground hard, after dropping more than twenty-feet.

I lay dazed, bewildered and damaged. The earth at the bottom of the excavation was like hard concrete. I barely had time to extend my arms to keep from landing face-first. It felt like one of my ribs might have broken from the impact. I slowly, painfully crawled forward to check how bad I was injured. I was bruised and sore, but luckily nothing was broken. I crawled to the edge of the wall so I might hide if pipe man showed up. An area of my ribs was very tender, but I knew it would heal in time. Time heals wounds.

I waited and waited, motionless, and waited some more. I glued myself along the corner where the earth wall met with the floor of the huge rectangular excavation. The most troubling part about the hole was that the walls were straight up for twenty-feet. I would need a ladder or a treble hook with a rope to climb out, and had neither. "Son of a bitch" I mumbled out loud, trying to scale the wall. It was too steep, too hard, too smooth and too dry. I could not even dig into the surface, it was like earth concrete. I moved to the corner where two walls met. I tried to prop myself against both walls, using them for leverage, but it was futile. I could not even get both feet up without sliding to the ground. It was like being trapped in a large concrete box with no lid. I ruled out shouting for help because the only ones who would hear me wanted to kill me.

After about two hours of trying to scale the walls, I was exhausted. I laid on my back looking up at the glowing Manila moon in all of its eerie radiance. I thought about Seven, lucky Seven. Was I duped into walking back and forth to the cemetery all night by a pint-sized ghost? I really had no strong opinion on ghosts before tonight. Now I was a believer and I did not like them too much. Why the hell did the kid trick me into going to his mom, a complete stranger, two years to the date he had died? Why me? The kid seemed normal enough, I mean, like a real kid. He walked and talked like a real kid. The white eyes that flickered in to view every now and then should probably have been a clue. Now his statement about living people scaring him more than dead ones also made more sense. What the hell would he do with my hundred peso bill if he was a ghost? Did onlookers just see me talking to myself? It was all very weird, but maybe having an Aswang demon lodging in my head made me more susceptible to the schemes of other spirits. I tried to close my eyes and get some sleep. Maybe in the morning a worker or someone would see me down here and help me, maybe.

I entered that tenuous space between consciousness and sleep, drifting in and out. I must have slept some because I am unsure how much time elapsed, but I opened one eye and I saw the moon, and was startled to see Seven peering down at me. His neck and head were looking over from the top of the hole. How long was he watching me? The moon shone brightly behind him and I bolted up shouting, "Hey! You little bastard; why did you trick me?"

"I'm Seven, but I'm nine," he answered, in a soft, calm voice, then he was gone. I called for him. I shouted for him. I even pleaded an apology to him. I wanted answers. I got nothing. The only thing I knew for certain was that he was seven, but he was nine, whatever the hell that meant. Why did he come back just to tell me that nonsense? Maybe he was trying to make me insane, or more insane? I lay back again, puzzled, frustrated and exhausted. I tried going back to sleep.

I rolled to my side, head against the hard dirt floor. I had nearly drifted off when I felt a knife stab me in the chin. It was a piercing, sharp pain. I opened my eyes and saw grey whiskers and beady eyes. I was face to face with a rat. I jumped to my feet and wiped my chin with my forearm. Blood dribbled down my arm and dripped onto the ground. My entire face hurt like hell, throbbing from the bite. I chased the rodent in anger, wanting to kill it in a furious rage, around the four walls of the rectangular pit. The vile vermin was much too fast for me to even get a clean kick at.

There was a crevice, a crack, merely two inches wide, at the base where two walls met and the rat wriggled itself into the crack. I kicked and clawed at the small opening, trying to widen it, but the hard earth would not budge. I heard a bark as I dug at the crack with my fingers. I looked up and saw the head of Blackie looking down at me. "Blackie!" I yelled. "Where you been, boy? You want to come down here and help me get a rat?" He just stared back at me and maybe it was the light of the moon playing tricks, but his eyes looked completely white. Then he backed away and I was alone again, still bleeding from the chin. I wanted to just go to sleep, but feared another visit from the rat. I removed my shirt, bundled it up, and crammed it into the crevice as deeply as I could. The little fucker might chew through the shirt, but it would take him an hour or two. I laid back down, putting the bottoms of my shoes over the shirt-filled crack, as extra insurance.

I didn't even care anymore about why Seven or Blackie showed up to observe me in my misery. My face throbbed in tremendous pain. I was exhausted. I lay back, sweating, and could feel the warm blood trickling down my chin. I wondered many things; why was I plagued by rats? Why was I on the other side of the world lying in a hole in a graveyard? Why was

I so happy to kill and torture people? Why did Lily lead me down this path, or why did I follow her? Why did I love Reshi so much that it superseded all of my rational thinking? I heard a bark and drifted into a dream.

I had a rope around my neck and stood, tippy-toed, on a narrow board. My wrists were tied together behind my back. The room was completely dark. A woman in a flowing white dress appeared. Her features were lithe, delicate and she moved gracefully. Her beautiful Asian face, with its elegant features came floating into view. It was Reshi, precious Reshi. She stood in front of me smiling and asked, "Hello Tim, do you love me?"

"Yes, I love you," I answered, hoping the correct answer might get the noose from around my neck.

"Then prove it; kiss me."

She puckered her lips where she stood. I stepped forward and the plank under my feet lowered like a see-saw, tightening the noose around my neck. Her soft, pouty lips were merely inches away. I wanted to kiss them badly, but it was very difficult getting any air. I took another half-step and my throat was completely sealed. I began to gasp for air.

Reshi smiled, saying, "I died for beauty, but was scarce. Adjusted in the tomb, when one who died for truth was lain, in an adjoining room."

I struggled to regain my footing and step backwards. The board tilted up, which was a relief since the lack of oxygen had me on the verge of passing out. I managed to back-step enough to gasp precious oxygen into my lungs. I regained my balance and took another step backwards.

"What's the matter, Tim? You don't love me?" she asked, looking like an intoxicating, voluptuous Asian angel of allurement.

"I do, but can you come closer to me?" I managed to ask.

She smiled and continued reciting the oddly familiar poem, "He questioned softly why I failed? 'For beauty,' I replied. 'And I for truth—the two are one; We bretheren are,' he said."

She puckered her lips again, seductively, and against all rational logic, I could not resist. A trademark of insane thinking is to make the same mistake and expect different results, and, dear reader, I insanely stepped forward again. The rope tightened around my throat and I found myself again in the throes of asphyxiation. I struggled to step backwards on the plank, but swayed off on one side and now dangled in the air, all of my weight pulling the rope into my neck.

As I hung there, slowly turning in the darkness, I heard Reshi continue her recitation, "And so, kinsmen met a-night, We talked between the rooms, Until the moss had reached our lips, And covered up our names."

On the verge of death, I recalled the poem. It was from the nineteenth-century, written by Emily Dickinson, the original gothic girl. Something either cut the rope or it snapped at that moment because I was now falling into the black void. My fall ended when I splashed into water.

The momentum carried me down into the water. I began to kick with my legs to break the surface and breathe in the precious air. I could see the glow of the moon as I neared the surface of the water. I broke the surface, bobbing and continuing to kick my legs as I gulped in the oxygen. It was difficult to stay above water with my hands still tied behind my back, but I managed. After regaining my breath, I scanned around for a way to shore. I turned to see Reshi, sitting in a black chair. She wore a white skirt and a loose white silky blouse. Her black hair flowed like liquid over the shoulders in the white blouse. "Reshi!" I shouted, "Please help me!"

She smiled, crossing her shapely, slender legs. She held a long, sturdy rod of bamboo in her hand and said, "Drowning is not so pitiful As the attempt to rise," and nimbly positioned the stick on top of my head, pushing me back under the water. I tried to kick my legs, but it was in vain. I began to panic, bending my head side to side and kicking more frantically with my legs, but her stick simply slipped to my shoulder holding me under. Finally, on the verge of drowning, the pressure relieved and I was able to break the surface. I gulped in the air.

"Please Reshi, help me!" I pleaded. She smiled and tapped me twice on top of the head with the stick, laughing, before pushing me under again. I struggled to rise upwards, arching my back and kicking my legs. Just before surrendering and gulping water into my lungs, she relieved the pressure and I broke surface to breathe again. The moonlight shone over her radiant refinement, as she toyed playfully with the bamboo.

She looked at me, saying, "Three times, tis said, a sinking man Comes up to face the skies, Where hope and he part company-". Then she rose from the black chair, laughing wildly, and put the tip of the bamboo against my forehead, plunging me under deeper this time. No matter how much I twisted, turned or kicked, it was useless. The stick held me under. As I screamed, I could feel water pouring into my mouth as I swallowed it in one final surrendered liquid breath.

I regained consciousness to the sound of an organ playing a funeral dirge. My body was immobile, stiff lying prone in a coffin. I could not move but I was aware of everything around me. There were people approaching the coffin, stopping, and looking down at me in sadness and pity. Reshi appeared first, with moist eyes. She was wearing a red dress with a shiny black belt. The dress made a wondrous display of her ample cleavage. She leaned over and I could see her breasts in my entire range of vision. My brain sent a message to my machinery about an erection, but I could feel nothing down there. Even in a comatose state though, Reshi was easy on the eyes. She stroked my cheek with the back of her fingers, saying, "It was fun while it lasted."

Next were Berto and Sonny, as they looked down at me, I could smell the San Miguel on their breath. Their faces were sad, and I wanted to tell them, "Guys, I'm alive!" but I could not move to save myself, not even a lip or an eyebrow.

"Tim, you were one hell of a killer, killer," said Sonny and I felt proud because Sonny did not give away compliments easy.

"Yeah," added Berto, "wherever you are, we miss you man."

Next appeared Jolen and Lily. Lily wore a flowing, airy white dress with a black opal pendant hanging just above her cleavage. She looked radiant, even in my death. Jolen leaned over, his contagious, knowing smile always a welcome sight, "Tim, my friend, I will miss you but you will always be in my heart." I wanted to tell him that I felt the same way, but I could not.

Then Lily leaned over, her long silk black hair flowed downwards, instantly creating two private walls of lustrous black silk between her hazel eyes and my own. The pendant swayed in a hypnotic manner as she spoke softly to me, saying, "I felt a funeral in my brain, And mourners, to and fro, Kept treading, treading, till it seemed That sense was breaking through, And then a plank in reason, broke, And I dropped down and down." Lily then stood back solemnly and the coffin lid slammed shut and I was in darkness.

I bolted upright, realizing it was another nightmare. The moon was still in the sky. I felt my chin and the soreness and bleeding served as an unpleasant reminder that real life was just as bizarre as the real deaths in my nightmares. I looked upwards and was startled to see Seven and Blackie together. Seven had his small arm around Blackie, holding him affectionately. They both stared down at me and their eyes were white as zombies. It was unsettling, four white eyes piercing my soul and who knew how long they were up there just staring down at me? I didn't care anymore even what they were or why they were there. I was just frustrated and worn out. I stared back at them, silently and got to my feet and walked right under the edge they looked down from. There was no doubting the whiteness of their eyes as we continued our silent staring contest. The only doubts that occurred to me were if my own eyes were just as white as theirs.

I hoped not, but it wouldn't have surprised me. Hell, at this point, nothing surprised me. After five minutes of silent staring, they both slowly turned away and were gone.

I had to get out of the hole. I tried to climb by getting some footing with my left foot on the portion of my shirt that was jammed into the crevice. From there, my right foot managed to find a small ledge, not even one-inch wide, on the wall of earth. There was also a lump in the wall that allowed my right hand to partially get some grip. With some struggling, straining, adjusting and persistence, I was able to climb my way out of the hole, rolling out at the top onto the grassy graveyard ground. I heard the crow of a cock in the distance and knew it would soon be morning light.

I got to my feet. I was soiled, sweat soaked with blood dribbling from my chin, running down my neck and across my chest. As I walked through the cemetery, more cocks crowed. I kept a path in the middle of the graveyard, avoiding the shanties and sakla games. It was that eerie time of night when dawn is near but not near enough. There was a light fog rising from the ground and making everything glisten with moisture. I did a quick peso inventory of my pocket to make sure I had money for a cab. I wasn't sure how a cab driver was going to react to a passenger covered in dirt and blood, but I didn't care.

A large bat swooped near my head and I screamed and ducked. As I crouched, from the corner of my left eye, a cloaked, black figure glided by. When I turned to see it fully, it darted behind a small mausoleum. Another bat swooped closely and I heard footsteps approaching from behind. I immediately began running, without looking back. I dodged tombstones and statues in my path. As I ran, more shrouded black figures glided on both sides of me, at a distance but moving in my general direction. I simply sprinted the entire distance to the hole in the fence, being careful not to high jump into any excavations.

I made it back to Kalayaan Avenue and quickly managed to flag down a cab. I held the money in my hand, as I was out of breath, bloody, sweaty, shirtless and grungy. The money helped the driver be less concerned about my disheveled appearance. I got into the back of the cab and told the driver Caloocan. As we pulled away, I saw a young boy on the side of the road. He waved to me in slow motion. I returned his wave. His eyes were completely white. It was Seven, lucky Seven.

CHAPTER X
Sweet Black Angel

As I live and am a man,
this is an unexaggerated tale
—my dreams become the substances of my life.

—Samuel Taylor Coleridge

Free at last, free at last! Good work Kinsey, you got me back with the general population of craziezies! I will hereby offer my sincerest condolences for the whole credit card fiasco. That must have been a humdinger when you got that bill, huh? I'm hypothesizing that you will get reimbursed from the Visa megalopolis, since your card was stolen and misused and all. Let bygones be bygones Kinsey. Actually, as you know, your card was never stolen and if you're looking to blame someone, blame that pied piper of piousness, Dr. Taylor. He was the kingpin, the mastermind, who agreed to deliver my private note to Mac. Isn't Mac great? He might be crazy as hell to find fun in masturbating in the footprints of the nurses, but he's a wizard with computers. He just waited until after you did a little shopping online and went in behind you and got all the pertinent information. Old Macdonald had a farm, EIEIO, and on that farm he fished your account, EIEIO. Don't blame Mac though, and don't blame yours truly, Kinsey. I know it's tempting. Blame Taylor. Do it. You know better by now than to hold it against Mac or me. It's the law of karma, baby. Bring bad shit our way and worse shit will come back at you. You can't win, and do you know why? It's for one simple but vital reason. We have absolutely nothing to lose.

Mac just waited for you to order some gay stuff, then he did his thing. That's how, within a few days, every nutsack in the joint had memberships to porn websites of their choice. It's probably a good thing there are only two computers in our recreation room or the damage might have been worse. Were you surprised to see Cochran and Stablein both wide awake at the computers and strokin' to the oldies when you were making your nightly rounds? Hahaha! Cochran joined some site with midgets and animals claiming he has exquisite taste. Even Fleckles joined some vintage, historical black and white photo porn site. It was good for them. Let them blow off some steam, a whole lot of steam. Shows they're not completely crazy, too. Just an FYI, Dandelion ordered a bunch of sex toys so there might be some packages coming in still. Don't worry about it.

The important thing is you did the right thing by getting me the out of solitary. I don't mind being alone, but that was just ridiculous, fifty-eight days. Now we need to make sure it never happens again, Kinsey. I'll do my part, you do yours. Hell, you're getting more shit to read than you were before, right? You made the right choice and I hope there are no hard feelings. It's a win-win Kinsey. We're all winners.

The cab took me back to the Caloocan warehouse. I made my way to the cot room, exhausted after a strange night in the cemetery. Jolen was up early, doing his morning sit-ups. He looked at me and did an exaggerated double-take with his head. "Looks like you had quite a night!" he said, smiling.

"Brother, you can't even imagine," I replied. "I need a shower and a few hours of sleep."

"Are you okay?"

"I'm not sure. I was tricked by a ghost, chased by a guy with a pipe, bit by a rat and stuck in a hole in a graveyard and a bunch of other shit. I think I'm losing my mind. I can't tell anymore between what is real and what is unreal."

"Like your mind is playing tricks on you?" he asked.

"Exactly, and my thinking gets pulled in all sorts of directions. I'm losing confidence in trusting myself as a normal person."

"There are no normal people, my friend. There is just love and death. Everything else is a sideshow."

"Maybe so, but not knowing what is real really sucks."

"Well, start with something basic. You love Lily, right?"

"Well, I love being a part of the syndicate. You all are like family."

"Then go with that, since you know it is real, let it motivate everything you do," he suggested.

I took a shower and finally got the bleeding to stop. Jolen went out for a run and I desperately needed to get a few hours of sleep. I laid back in the cot, looking at Lily's painting and considered Jolen's view on life being motivated by only love or death. I could also visualize the concept in the painting, with the red representing love and the black representing death. The black was constant, always present. It was the painting in its natural state, ground zero. The blanket we all rise from and eventually go back to. The love was fluid, active and in motion. The contrast made it abundantly clear that love needed death in order to thrive and flourish. The red circles moved and orbited with intensity and energy. The theme of the painting seemed to be that we all belong to death, but love is the gift that gets things done.

I'm not sure how long I slept for, but I must have been restless to roll out of my cot and hit the floor. I had barely been awakened by the fall, when I went to climb back on my cot. I saw something there that defied all of the rules of reason. Dear reader, as I knelt beside my bed to get back in, I saw myself sleeping on the bed! I thought someone else was in my bed somehow, but the bite mark on the chin and the replica of my face was irrefutable evidence. I had a slight déjà vu feeling going back to the feeling I had when I first heard my voice recorded on a tape recorder. It was a weird feeling because I wanted to deny it was my voice, but I could not. Seeing myself was even more alarming, since there was no room for denial. I had read accounts of astral projection where people claimed to leave their bodies under times of extreme stress or pain. The accounts were interesting, but I considered them to be somehow a trick of the dreaming mind. Now, I was more persuaded. I felt deep down that it would be a huge mistake to try to wake myself up.

I looked around the room, remembering my mother's story she once told about leaving her body while giving birth. I disregarded her tale as the delusions of a woman in intense pain and under the affect of anesthesia. Now, looking around the room and seeing myself in the cot, I knew she was telling the truth. After all, it was me she was giving birth to. I moved out of the room and down the hallway. Things seemed brighter and I moved clumsily at first, but quickly adapted to the new awareness. I walked through the warehouse and saw one of the black apparitions from the cemetery, a cloaked figure in black floated off to the side, I hurried to the back door. It would not open but when I willed myself outside, I easily went through the door and was outside.

I began to walk around the perimeter of the building. When I turned the first corner, I encountered a young girl. The fact that she was wearing a pink ballerina outfit, complete with tutu and tights did not strike me as odd as how the outfit showed wear and was slightly stretched out and a bit too big on her. It also had some splotchy stained areas, frayed and tattered. "Hello," I said to her. She sniffled with her head lowered, looking down at her soiled ballerina slippers. "What's wrong?"

"I can't find my daddy; will you help me?" she asked. I was suspicious, hesitant after my episode with lucky Seven.

"Are you a ghost?" I asked, seeing no sense in beating around the bush.

She quit sobbing and looked up at me, "I'm just like you, mister. I got kind of lost trying to find my daddy, though. Will you help me?"

Either some force knew I had a weakness of caving in to kids or I was just a victim of circumstance. In any case, I would help her. "Where did you lose him?"

"We came here from the province of Capiz. My daddy wanted to bring me here because I dance. We were at the dance studio where I had practice then he was just gone," she answered.

"Why don't you just go back and wait for him?" I suggested.

"Please walk with me," she sniffled, "I know how to get back, but I hate walking alone."

"Okay, let's go to the studio. How far is it?"

"It's just up the street, come on," she said, taking me by the hand.

We proceeded to walk up D Aquino for a few blocks. "What's your name?"

"I'm Tickie, but my nickname is Tik Tik," she said, now much happier.

"I'm Tim, but my nickname is Tim Tim. You can call me Tim Tim, Tik Tik," I teased, as she giggled.

"Tik Tik and Tim Tim," she said, now laughing harder. Her laughter was contagious enough to make both of us laugh.

"What kind of dancing do you do, Tik Tik?" I asked.

"Ballet, I'm going to be a ballerina" she said, matter-of-factly.

"Good for you" I replied, as we turned onto Ninth Avenue for one block then continued up P Sevilla Street. After walking a few more blocks, we arrived at the HMT Dance Studio. "Come watch, Tim, they're practicing turn-outs," she said, excitedly. We went inside to the sound of piano music and eight girls dancing side by side in a row. My guess was that turn-outs had something to do with foot position, since all of their feet were turned way out as they moved. "I can pique and pirouette" she stated, proudly, "want to see?"

"Sure, Tik Tik, let's see you go pique pique," I said, as she smiled and trotted in line with the practicing dancers. When it came to dancing, Tik Tik knew her stuff, blending right in with perfect synchronization to the other young, graceful ballerinas. Her outfit may have been more worn and tattered than the rest, but she could certainly hold her own dancing. She twirled, dipped and spun effortlessly and with precision. They practiced for twenty minutes and she continued to spin on her own, faster and faster, for a moment, it looked as if she had sprouted wings. Then she went near the slender Filipina instructor before coming to where I was. She looked visibly upset, with tears at her eyes "My daddy is in the hospital."

"What happened?" I asked.

"I don't know. Can you go to the hospital with me, Tim Tim?"

"If you know where it is, let's go."

"It's General," she said, taking my hand in her small hand and pulling me towards the door. I had no idea where the hospital was or what had happened to her dad, but I liked Tik Tik and wanted to help her, so, on we walked. The hospital was on A Mabini Street and Tik Tik and I arrived into the waiting/reception area. "My daddy is in room 128. He only brought me here a few days ago from Capiz. I hope he's okay," she stated, pulling me by the hand past the receptionist's desk and into the long hallway. The lights were very bright against the white floor of the hallway and the sting of disinfectant smell hung in the air. We came to room 128 and entered, there were bags of intravenous solutions hanging from a metal stand beside the bed of the first patient in the room, an elderly man lying with his eyes closed. The patient on the second bed in the room was a woman in the later stage of pregnancy.

"We will let him sleep for awhile. Can you wait with me?" she asked, whispering.

"Sure," I answered, feeling sympathy for the little ballerina. We sat in chairs alongside the bed. It did not look like her father was going to come around anytime soon. My guess was that one of the liquids going through a tube into his arm contained some kind of sedative. However, this theory was proven wrong twenty minutes later, when the man sat up, eyes wide open, and pointed towards the sleeping pregnant woman in the other bed. He was grinning eerily as he pointed. Tik Tik acknowledged his pointing by nodding her head and smiling back at him.

She tippy-toed over to the woman's bed and a small set of crooked wings sprouted from her back. Her wings began fluttering, making a low hum, as she rose in the air and remained stationary over the woman, then slowly descended on her. Each of her feet lightly landed on each of the woman's thighs as she squatted, looking down at her large stomach. I looked back at Tik Tik's father and he was looking at me, smiling, but his eyes were completely white.

"Alright, what the hell's going on?" I asked. He lifted a bony finger to his lips as a gesture for me to remain quiet. I looked across the room to see Tik Tik still perched above the woman's stomach, her wings lightly humming to keep the weight less noticeable and not awaken the woman. Tik Tik, still perched above the sleeping woman's stomach, extended her tongue and it continued to extend, like a long pink tube that narrowed to a sharp point at the tip.

Her tongue penetrated the woman's stomach and she looked to be drinking liquid, as if sipping through a flesh straw. As she slurped and swallowed, she made a sound of "tick tick, tick tick, tick tick . . . " I now understood her name a little better, but was completely baffled at what the hell was going on. The whole scenario became frightening enough that I rushed out of the room, down the hall and out of the hospital. I ran towards the warehouse, and as I approached, something began crowding in through my perception. It was Jolen's voice, yelling.

"Tim! Tim!' he shouted, "Chill the fuck out!" I had no idea why he was shouting at me. I also had no idea why I was crammed under my cot staring at a puddle of my own drool.

"What?" I asked.

"Dude, you've been having convulsions for the last thirty minutes and speaking in weird voices, like the Exorcist and shit."

I trusted Jolen. He would not just make things like this up, and my throat was torn raw. I was confused and the best guess I could make was that something else had taken control of my body while I was having an out-of-body experience.

"Man, something weird just happened," I confessed.

"I'll say," began Jolen, "You were growling in a low deep voice, deeper than your own and speaking some language that wasn't Tagalog or English. It was scary as hell! Your eyes were rolled back in your head, too."

"It was completely messed up," I said, after crawling out from under the metal frame of the cot. I sat on the mattress, rubbing my head to regain a few marbles. "I like left my body for awhile. I fell asleep and rolled out of the bed and when I climbed off of the floor to get back into bed, I saw myself lying in the bed still!"

"I heard of stories like that, they call it astral projection," said Jolen, matter-of-factly.

"Then it got more fucked up. I met a little girl outside of the warehouse. I might have been a spirit body or something, but it felt real, like normal. We walked up to a dance studio and then went to a hospital because she was supposed to visit her dad there. The weird part was that she sprouted wings and flew up on top of a pregnant lady, then her tongue came down and penetrated the lady's stomach, and she started sucking through her tongue, like she was sucking the baby out of the lady's stomach through a straw!"

Jolen's face revealed more shock than disbelief. "Did it sound like 'tick tick tick' when she did it?"

"How did you know that? She even told me her name was Tick Tick!"

"She was from the provinces?"

"Yes; province of Capiz, how do you know all this shit?"

"I'm going to the hospital to check on this; it was General?"

"Yes, room 128"

"I need to confirm the miscarriage. I might have good news and bad news for you when I return," he said, quickly putting his shoes on.

"Do you want me to come?"

"No, you've been through enough, just, well, wait here, I won't be long. Get a bite to eat," he suggested, before quickly leaving.

I heated up noodles and hoped the spicy broth would soothe my raw throat. I ate slowly, thinking about all of the bizarre events that seemed to be occurring with greater ferocity and frequency. I missed my old life. My normal life I had before coming here, just as a regular, taxpaying citizen of the United States. Because of the crimes I have committed and the things I have seen and experienced, I knew I could never regain my old, normal life. I was past the point of return. I had lost hope. Without hope, it is hard to find a reason to keep on keeping on. The hope I did have was nearly as pointless, but it was easier to keep the flames fanned; the hope that I could somehow be with Reshi someday. I held a hope that her heart might feel like mine once I confess my desire for her, as unlikely as it might be. Maybe this was all just one big test Lily was putting me through, orchestrated to test my fortitude and mettle, my devotion. Anything was possible with a scheming, fickle-hearted and duplicitous woman like Lily.

Jolen returned, breathing hard, as if he had jogged the entire way. "Well?" I asked, "Did you find anything out?"

"Yes, the woman lost her baby. There was a puncture wound in her stomach and the fetus lost blood through hemorrhaging, or at least that's the medical take on it. Now, if your body was here freaking out when it happened, then somehow part of your self was at the hospital too. I could only get so much information because I pretended to be her concerned son, and had to leave quickly when they began asking me too many questions. I also didn't want the lady to suffer any more, so I asked them not to tell her I was even there."

"Holy shit, was there an old guy in the other bed in the room?"

"No, just an empty bed."

"Damn, you didn't see any old guy or a little girl dressed in ballerina clothes?"

"No; but I do believe your story. It was Aswang, dark spirits that can assume any shape of animals or people. They are known to fly and use their tongues to drink the blood from unborn babies when the pregnant moms are sleeping."

"How the fuck do you know about this? You said there was good news and bad news, what's the good news? All I can see is plenty of bad."

"Well, we might know what's wrong with you. You have Aswang. You are now probably a victim of Aswang possession. I've heard lots of stories, since I was little. Living with you and hearing about what you are going through, it would make perfect sense."

"Aswang?" I asked.

"Aswang are known here as shape-shifting spirits. They have a fondness for the blood of unborn babies, but also enjoy getting inside people's heads and making them insane. Like in your country when people speak of demonic possession. They are said to be capable of appearing as any animal or person, young or old. They are sometimes recognized by their black tongues or white eyes. Usually the animals they appear as look flawed or deformed somehow and they're black or have black tongues."

"White eyes? I've seen plenty of those since I've been here, but it all sounds too hokey, like the boogey man or something. I mean the weird shit that has been happening has me open-minded, but this Aswang sounds more like an urban legend or farfetched monster story."

"It might be, but what other explanation do you have? Maybe it's inside you somehow. I'm pretty sure Lily has it, too; she hides it well but there have been moments. When you were doing the Exorcist thing under your cot, I mean, your eyes were white and the voice coming out of your mouth was not your voice."

"Maybe," I replied, "I guess if what you are saying is true, it leaves two questions; one, how did I get it? And, two, how do I get rid of it?"

Jolen smiled, "I remember hearing that people can become Aswang from eating a black baby chicken. I also heard that it can transfer from person to person. If someone has it, they can spread it to you, usually through intercourse. As far as getting rid of it, I'm not sure. I remember hearing about a fortune teller who dealt with Aswang, a lady in Quiapo. She's a manghuhula at the Plaza Miranda. Rumor has it that she used to treat cases of Aswang possession in Davao. I heard about her years ago, so I don't know if she's still at the plaza or not. You want to try to find her?"

"I'm game for anything that might help. I'm losing my mind."

"Okay, I have to run an errand and then we will go. Give me about an hour," he said, before leaving.

I spent the time thinking about Aswang. Could such a thing exist? Was it responsible for my dysfunctional relationship with sanity? I recalled back to when I arrived in Manila, before I was tainted with lunacy. It was difficult to remember the innocence I arrived here with as a simple tourist in search of pleasure, with an innocent friend who I watched savagely murdered. I was now out of innocence. There was no way back. My pleasures were far more sinister than I could have ever imagined. The first rat that I had locked eyes with from across the swimming pool, the one who warned me to get the fuck out of Manila, maybe I should have taken the hint? Did Lily transfer Aswang into me when we had sex? There was the sudden blood lust for torture and murder. There were the nightmares, the funhouse, Blackie, Lucy, Tik Tik and Seven. Learning I was contaminated by Aswang would help to explain a lot, but would the knowledge be of any real benefit?

We met up with Madame Aurang as she sat at her table at the busy Plaza Miranda. There were many tables of alleged fortune tellers. Jolen approached her and spoke to her in Tagalog, occasionally pointing in my direction. Madame motioned me forward. She was middle-aged, wearing a simple white blouse and jeans. There was nothing about her or on her table that would indicate that she was a fortune teller of some renown. She appeared very down-to-earth and friendly. I felt at ease with her right off the bat. There was no weird jewelry, no dangling crystal earrings or zodiac bandanas; she just looked modest and humble, particularly when compared to the soothsayers at tables near her.

"Can I see your left hand?" she asked, in perfect English. I gave her my hand, assuming she was going to study the lines on it. She held my hand and reached into her satchel bag, pulling out a black, smooth stone. She placed the stone in the center of my open palm and folded my fingers around it. "Squeeze the stone," she directed. As I squeezed, I began to feel a burning sensation, first in my hand, as if the stone were heated in a fire prior to being in my hand. It became unbearably, scorching hot, the sensation traveling up my left arm. I dropped the stone on her table and waved my hand in the air hoping to cool it down. Madame Aurang showed no reaction, except a smile, a knowing smile. "You have a spirit, maybe more than one," she revealed, calmly, but with certainty. "Have there been lots of things happening to you that you do not understand?"

"Has there?" I replied. "I don't even know where to start. I just think I am losing my mind, like going crazy. It is like something wants me dead, but it will settle for making me miserable and just keeps me confused as hell."

"Have you been dreaming?" she asked.

"More than I want to, and with more intensity than I can control; my dreams are all nightmares, and worse since it has gotten to the point that I cannot tell when I am dreaming and when I am awake. How come the stone burned my hand when I squeezed it?"

She looked at me, surmising my up and down, before sighing lightly, "it was soaked in garlic salt and brine. I keep it handy as an amulet, as protection against Aswang. Tell me, have you been seeing certain animals frequently?"

"Yes, well, rats and a dog, Blackie," I answered. "Blackie is big and calm and usually comes out at night." I didn't want to share that he often shows up as I'm burying bodies and tried to think of something else, for fear she might read my mind and change her mind about helping me. "Sometimes, when he barks, it kind of launches me into a dream."

"I see," she stated. "What happened to your chin?"

"I was bit by a rat. I've also been bit on the hand, wrist and ankle."

"I must be honest with you. I do not know if I can help you," she said, before speaking to Jolen in Tagalog for a few minutes.

"Is it because Aswang is inside me?" I asked, interrupting them.

"Yes, exactly," she answered, "you are thoroughly filled with Aswang. I have not dealt with a case like you have in many years. I can try to help you, but I need to tell you that there is a chance you could die. There is a chance I could die. I also have no idea how long it might take. I will require much payment and need three days to prepare myself."

"How much money?"

Ten thousand pesos for our first session; meet me here in three days, at nine in the morning. Bring the payment.

"Thank you, I will be here." I replied, extending my hand to finalize our agreement. She kept her smile, looking at my hand and politely shook her head no, as she pushed a bit back from the table.

As Jolen and I were on our way back to Caloocan, I felt hopeful, relieved at the prospect of finally having my mind back to normal, with no more nightmares, blackouts and unpredictable episodes. "What was madame talking to you about in Tagalog?" I asked, curious.

"She was just asking about your situation. She said you are possessed by Aswang and she has never dealt with a case like yours, a foreigner."

"Do you think she's just acting dramatic to try to get more money?"

"I don't think so," he replied, "I mean, if she's just working on you she is going to miss out on making money from other clients during that time. Plus, she said that dealing with Aswang possession is very dangerous. It's more risky than just flipping tarot cards or something. When she said you could die, she wasn't joking; I'm guessing she knows that she could die too. Most Filipinos have some knowledge of Aswang; and while the stories usually involve some kind of fake sounding flying predator that sucks the blood from babies; nearly all of us know someone or have a relative or have a relative or friend who knows someone that has been affected in harmful ways by the dark demon of Aswang."

"That must be why she didn't even want to shake my hand."

"Yes, and the fact that she knows you jerk off with that hand," he said, as we both laughed.

Three days later, I met Madame Aurang at the Plaza Miranda. She looked thinner and frailer than just three days prior. She also emitted a pungent smell of garlic. "Don't mind the smell," she said, apparently reading my thoughts. "I have to protect and shield myself by smearing garlic pulp over my body."

We walked a few blocks from the plaza, to an old house and entered. The living room was dark, except for a loosely formed circle of jars with candles inside of them. Inside the circle of candles was a more exact circle of poured salt, with a gap. "Once you remove your shoes, you may enter the sacred circle through the gap," she instructed. "Once inside, just lie flat on your back, with arms and legs slightly outwards."

I followed her instructions and entered the circle through the gap. Madame followed behind me and carefully connected the two open points of the circle, closing the gap by pouring down more salt. I got comfortable on the floor and she knelt beside me, gently stroking my forehead with the palm of her hand. She placed an egg on my abdomen, over my belly button. She then began to recite something in Tagalog. It sounded like some formulaic prayer or spell, with certain phrases continually repeated over and over. The sing-song repetition and pattern proved hypnotic. I felt my body enter a mode of complete relaxation. My limbs felt heavier and as she continued her rhythmic incantation, a pleasant, light buzzing sound began to vibrate in my ears. The egg on my stomch felt heavier, but comforting. I was in a state of complete relaxation, subdued to the point where Madame's voice was heard as if it were from a far distance, like it was being faintly heard from another room. I began to dream.

I was in my old house where I grew up. I was young, maybe six years old. Our house had a basement where the washer and dryer were kept. I was always afraid of going down to the basement. The basement was damp, musty, with cobwebs and dark. It was also always five degrees cooler than the rest of the house. Just the smell of the basement terrified me. It was my one great childhood fear, to go down in the basement. I would not do it. The only way I could do it was if I clung to my mother's leg.

My mom was cooking at the stove as I played with some toy cars on the floor. It was like traveling back in time. "Tim, you're now almost seven. It's time you helped me out more around here. I want you to go downstairs, take the clothes from the dryer, put them in a basket, and carry it up here."

The only words I heard were "go downstairs" and fright surged through my body. I wanted to help her; I really did, but anything besides going down into that basement. I would rather she asked me to jump from the roof of the house into the laundry basket than to go down to the basement.

"I can't do it" I told her.

"You will do it," she replied, in a tone of voice that left no room for compromise. I knew she was not going to budge. I swallowed hard and nervously surveyed the basement door. "Now go!"

I took a deep breath and walked towards the door. I knew my fear was unjustified, but, deep down, I could not get around the idea that there was something horrible about the cellar. It was a bad place, a place I should never be in alone, a place where bad shit goes down. I summoned all the courage I could fake, which was not much and feebly attempted to go down the stairs. I walked down two steps and froze. The evil, damp smell rose up from the darkness below.

"Just go" said my mom, in a bossy way. I tried to imagine other things, to think I was somewhere else. Maybe if I could relocate in my mind, I could get down there and back with the laundry. I told myself I was going down the steps to a playground and it worked, until I was five more steps down. I froze again, in shock. I had the certainty that something menacing was approaching me from down there. The hair on my head stood on end. I bounded back up the stairs, faster with each step. My mom glared at me in anger. "What's wrong with you?" she screamed, "I cannot believe this! We're going to the doctor next week. Enough is enough!"

The next thing I knew, my mom and dad hauled me into the city to see a child psychologist, Dr. Kryptoforski. He was a large, bald, intimidating looking man. My dad said he used to be a football player at Boston College. He wanted to meet with me, then my parents, then all of us together. It was his procedure.

"So, Tim, tell me; what's the deal? You're afraid to go down into your basement?"

"Yeah, I just have a bad feeling, like there's something down there and it wants to kill me."

"You go down there when your parents are down there, right?"

"Yeah"

"And nothing ever happened?"

"Nope; but it's different when I'm by myself."

"I see. Don't you think the danger might just be something you make up in your head?" he asked.

"No, I can feel it, like in my stomach."

"Well, do you think whatever you are afraid of down there wants to hurt you or just scare you?" he pressed.

"It wants to kill me and that's what scares me. I just don't want to go down there. I don't see what the big deal is," I argued.

"Okay, I think I have a solution," he said, rubbing his head with one hand, deep in thought. His eyes then darted around the room and settled back on me. "I have an idea that I need to run by your parents. Do you trust me, Tim?"

"I guess, but I don't want to go into the basement."

"Okay, we will work through this, easy. There's nothing to worry about."

Dr. Kryptoforski sent me out to the waiting room and called my mother and father in. There was a toy box and a kid's table, but I had no interest in playing. My future was at stake. I wanted to know what the hell the doctor had planned. I leaned my ear against the door and eavesdropped.

"Why do you guys think Timmy is afraid to go into the basement by himself? Has anything ever happened down there?"

"Not a thing" said my dad.

"He just gets terrified," added my mom.

"Well, are there any stories or scary movies he has seen that might have influenced him?"

"No, we don't let him watch things like that."

"Well," said the doctor, "I have an idea. You may not want to try it, but if you go along with it, I'll need to know both of you are on board. I must warn you, it will sound harsh, dated even; however, I have had high success rates with this direct approach in dealing with adolescent phobias."

"Well, you're the expert," said my dad, "what do you suggest?"

"As cruel as it sounds, I recommend locking him in the basement for a minimum of four hours. This will enable him to fully meet, confront and, hopefully, overcome his irrational fear."

"He will go berserk. It's too cruel," protested my mom, thankfully.

"I understand completely," began the doctor, "and if it were my son and I was being asked to do something that sounds so drastic, I would have similar reservations. Your apprehension is natural and completely understandable. The success rate of curing these kinds of phobias, however, is very high, particularly for his age group. The indifference of it goes against all of your maternal instincts, which makes perfect sense, but letting go in this instance could allow for a conclusive cure.

"I won't be able to deal with him screaming and banging on the door for four hours," she confessed.

"Well, the only way it will really work is if you two leave the house for four hours. Otherwise, one of you will cave in to his pleas of mercy. If, however, he hears both of you leave in the car, it will force him to endure the situation, ultimately realizing that there is nothing to be afraid of."

"This sounds insane," protested my mom.

"Dear, he is an expert, let's consider it" said my father.

"If you both agree, just let me know the day and time so that I can be available, just in case anything unforeseen occurs, you can call me."

"I say we try it," said dad.

"I know, but it just sounds so cruel. I feel horrible to lock him down there and leave."

"I know, honey, but in the end it is for his own good. Can we try it?"

"Okay," she conceded. They agreed the date would be Saturday at noon.

I really didn't like what I was hearing. The main thing on my mind was how I was going to get out of this. Running away came to mind, but I had no place to go. I didn't stand a chance if mom was on board, since she was my only hope. The rest of the week was something of a blur. I could not concentrate at school. I could not sleep at night. I could barely eat, since the constant worrying curbed my appetite.

Saturday morning came and I accepted my fate. I was curious what kind of approach my old man would use to get me in the basement. Would he be angry and forceful, or would it be more of a bribe. Turns out, it was neither.

He simply called me to the basement and I went there, dazed. "This is for your own good," he stated, solemnly. Then he turned, went up the stairs, closed the door and I heard the click of it locking. The strange thing was, after worrying so much all week, I was out of fear. I wasn't scared. I just took a seat on the stairs.

Next, I heard my mom and dad talking, and the door opening, then the car doors slamming shut. The engine started and I heard the crunch of gravel under the tires of the car as it backed out of the driveway. I sat in the stillness, alone, or so I thought.

"Meow," came a soft sound from the furthest corner of the basement, which was also the darkest corner.

"Strange," I thought, "how did a cat get down here?" Perhaps, even stranger, I was not really terrified of being locked in the dark, musty basement. I sat on the stairs, growing mostly bored after fifteen minutes. I heard the cat meow again. I decided to go and find it, since I had more than three hours remaining.

"Here kitty kitty" I said, hoping he might come to me at the stairs.

"Meow" it returned, from the dark corner. I tried coaxing him out of the darkness, again and again, but no luck; he wasn't going to budge, only returning a soft "meow" every three minutes or so. I ventured towards the dark corner in a crouch. I could hear friendly purring and moved closer towards it, blindly reaching out with my hands, until something suddenly grabbed my wrist in the darkness and I screamed.

"Hehehe" came an evil, taunting, menacing laugh. My arm recoiled in shock. Out of the darkness, a familiar looking face appeared. It was Dr. Kryptoforski. Part of me felt a sudden relief, thinking maybe this was part of the therapy. After all, he was a licensed professional with the respect of many people, including my parents. However, his evil face did not match his respectable reputation. He looked weird, though, wearing a white lab coat and nothing else. His bare calves pulsated with veins as he held me by the arm. He grinned maliciously, like he knew a secret that nobody else was aware of. I had a sense that he was going to kill me. It showed in his crazed eyes.

He clubbed me on the side of the head, sending me sprawling sideways across the concrete floor. I saw a burst of color when his hard fist impacted against my skull. Before I could scramble to my feet, he yanked my arm and held me captive in a headlock, where all I could see was his gargantuan calf muscles.

"Help!" I shouted, "Why are you doing this?" I asked. All of my fears about the basement were now justified. In fact, they were more terrifying than I had ever imagined.

"I loved my bird," said Dr. Kryptoforski, not so much to me, but just as a random confession. "I had to kill it. Fuuuck," he said, dragging out the vowel of the cuss word. He pulled me over to a work bench. "I ate my bird. I ate my bird after I killed it. Fuuuck."

I struggled to get my head free and he gripped it tighter and bounced it off of the bench a few times. The pain was intense. I momentarily forgot who or what I was. When I regained my senses, he was wearing a latex glove and stretching my tongue out of my mouth. It hurt so much that water was pouring from my eyes. The rubber material of the glove made it impossible to retract my tongue. He pulled my tongue over the work bench, grabbed a Phillip's head screwdriver with his free hand, and plunged it through my tongue where it pierced the wood on the bench. My face was numb from the searing pain. I tried to scream, but could only moan with my tongue now nailed to the work bench.

"I loved my bird. I killed it," he repeated, before tapping the handle of the Phillip's head with a hammer to drive it deeper into the wood. "I killed it and then I ate it. Fuuuck," he drawled, putting the hammer down and picking up a razor, Exacto knife. He brought the blade across the tip of my tongue, slicing it off. He picked up the pink, flesh square between his thumb and index finger, turning it and scrutinizing it with a tilted head. Blood began to form in a pool in front of my face from my severed tongue.

He popped the morsel into his mouth and began to chew. I suddenly felt like I was suffocating. Something was in my throat. It was wriggling. I was choking, gasping for air through the blockage. I began to gag and cough. Dr. Kryptoforski continued slowly chewing the piece of my tongue, smiling at me as I gagged. I dry-heaved with a burst of air, dislodging the blockage. On the bench in front of what remained of my nailed tongue was a ball of feathers in blood, slime and saliva. It began to move. It was a tiny black chick and it nearly met me at eye level.

Dr. Kryptoforski finished chewing and swallowing the portion of tongue. "I loved my bird," he said, "But I killed it and ate it." He picked up the tiny chick and surveyed it from different angles, before putting the entire creature into his mouth and chewing with force. The pain in my tongue and throat was unrelenting. A pool of my blood now filled the counter top. I became cross-eyed staring at the handle of the screwdriver, and then I was able to open my eyes.

I found myself crouched in the circle of candles. Madame Aurang lay in front of me. Her chest cavity was violently ripped open and there was blood oozing everywhere. I was holding her half-eaten, slimy heart in my bloody hands. I was chewing slowly, mindlessly, at the raw, grisly meat. "What the fuck?" I asked myself, spitting the portion out that remained in my mouth and trying to figure out what in the hell had happened.

Apparently, sometime during my vision of childhood basement fear, I had murdered Madame Aurang, carving her heart out of her chest with the aid of a broken candle jar, the glass now lying in the pool of blood around her corpse. It seemed Madame Aurang was correct about people can dying during rites of Aswang exorcism. I did not remember one detail of the murder, but it looked like Aswang was the winner here. I dropped what remained of her heart and it splashed in the puddle of blood at my feet. I walked out of the circle of burning candles and left the house. A common cliché came to mind to help me keep calm about the Aswang inside of me. *If you can't beat 'em, eat 'em.*

CHAPTER XI
Tumbling Dice

Tis now the very witching time of night,
When churchyards yawn and hell itself breathes out
Contagion to this world: now could I drink hot blood,
And do such bitter business, as the day
Would quake to look on.

Hamlet, Act III, scene ii

Screw you and the horse that rode in on you, Kinsey. If you like reading it, fine. Just enjoy it and stop asking if everything is true. It's downright annoying. I do appreciate you going to bat for me on the unjustified assault charge and for helping to get me out of solitary. I'm also glad you enjoy reading this crap, but let's not forget one key thing here. I'm not writing for your entertainment. I write because I have to. I have to drain my theological and immoral infections. I have to pour the pus onto the page. It's good medicine for me.

I also know you want to keep me here and its okay. Hell, this place isn't so bad and it proves that sanity is relative only to the degree of insanity. If you think about it, the majority of us are just here because we never learned to play well with others, not because our brains turned to batshit. Society needs a safe place to store us and keep us doped up and tranquilized. It's like we committed crimes that society can't figure out, so they lock us up in here instead of prison. The message sent is simply that nonconformity is a crime, and we are the guilty.

Kinsey, I'm going to be going away. I have considered killing you, was relishing the idea actually. Had many visualizations of the murder going through my head and was hard pressed to choose which one, since I liked them all. Somehow, you're safe now. Maybe I had a change of heart. Maybe you inhaled a sulfurous spirit. Don't get paranoid or anything, but Aswang travels through people and knowledge of it makes it highly contagious. Have you had times of not remembering things? It's progressive. When you snap out of a trance and realize you are eating a heart carved out of someone's chest, then you'll know for sure. Until then, enjoy the ride.

When I vanish, don't you say a word to anyone or offer tips about where you think I am. Just let it go. I might write to you, but keep it to yourself. Everyone else that works here can kiss my ass.

"What the hell happened to you now?" asked Jolen, beginning to laugh and shake his head, "Every time you come home you're a bloody mess."

"I ate her heart," I confessed.

Jolen didn't look surprised or disappointed, "Well, how was it?" he asked.

"Chewy," I replied, "I went into a blackout and don't even remember doing it. When I came back to myself, she was on the floor all cut open and I was chewing on it."

"At least you're eating fresh. That's important. Get cleaned up and we'll play some ping pong," he said.

Right then, I wanted to hug Jolen. I felt horrible to know I killed an innocent lady, carved her heart out of her chest and ate half of it. Anyone else would have backed away calling me a degenerate psychopath, but Jolen stuck by me. He seemed to understand the fact that I did not remember doing it. I went and got cleaned up and then lost twelve games of ping pong to him. It was the least I could do.

That night, Berto and I hung out for awhile at the Giraffe. Lily said she would meet us there later. As we talked at the bar, I felt restless. There was a humming noise in my ears. "What's wrong man?" he asked me.

I had to smile at the irony of thinking to myself that I didn't have the heart to tell him that I ate an innocent woman's heart that morning. "I don't know. Maybe it's the full moon or the fact that Jolen kicked my ass so many times at ping pong today."

"Yeah," he sympathized, "we really need to rig that little shit's paddle or something. Maybe smear it down with bacon grease or something." We both laughed.

I could tell Berto had received an important text message by the way his facial expression turned serious as he read it. "Awh damn," he let out, in disappointment.

"What's wrong?"

"Nothing" he answered.

"Yeah, right," I replied.

"Fucking Paul; here, look," he said, handing me the cell. The text message on the screen was from Lily. It read: 'Fucking German was acting inappropriate, causing a scene here, drunk, trying to pull me by the arm to his car. I planned to come by the Giraffe tonight, but I'm going home.'"

As I read the message, my blood began to rage. I became instantly infuriated and no longer capable of rational thought. I handed Berto his phone and walked out of the bar. The German was a dead man.

I knew Lily was at a political fundraising dinner at a convention center only four blocks away. I began to run. I'm not sure if it was Berto calling after me, but my pocket knife was already in my right hand and fully extended. The blind fury in my mind was zeroed in on one goal.

I ran the entire four blocks, the rage increasing the closer I got to the convention center. Things were blurry as I approached. There were men in suits and women in formal dresses, mingling in small groups outside. I saw Lily, looking beautiful, but shaken, in a white dress. Then I saw the German talking to another man. His arms were making the usual gestures as he spoke, apparently trying to justify his recent behavior. I could tell he had had too much to drink because he spoke loud and slurred his words. He also failed to notice me approaching. I came to an abrupt stop at an arm's length in front of him. I turned on my heel, smiling, to face him and swung the blade upwards towards his throat, while simultaneously batting him on the opposite side of the head with my free hand.

As the blade plunged through the side of his neck, his eyes widened with the epiphany that he realized his life would soon be over. I relished the expression, dear reader, it said so much, even in his drunken state; the sober reality of acknowledging his death was evident. I loved it. I wanted to freeze the moment forever. This instant when the pickled, proud, pompous and perverted prick, used to always getting his way because of his money, became enlightened as to how weak he actually was. For him there would be no more ego trips of treating women like property, having his way with them like toys. Now he was the toy, soon to be put in the toy box, forever.

There were screams and shouts in the background. People were running and screaming for help and police. I couldn't really hear them or even see them. I was too focused. It was like everything around me was just extemporaneous, trivial, as I gazed into the dying German's eyes. That's where the beauty was and it captivated all of my attention. Blood began to trickle downwards from where the blade was lodged in his throat, the warm red liquid felt comforting running over my hand. His head was bent nearly sideways as I released the grip on it. On the opposite side of his neck, I could see the tip of the blade poking through.

I pulled the knife out from throat, grabbing his dress shirt in the chest area with my free hand, and pulled him forward while thrusting the blade into his stomach. His face rested on my shoulder, as I twisted the blade as deep as possible. The stream of blood from his neck was now spurting sideways, timed to his heartbeat, and ran down my shirt.

He managed to push away from me, taking a step backwards, and attempted a wide-eyed scream. I retracted the blood laden blade from his belly and forcefully swung it overhead, directly into his gaping mouth, mid-scream. It entered so deep that my fist impacted against his lips. As his eyes widened and his scream turned to a blood gargle, I could not help but to begin laughing, hysterical, maniacal and malicious laughter. It felt very good to stab a loudmouth right in the mouth. It felt perfect, in fact. As I twisted the blade, blood began to pour over his bottom lip. I relished in my frenzy, like a shark swimming in blood, I saw something that instantly ruined my joy. I saw Lily was not happy with my deed.

She looked at me coldly, with an indifferent glare that said more than words could. I knew instantly that I had royally fucked up. I had gone too far. She never gave any order to make this hit and doing it so publicly, in front of more than twenty witnesses, only compounded the screw up. I suddenly knew that what I believed would be a heroic act, was seen as mere defiance to Lily. It was the last thing I wanted to do, and it was already done. I yanked the knife from his mouth as he collapsed to the pavement. I began running with no destination in mind, albeit the nearest darkness. I was now like a cockroach and I was as dead as Paul. Lily's disapproving eyes told me so.

I continued running. I only knew that I had to get distance away from the crime and the witnesses. Thoughts raced as I ran and a committee inside my head was holding something of a debate. How would I survive on my own? Where would I sleep? What would I eat? How could I support myself? I finally resolved that these were all matters I could worry about later. I only knew that returning to the Caloocan warehouse was out of the question. The rules of the syndicate were always stronger than any bonds of friendship. It's just the Asian mafia way. I'd broken the rules and was now an outcast, an exile in Manila. I was as good as dead.

I saw some people boarding a jeepney ahead and fell in behind them. It was crowded and smelled like an anchovie's cunt, but at least nobody seemed to mind or notice that I was soaking in blood. I passed my pesos up to the driver, rested my head into my hands and with my elbows braced upon my knees, I began to consider what the hell I was going to do next. Berto's continual warnings about not acting on anything unless Lily gave the okay echoed in my head again and again. I tried to justify killing the German and how Lily was wrong to think I did a bad thing. But the look on her face, the expression in her cold eyes said otherwise. Besides, in Manila, Lily was right even if she was wrong. I had nothing left to offer the syndicate. I was a dead man. Worst of all, I knew Lily only saw me as a problem to be exterminated, a vermin.

I didn't regret killing the German, it was downright satisfying, but I did regret doing it so compulsively and with no consideration of potential consequences. I was supposed to be Lily's soldier, a relentless warrior who never questioned how or why, but just got the things she wanted done. It was a perfect machine-like chemistry, because she was a natural leader, and I was bound to the syndicate. The worst part was that I knew she would have given the green light on killing the German had I only waited a bit. Now, it was too late. I acted crazily and there is no going back to change it. It wasn't just a defiance of her leadership, but alienation from my only sense of family, the syndicate. Dear reader, I fucked up irrevocably.

I hopped off of the jeepney in Pasay City, and, for lack of an immediate better plan, began walking down Roxas Boulevard. I somehow felt safer near Manila Bay. They could only come at me from three sides. I kept my eye out for a safe place to hide-out. I knew there would be things like food and water to worry about soon, but first things first. I needed a safe place to hide. From Roxas, I continued walking towards the bay, until coming upon a large, coliseum-like structure, elevated and majestically surrounded on all sides by huge, square concrete pillars. For the most part, the structure looked abandoned, at least on this night. It looked safe, though there were some posters advertising theater performances later in the week. Fuck it, I could disappear when it was show time.

Walking up the circular driveway, the building appeared more massive and ancient, like the Acropolis at Athens. Each pillar loomed larger as I walked under them. They were at least fifty-feet high and the ceiling going around the perimeter of the building had a waffle-like pattern of concrete. It was evident that someone had carefully and meticulously thought through the details in the design of this spectacular building. The height, size and geometric precision made it breathtaking to walk around. At one of the corners, I leaned my back against a pillar and slid to the ground. The concrete felt cool to the touch, and the elevated foundation made for a slight steady breeze coming off of the bay. This was camp for the night, and possibly a few more. I sat trying to gather my rampant thoughts, or at least structure them simple. There was so much on my mind, mainly involving aspects of regret. I let go and tried to relax.

I must have dozed off for awhile, since I was now curled up on the concrete, attempting to use one folded arm as a kind of pillow. I was exhausted enough to fall asleep immediately. I'm not sure how long I was out for when the sound of steady footsteps could be heard in the distance. The sound of footsteps on concrete grew louder. Slow, heavy, rhythmic footsteps were the only sound heard in the darkness of the night.

My first thought was to haul ass and take off running. Nobody would be out parading around a building this late at night unless it was a cop or a criminal. I decided to take my chances and just pretend like I was asleep. I kept one eye opened, looking down the massive corridor. I saw a man, a worker wearing a tool belt. He was walking away from me and turned the far corner before I could see more of him. I wondered out loud, "why the hell is a construction worker out here this late?" I thought of going somewhere else to sleep, like in the surrounding foliage, but I had enough encounters with biting rats lately to scratch that idea. Besides, he didn't seem very bothered with me sleeping where I was. I closed my eyes again.

I'm not sure how much time had passed until the "clump clump" sound of footsteps woke me up again, only growing slightly louder with each step. I again opened my eyes and saw the construction worker making his way towards me down the long concrete hallway. Apparently he was walking around the building. I debated again whether to get up and run into the surrounding trees. Staying right where I was would look less suspicious. I planned to simply tell him that I was just a tourist who got too drunk and needed to sleep it off, just another wasted tourist doing fucked up things.

He approached me, closer and closer; the footsteps growing louder and louder. He did not stop, or even slow down. He simply turned the corner and began walking away down the long hallway where I had originally seen him. A few of the tools hanging off his belt, the level and the hammer, made clanging noises as they swayed with his walk. On an impulse, I decided to make myself known to him.

"Sir, excuse me," I said, rising to my feet. He continued walking as if he heard nothing. I followed after him, "Hey!" I shouted.

He stopped, turned his head towards me, calm and smiling. "Do you . . ." I began, until noticing that both his eyes were completely white and glazed over. He turned away and continued walking. I was only mildly frightened. I was kind of desensitized to white-zombie eyes by now. I simply went back to my spot and tried to get some more rest. I wasn't really sure if this worker making laps around the building was a ghost or my imagination or real. His footsteps and the jangling of his tools sure sounded real. In any case, he seemed like he wasn't interested in bothering me. He just wanted to walk his laps. I curled back up on the cool concrete and was nearly asleep, when I heard the single bark of a dog.

I rose up to my feet and saw the worker standing at the door to the building. He motioned slowly for me to come with him and I followed after him. He entered the building and before following him inside, I looked back down the concrete corridor. I was puzzled to see Blackie again, my come and go dog, sitting stoutly upright, staring at me. Even more puzzling was seeing my still sleeping body lying beside him. Before I tried to sort it all out, the workman motioned to me from inside to keep following him. I let the temporary confusion of seeing Blackie, and my sleeping body beside him, go. I followed the worker inside, where it was very dark. He came to a large scaffold that climbed up into the vast open darkness of the theater. He began climbing, tools jangling, and stopped about ten rungs up to motion towards me to follow him. For some reason, I trusted the guy. After all, he was a working man. The fact that it was pitch black dark and we were the only ones inside during the middle of the night didn't even phase my reasoning.

I climbed behind him. Every five rungs he would stop to look back and make sure that I was still climbing behind him. After ascending at least thirty more rungs up into the darkness, he climbed through the bars onto a large sheet of wood. As I approached, he offered his hand to assist me. I grasped it and it felt clammy and cold to the touch. He helped pull me through the gap where I crawled on the wood platform before standing to my feet. I tried looking out over the theater space, but there was only blackness.

"Damn," I spoke to him, "This place is huge. How long have you been working here?"

He turned to me, smiling, with alabaster eyes, "Since 1981" he answered.

"That's a long time," I responded.

"Not really, but you will relieve me now. My shift has ended."

He began to laugh, and with the blanched eyes and how it echoed through the infinite space, it became eerily frightening. The scaffolding began to vibrate and shake under my feet. I fell to my knees and crawled to grasp one of the bars. The entire structure was now leaning in the darkness. "Hang on Americano," the workman said, still standing with a creepy, knowing smile, "You're in for one hell of a ride!"

The scaffold tower was now gaining momentum as it fell into the darkness. As the speed of the fall became unbearable, I released my grip on the bar. Terror rose from my stomach to my chest as I fell through the darkness, fearing the eventual landing. I looked and listened for the workman, but I was falling alone.

An odd sensation occurred upon hitting the ground. There was a splat, but I continued into the floor, sinking into a wet, cool thick mixture. I was submerged in quicksand-like cement, struggling to at least get my head above the surface in order to breathe again. The harder I tried to move my arms and my legs, the more resistant the thick material became. I could not get traction or leverage to break the surface. With the physical claustrophobia came mental anguish leading to panic. I continued my life or death struggle in the thick sediment when something landed on me from above, pushing me down deeper into the thick abyss.

I needed to breathe but it was hopeless. I could feel the limbs moving of others who were also struggling beside me and above me, frantically. In desperation, I inhaled the thick, grainy sludge, resigned to drown in it as it filled my mouth and oozed into my throat. I just wanted to die quickly, putting an end to the pain and the panic. Why the hell did the worker lure me into this disaster? Why the hell did I follow him? And, most importantly, why wasn't I dead yet? The liquid was hardening in my mouth and throat. It was now impossible to move my limbs. The damp sludge had solidified; I was frozen, trapped in solid, hardened concrete. I was also unable to just die and be done with it all. The agony of this realization became unbearable. I thought of the workman and how he mentioned being here since 1981 and how he said that I was now his relief. Some fucking relief for me! I screamed as loud as I possibly could, mentally.

When one is trapped and near death, there comes a breaking point. It's the point where you resign yourself to death. Reaching this point and then finding that you cannot die is torturous. The mental anguish of staying physically trapped, stock-still in hardened concrete easily takes one beyond the endurance of sanity. My mind screamed and convulsed with each passing minute and, dear reader, there were many, many minutes. In the depth of panic, I thought of Hamlet's contemplation of "to die, to sleep; To sleep perchance to dream . . . . For in that sleep of death what dreams may come," and I now knew the dreams involved in the sleep of death. They were dark, desolate nightmares; dreams filled with terror so brutal that going insane was the only way to endure it. Did I go insane as a coping mechanism, to deal with my body being fixed under hardened concrete? Or did my predicament itself drive me over the brink of sanity? Either way, the terror continued unabated. I had entered an eternal anguish greater than any hell my imagination could have concocted.

Suddenly, I was able to move my arm. I felt a breeze. I was outside on the pavement, waking up with the first signs of the approaching dawn. I asked myself out loud, "What the hell was *that* all about?" Whatever the horrendous experience was, it was more than a mere dream. My body felt somewhat rested, but my mind was drained, recovering from the lengthy anguish. It seemed the intensity of the terror had burned me out mentally. My thoughts were disorganized and rudimentary, but I was pleased to be able to move and breathe once more.

There was no sign of my foul-weather friend, Blackie. Weird things always happened when he comes around, but I love that damn dog all the same. He's loyal, if little else. The construction worker was also long gone. I walked to the entrance and tried the doors but now they were locked. I needed to get cleaned up and looked ahead, over Manila Bay. It was time to wake up as well. It was time to go for a swim. I walked a short distance to the shore and plunged in with my clothes on. I needed to wash all the blood stains away from the German, though near the shoreline, the water was not the cleanest. Plastic bottles and debris bobbed along the edge, but after swimming out a hundred yards, the water was just fine, still, calm and tranquil. I floated on my back, absorbing the beauty of the Manila morning sky.

I had one single plan, to get something to eat. I was down to 200, now soggy, pesos in my pocket, so my first meal as a fugitive shouldn't be too difficult to get. Dinner might prove more difficult, but I could worry about dinner when it was dinner time. I swam into shore and sat on some rocks for awhile, letting my clothes drip dry and wallowing in my misery about not being able to work with the syndicate. My heart ached. I still needed to keep my head, though. I had to be leery of the police and the syndicate. I would have to mingle with the regular folks and avoid the cops and criminals. Once I drip dried a bit, I made my way up to Roxas Boulevard and worked my way to Mabini Street. It was familiar turf since it was where I first stayed before the whole nightmare began. It was also more good reason to proceed with caution.

As I walked down Mabini, I could hear someone shouting from a block behind me. "Hey, Americanooo!" I continued walking, not even glancing back, hoping they would not continue or that they were calling for someone else. I was in no mood or condition to attract attention of any kind. "Hey, you walking, yeah, you Americanooo!" he shouted, again, dragging out the end of the word like a drunken moron. I turned and saw a clean-cut guy in his thirties, wearing a drink-stained wrinkled polo shirt and wearing a goofy smile. "Hey, my name's Don," he said, acting like I should be excited to meet him. "How's it going, man?"

"Uhm, hi," I began, coldly, "It's going" I replied, trying to avoid conversation. Someone so enthusiastic so early in the morning could not be trusted.

"This place is fucking awesome, isn't it?" he asked. "I'm from Youngstown, Ohio. Where you from?"

"My name's Tim. I'm originally from Pennsylvania," I replied, deciding that it might not hurt to make a new friend, particularly when considering my net worth was down to 200 pesos. "Yes, this place is something; what brings you here?"

His smile grew, "It's a long, sad story, but the short version is that I met a gal on the internets and came here to see her, but found out once I got here she works as a stripper. Ain't life a bitch?"

"Yeah," I laughed, "Did you plan to marry her or something?"

"Nah, I'm already married, but I was sort of planning a honeymoon. Can't trust those damn internets. Say, you want a drink? I'm buying!"

"It's like seven in the morning; are you nuts?"

"Yeah buddy," he began, doing a little dance on the sidewalk, "I'm a fuckin' train wreck."

"Well, I was just looking for somewhere to get a cheap breakfast," I said.

"Come on, dude, I'm taking you to the best fried chicken place in the fucking world, Max's Fried Chicken. It doesn't get any better!"

"Sounds good, but isn't it kind of early for fried chicken?" He turned to watch a jeepney beeping his way down the road, then looked upwards at the sky. "What time is it again?"

"Morning, like 7 or 8" I answered.

"And what day is it?"

"Thursday" I answered.

"Oh yeah, noodle Thursday!" he shouted, making no sense whatsoever. "I know a place we can go, my treat! Buddy, fuck the chicken; say hello to noodle Thursday!" While I was not nearly as excited as he was about noodle Thursday, I did like hearing him say "my treat".

"You're screaming about it like it's some kind of major holiday; where do you get noodles?" I asked, curious.

"Two words: Dragon Noodle Center, oh yeah!"

I didn't want to dampen his spirits by pointing out it was three words, "Sounds good; how do we get there?"

Without looking in both directions, he suddenly walked right out into the street, nearly getting hit by two cars and a horn blaring jeepney. Apparently, noodle Thursday was very important to him. After nearly being killed, he flagged down a speeding taxi by standing directly in front of its path and raising his hand. The angry driver had no choice but to slam on his brakes.

"Damn, you almost got yourself killed!" I said.

"It's worth it," he answered, "noodle Thursday." This new friend was crazy, but I liked his enthusiasm. The driver of the cab began protesting because he said he was on his way to pick up a passenger, but Don handed him a large enough peso bill to help him change his mind. "Dragon Noodle Center," he yelled to the driver, "Step on it!"

The driver and I made eye contact in his rear-view mirror and we both could not help to burst out laughing at the same time at how retarded the request sounded. The driver shook his head from side to side laughing before regaining his composure and pretending to play along. "Dragon Noodle Center, you got it!" he replied to Don, acting as if he were about to get a woman in labor to the hospital on time. He punched the gas, cut the wheel and almost sideswiped a car while blowing the horn. He was hunched over the steering wheel as if it were the Indianapolis 500.

Don was excited, "That's it man! Go! Go! Go!"

"Dragon Noodle Center!" shouted our driver, as he careened around another car, narrowly missing an old man on a bicycle and pounding on his horn the entire time. The exaggerated stock car driving lasted for only half of a block before he shot up on the sidewalk and parked in front of the Dragon Noodle Center.

"Uhm, we were not even a block away from the place. We could have just walked and avoided the whiplash," I said.

Don seemed unfazed about paying a large amount of pesos to be driven only half of a block. "Ordinarily, yes, but this is worth every fucking peso!" he exclaimed, tugging on the door to find it locked. He read the sign, "Fuck me, they don't even open for another hour. Guess we'll just have to wait." And there we sat, until the owners came to unlock the door an hour later.

As we sat down, a few other customers entered, "See, you know it's good noodle activity when the Asians eat here."

"Don, the Philippines is part of Asia, right?" I asked.

"Trust me on it. Asians invented Noodle Thursday." I didn't argue with him. He was right about one thing, the noodles here were delicious. We ordered lugaw (congee) served with bitso bisto and egg.

"That raw egg in there will put lead in the old pencil," advised Don, before continuing to slurp at his bowl. I wasn't sure of his theory, but the noodles were very delectable. It felt weird to just be hanging out with a tourist from the States. I felt as if I were an actor pretending to be a tourist, since I had been through lots of bizarre events here. It was refreshing to just be accepted as another bumbling, foolish tourist. Maybe a change of environment was what I needed to make the demon in my head disappear. Maybe. I no longer felt like a killer. I no longer felt insane. I was barely heartsick over being banished from the family, the most influential syndicate in Manila. I knew all of my baggage would eventually return, but, for now at least, I was enjoying the peace of just living in the moment and remaining an anonymous tourist.

"Hey, what are you planning on doing today?" he asked.

"I'm not really sure," I replied, "my schedule is open."

"Well, you should hang out with us. I brought a guy from work here with me, Bob, he's cool. Why don't you hang with us today? Don't be afraid, homie!"

"Maybe," I answered, "what's on your agenda?"

"Well, Bob usually doesn't get up till about noon, but after lunch we'll probably just party like rock stars."

"Sounds good; I'm not a drinker, but I'll hang with you guys."

"Cool, I'll drink your share. I'm a fucking train wreck," announced Don, prior to taking a sip of beer for emphasis. "Once we finish eating here, we can go see if Bob's still alive. I might move here some day, become a sex-pat."

We finished our meals and walked the few blocks to Robinson's Mall where the Pearl Lane hotel was located. We entered the small room and saw

Bob, still sound asleep and snoring. "Hey, want to see something funny as shit?" asked Don, whispering and grinning.

"Sure," I answered, not quite sure what he had in mind but judging by the grin it had the potential to be something entertaining.

Don pulled a lighter from his pocket and tippy-toed towards his sleeping roommate. He flicked the lighter and extended it towards Bob's feet. His socks looked (and smelled) like they had seen better days. One of them hung over his toes by a few inches, drooping and looking dry and worn out. Don ignited the drooping sock and the flame quickly was rising towards Bob's toes. Don began grinning like a mad pyromaniac, pocketing the lighter and stepping back to admire his combustible handiwork. "Better get back," he advised, "Dude's gonna be pissed and might start swinging." Bob looked like a pretty big guy. I stepped back. The sock was catching fire as if it were sprinkled with gunpowder. Now, his entire foot was aflame.

"Fuck!" shouted Bob, rapidly bicycling his legs, which only made the flame grow, and trying to figure out the source of the pain. He jumped from the bed, still trying to figure out why his foot was ablaze, momentarily staring down at it as it continued burning. He then ran for the bathroom and plunged his flaming foot in the toilet, where a sizzle was heard and a sigh of relief. "What the fuck's wrong with you?" he screamed, angrily, from the bathroom.

Don was doubled-over in laughter. Out of courtesy of not even having met Bob yet, I tried my hardest not to laugh. There's just something about seeing a pissed-off large guy with one smoldering foot in a toilet that makes not laughing difficult, especially with Don howling like a madman. "That was fucked up!" shouted Bob.

Don finally managed to ease up on the laughter, "I'm sorry, man; I was just going to wake you up with a hot-foot but your crusty sock just went up like gunpowder."

"Yeah, real fucking funny; I'll get you back, pecker-head. Who's this?" he asked, pointing at me.

"Bob, meet Tim; Tim, this is Bob. Tim grew up not too far away from the center of the universe, Youngstown," informed Don.

"Well, nice to meet you, Tim," said Bob, "I'd shake your hand but I think I need to soak my charred foot a little longer."

"No problem," I replied, "Nice to meet you, Bob."

"Dude, get cleaned up," said Don, Let's go get some lechon and pound some beers," said Don.

"That sounds like a noble plan of action," answered Bob, "Give me fifteen to shit, shower and shave."

As we waited for Bob to get spruced up, Don asked, "You never told me what brought you here to Manila in the first place, Tim?"

"Oh, pretty much the same story as you. I met a girl on the internet and we were penpals for a few years. I finally decided to come and see her." I answered, not really wanting to divulge any true information about how long I was here and the crowd I ran with. Luckily, Bob soon diverted Don's attention away from asking me any more personal details.

"Dude, the fucking toilet's clogged," he exclaimed, while bursting out of the bathroom in a towel. Water came seeping out of the doorway behind him.

"No, dude, not again!" moaned Don, as a turd floated out from the doorway, like a small brown canoe riding the advancing water. "This is like the fourth fucking time you clogged it in a week!" He pointed at the turd, "That's disgusting! They're going to throw us out of here and I don't blame them!"

Bob just looked downwards, sheepishly, "I think it's the Asian plumbing," he offered.

"Right, and it was the Asian plumbing at the Holiday Inn in Detroit too?" asked Don, shaking his head.

We alerted the front desk and got the situation somewhat cleared up before going to the Aristocrat for lechon. Don and Bob began drinking heavily. And they continued drinking heavily through the heat of the Manila afternoon. At some point, I told them about swimming in the bay in the morning and they both got the idea fixed in their heads that they wanted to see the bay.

I took them back down near the Manila Film Center and we arrived there just in time to witness the most glorious sunset in the world, the transcendent Manila Bay sunset. We sat behind the Film center and watched just as the fiery orange sun neared the edge of the horizon. It was majestic, tranquil and hypnotic, completely breathtaking in its beauty. There were streaks of yellows, oranges and reds blended into the sky over the vast water. Nobody said a word, as we took in the picaresque beauty. As the sun was halfway disappeared into the horizon, Don affectionately put his arm around Bob and the two remained that way for a good ten minutes in silence, enraptured with the view. All of the traffic noise, confusion, clogged toilets and hustle bustle was temporarily forgotten as these two regular bumbling American tourists absorbed the glorious dusk that can only be found in one city in the world, Manila.

When darkness came, Don wanted to go to the Bedrock Bar near Robinson's Mall. They enjoyed their beer by the bucket, five bottles in ice at a time. By ten in the evening, they were both extremely intoxicated. Don approached an attractive Filipina, "Hi. My name is Don."

"Hello Don, I'm Celeste" she replied, smiling beautifully.

"Hi Celeste," exclaimed Don, regaining his balance, "You want to see a magic trick?"

"Maybe" she giggled.

"It's thoroughly amazing; I can make my penis levitate."

"Oooh" she laughed.

Once she and Don talked for awhile, he came back to where Bob and I sat to tell us of the new game plan. "Fellas, Celeste has some friends she wants to go and see, female friends, and they're at a club in Quezon City. Let's take a cab there and see what's up!"

It sounded like a fun plan, but my head was acting up. A black feeling was growing in there. I was kind of drifting in and out, without so much as a single drink. I was feeling the return of a grievous angel. I was feeling in the mood for homicide, not Don or Bob, but someone. If Juvi was the driver of the cab we flagged down, I would have to kill him. I missed Reshi. I was exiled, though. Ironically, she probably was under orders to kill me now. I really missed her.

The cab driver was not Juvi. I became disinterested in friendship or conversation during the ride to Quezon City. I knew going to a club was a bad idea. I needed to get alone and let the demon run its course, away from other people. We were on our way to a club called Temple. When we arrived there, I knew I had to go somewhere else.

"Fellas," I said, "I'll meet back up with you. I have a friend a few blocks from here I'm going to go visit for a bit," I lied. Hell, I had no idea where I was or where I was going. I only knew that I needed to get away. I began walking down Timog Avenue, alone and on edge. Two blocks later, I saw a large rat running along the curb of the street. It climbed the curb, stopped momentarily, and our eyes locked. Something told me I knew this rat. He shot across the sidewalk so quickly, I questioned even seeing him. I walked towards the abandoned street he ran down. It was the corner of Tomas Morato Avenue. I pulled on a metal door and it opened. The corridor was pitch black and smelled musty. Like some kind of vault that held death and had not been entered in a long time. It felt like the right place for me to spend the night, and the price was in my budget.

The dark, narrow corridor led to a flight of stairs. I used the walls as guides and walked up the stairs, entering a spacious area. I kept along the wall to avoid walking into anything in the pitch blackness. I could hear the familiar scurrying sound of rats, nothing new but making me less inclined to sleep on the floor. I bumped into a counter in the darkness, a bar. While it wouldn't be absolutely rat free, it would make it more difficult for them to bite me. I climbed up on the bar and laid down, relaxing and looking up into the black void. Soon, I was able to close my eyes, the only sounds being an occasional squeak and scurry across the floor. I felt right at home and decided it was good to spend the night here.

I'm not certain how long I was asleep before the first burst of light and song woke me up. There was a bright flash, a disco beat, people dancing, lights reflecting from a spinning silver ball, casting a pattern of colored diamonds on the walls. It was like instantly being in the middle of, seeing and hearing, a crowded dance club at midnight on a typical Friday night. People were dressed up, spinning, twirling, gyrating their arms and legs in fluid, rhythmic motion. The throbbing music shook the building. The place was fully alive for fifteen seconds, then, suddenly it was quiet darkness again.

The disco flashes returned, one about every twenty minutes, but they lasted only a mere fifteen seconds. Again and again, over the next few hours, just as I would enter sleep, they would come. I got to where I was desensitized to the interruption and able to just sleep through them, but they became louder and weirder and the air grew thick. I woke up, coughing, gagging and gasping for air. My eyes were burning like they were filled with soap. There was thick smoke throughout the building. Then it was all quiet, dark, and I could breathe freely again. I shook it off and resumed sleeping.

When the next disco flash scene appeared, there was no music and the bright lights were clouded with black smoke, and flames. The music was replaced by the shrill sounds of agonized screams, like a wailing of banshees. The smell was nauseating, a sweet, putrid, burnt steak stench with hints of sulfur. It was a distinctive, unforgettable smell and instantly recognizable as the aroma of charred human flesh. Through the smoke and the screams, I could see bodies on the floor, charred bodies against the blazing wall and staggering figures fighting their certain oncoming death by asphyxiation. I had to get out, but the entrance to the stairwell was heaped with bodies. Then everything went black, and quiet. There were no more screams of panic and pain. Even the thick smoke in the air vanished without a trace.

The nauseating smell of burnt flesh was gone and I no longer was gagging and dry-heaving. My ears were still ringing from the shrill screams of terror heard from those burning to death. I didn't know what had happened here, but it was some bad shit. I needed to get out of here. I felt around in the darkness to locate the wall, which was blazing orange only moments before. Once I found the wall, I was able to make my way to the stairwell, and cautiously made my way down the stairs and back to the door where I had entered.

I pushed on the door, but it would not budge. I pushed and pulled numerous times. I backed up, got a running start, and rammed it. I tried kicking it. I pushed, pulled and blasted it with my elbow. I leaned my back against it and pushed with my legs, all to no avail. After countless failed attempts to get the door open, there was a cracking noise. Suddenly, I was in the scene of a disastrous fire. There were screams of agony, thick smoke and bodies all over the place. The heat was intense. All around me were piles of stacked, lifeless bodies. They were waist-high, on top of one another, all the way to the exit door. I began to gag from breathing in smoke and was becoming dizzy. Water poured out of my eyes from the burning irritation. I found myself having to climb on top of the bodies and over them on my hands and knees. I finally got to the bottom of the stairs, but here the piled bodies were even more densely stacked. In fact, the entire stairwell was filled with dead bodies; hundreds of panic-struck contorted faces trying to get out of the burning building. All were caught clamoring for the one exit door, which, for some reason, would not open. I crawled over bodies, stopping to dry-heave from the smoke and death stench, and made it back to the locked exit door. I could no longer breathe. Smoke filled my lungs, then, silence.

I was on the floor. It was dark. The screaming had stopped and the smoke was instantly gone. I tried the door again, but it was still locked. How did it open so easy when I came in? I made my way back up the stairs and found the bar, where I climbed up and laid back down. I was soon able to sleep again. I would play with the locked door in the morning. I would also tolerate the next burst of a fire scene as it came, and if it woke me. They only lasted about fifteen seconds. They were, however, increasing in intensity as the night wore on, people being burned alive, the pitiful wails and the smell of their roasted flesh all made it seem longer than fifteen seconds. The glimpses might haunt me forever. Well, unless the demon is running my brain, then nothing really frightens me. It's sort of like finding safety and comfort from inside the mouth of a shark. My Aswang demon doesn't give a flaming fuck.

At some point during my sleep, I rolled off of the bar. It was a long drop to the floor. The fall didn't hurt me, but was just annoying. When I stood up to climb back on the bar, I saw myself flat on my back, already sleeping. "Great, I'm outside of my body again," I thought, then, "Maybe I can visit Lily like this and she won't be able to see me or kill me. I can tell her how sorry I am." And, in my astral state, that was my plan. I walked down the stairs, through the door and was out on the street again.

I continued to walk on Tomas Morato Avenue. While I knew that I was outside of the confines of my sleeping body, my sense of awareness and perception seemed fairly normal. Maybe I was used to functioning in my spirit body while the demon occupied my head. Everything looked and felt normal or the way it usually does, just slightly different. There was a greater sensitivity to inanimate objects. I was aware of them as energy, atoms in motion, not just as things or objects that were lifeless. Everything was alive, but similar to always. I continued walking, block after block, down Tomas Morato. After crossing the intersection of Aurora Boulevard, things began to look darker and eerier. The trees on both sides of the road looked hauntingly human in the darkness and pale glow of moonlight. Not exactly human, but twisted, gnarled and sinewy like deformed human limbs. I could also here occasional whispers. Maybe it was just the night breeze, maybe.

I saw someone walking away from me about one block ahead. It appeared to be a woman, judging by the white, flowing, luminescent gown and long black hair. A car approached and as the headlights shone a path, illuminating the dark stretch of road, I lost sight of the woman. After the car rolled by, she was nowhere to be found. Did she go off into the trees? Maybe she needed help? It was certainly plausible, since it was so late at night. One thing was certain, the car never slowed down for her, so she didn't disappear into the vehicle.

I decided to walk off of the road and head into the twisting, whispering balete trees. The night grew even darker once the canopy of trees shielded out the moonlight. The whispering also became distinctively louder, or was it just the breeze? I sat down on the partially exposed roots of a huge tree and just relaxed. I took a deep breath, leaned back, and rested my head against the firm base of the tree. A low humming noise rang in my ears and my body became completely relaxed. It felt as if there were some kind of energy exchange coming through the tree and fusing itself with my body. It felt better than the best massage and it was from a tree.

As I sat in a relaxed trance-like state, I again spotted the lady in white. She was near the road, her gown flowing in the breeze, but moving towards me. Part of me should have been cautious or frightened, but the tree had a narcotic affect over me. I was at peace. In fact, I completely bypassed all reason and was hoping to maybe get laid. I remained seated, still and hopeful. As she came closer, I could see her willowy frame and her beautiful flowing black silky hair.

I remained where I was and she approached slowly, gracefully. I felt strangely calm as she stood about ten-yards directly in front of me. Her head was slightly bowed forward and her black hair hung from the sides. Her slender figure looked attractive as hell, but I was hoping to see her face.

"Hi, my name is Tim. Do you need help or anything?" I asked.

She leaned her head back and her long hair slowly parted to reveal a pale, glowing face. The odd part was that the face was featureless. There were no eyes, no ears or mouth and, as frightening as she appeared, the overall impression was one of beauty.

"Where were you when I needed help?" she asked, in a slightly angry, serious tone. Her mouth did not speak, there was no mouth. Her voice just appeared in my head as if she were speaking.

"I'm not sure what you mean," I replied, "but I'm here now if you need help. Did your car break down or something?"

"No, I was raped and tortured!" she screamed in my head. "The fucking driver used and abused me and, worst of all, nobody even cares!"

I wasn't sure how to respond. Her anger rose into a vengeful rage that was frightening. As I considered carefully what to say, she was gone again. I looked around, scanning both sides of my field of vision for a white figure, but there was nothing. I heard a car approaching from up the road. It slowed to a stop and I saw the silhouette of a glowing white figure approach. It was a taxi and apparently she was getting a ride to wherever she was going. I leaned back and soon fell asleep.

The sound of the impact was a crash that made me jump to my feet. There was a car smashed into a tree at the side of the road. The crunching of metal and shattering of glass pierced the quiet solitude of the desolate stretch of road. Instinctively, I ran towards the car to see how badly the occupants were hurt. I did not know how I could help them, but felt doing something was better than doing nothing. It was a taxi, but I wasn't sure if it was the same one I saw earlier. This one was going the opposite way on the road when it slammed into the tree.

The first thing I noticed was the hissing sound coming from the smashed radiator and fluid was leaking out around where the front end had partially wrapped itself around the solid base of the tree. The windshield was shattered and nobody was visible inside, not even a driver. I could see blood on the driver's side window. I opened the door and a head fell to the ground and rolled just a bit. A body was slumped over the steering wheel, a decapitated body. Fresh blood was still sprouting from the exposed neck. Somehow the cab driver had lost his head and it seemed to be before the crash even occurred. There was nothing about the shattered windshield or smashed front-end that would cause one's head to be severed from the body. I noticed a figure, the lady in white, walking away from the scene of the accident. She walked calmly, holding what looked like a wire or guitar string in her delicate hand. The guitar string swayed rhythmically as she walked.

"Hey!" I shouted to her. "Were you in this taxi? What happened to the driver?"

She stopped and turned slowly until facing me, faceless. She dropped the piece of wire onto the ground and brought her lithe hand up to her neck, extending one long finger, and made a slow motion from one side of her petite neck to the other. It was a symbol of death and she emphasized the gesture by mouthing "I killed him."

"Why?" I asked.

"Because he's a fucking taxi driver and he earned his fare. It's neat how a tiny wire can cut right through a human neck," and then she laughed, turned away and continued walking. I really needed to get out of this place. I couldn't really remember how or why I was here, or the series of events leading me here in the first place. Besides, there wasn't much I could do for the headless cab driver. He didn't need an ambulance, just a hearse. I began to walk.

About half a block down the road, I felt a tap on my shoulder. I turned to see the faceless face of the lady in white. Her gown reflected the glow of the moonlight, as if it were a luminescent material. As I looked at her face, some features began to appear. There were teeth and eye sockets and holes at the nose. It was the face of a grinning skull, surrounded by beautiful black, flowing hair. I wasn't afraid, but something held me in place. Her grinning skull face was somehow captivating and beautiful. I was mesmerized and frozen, lustful and afraid. She brought one hand up and curled it behind my neck, gently rubbing the back of my neck with what felt like tenderness.

"Open wide, Tim," she spoke, in a sultry voice, inaudible but clear as a bell in my mind. I obediently opened my mouth wide. She brought up her other hand and extended two fingers then jammed them into my mouth. They went in deeper and deeper, somehow becoming longer. Her fingers were lodged in my throat, blocking the passage of air. I tried to yank my head backwards, but her grip on my neck made movement impossible. As I strained, struggling to breathe, she moved her smiling skull face up closer, within an inch of my face. I could smell her death breath. I knew that my own death was imminent, and her skull was a symbol of my own skull. I could no longer breathe and lost consciousness.

I came to lying on my back on top of the bar. I was still unable to breathe and, in my panic, I reached up to my mouth and found a string. I pulled it, frantically, and a dead baby rat was dislodged from my throat. The string was his tail and the body was covered in my bloody throat phlegm. I gasped in the precious oxygen while throwing the slime laden rodent across the room. What happened? My best guess was that the demon took over while I was outside of my body or else the demon forced my astral body out of my physical one. I don't have a clue. All I know is that coming to with a baby rat stuck in your throat isn't such a great way to start the day.

I spit some nasty hair and rat funk out of my mouth. There were bumps on the back of my head. Maybe it was bounced off of the bar or maybe I was banging it when I couldn't breathe. Everything was wrong. No sense in trying to make sense out of chaos when my brain is in chaos. I walked down the stairs and pushed on the metal door and it swung open easily. The bright sun burned my eyes as I exited the building. It was time to catch a jeepney back to Malate and see if I could find Bob and Don. Maybe I could get something to eat or at least borrow a few pesos. Why not? It was something to do and as Bob Dylan once said, "when you ain't got nothing to lose, you ain't got nothing to lose."

CHAPTER XII
Happy

An idea, like a ghost, must be spoken to a little before it will explain itself.

—Charles Dickens

    I tried to give you some head's up about my getting out of here, Kinsey. You could probably sense it wouldn't be long till I was gone, but I bet you didn't expect such a dazzling departure, did you? Luckily for you, I don't mind typing up my notes while I'm roaming. I'll send you e-mails via Mac, but don't mess it up by telling anyone. Besides, you're feeling some Aswang action, aren't you? Side effects may include trouble sleeping, ghostly interactions, astral projection, lots of rats, a penchant for homicide, frequent thoughts of suicide, a taste for blood, black dogs and blackouts. I haven't found a cure. My advice is just, when it takes over, try to get somewhere by yourself and expect some weird shit to happen. Usually if it takes completely over, you can sense it coming. You'll feel like killing someone. Spirits and ghosts start coming around (don't scoff, having Aswang is like a ghost magnet). Just find a place to be alone and minimize the damage.

    Now, if you're thinking of being some kind of hero and telling the authorities you have contact with me, don't. Dr. Taylor was a prick who had it in for me, we both know that. Hell, you can get his job now, too. They ain't going to pin any medal on your chest for ratting me out. I'll stay in touch with you and Dan through Mac. Those porn subscriptions on your credit card were mild compared to what he's capable of. You haven't seen ugly yet. Those nuts in D wing would do anything for me. And what about Dr. Taylor's murder? Nobody has any proof of who killed him. He wanted to meet with me, alone, for Bible study. What the hell? His skull could have been bashed in and his windpipe ripped out of his throat before I even got to his office. It's a shame, really. They used to believe, back in the Neo-classical age, that murder brought extra wrath if committed while the victim was at prayers or devotions. Apparently, the times have changed. Nowadays all the crazies out there don't think twice about it. They see prayer as an excellent time for savage murder. I didn't kill the sanctimonious prick during his prayers, but there is power in the blood, apparently. I saw it everywhere. You saw it, too, yes? Weren't you the first one to find him? The spirit in your head likes seeing that red color, huh? It's like being a kid and finding a few dollars on the ground. Just be glad you're okay, Kinsey. Rat me out and there will be more spiritual cleansing. I'm always a few steps ahead of you, Kinsey. Forgetting that could prove lethal.

I made it back to the Pearl and had to knock on Bob and Dan's door, on and off, for a good fifteen minutes before there were any signs of life.

"What's up amigo?" asked Don, looking a bit hung-over, "Where did you go last night? We had a wild time!"

"I got tired and ended up just crashing at my friend's house. What'd you guys end up doing?" I asked.

"Oh man, you missed it," he began, allowing me inside, "Bob picked up this hot chick, buying her drinks, making out with her and shit. It was all fun and games until he found out she had a penis!" he said, laughing and shaking his head.

"Wow;" I replied, laughing, "He kind of has bad luck follow him around; how did he take it?"

Don continued laughing, "Straight up the ass! She or he came back with us," he revealed, pointing towards Bob's door, which was shut.

"What about Celeste?" I asked.

"I don't really remember. I was hammered," he revealed. "I think I got her phone number and am supposed to call her today, but I'm not sure. I'm a freaking train wreck!"

"Sounds like calling her is a worthy plan," I said, "She was hot."

"Yes, and I'm fairly sure she isn't carrying the added feature that Bob's chick had. Hey, how come you're here so early? They kick you out of your hotel or something?"

I wasn't sure how to answer but I felt this might be a good time to come clean, a little. It wasn't like I had anywhere else ago and I also had nothing to lose. "Well, I had some messed up shit happen. I mean, like real messed up. I lost my wallet, my passport, the whole she-bang."

"Were you ripped off? Did you tell the cops?" asked Don.

"Yeah," I lied, "but for now I have nothing and nowhere to stay. I'm just taking one day at a time."

"Shit bro," sympathized Don, "we'll find some clothes and you can shower and sleep on the couch here until we leave. Maybe you should visit the U.S. Embassy and tell them your situation."

His suggestion sounded sensible enough and the idea had been there since the beginning of this nightmare, but I knew the syndicate would have eyes either outside or inside. I might as well stroll into the warehouse in Caloocan with a bulls-eye on my chest. I simply knew way too much and crossed Lily way too publicly. I didn't stand a chance. If I wanted to stay alive, I'd have to survive in the nooks and crannies of Manila until an opportunity appeared. "Yes, I'll have to go down there and tell them my sad story," I said, knowing full well I would not.

"Well, dude, you can crash on the couch here for awhile. I'm going back to sleep," said Don, "Later we'll get lunch and you can hit the embassy."

I lay on the couch, which was a relief, but my brain kept grinding. If I told the embassy I was kidnapped, the syndicate might slip out proof that I committed murders with pleasure. My chances of ever getting back to the U.S. were slim to none. Lily held my passport. I would have to survive, for now, in Manila. I closed my eyes and soon fell asleep. I'm not sure how long I was out until I heard Don and Bob arguing.

"Dude, not again!" shouted Don. It was like déjà vu as Bob stood by the bathroom doorway, water running out of the door by his feet. Not wanting to see the tempers escalate, I rolled off of the couch.

"I'll go tell the front desk," I announced, heading out the door still half-asleep. I went down and explained to the receptionist that 211 had a problem with the toilet. It was no big deal and she said that someone would be up to look at it soon. What was a big deal, however, was when I returned to 211 to find a Korean couple. They were as startled as I was when I walked in on them.

"Where's Don and Bob?" I asked.

"Get out of our room," yelled the man, angrily, "I will call the police!" he warned, in broken English. I looked around for any familiar sign, some clothing or luggage. I kept thinking that they had to be playing some kind of a practical joke on me. Clearly, there was evidence to show that this couple had been staying here for awhile. I walked back out to the door to double-check the number, but it was the same. "What the hell was going on here? How could they just vanish?" I asked myself.

"Uhm, I'm sorry, sir," I said to the Korean man, "I must have the rooms mixed up." I closed their door, slowly walking backwards down the hall to see if everything looked the same as it did before. I thought maybe somehow I had the floors mixed up, so I went up to 311 and knocked. A Filipino man opened the door.

"Uhm, I'm looking for two American guys who had a room here somewhere. I'm sorry to bother you."

"Well, they aren't here; good luck with that," he said, closing the door.

I went up the other four floors with similarly confusing results. "What the hell happened? Did they vanish just like ghosts? Did I just imagine I was with them? Maybe I had the room number mixed up?" These were among the questions running through my head. For lack of a better plan, I decided to wait for them in the lobby. After sitting there for twenty minutes, I could not help but to go back up to room 211. I didn't want to knock on the door again, since the guy was already pissed, so I just loitered around in the hallway. It was inconceivable to me that Don and Bob could just vanish from their room into thin air. I could hear the Korean couple talking from behind the closed door. Don and Bob were not in there. I went back down to the lobby.

A fairly attractive Filipina in tight jeans and a black tank-top motioned for me from the entrance. Her long black hair and ample breasts helped persuade me to approach. She smiled at me in a way that seemed beyond putting on a pleasant appearance. There was a twinkle in her eyes that made it feel as if I knew her from somewhere, but I could not place her. I returned her smile as I approached, "Hello, I'm Tim, did you want to see me?"

"Yes, very much, Mr. Tim; I'm Tessa. I need to talk to you about something. Could we go somewhere more private?" she asked.

I looked her up and down, trying to ascertain her possible motives. My guess was that she was going to solicit me for sex in exchange for money. I figured she saw a white guy and just assumed I had money and was horny.

"Well, Tessa, I want to be up front with you. I really don't have any money. I mean I have enough that we can get a few coffees, but, not, well, for other things. It doesn't mean that I don't think you are attractive, though."

She began to laugh, "You're cute," she said, touching my arm, "I'm not a hooker. I really just want to talk to you. Is that okay?"

We walked across the busy street and into Robinson's Mall and entered the dark, aromatic Starbucks coffee shop. I brought our coffees to a table she had chosen near the window. Just outside we could see a group of girls sitting at a picnic table, talking and laughing. I noticed one of the girls was built huskily, and even in a skirt, she had the build and features of a man.

"Looks like one of those girls is a guy, huh?" I asked, nodding towards the window. The other three were remarkably pretty, making the ugly duckling even uglier. I scrutinized the other three, but came to the conclusion that they had to be natural born women. Tessa could read my confusion.

"It helps to look at the hands," she said, calmly, "If the hands are disproportionately large, it's a sign. Also look for an Adam's apple, or jewelry that covers the area. Hearing the voice can help too. They are all boys out there, but most of them, well, three out of four, are very pretty as girls, don't you think?"

"Yeah, well, very much so. It's a common thing here, gender changing, in Manila, isn't it?"

"Yes, I suppose in some ways our culture here is more tolerant about sexual preferences and changing gender identities than in many other parts of the world. Take myself, don't you recognize me? You already know who I am."

"I can't say I do," I answered, looking out the window to the group of girls, "That one in the red blouse, there is no way she is a man. I mean, she's hot as hell," I observed.

"She is very pretty, isn't she?" agreed Tessa, "I think her having a penis is meaningless, really. I mean, if anything, it only makes her more interesting. Nothing in Manila is really how it appears to be," she said, laughing.

"So, the one in red out there is really a boy?" I asked.

"Let me put it this way," she began, "If I was a guy, and I once was, I would do her in a heartbeat."

Now I was even more confused, "What do you mean? You're a guy?"

"Yes, in fact you know me; well, before there was a contract on your head that is."

Now she had my undivided attention. How did she know there was a contract out on me? Was she with the syndicate? "Okay, Tessa," I whispered, leaning closer over the table, "Who are you and how do you know anything about a contract?"

"I'm sorry," she giggled, "you got so serious all of a sudden. Look closely at me, Tim. Can't you see who I am?"

I stared at her face, silently, and could feel an odd familiarity but it was just out of my grasp to make any connection. "You somehow look familiar, but I can't place it. I'm stumped."

"Well, you know me as the man I am today, Berto."

"What the hell?" I asked, incredulously, "No way! Berto?" I looked at her closely and the resemblance unfolded before my eyes, as if a veil had been lifted. "I'm real confused. If you are Berto, how are you female? You mean you're his sister, right?"

"Well," she began, taking a deep breath, "remember that nothing is as it appears to be, especially here in Manila. Tim, would you believe me if I told you I was a ghost? When Berto became a man, he basically killed the woman he once was and here I am now."

"I'm sorry, Tessa; I've been through tons of weird shit since landing here in Manila. I can't buy it, though. I mean, you're right here, in plain sight, drinking coffee with me. How in the hell can you be a ghost?"

She chuckled, "I'm sorry if I don't fit in neatly with your ghost qualifications rule book, Tim. Maybe this will persuade you, look into my eyes."

I stared into her eyes, when they suddenly glazed over, becoming white. Her eyes looked just like the ghost kid, Seven, and the ghost construction worker. They flittered and shifted again back to normal. "See, Tim, a ghost is usually someone who died unexpectedly, traumatic or someone who feels very strongly that they have unfinished business here. As for my physical presence appearing normal, you probably know as well as I do that the spirit of Aswang possesses you. Aswang acts as a magnet for wandering spirits. Aswang provides a crossroads or a meeting point between the dead and the living."

"I'm not sure what to think. I mean, I don't even know what's real or unreal anymore. I really don't want Aswang inside me and I don't know how much longer I can live with it. I feel like it wants to keep me confused and destroy me," I confessed.

"Yes, I know the feeling of internal confusion, like Berto put me through. Actually, you don't know this, but I have been following you for some time now. I even helped you out on occasion," she revealed, giggling. "When you were stuck in that big hole in the cemetery all night, I kind of made notches in the wall and directed your attention towards them. I also helped you get back to your body when you were trapped in the hardened concrete. I acted as a guardian spirit sometimes, but for my own selfish reasons."

"So you've been following me? This just all seems too weird. Are you possessed by Aswang too?"

She smiled, "Aswang possesses the living, not the dead. But, yes, I have been around you because your possession makes it easy for spirits to interact with you and other people around you, invisibly or as I am now."

"Can other people here in the coffee shop, can they see you now or do I just look like a nut talking to an imaginary friend here?"

Tessa smiled, twirling her hair with the fingers of her right hand, "It's a good question. Rest assured that when you can see me, everyone around you can also see me. But since I am a spirit, nobody really notices details about me. If they took pictures of me, they would only see an orb of light. Everyone can see you are talking with me, though. Nobody will think you are crazy."

"Were you around when I was doing dirty deeds for the syndicate?"

"You mean, killing people? Yes; that was kind of hot," she answered. "I was also there when you dug up a corpse, which was kind of not hot."

"I didn't know what I was doing. Sonny was pissed!"

"Don't worry about it," she assured, "when Aswang takes over, you're not really responsible for what you do. You can't feel guilt for things you don't realize you're doing, right? I must say, though, you are very skillful at killing people, quickly and efficiently. I was thinking of using your services, but I have a more interesting plan."

"I hope your plan at least involves food and lodging. Who do you want killed?" I asked.

"Berto, it's only fair since he killed me, tit for tic-tac. I'm not really a woman who forgives. I want to mess him up. I think we can help each other."

"What do you have in mind?" I asked.

"Well, you want to get back to the U.S., yes?"

"Yes, they will kill me if I stay here. I'm an exile in Manila and it's only a matter of time until they find me."

"And I want to mess Berto up, not just physically, but I want to toy with his mind. I need your help to make it happen."

"Hey, if it will get me back to the U.S., let's hear it; I'm in."

"I will help you get your passport and a plane ticket. You will help me get revenge on Berto."

"I don't want to kill Berto. I mean, he is, or was, my close friend. I don't want to fuck with him," I resolved.

"I do, literally. I will need you to be nearby for reasons you don't fully understand. Because Aswang lives in you, well, think of it as a battery pack.

For me to go from immaterial to material and interact with the living, I need to be in close proximity of Aswang," she explained.

"So, you need me nearby when you kill Berto?"

She laughed, "I'm a lover, not a fighter. I need you nearby when I fuck Berto."

Now I was confused, "But you are, or once were, Berto?"

"Exactly, and it's going to mess him up to realize he screwed himself," she said, still laughing.

"Okay," I replied, "I'm still unclear on how me watching you screw Berto is going to get me my passport and a plane ticket."

"Come on," she teased, "it's not like you won't enjoy some voyeuristic action."

"Well, maybe," I chuckled, "but I'm sure Berto will try to kill me if he sees me. We were pretty close, but with Lily's syndicate, business is business and business comes first. If she wants me dead, he wants me dead. And how will it help me get home?"

"Just trust me. I'm going to give you some things, like evidence, that he was once a woman. I know him very well. I mean, Lily probably won't mind, or Jolen; but Sonny is old fashioned and will never look at him the same way. I'm sure Berto will do anything to keep the syndicate from knowing."

"So I will blackmail him?"

"Yeah, leave him a package, a note and a drop-off location. You will not even have to see him, ideally."

Tessa's information was still hard to digest. I found myself alternating between disbelief at the absurdity of it all and hopefulness of being able to escape Manila with my life. Maybe Aswang would leave me if I traveled as far away as the U.S. I would find out if and when the time ever came. For now, I only needed to escape Manila and save my ass. As outlandish as the whole deal sounded, I hoped for the best. Hell, maybe it was all an elaborate trap but even Lily wouldn't invent something this bizarre. I also noticed a childhood scar from an incident that Berto had told me about involving falling on broken glass as a child. Tessa had the exact same scar. "Okay, I'm in; let's do this," I said.

"I have a friend who will meet you tonight, around midnight. Go to the Manila North Cemetery and just wait there. I know it's large, but he will find you there."

"Okay," I answered, silently wondering what I would do the rest of the day.

"You wish you had a place to sleep and clean up, and food, don't you?"

I was startled at how well Tessa read my mind, "Well, it does suck being broke and on the run."

"I'm going to help with that. I have to go now. Once I'm gone, you will find a 1000 peso bill under the table. It's yours, just be sure to be in the North Cemetery around midnight," she said, before rising and giving me a peck on the cheek and walking out of Starbucks.

I took a long sip of the dark brew, slid my chair back, sure enough, there was a bill on the floor under the table. I picked it up, tucked it away and meandered out into the mall. It was time to get some sugar-cured bacon. I could get enough to keep some in my pocket for the jeepney ride up to North Cemetery.

I arrived a few hours early, making my way to the flat stone slab of a mausoleum where I laid back and enjoyed the celestial display offered by the night sky of Manila. Through the haze of the moon's glow, the stars twinkled like yellow neon lights. I didn't quite fall asleep, but I was very relaxed, more relaxed than I had felt in a very long time. A unique and scarce feeling that everything was going to be okay settled upon me.

After what felt like hours, I decided to walk around a little. I slid down from the concrete and stood with my feet planted on the ground. Something suddenly reached upwards, grasping my right leg just above the ankle. A jolt of electrical adrenalin coursed through my body. I screamed in shock. I looked down, fearing what I might see.

I jerked my leg away. There was a man, an older guy, in his mid-sixties, crawling on the grass. It looked as if he had somehow emerged from below the ground. I took five good steps backwards, watching him, as he remained on his hands and knees, coughing.

"What the hell, old man?" I exclaimed, "You scared the shit out of me!"

He raised a wiry arm, making a stop talking gesture with the palm of his hand. "I'm sorry, son, I didn't mean to startle you like that," he said, before wiping the drool from his mouth and slowly attempting to rise to his feet. I moved in, taking him by the arm and helped him to his feet. He was a frail old man, weighing about a mere 120 pounds. ""Gabriel's the name, boxing's the game," he said, extending his hand to shake. I had to chuckle, thinking of this frail old man, who could barely breathe, trying to box. I doubted if he could box his way out of a wet paper bag.

"Are you the friend Tessa told me about?" I asked, unsure if the old guy was a zombie since it appeared like he came out of the ground. "I was with her earlier and she said someone would meet me here," I added.

"I like that girl; you know, she's my best friend's grand-daughter and, well, since I don't have any kids of my own, I've taken a shine to her. It's a shame that her male half got rid of her, but I'm sure she will have the last laugh. She's a fighter, that girl!"

"Yes, she's very nice," I replied, "and has an independent spirit. How the hell did you come up from the ground?"

"Well," he began, eyes drifting over my head, somewhere beyond me, "Her grandfather was a hell of a guy. You think she's independent? Her grandfather didn't take shit from anybody," he said, beginning to reminisce with a twinkle in his eye. "We once had a job together moving furniture and some big wheel politician wanted to inflate his ego by bossing her grand-dad, Bones, we called him, around. So this hotshot starts barking orders and pointing and talking down to us and Bones says, 'Screw this,' and walks up and grabs the bigshot's hand and snaps one of his fingers back. I mean, snaps it, one finger, like a dry stick or something, while just smiling at the guy! I couldn't stop laughing! Of course, we were both out of a job, but, damn, it was worth it. Yeah. I think Tess is a bit like old Bones was."

I couldn't help but to chuckle at his story. "That's quite a tale. Bones sounds like a real character. I'm still wondering how the hell you came up out of the ground though?"

"Ah, don't worry about that, it's nothing. To you it looks like I came up from the ground, but when you're a spirit it's just another way to get around. All the rules are different for spirits. So, are you a boxing fan?"

"Oh yeah," I answered, "I was a wrestler back in school, but if they would have offered boxing, I would have done that too."

"I knew I liked you. Those are real sports, there, boxing and wrestling. Boxers don't play with balls, they have them."

"Yes," I agreed, chuckling.

"Would you believe I was once the feather-weight world champion for seven years running?" he asked, before crouching into a boxer's stance.

"No shit?" I asked, wanting to believe him.

"Yeah, I was known as the Flash. I was as famous as Pacquiao before Pacquiao was even born. In the mid-fifties I pounded the piss out of the reigning world-champ at the time, Sandy Saddler. Then I had to scrap it out with the Mexican, Gomez here in Manila and overseas in San Francisco."

As I listened to Flash, I realized that, he was, in fact, telling the truth. The sincerity showed in his eyes. He didn't really come across as bragging, but more of just telling it like it was from the perspective of a tough old

boxer. The irony struck me of how the dead could be more honest than
the living.

"Did Tessa say why I was supposed to meet you?" I asked, after allowing
him ample time to share more details from his impressive glory days as a
fighter. He sadly shared how he took to smoking once he retired from the
ring and ended up with lung cancer in a short span of time.

"Yes, and lucky for you, there are two things working in your favor."

"What's that?" I asked.

"Well, folks are always dying and you don't have any luggage," he
said, laughing until it turned into coughing. I really had no clue what the
hell he was talking about, but I trusted him and I hung in there. "Tessa
asked me to find you places to stay in the city for as long as you need
them. I'd do anything for that girl, so I didn't ask why. Now, I can get
you places, but there's good news and bad news about it. Which do you
want first?"

"The bad."

"Well, two things, you're going to be sharing these places with recently
deceased people. And, second, you will need a new place every day or two,
since the dead person will be discovered as being dead within a day or two.
I will try to find ones that die away from their homes, but usually relatives
will be swooping on their house like vultures in a hurry, so there is an
advantage to sharing a place with a dead body."

"I have to stay with dead bodies?" I asked.

"Sure, it's no big deal. Shit, they're recently dead so it isn't like they
will smell or anything. Just be careful about everything. You'll only go in
at night and leave at night, real early in the morning, and quiet as a church
mouse because you don't want a witness thinking you killed anybody. Just
eat, sleep and get cleaned up, but no noise or anything that might draw
attention. Don't even turn on lights. Are we clear?"

"Clear as a bell."

"Okay, tonight we're going over to Chinatown. You will be staying in
Lin Xang's apartment. Lin died from a sudden heart attack just about four
hours ago. Nobody will be looking for him until tomorrow."

"So the guy will be there, dead, in the apartment?" I asked.

"Well he won't be keeping you up all night. Just step over him as necessary."

"Alright," I agreed, not having many options. We walked out of the
cemetery, making our way towards Chinatown. Over the noise of traffic
and horns beeping, I had the urge to get more answers. "So, uh, Flash, how
do you know this guy is dead?"

"Well, how do you think? He told me," he answered, seemingly immune to the irony.

"Like his ghost told you?"

"What's all this ghost shit?" he asked, impatiently, before coughing a bit. "All I know are spirits, it's just that yours is trapped in your body for now, with Aswang riding shotgun," he added, laughing and coughing.

"Okay," I replied, as we continued walking, "So his spirit told you?"

"Well, sort of, but just know that everything is different in the world of spirit. I mean everything, time, space, movement, communication, the whole shebang. You can't even guess what it's like until you experience it. Hey, there's your apartment," he said, pointing up to a window above an appliance shop. "It's number 216 and the door should be unlocked. Tess told me to tell you she will meet you outside here at ten in the morning. Go get 'em, tiger. Get some rest and get cleaned up. Remember, no lights and no noise."

"Okay, got it," I replied, approaching the door at the sidewalk. I entered and began walking up the wooden steps inside. I could hear cars out on Juan Luna Street, beeping their horns, as I reached 216 and I wasn't clear on how Flash knew, but when I turned the doorknob and pushed, the door opened. It felt oddly forbidden to just be walking into a strange apartment, belonging to a person I had never met. The lights were off, but a dim pallor glowed through the windows from the street.

The apartment looked clean, neat and orderly. A mild smell of cabbage hung in the air. The hallway leading into the kitchen and dining room was a bit darker. I waited a few minutes, hoping my eyes would adjust better to the darkness.

I felt relieved to finally have a roof over my head and a place with running water. I was in dire need of a shower and some food. My first stop would be to look over the kitchen to see what might be available. If the guy was dead, he wouldn't be having much appetite. The only problem was that somewhere in here was a dead body. I needed to find it just for the sake of avoiding tripping over it. I narrowed my eyes, surveying the floor of the dark hallway and just about halfway, there was the feint outline of a body, a body curled on its side in the fetal position.

I approached slowly, stopping to step over it. The hair on the back of my neck stood on edge as I had a brief moment of terror. I felt a hand clasp my ankle, suddenly, with a powerful grip. I screamed, but when I looked down, the body was still and the sensation was gone. Maybe my imagination combined with fear to play tricks on me, maybe. It felt quite real, real enough to almost give me a heart attack. I nimbly stepped over the body, who appeared to be an elderly Chinese man in his upper-seventies. I went towards the kitchen without looking back.

There were plenty of dry noodles and canned goods in the cupboard. In the refrigerator I found a bowl of leftover noodles with chicken. I searched for a fork and began to eat them, cold. I was pleasantly surprised at how good they tasted. I ate ravenously, finishing the entire bowl in minutes. After eating, I took a much needed shower and searched around for some clean clothes that were tight, but doable. I then laid on the small couch, in the darkness, and soon fell asleep.

Surprisingly, there was no trouble falling asleep. Even more surprising, I had a dream that was pleasant, way beyond pleasant, in fact. It was the erotic dream of a teenage boy going through puberty, intense and lust-driven. The reason was unclear to me, but in my dream, I was escorted to a jail cell. What was clear was that while I sat on a bench in the cell, I could hear the click clack clump of female shoes. The sound alone was erotic and grew more stimulating the closer it got.

A female cop stood in front of the bars of my cell. She wore a tight, leather shorts jumpsuit with a zipper running down the center of the front, unzipped to show cleavage of her ample, golden breasts. She had on a police cap with a badge in the center and high, shiny black leather boots. She held a night-stick and handcuffs were at her side. Her waist was narrow and her tits and hips were curvy, with athletic, muscular legs. Her flawless face, with light blue eye-shadow gave her a "do me now" appearance as she stood in front of my cell, smiling. I looked closer and realized it was Reshi!

"On your knees, prisoner," she ordered, in a sultry voice that made me instantly aroused. I proceeded to go to my knees and noticed that her stern, gorgeous face, gave way to an approving smile. As I watched her unlock the cell door, she scolded me, "head down, prisoner; eyes on the floor!"

I lowered my gaze and she moved closer, her shiny black boots were now directly in my field of vision. "You will do as I tell you without saying a word. Just nod your head like a good doggie. Are we clear?" I nodded my head affirmative. "Now clean the top of each boot with your tongue," she ordered, before sitting down on the bench and spreading her legs with her boot soles flat on the cement. "Come doggie," she called, patting the leather shorts at the very top of her shapely thighs. "Do you want me?"

"Yes!" I exclaimed, feeling as if someone were about to give me one-million dollars.

"No speaking," she scolded, "just nod your head like a good doggie should."

I nodded my head rapidly, with enough enthusiasm that she chuckled. "Okay, you may enter me. Now remember, good doggies stop when I say stop and do not finish unless I give them permission." She said, while slowly undressing down to her panties and boots.

I was ready as I approached her hourglass-shaped body. "Now remove my panties," she said, "good doggies use their teeth," she added, while lying on a wooden bench and moving her hips.

I gripped one side of the panties near the waist band and clenched it in my teeth, looking at her perfectly shaped ass while pulling one side down to her knee. I moved to the other side of her hips. A part of me wanted to hurry up and just rip her panties right off and plow myself into her, but another part was enjoying the slow build-up of the tease. I clenched the other side of her panties in my teeth and slid them down to her knees. She lay flat, lifting both of her shapely legs, straightened and allowing me to slide the panties all the way to her boots, where I pulled each side over the heel, allowing them to drop to the floor. I wanted to devour the panties on the spot, but knew there were better things in store.

"Enter me, doggie boy." And I buried my bone in paradise.

Afterwards she asked, "You belong to Mistress Reshi now, don't you, boy?"

Her question excited me again. I had switched loyalties. I now belonged to Reshi. "Yes," I replied.

"Yes, what, pet?"

"Yes, I belong to beautiful Mistress Reshi!" I said, suddenly realizing that Reshi was the one and only leading lady that I should have been serving all along. It dawned on me that I had wanted her since I first laid eyes on her. Lily was a mere stepping stone along the path to precious Reshi.

I woke up with disappointment, realizing it was only a bizarre, vivid dream and it was difficult to sleep through the rest of the night. I remembered where I was and was worried of being discovered. I could not stop thinking about the dream of Reshi and how real it all had seemed. Dear reader, I was losing my mind. Murder, torture and eating a woman's heart could all be forgotten and buried deep within the psyche somewhere, so deep that they might never return. But this was just too much. It wouldn't digest. I couldn't accept it. I knew that peace would be out of reach. Spending the night in a strange place with a dead body makes a person think a lot. The further I was from my syndicate family, the more hopeless my life had become. I only knew two things with any certainty, Tessa would be meeting me outside at ten and I missed Reshi.

CHAPTER XIII
Hip Shake

Call no man happy till he is dead.

—Aeschylus

Kinsey,

> You say that you aren't in control of yourself at times? You say you're suffering from chronic horrible nightmares, the worst you ever had? You say you black-out sometimes, not remembering what you've done? You say that there's a black dog and rats that always appear in your dreams? Well, all I can say is, lucky you. It sounds like you have what I have, so buckle up and hold on. You're in for one hell of a ride. Cheer up, though, it's not really so bad if you look at it the right way. In fact, it can be damn interesting. Life is never boring when you're possessed by Aswang. It can be cheap and miserable and confusing, but rarely dull. Wait until you come out of a black-out and find that you're in the midst of eating the heart of a human you murdered, talk about exciting! That's good stuff!
>
> And what is this crap about you feel like you need to come and see me? What for? Don't you recall what happened to Dr. Taylor, the head honcho there? I bashed your boss's brains in with a bible, that's what happened. Why do you think I'd treat you any different? You have to keep things in perspective, champ. You're a night supervisor at the loony bin and I'm just one of the loonies. Granted, I escaped

198

and got out of there, but I'm still a psychotic loony. The loony bin phase of my life is now way behind me. I've moved on. Greener pastures unfold and all that shit.

In any case, you have Aswang in your blood now. There's nothing you can do about it. It's best to just accept that you're possessed and go with the flow. You try resisting and fighting and Aswang will really make you its bitch. If you feel you have to see me, come and try to find me. You're not going to get any encouraging, warm invitation. And if you do somehow manage to find me, I can't guarantee that I might not just kill you. Depends on my mood at the time, I guess. It's up to you, though. Like Smokey the Bear always says, 'Only you can prevent forest fires.'

Sincerely,
The Midnight Rambler

I headed out in the morning light, leaving the apartment and going in search of Jollibee, where I could kill some time and get some breakfast. I hardly slept and my mind was heavy and sluggishly broody, but I tried to keep upbeat. In Manila, it's what's on the outside that counts. Put forth a good appearance and a fake smile and you can go places. I sat in Jollibee and made up fictional lives for people around me. It's a great way to pass the time and keeps myself from thinking about myself.

Around ten in the morning, I walked down Juan Luna Street and went about two blocks before Tessa suddenly appeared, walking right beside me. "Good morning, handsome. Going my way?" she teased.

"Hey Tessa; how are you?"

"I'm fine," she replied, "thank you for asking. You had a good night? Flash found you a place?"

I did not wish to go into any details about the previous night's activities. "Yes, Flash took good care of me. He's quite a character, isn't he?"

"He is, I love that old man to death, or maybe I should say, in death," she laughed.

"He was really a great boxer?"

"Yes, back in the day, as great as Paquiao."

"He sure as hell didn't like me using the word 'ghost'," I said, chuckling.

"No, he wouldn't. He's old school and likes accuracy. We're spirits," she said, stopping and waving her arm towards the busy street traffic. "I mean, when I look around, there really are no people here, just all spirits. They just look greener when they are still stuck in their bodies."

"Do I look green too?"

"No, you're special," she laughed, clutching my arm, "You look black, big and turbulent. You have Aswang."

"So I'm different than other people here?"

"Of course; I mean, in the human world, you feel like an outcast who is losing his mind, yes?"

I agreed by nodding my head.

"In the spirit world, you are already powerful. You have Aswang, and that's hot! The human world is just a big mind deception anyways. It's the spirit world that is the true foundation for everything."

"Can other people catch Aswang from me? Is it contagious?" I asked.

"Sometimes, it can spread easiest through sex, but also in ideas, or blood. Having sex with someone creates an opening and if one partner wills the Aswang to spread into the other, it will. Also, a person sharing ideas with an Aswang possessed person could receive the spirit, and just a drop or two of mixed blood would spread Aswang as well. There are not really any strict rules, like science. If someone is around Aswang, then they are vulnerable. Aswang choose whoever they wish."

"Well, I thought I got it when some crazy Japanese chick grabbed me and released her sulfur smelling breath into my mouth, but now I realize that Lily gave it to me way back in Boracay when we first fucked," I revealed. "What a deceitful, fickle-hearted bitch!"

"Well, she has Aswang, what do you expect? Girls play with a guy's mind. Women explore a guy's mind. Ladies with Aswang corrupt a guy's mind, and sell their souls. You probably feel corrupt as a human, but you're powerful in the spirit world, trust me."

We took a taxi to Makati, getting out a few blocks from Berto's house. The sweltering heat of Manila, the smell of durian in the air and the chaotic traffic made the walk seem longer than it actually was.

"He won't be home for awhile, but we need to go inside to find you a good hiding place," advised Tessa.

"Okay, but, uh, Tessa, you do realize that he will try to kill me if he sees me, right?"

"He'll never see you. Quit worrying, you have a ghost on your side. Oops, I meant spirit," she laughed, turning the doorknob with a click and simply opening the locked door. Inside we were greeted loudly by at least a half-dozen tropical birds, some talking, some squawking and others just singing. On the computer monitor "Milf Mania" bold text flashed, announcing the wondrous offerings of its website with pictures of nude women performing multiple sex acts. "Well, well, well, looks like the horny prick is trying to become a typical man," said Tessa. "When was the last time you had sex, Tim?"

"Uhm, don't worry about it," I answered, wondering if the previous night's dream counted. "It's just something I don't like to share," I added, "And besides, the only woman I really lust after is with a syndicate that wants to kill me."

"Lily?"

"No, it's Reshi."

Tessa sighed, smiling, "Reshi is very beautiful, isn't she? Well, we want who we want and logic is powerless over it when it's the real deal. What you will see tonight, however, won't be want, just raw sex."

I chuckled, "I should probably say that I won't watch, but, hell, I probably will. Maybe I am a pervert, but it isn't every day that I get to see my old buddy screwing a ghost, a ghost of his old self. That's kind of kinky, ghost incest!"

"Okay then, there's a closet in the bedroom you can hide in tonight while I seduce him in bed. I don't know for sure how long it will be, but keep a bottle of water handy if you get thirsty."

"I just can't make any noise?"

"Right."

"What if he needs something in the closet?"

"He won't. I'm a spirit; we can persuade people to keep out or go into places."

"Alright, I'm game."

"Good, after I screw him, I'm going to make him go for a walk with me. Just wait a few minutes and leave after we leave. Turn right and walk down the street, Flash will find you. Once you get farther down the street, away from me, I will become immaterial and vanish before his eyes."

"Leave after you leave and turn right, got it."

The closet was small, but had adequate room to stand and stretch as needed. I waited until five in the afternoon when Berto finished work, then settled in for my shift in the closet. I knew he'd probably stop at the Giraffe for a few hours on his way home, as was his standard procedure, but was not certain. It was best not to take any chances.

It was three long hours until he arrived. The birds began talking to him when he came in the door and he talked back to them. I could hear and smell him cooking, what seemed to be a fish and rice combination. I then heard the television and, eventually, loud yawning. I knew he would sleep soon. I waited, nearly dozing off myself. The television was turned off and I heard him get into his bed. I waited in the darkness.

His snoring pattern went on for some time. I had doubts if Tessa was even going to show up, but then I heard her presence in the room. I squinted to see through the lattice of the closet door. With the glow of light coming through the window, it was easy to see Tessa. She stood at the foot of the bed, smiling. It was the malicious smile of a scorned woman bent on revenge.

She wore a white nightgown, nearly transparent, and the moonlight shining through silhouetted her curvaceous figure. She leaned slightly over the foot of the bed and her breasts appeared to grow as they hung forward, her nipples gently appearing through the fabric. She kitty crawled upwards, slowly between Berto's legs, and swiftly pulled his boxers down, making kissing sounds.

"Why are you here?" he asked, breaking the silence while breathing heavy.

"Because you still love me," replied Tessa, with assurance.

Berto looked puzzled, "I'm confused. This is impossible. You are who I once was."

"Just enjoy me. Fuck me hard. Everything is possible, even the word impossible says I'm possible," she whispered, putting Berto's apprehension and worries to rest. She straddled his prone body and lowered herself slowly as he penetrated her. She rode him and picked up rhythm. He squeezed her tits as she moaned. After five minutes, he arched his back and moaned loud enough to be heard by a cargo ship on the bay.

"That was hot," she said, afterwards, as they lay side by side.

"That's what she said," quipped Berto, before turning serious, "hey, who are you and how did you get in here?"

"You know who I am," said Tessa, grinning at him. "I'm the woman you left behind."

"I know, but how in the hell can you still be here if I'm here?" he asked, rubbing his head in confusion.

"Come with me. I will explain it," she said, sitting up on the edge of the bed. She rose and walked across the room, putting on a robe and sandals. "Come" she insisted.

"Alright" sighed Berto, rolling out of the bed and putting on his clothes that were in a pile on the floor. "How far are we going?"

"Just come; only a short walk" she said, leading the way out of the house as Berto followed. I waited to hear the door close. I knew it was safe to finally get the hell out. I left the house and turned right, walking down the street at a brisk pace.

It wasn't until I was nearly six blocks away that Flash waved to me from a field of overgrown grass, littered with debris. He was smiling the smile that always made it good to see him again. "Tim; how are you doing? Mabuhay!" he yelled.

"Flash; good to see you!"

"Yes," he replied, "and it's good to be seen, usually I'm not! Got a new place for you tonight; cut through this field with me. Once we get to Harrison, there's a little joint down the road from there; top-notch, and you'll have your own Jacuzzi."

"Sounds outstanding, Flash, who's my roommate?"

"Ah, just another heart attack; middle-aged guy from Cebu who was visiting family here in Manila and, whammo, the grim reaper scythed him about an hour ago. He's on the middle of the marble floor, so just slide him to the side and you'll have run of the place. You can't go in or out, but he's got some adobo in the fridge and there's a microwave there. The world is your oyster!"

I chuckled as we walked, "So the guy just died; how old was he?"

"Mid forties; it's a strange thing, if they're under fifty and have a heart attack, they die. Kind of the opposite of what you might expect. You're the scholar, what do they call that shit?"

"Ironic" I replied.

"Yeah," agreed Flash, "that's just what it is, it's ironic!"

"Kind of like an old, dead boxer being the one who helps me stay alive," I teased.

"Watch it, pal, I might be old by your standards, but I'm still young and full of piss and vinegar by mine," he said, before throwing a quick jab at my chin with his right fist and cuffing me on the ear with his left. He was not exaggerating. His hands were still lightning quick and precise. I certainly had no desire to box with him.

We exited the field and started walking down Harrison. It was a busy area, abundant with seedy bars and young women loitering around the entrances. Two expats walked past us, their arms around their young catches of the evening. We continued down Harrison, "That guy has it tough," said Flash, pointing at a skinny, stray yellow dog. "He's got lots of competition for street scraps and that's if nobody goes Chinese and tries to eat him. Better to be a stray in Manila than a stray in Shanghai, I always say."

"This place looks alright," I stated, looking at the jungle themed exterior of the hotel.

"Only the best for you, Tim; hey, a young, healthy, handsome guy like yourself, aren't you interested in picking up one of those barroom beauties and doing the old you know what with her? Hell, when I was your age, well, just you know that I was getting mine."

"When you were my age, you just drug them into your cave by their hair, right?" I teased.

"By their pussy hair, maybe," he grinned. "So what's your excuse?"

I hesitated to answer, "Well, I know this is lame but there's only one girl I'm really lusting for. Anything else would seem like a step backwards."

Flash scoffed, waving his hand, "Damn, I'm just talking about fucking, son," he admonished. "Not only does it feel great, but it's good exercise and builds stamina. You notice these heart attack fellas are all single, right?" he asked, cracking his knuckles outwards. "Now I don't mean to pry, Tim, but it's Filipino nature to take an interest in other people, so just who is this lucky girl that you're so devoted to?"

"Ah, it's okay Flash, her name is Reshi. She's an actress and a model, just a radiant, elegant beauty."

"Well, she sounds real nice, but why aren't you with her?"

"Cause she is under orders to kill me."

"Yeah," reflected Flash, "That could be a problem. Kind of ironic, too, isn't it? I might just be spitting coconuts here, but is it worth it to be devoted to a gal who wants you dead?"

"Probably not, but my heart doesn't want to change. It's ironic, isn't it?"

"No, more like moronic," he retorted, as we both laughed. "I'll go as far to agree with you on one thing though; it's a bitch trying to control the heart. I always wished I could knock it out just to avoid the stupid shit it brings."

"Well, Flash, since this is a hotel, I'll have to check out before morning light, right?"

"Yes, we'll get you a new place tomorrow. There are people dying to get out of Manila every day, so vacancy is never a problem."

"I like Manila, love it here. I just wish certain people didn't want me dead."

"Hey, room 118; the door's open. I'll see you tomorrow sometime. Tessa said to meet her at the Mall of Asia at ten, in front of the fountain. Goodnight, my friend."

"Okay, Flash, good night, and thanks again."

"Ah, thank Tessa, that girl's a sweetheart," he said, before turning away and walking into the darkness.

I walked past the front office. Room 118 was off to the side of the building, where it was very dark. The door was unlocked and the lights were on inside. There were two beds in the spacious rectangular room. The kitchen was near the back and had a full-sized refrigerator with a microwave on top of it. A large, shirtless Filipino man lied face down on the floor. "Too much pork tocino and adobo for you, buddy," I said, before grabbing his torso and sliding him against the wall, out of the way. Both beds were made and unused. I walked further back past the kitchen and entered an archway where, to the left, was a bathroom and to the right, a separate room containing a large Jacuzzi tub, like a small swimming pool. "Hell yeah!" I exclaimed.

I ate the leftovers in the fridge while filling the Jacuzzi with water. When full, I flipped the switch and crawled into the swirling, pulsating warm water. As I sat, contemplating my circumstances, I felt some gratitude. Sure I had a lot of immediate problems and I was hijacking the hotel room of a dead guy, but at least my current life was never dull or routine. I always was able to find food, I had shelter and I was traveling the world and meeting new people, even if some of them were dead or spirits. Who else from back home could claim such an interesting life? It wasn't always pretty and it sure wasn't always comfortable, but it was hardly ever dull. This lack of boredom was probably the silver lining around the dark cloud of being possessed by Aswang.

I floated in the water, letting the powerful jets do their magic on my body. I drifted in and out of consciousness while becoming completely relaxed in the swirling luxury of the tub. I relaxed in the water for at least an hour. I became a comatose jellyfish by the time I had to get out. I also felt relaxed enough to sleep. I quickly dried off with a towel and headed to bed.

What followed was the best sleep I had in a very long time. Two hours of uninterrupted bliss. Until a voice pierced the darkness, saying "Mabuhay!" I sat up, looking around the dark room.

"Who's there?" I asked.

"Jonathan," he answered, sitting in a chair halfway across the room. I could only make out a dark silhouette. "You have Aswang inside of you," he stated, matter-of-factly.

"Jonathan," I replied, "Are you a spirit?"

"Aswang will devour you," he said, oblivious to my question.

"He already has, Jonathan, now why the hell are you in my room?" I asked, growing more irritated.

"Halika, sumame ka sa amin. Maganda dito. Walang mananakit sa iyo."

I suddenly asked, *Makakababalik ba ako kung magbago ang isip ko?*

He chuckled, gently shaking his head in the dark room, "Sa oras na sumama ka sa amin, hindi ka na makakabalik at di morin gugustuking bumalik."

Kung ganun, hindi muna ako makakasanra sa inyo.

As the last few words left my mouth, I realized that I was speaking a language that I did not even know. It was as if someone or something was speaking through me. Jonathan was asking me to join him, how, I'm not sure. I believe it would require my life, as I knew it, to end. I asked him if I could return back after joining him. He said there was no return. It was a one-way trip. As easily as he appeared, he was gone. I called for him, but nothing. I was alone again. I felt strangely violated. Not just because of a spirit coming into my room, but also from the inside. Something spoke Tagalog through me. I felt used; but I still managed to be able to get some more sleep.

When the sun peeped through the window, I made my way out of the room. Leaving the hotel, I went around the corner and down the street. I caught a taxi to the Mall of Asia. It was six in the morning and the mall didn't even open till ten. I sat behind the mall for four hours, with a scenic view of Manila Bay. The rising of the sun cast an orange reflection on the surface of the water. There is something about Manila Bay that makes daydreaming come easy. The haze just above the water's surface and the sun's reflection through the haze, with the occasional small sailboat bobbing along the water surface, lends tranquility to the mind, even to the most disturbed mind that has no control over itself. I daydreamed for three hours and was never bored. I walked to the front of the mall and waited on a concrete bench near the fountain. Without noticing her arrival, Tessa was sitting beside me.

"Tim, there are two envelopes here. They both contain identical copies, pictures of Berto, pre-op and post-op. There are also medical records from Japan of the sex change operation, translated into Tagalog," she said, handing me the large gold envelopes.

"Wow, Tessa, you really did your homework here. Should I just try to arrange a meeting with him?"

"No; it's not necessary. All you really need to do is write on one of the envelopes that you have identical copies and that you want your passport and a plane ticket, give a drop-off location and a deadline. The rest is up to him. His head will already be messed up from screwing himself last night, so the envelope should put him into fast action."

"Well, thank you for your help. I'll get it in his mailbox today."

"No problem, Tim, my job is done. I wish you the best of luck, with everything. Flash will continue to help you for as long as you need and if you need me again, just let Flash know, okay?"

"Okay," I said, before embracing her in a hug. "Tessa, what's it like?"

"What, to be on the other side?"

"Yes, what's it like in your world?"

She smiled, "It's same same, but different."

I chuckled at the nonsensical answer, "Okay, so will I ever see you again?"

"Someday, Tim, someday," she answered, before walking into the crowd of people near the mall.

I borrowed a pen from a security guard and scrawled my demands on the outside of one of the envelopes. I simply made my requests with no explanation of how or why I had the sensitive documents. I went to the taxi stand and had the driver wait at Berto's house while I dropped off the envelope. From there, I had the driver take me to Café Adratico where I could get my fill of crispy pata. I devoured everything, the skin, the fat, the cartilage, only leaving the bone. I walked down Roxas after eating. People loitered around the doorways of a few clubs and a group of teenagers were playing basketball. I walked around the court and entered a dark club that sat behind it. The court had seen better days. It was just a rectangle of cracked concrete with rusted hoops at each end. Two teams of six, mostly shirtless, players were playing and they made it appear as if this was the most important game in the world. I ordered a Coke and sat, watching the game of the century.

The ball went back and forth. When one team would score, the other team would quickly answer back. There were short passes, bounce passes, hook shots, lay-ups all executed with finesse and precision. What these guys lacked in height, they made up for in accurate technique and unflinching stamina. I wasn't even much of a basketball fan, but I liked the way these guys played. There were no fouls, or at least none that were called. There were also no breaks, just constant back and forth action. About thirty minutes into the game, it began to rain, hard. The sky turned dark and ominous complete with cracks of thunder and flashes of lightning. The players could have cared less. They continued their game as if it wasn't even raining. Within minutes, it began pouring. Clothes and shoes were soaked, puddles formed on the court. The players just splashed through the puddles and water, working towards the basket, oblivious to the rain. It was admirable, tough and showed a love of the game that I never witnessed on any neighborhood basketball courts in the U.S.

"Well," said Flash, suddenly appearing right next to me in the dark bar. "It sure isn't boxing, but they play it damn tough, don't they?"

"They sure do; how are you doing, Flash? You kind of snuck up on me there!"

"Yeah, don't underestimate my footwork, kid, it'll get ya. Got a nice place for you tonight; you'll be rubbing elbows with the rich and corrupt."

"Sounds awesome," I replied.

"Yeah, and even better, it's only about three blocks down the street," he said, sliding me the plastic rectangular key across the table. "Diamond Hotel, room 1422; the guy croaked about an hour ago, but nobody will know until tomorrow morning when the maids find him. The room is big, plush and has a fantastic view of the bay."

"Thanks Flash," I said, pocketing the key, "Guess I'll see you sometime tomorrow." I walked into the rain, lightly jogging down Roxas until coming to the half-circle entrance to the Diamond. There were security guards at a blockade checking out every vehicle that entered. They had more guards at the doors checking everyone who entered and their belongings, even a metal-detector to walk through. Some of the guards had dogs with them, Diamond dogs. In light of being wanted by the police for murder, the stringent security here was making me extremely nervous. However, they had all seen me and I was near the entrance. Turning away now would only arouse suspicion. Besides, these guys didn't look like the Manila police, most likely just a security outfit that held a contract with the hotel management. I entered, walking through the metal detector and flashing the room key to show I belonged there.

Once in the lobby, adrenalin continued to course through my veins. I was a wanted man and there were a hell of a lot of people, dressed well. My disheveled appearance combined with being soaking wet set me apart from the clientele. Even the workers wore suits and business dresses. "Screw it," I said to myself, and walked with authority. Experience has shown me that people don't question if you belong in a place or not if you walk with confidence and authority, and act like you know exactly where you're going. I found the elevators, pushed the up button and, when the doors opened, waited for an attractive hotel receptionist to come out before I went in. One thing was certain as I roamed the hallway looking for 1422, this was a smoking floor.

I entered the room. There was a suitcase, a briefcase on the floor and a Japanese man collapsed on the undisturbed bed, facedown. He looked to be around sixty, balding. I lifted him with both arms, all 160 pounds of him, and gently placed him on the carpeted floor near the closet door, where I was able to fit him inside after opening the two sliding doors and nudging the body with my feet.

The room looked very nice, untouched. Two rows of fancy ornamented pillows lined the headboard of the bed. I locked the door, walked to the bed, and fell backwards on it, soaking in the comfort and luxury. I laid there motionless and relaxed, soon falling asleep.

The ringing of a phone penetrated my sleep and prompted me awake, groggily, without thinking, I picked up the receiver. "Hello?" I muttered into the phone.

"Mr. Soto, you have a call from Lily," said the hotel receptionist.

Against better judgment, or in spite of better judgment, I said, "okay". The wait for the line to switch over made two seconds feel like an eternity.

I sat up, rubbing the grogginess away from my head with my free hand. The phone line clicked over. "Tim, we need to talk," she said. Her voice sounded amazingly familiar, but cold and lethal. A floodgate of repressed memories momentarily burst open somewhere inside of me. Hearing her voice again sky-rocketed my brain beyond the clouds and into another dimension; but it suddenly dawned on me, "How the hell does she know I am in this hotel room?" My brain was now racing to sort it all out.

"Tim, I sent Sonny to pick you up. Go with him so we can talk in person. I miss you."

I wanted to believe her, especially that last tidbit. There was a major struggle between my heart and my head. I wanted to believe, yet logic hinted some queries; why would she miss me? She seemed able to turn her heart on or off at will. Then I recalled the look on her face as I drove my blade into the loudmouthed drunken German. The image returned. Her eyes were cold and murderous. I knew the look; it was a look I had seen directed at past victims, but this time it was all for me. It was the green light for murder look in her eyes and it was non-negotiable. All of these thoughts rushed through my mind as I still held the phone and I debated to even respond, then yelled, "You'll miss me more when I'm gone for good, you phony cunt!" and slammed the receiver down.

Adrenalin coursed through my veins. Someone working at the hotel tipped off the syndicate. Maybe the guards or the cute receptionist at the elevator; in any case, my picture was now making the rounds, and the syndicate had tentacles everywhere. In Manila, the syndicate always gets what the syndicate wants. It was fight or flight and I knew Sonny was coming prepared. I had to get the hell out of dodge fast. I ran to the door, opened it and saw Sonny coming out of the elevator down the hall. I knew he probably had a key, so locking the room was futile. I left the room, sprinting away from him down the carpeted hallway.

"Tim!" he yelled, "Lily just wants to talk to you, that's it!"

I continued sprinting to the stairs and began leaping down them, six at a time. Sonny was one tough bastard, but he was a little too old to catch me in a foot race, especially one involving fourteen flights of stairs.

"Tim, stop running!" he shouted from above, his voice resonating down the stairwell chamber. "We just want to hide you from the cops, get you back home!"

I slowed down and leaned over the handrail, looking up. I saw him trying to steady his gun on my head. I quickly jumped back against the wall. "Go fuck yourself, Sonny!" I yelled, while continuing down the stairs and staying close to the far wall. He was going to have to be a hell of a shot to get me here. I reached the second floor and exited the stairwell, knowing Sonny would have henchmen waiting in the lobby.

There was a metal door going to the pool area and I burst through it and ran down a metal spiral staircase to the pool patio area. There was a family of four enjoying the pool, splashing and laughing under the huge waterfall that spilled into the pool. I sprinted past them to the far edge of the pool patio and climbed the twelve-foot high wooden fence wall, landing on the other side and collapsing momentarily on the pavement, facing Roxas Avenue. I got up and ran across all lanes of Roxas, to the bayfront walk area and continued running. In desperation, and knowing it was only a matter of time until Sonny drove up and put a bullet in my head, I ran back to square one, the Manila Film Center.

The combination of being out of breath from running for my life and the stress of having such a close call made me double-over, hands on my knees, gasping for air and trying not to vomit. I needed to unwind a bit after running so far, so fast. It's an odd feeling to run in public and think that any second your head could explode with the help of a well aimed bullet. It kind of motivates a person to run further and faster than they thought they were capable of. I walked around the perimeter of the large building, breathing deeply as I walked. On the third side of the large corridor, I began to think how everything was like a circle. I was making a circle just walking around the building. Also, I had ended up at this building on my first night as a fugitive from the syndicate, when I slit the German's throat, and now, here I was again. I wondered if the circle would ever take me back to the United States, or was that circle broken?

I decided against sleeping in the corridor. I wasn't in the mood to play around with any weird construction worker ghost again. I decided to take my chances in the patch of woods next to the building. I'd risk the critters and bugs as opposed to the sheer terror of being buried alive in concrete like last time.

I walked into the brush, crouching and clearing openings with my hands. After a short ways, I came to a small clearing. I swept away the rocks, dead limbs and debris with my feet. The small clearing felt secluded and safe, so I lay on my back and began to star gaze up into the clear Manila night sky. I thought about the syndicate. I wondered if there was any way possible that Lily did just want to talk to me. I thought of how she said she missed me and replayed it through my head over and over. What if it were true? She did seem to love me back in the beginning, there had to be something about me she liked? But why would Sonny have a gun? Sonny always carried a gun, but he was aiming it at me. No, no matter how much I wanted to believe that she missed me, that she only wanted to talk, I had to remember just who it was. Lily was heartless with keen intelligence, a calculating, shrewd, deceptive syndicate leader. But, damn, I still missed being part of the syndicate family. I missed the sense of belonging.

I fell asleep under the night sky for some amount of time, until I began to hear a heavy "whooshing" sound, repeatedly. The sound was accompanied by warm breezes being blown across my body. The slow flapping came closer and the gusts of air blew with more force. As I opened my eyes, it was on me.

Two talons gripped each of my shoulders like strong hands, and held me in place with the strength of a vice. The large wings continued to gently flap, until the large creature was evenly balanced on my chest. I could not move. The brute strength and unrelenting grip of the winged beast were overwhelming, crushing.

I looked up at the creature and saw the shiny slick black beak of a bird, but the head was shaped more like a horse. The eyes glowed red in the darkness, like two neon cherry diamonds. Holding me in his power, he lowered his head, gazing into my frightened, shocked eyes. There were curled ram's horns on each side of his head. I could feel his warm breath against the skin of my face. It smelled of thick smoke and sulfur. The creature's gaze was menacing, all knowing, all powerful and malicious. A slight diabolical grin showed no mercy or trace of compassion. The beast only desired to devour and destroy me. I released a scream that erupted from down in my stomach. It was all that I could do. The agony of being on the brink of death, combined with the manic scream, opened a plank in my ability to think rationally and the floodgates of darkness erupted in my mind.

I do not know how long the black-out lasted. I looked up while pinned to the ground with a malicious, strong winged creature on my chest. A hollow tongue, like a drinking straw, extended from the birdlike beast's beak, going all the way into my mouth. I stared in shock at his glowing red eyes. They were fueled with menace. His tongue went back to his mouth like a collapsing telescope of flesh. His wings began to flap and the weight on my chest became lighter. I was relieved to watch him slowly ascend up into the night sky, above the surrounding tree tops and beyond my field of vision. I felt violated and confused. I was glad that he was gone.

I could not sleep the rest of the night. I had no idea why the demonic bird had subdued me or what he was doing with his tongue in my throat. I feared the beast might return. I moved to an area thick with overgrowth and vines. And there I waited, confused and cautious, until the sun broke through the darkness.

I walked out of the woods and saw Flash standing in front of a column at the Film Center. "You had a close call, huh, kid?"

"Yeah Flash," I replied, happy to see a friendly face, "The syndicate found me at the Diamond somehow."

"It happens; I have a house for you. Just became open so you should be good for two days and two nights, you interested?"

"Yes, of course" I answered, with relief. We walked up to Roxas and caught a taxi. Flash gave the driver the address as we headed over a small bridge into the thick Makati traffic. I was grateful that Flash showed up so early and to know I had a safe house for at least two days. There was way less chance of the syndicate finding me in a random house as opposed to a big name hotel.

The neighborhood, however, began to look all too familiar. The car was slowly going down Berto's street, and then stopped in front of his house. I was nervous it was some kind of set-up, but this was Flash, I trusted him. I looked at him for any signs of betrayal, but nothing. I debated telling him this house belonged to an active member of the syndicate, a member I was currently trying to blackmail and who was once Tessa. "And this is where you get off," said Flash, smiling.

I decided to keep my mouth shut. The suspense was getting to me. I knew Flash was only concerned with finding me places to stay, but wasn't involved in the details of the syndicate and its members. "Okay buddy, see you in two days," I replied, getting out of the cab as it slowly went down the road. I wondered what the driver might think if Flash just vanished from the back seat and chuckled to myself.

I approached Berto's door. A door I had entered on many occasions. I turned the handle and went inside. In the middle of the living room, dangling by a rope, in awkward stillness, was the lifeless body of Berto.

Chapter XIIII
Soul Survivor

But what is Hope? Nothing but the paint on the face of
Existence; the least touch of truth rubs it off, and then we see
what a hollow-cheeked harlot we have got hold of.

—Lord Byron

Kinsey,

*What are you thinking? You quit your job at the funny farm
and bought a one-way ticket to Manila? One the one hand, I am
impressed. You're gambling with the security and sanity of your
future. I don't know how long you worked at the nuthouse. It seemed
like you had it good there, cushy duty, job security and a steady
paycheck. You could have easily coasted your days out there into
an idyllic retirement. Hell, you had to be like the head honcho
there after Dr. Taylor's unfortunate murder, weren't you? It makes
absolutely no sense to throw it all away and that's exactly what I find
impressive. You gave up damn near everything to fly across the world
to nothing. Oh yeah.*

*Hell, I'm not one to judge. Besides, with Aswang running
around in your head it would have only been a matter of time before
you messed up on the job and killed somebody or yourself. Maybe you
should have killed Mac! That would have been outstanding; plus,
you owed him one for stealing your credit card and getting every nut
in there a subscription to their porn website of choice. Imagine the*

change of going from being the man in charge to becoming one of the
patients, can you imagine? No, you probably made the right call by
leaving, but the wrong one in choosing to go to Manila.

    First of all, you never even traveled, so you have no idea what
Manila is like. It's busy, busier than New York City on steroids.
Secondly, I don't have any magic cure for you. You have Aswang.
I have Aswang. We're both possessed and crazy as bat shit. The last
thing I want to do is hang around with another fucked up person.
That being said, I will tell you that I'm not even in Manila. I'm not
even in the Philippines. I'm not telling you where I am, but I am
telling you where I am not. I'm not in Manila.

    You wanted to keep reading my drivel and look what happened.
I told you it was none of your business from the very beginning.
Would you listen? No, you just thought since you were in charge and
bored at work there, you'd kill the time reading the adventures of a
nut case. Now the table seems to have turned and I'm reading the
e-mails of a nut case. If all you want is to keep reading my stories, I
will send them by e-mail. Do not try to find me because if you do I
will probably kill you. Who knows? Time changes everything.

                                          Sincerely,
                             Mad Brained Bear

I tilted the chair upright that Berto had used as his launch pad. His body slowly turned under the strain of the rope. I went to the kitchen and got a knife, hacking through the rope until his body collapsed in a pile onto the floor. I thought about how, just a few nights before, I watched him screwing Tessa. Now here he was devoid of life. He also smelled like the hanging had caused him to shit himself.

    At least there was no blood or mess. Hanging and heart attack victims were pretty clean, just a body to tuck away. I dragged Berto, noose still tightly on his neck, to a spot on the floor across from his couch next to the television stand. I also went and found a spare bed-sheet from the closet and draped it over his body. It wouldn't contain the shit smell much but at least I wouldn't have to look at him. When it's a stranger, being with a dead body is no big deal, but when it's someone you know, that's a different story.

    I began to go through the house, hoping that maybe by some small chance he had put the plane ticket and passport somewhere before he decided to kill himself. I went through a basket of bills and receipts with no luck. A drawer on the nightstand beside his bed revealed two handguns. On the dresser were some random pictures, including one of myself that was taken at the Mirage before the nightmare even began. On the back of the photo were all of my statistics, name, birth date, hair color, eye color, weight, height and even complexion. There was also an asterisk with a note that 50,000 pesos would be awarded to anyone who gave a tip leading to my capture. Now I knew how I was spotted at the Diamond.

I continued searching the entire house with no luck. I sifted through every box, flipped the pages of every book, checked in the freezer, even felt my way along the plumbing under the sink. As I was lifting the mattress to look under it, I felt something grip my neck from behind, like a clammy, cool hand. I yelled and turned, and there was nothing there. I felt a slight breeze of energy, cooler air rush past me. Something weird was going on. I let it go and continued my search for any documents. He must have destroyed or burned the envelope of documents I left in the mail because they were not here.

I took a bottle of water from the fridge and sat on the couch, sipping and thinking. All of my high hopes about getting back to the States and away from the chaos and danger were crumbling. There's no mileage in blackmailing a dead man. At least I'm the first to know he is dead. I sat thinking, trying to figure out if there was any way to use the awareness of his death to my advantage. As I concentrated, the sheet covering Berto's corpse began to move, like he was scratching an itch under it. I stood up, "Berto, are you alive?" I asked, "Berto?"

I waited in silence, on edge, but there was no response and no further movement from under the sheet. As I walked up closer, to determine if maybe my eyes were just deceiving me, I heard an object fall in the bedroom. It sounded like it might have been a small coin or something similar, I ran to the bedroom and looked around. There was a pen on the floor, and apparently it had rolled off the dresser.

I picked up the pen and was putting it back on the dresser when I noticed some writing on the photo. There was a crudely drawn caricature of myself with "Timmy" written under it. "Who the hell is here?" I demanded. "Who's screwing around doing grade school shit?" I looked at the drawing again. It revealed some degree of skill. When I looked up from the drawing, I briefly saw a reflection in the mirror of a man standing right behind me, grinning. I spun on my heels, turning to confront him, but there was nobody there. "Who are you?" I shouted. Suddenly the television came on. It was a basketball game and the volume was loud. As I went to turn the television off, the doorbell rang.

My nerves were on edge. I wondered who the hell could be at the door. I left the television on and went back to the nightstand to retrieve one of the guns. I checked the clip and saw rounds. I tip-toed cautiously to the window near the door and slowly peeked through the blinds, but there was nobody in sight. I opened the door and looked around outside and found nothing. As I shut the door, I heard someone walking through the house. It was the sound of slow, deliberate, heavy footsteps on the hard wood floor.

I clutched the gun, wanting to fire only if I had to. I knew the blast would draw much unwanted attention. In Manila, everybody's business is everybody's business. The footsteps came close and closer. I could see the wooden planks of the floorboards sinking down as they creaked from the weight. I backed away, nervously. "Who are you?" I demanded. They continued to stroll towards me.

The footsteps stopped when they were right beside me. I could feel cool air around my neck and a muffled whisper in my ear, "Go on, do it."

"Do what? Who the hell are you?"

I was answered by the feint sound of giggling. "You know," a malicious tone replied, "blow your head off. Do it."

"Leave me the fuck alone, whoever or whatever you are!" I shouted, but the entity only chuckled.

"What else do you have to live for?" I mean, think about it, friend. You've got nothing. No honey, no money and nothing is funny; hell, the family you love even wants you dead. Prove your love to them! Do it. Pull the trigger and end the headache."

I considered what he said and could agree with the logic, but then I thought of at least seeing, possibly speaking to Reshi again. The idea gave me hope. "No, screw you!" I replied, wondering how in the hell this ghost knew so much about my haphazard life. I also wondered how he could be so persuasive. "Just tell me who you are."

"I'm your only friend," he answered, in a voice that was somehow serpent-like. "I'm on your side, sincerely," said a whispered hiss.

"Then why the hell do you want me to shoot myself?"

There was no response, just silence. From the corner of my eye, I saw the sheet covering Berto's corpse move again. The sound of the television was of a man whispering repeatedly, "Do it, do it, do it . . . . " I sprinted to Berto's corpse and yanked the sheet off, revealing Berto looking at me with white eyes, dead eyes, grinning at me from his curled position on the floor. His arm was bent with his hand gestured like a gun, pointing at his temple. He continued to grin while slowly bringing his thumb down, over and over, gesturing shooting himself in the head. The television never changed scenes and the voice continued, "Do it, do it, do it . . . . " I draped the sheet back over the sickly, white-eyed corpse of Berto and raised the gun.

I pointed it at the television, but considered the consequences before pulling the trigger. I decided to put the damn gun back in the drawer, mainly to avoid being persuaded into using it on myself. I needed to get away from the spirits, the voices, but I was stuck in the house for lack of anywhere else to go. I crouched down in a corner of the bedroom, closing my eyes and covering my ears. I slowly rocked back and forth, trying to take my mind off of all things haunted. I began to think of Reshi, and her beauty; for me, she was (and remains) the pinnacle of the standard of beauty. I have no idea how much time elapsed as I sat there, rocking to and fro on the hard wood floor, when I felt a nudge from a light kick on my leg. I opened my eyes and looked up to see Jolen, smiling down at me.

"See no evil, hear no evil," said the jubilant, teasing voice, bursting through my lengthy trance hangover. I quickly scrambled to my feet, going after the gun.

"How have you been, Tim?" he asked.

I stopped, looking at his friendly, disarming smile. "Uhm, aren't you supposed to kill me? I know Lily wants me dead."

Jolen chuckled, "You know me better than that, don't you? I love my friends more than my membership in any organization. I stick by my friends, which you are one. I was worried about you, for sure. You can't blame, Lily, though, since you did bring lots of unwanted attention to the syndicate. I just came by to get Berto. He was supposed to meet me. You're the last person I expected to see here. Where is he?"

I quickly forgot all about defending myself with the gun. Jolen was always honest with me, always. I pointed towards the sheet, "He's dead. He had hung himself before I got here. I just found him hanging by the rope when I got here this morning."

Jolen looked astonished by the sad news. He walked over to the corpse and pulled the sheet back. Berto's body was now limp and the eyes were closed. "Why would he do this? Was there a note or anything? And what the hell are you doing here in the first place?"

"It's a long strange story. Did you know Berto was born a girl?"

Jolen, began to chuckle, "If you're making up a story, this is one hell of a start. Do continue, please."

"Alright, this is going to sound like made-up fantasy crap, but it is what really happened. I never had to lie to you before and I've always respected our friendship," I began.

"And you're always involved in some crazy ass shit, so let's hear it," Jolen replied.

"Well, the short version is that Berto was once a woman. The spirit or ghost or whatever of his female person visited me because she wanted revenge on him."

"She wanted to kill him?" asked Jolen.

"Close, she wanted to fuck him," I replied, as he began chuckling again and shaking his head.

"I missed hearing this weird shit, my friend, please proceed."

"Okay, so Berto's female self was pissed and wanted revenge."

"And it looks like she got it," said Jolen, nodding his head towards Berto's corpse. "Why didn't she just do a Lorena Bobbit and cut his dick off? So, she fucked him to death or what?"

"No, like I said, he hung himself, but after she screwed him."

"I just can't see Berto killing himself, he was happy go lucky. It doesn't add up."

"Well," I confessed, "there's some more, too. I was blackmailing him just because I wanted to get my passport and a plane ticket and get the hell out of here. It was a matter of life and death for me. I had evidence of his sex change operation and told him the syndicate would know unless he got me my ticket out. So, I feel responsible. Even if the guy was trying to kill me, it was just syndicate business. He was still my friend and I didn't wish him dead."

"Well, you had to do what you had to do. Hell, you got an evil spirit in you so what can anyone expect? It's kind of cool that it allows you to be able to talk to ghosts and interact with them."

"Yeah," I agreed, "but not all of the ghosts are friendly."

"So, you watched Berto fuck his female ghost?"

"Yes, I had to hide in the closet and be nearby for her to appear in physical form. The Aswang can give spirits more energy, so as long as I was near, she appeared just as a regular girl. It was pretty hot. She was riding him for awhile."

"Would you have banged her if you didn't know it was once Berto?" asked Jolen, smiling.

"Oh yeah" I answered.

"Would you have banged Berto?" he asked, grinning, and we both began to laugh. It was always easy to laugh with Jolen, it felt like old times again. I had forgotten how much I missed him.

"This sucks though; even if we all knew he was a chick, it's not a big deal," said Jolen. "This really sucks." His phone chimed at an incoming text message, which he looked at, "Oh shit, my friend, Lily is on her way here."

"Oh no; I need to leave," I said.

"Well, wait, hold up, I'm not sure how close she is, but just hide here. You don't want to be spotted out there. I'll talk to her and get her out soon, so the place will be yours again. Besides, where the hell would you go?"

"Alright," I resolved, "I trust you. You're like the only person here I ever could trust. What will you tell her about Berto?"

"There's not much to tell. He decided to end his life and was successful."

We heard a knock at the door, "Shit, she's here, hide!" whispered Jolen.

With adrenalin rushing, I scanned around the area like a kid caught up in an intense game of hide and seek. I peeked under the bed, saw room and slid underneath it. I heard the front door open. Sonny and Lily entered.

"So what the fuck happened?" asked Lily, apparently Jolen had told her about Berto by text. Her heels clicked seductively as she walked across the hard wood floor.

"I knocked," began Jolen, "and there was no answer, so I peeked through the window and saw him dangling from the rope."

"Why in the world would he commit suicide?" she asked, angrily. "There's no way. I mean, he was a happy guy. Does this make sense to you?" she asked, before walking to the corpse and lifting the sheet. "Something happened, or someone killed him and made it look like a suicide. Fuck! Sonny, put the body in the van. We'll take care of his funeral our own way. And we'll get to the bottom of this our own way too."

"I can't believe it myself," said Jolen. "And there was no note or anything."

Lily walked closer towards the bed. She stood still for awhile, silent. Turning, she began to speak to Jolen, but I was having trouble concentrating on what was being said. Seeing her feet in the heels, with red toe-nails and the ankle bracelet she always wore on her right ankle was reminding me of belonging to the syndicate. I began to get aroused just looking at the stylish heels and imagining it was Reshi's beautiful feet inside of them.

There were two wide straps that crossed over the upper part of her toes. They narrowed and were bound together in the center, at the bridge of her second and third toe, forming a long "x" across the top of her delicately majestic foot, like a cross-roads. Midway up the elevated shoe was a single wide band, on each side of her foot that rose up to the base of her ankle and crisscrossed at the top of her foot. The bands narrowed after they crossed into a thin strap that circled her ankle, and buckled with delicately small but elegant gold rectangular buckle. At her heel, a strap ran up the back, straight up, with an eyelet at the top for the smaller band to thread through. The straps were white and the sole was eggshell in color. The four-inch high heels were tapered, narrowed to a point at the tip and had symmetrical black lines for an appearance of thinly layered wood.

"So, what do you think?" she asked Jolen, as Sonny secured the sheet around the corpse to drag it out to the van. Her feet were close enough to the bed that I could have reached out and touched them. She was standing right in front of my field of vision. Just hearing the unique tone of her voice was enough to stir up memories of better times. Her voice brought it all back to me, the longing for belonging. The demon in my brain responded to her voice and convinced me it was angelic, the most precious voice in the world. With her close proximity also came the scent of her perfume. It was an aroma of intrigue, lust and elegance. Lily's tastes were refined and distinctive. She only wore the best, in clothing, shoes, perfume and jewelry and her taste was not simply based on what was the most popular or expensive, she had a knack of sifting through the falsities and finding the best. I began to grow aroused looking at her feet. The Aswang in my head was fully aroused and longed to touch, to caress her perfectly shaped feet. I wanted to hold them, to kiss them. It was a temptation that I knew would end in death. It was suicidal. I struggled to think of Reshi instead and the mental tug-of-war became a challenge between my desires and those of the Aswang within me.

"I really don't know," answered Jolen. "Maybe he had some kind of secret or something. It just sucks. I'm going to miss him."

"So you really think he killed himself?" as she adjusted her balance, making the left heel rise slightly from the floor and positioning the weight onto her delicate toes.

"Well, I only know what I saw. He was hanging by a rope," answered Jolen.

"Was the door locked?" she asked.

"No, I just came in the house. What are you thinking?" he asked her. Jolen and Lily shared a closeness that allowed them to know how the other felt without even speaking.

"I'm thinking that somehow, and I'm not entirely sure how, yet, that Tim was involved with this," she said. "We need to find that fucking vermin and kill him."

It was strange and frightening to hear her say my name, and with such venom. Suddenly, a cool chill of air was rising up from my legs. There was something, a presence, under the bed with me. It continued to climb my body and was now at my chest, a cold energy. I began to hear muffled whispering, directly into my ear. There was an itching in my ear but I did not dare to move. "Kiss her foot," said a muffled whisper from somewhere. "Do it, do it, do it!" Being unable to move, or cover my ears for fear of making the slightest noise, I closed my eyes and tried to ignore it.

"I don't know," replied Jolen, "but should we try to find any of Berto's family and let them know?"

I began to feel an irritating itch, like there was a small insect with many legs moving around inside of my ear. My desire to scratch it was so intense that tears began to form in my eyes, but I did not dare to move. "Do it, do it, do it . . . " the whispering voice persisted. It became difficult to tell if the whisper was inside or outside of my head, but I held still. I could endure this without giving away my hidden position, but from the corner of my eye, I saw a rat scurrying along the wall, quickly moving under the bed with me. A rodent was the last thing I wanted around me at this particular time. I could not move and I closed my eyes again.

"They will probably want to see the body; but, I know how you are about family so do what you feel is right, just leave the syndicate out of it."

I held perfectly still, feeling the rat bumping my body as it raced up my side. I wanted to flinch, to push it away but I could not make a sound. The pain of a bite would be impossible to endure, so I braced myself for the searing pain. The lengthy tail grazed my elbow and the large hideous creature stopped beside my face. It's tiny, beady eyes glowed red and the smell of death wafted from its mangy fur. It was the rat from the swimming pool at the Mirage. It stared at me the same way as before, with whiskers vibrating and bared his long, sharp teeth. I thought he might try to bite my face, but he extended his tongue, which was pitch black, and briefly ran it over his teeth. I waited, nervously losing all fascination with Lily's feet and only considering how I would manage to remain silent if this demon rat bit my face.

"He's loaded up," boomed Sonny's voice from the doorway.

"Okay, Jolen, you come with us and help Sonny get him buried. I need to make some calls. We need a replacement, someone that can hopefully fill at least one of Berto's shoes. We also need to find that fuckhead, Tim."

As they walked towards the door, I was able to back away slightly from the rat. When the door shut, my fear transformed to rage and I turned lethal. The rodent turned and scampered along the baseboard of the wall. I slid my way out from under the bed and searched for something, anything to kill the little menace with. I grabbed an unopened umbrella beside the door. It had a two-inch metal tip. I held it like a bayonet and began chasing him along the wall. I didn't just want to kill him. I wanted to give it a slow death. I was in the zone, the manic killing zone. Only two options now existed; either the rat would suffer and die, or I would die trying to make it suffer.

The creature darted and turned, running under a heavy chair in the living room. I flipped the chair with my left hand and attempted to spear him with the umbrella tip clutched in my right. I struck floor. I continued to chase it through the living room and into the kitchen, where it managed to squeeze itself behind the refrigerator. I dropped the umbrella, grabbed the top of the fridge with both hands and pulled it forward until the momentum brought it smashing to the floor in a cacophony of noise. I grabbed the umbrella and continued the frantic chase.

I was bent on killing the rat. It was the only thing that mattered to me. In some strange way, the zeal to murder and torture was a relief. It was an escape from the problems and nervous worries. The fever to kill made things simple, black and white; just kill or die trying. I would burn the entire house down if I had to. My purpose in life was to torture and exterminate this rat, the one with the beady red eyes and black tongue. It was taunting me, dear reader, and it would pay the price. I no longer was even aware of who I was. I only knew it must die. Everything got blurry as the chase continued. More furniture was toppled, including the television stand. The rat was a worthy foe, constantly darting in unexpected directions, causing me to strike floor. Finally, I managed to stomp on its fleshy, long tail and its agile dodging was severely limited. His tiny legs spun in place, as he was only able to slide in a half circle, like a furry wind-shield wiper. I raised the umbrella and managed to strike its rear leg area solidly, before it slipped free and hobbled less quickly. The squeal he released when I struck him was like music to my ears. I had injured the little varmint, and had also drawn blood.

I pounced like a predator and grabbed him with my right hand. He squealed and turned his head to bite my wrist, but I wanted him to know I was more animal than he. I brought him up and closed my mouth around the tip of his nose. I wanted to bite his head off, but I also wanted him to suffer, so I compromised and decided to bite off only half of his head, the dangerous half where his teeth were. His incisors wasted no time in penetrating through the tip of my tongue. The searing pain was so bad that as I screamed, tears flooded from my eyes. I bit back with unrelenting fury. I could hear and feel the texture of crunching bone as I chomped through the tip of his skull. I crunched my teeth through it like a wild animal, while pulling the evil little beast's body away from me. The break was clean and the rat's facial flesh ripped away as I continued to bite and pull the body further away from my face. I viciously turned my head sideways, making the severance complete. Blood spurted from the gaping carnage of rat flesh just below the creature's beady eyes.

His incisors were still completely pierced through my tongue. I dropped the bloody headed rodent to the floor and carefully extracted the long teeth out of my tongue. The pain was immense and only increased my rage. I threw the toothed tip, the diabolical snout, against the nearest wall. I spit blood from my mouth. There was blood everywhere, all down the front of my shirt, blood from my tongue and blood from biting through his nose. His blood was mixed with my blood. I didn't care. There was no disease or sickness he carried that could be worse than what I already had. If anything, the rat would be the one to suffer from my blood. Let that little critter get a taste of my Aswang juice.

I followed the trail of blood. The rat continued to run with the tip of his snout missing and with blood spilling out of the wound. The thing ran like a chicken with its head missing and scurried underneath the bed, where our original encounter had begun. I lunged headfirst on the floor, sliding on the smeared blood. He ran out the other side of the bed, oozing blood. He hit the wall and was moving slower. I crawled closer, grabbing his squirming, blood soaked body. It was a relief to know he could no longer bite me. I held him outwards and squeezed the middle of his body as hard as I possibly could. The blood, guts, and innards erupted from the tip of his head like a grotesque rodent volcano. It brought me joy, dear reader, so much joy, in fact, that I began to smear his bloody carcass, with the entrails hanging, all over my face. It was a primitive form of celebration, granted, but a tremendously satisfying one. This evil little rat who made my life a living hell since I arrived in

Manila was no longer a problem. He had struck me but I struck back with greater fury. It probably had some Aswang, evidenced by the beady eyes and black tongue, but the Aswang in me was greater, stronger and more powerful, all powerful. I had given myself over completely to the power of Aswang and the transformation was nearly complete. I was becoming Aswang.

A blast of water hit me in my face and made me begin to cough and choke. "Tim! Are you in there?" asked a loud voice that I could somehow recognize as being familiar. I continued coughing up the water and shaking my head into clarity. It was similar to being startled awake from a very deep sleep, but much stronger; like coming out of a coma. "Tim? Earth to Tim; do you read me?" the loud voice demanded.

It was Jolen. I focused my fuzzy vision on him, "Yes, yes," I answered. "What the hell happened?" I asked, looking around and noticing that the house was wrecked, furniture toppled, refrigerator toppled and blood all over the floor and on me.

"You've been out of your mind for the past twenty minutes since I got here. Are you sure you're okay now?"

"I think so."

"Why did you destroy the house and eat his bird?" he asked.

"Bird? I thought I killed the rat?" I replied, before noticing the colorful feathers on the floor around me, mixed in with the smeared blood.

"Well, when I came in here, just twenty minutes ago, you were on the floor eating it and smearing it around on your face. Your eyes were out there, like white. I asked why you killed the bird and you just kept repeating over and over in a strange voice, saying the same thing."

"What was I saying? I don't even remember anything."

"You kept saying, 'I loved my bird, so I killed it,' and repeating it, over and over and over. It was freaking me out. That's why I threw the pan of water in your face."

In my mind it was the rat I had killed, but apparently the bird was involved. I knew that anything could happen once I entered an Aswang blackout, so I didn't even try to explain or even rationalize, to myself or Jolen. The phrase he mentioned I recognized as coming from an earlier blackout about Dr. Kryptoforski. Why I was repeating his words I have no idea. Nothing made sense anymore.

"Jolen, I'm sorry. I'm just losing my mind. I didn't want to wreck the house or kill the bird. It's just the demon in me, the Aswang, takes over and I lose myself.

"I know, I'm used to your crazy ass shit," he said, smiling. At that moment I felt like Jolen was the best possible friend a person could ever have. He always stood by me, no matter what, and right now it meant the world to me.

"Well, Lily wants you dead, as you heard while you were hiding under the bed."

"Yes," I replied, sadly.

"I'm going to try something. I might be able to get you out of here in two days. Can you stay here without screwing up?"

"I will try," I replied, now feeling some hope.

"I have never gone behind Lily's back on anything, but my heart, for some reason, tells me this is the right thing to do. I will be back in two days. Get cleaned up, get some rest, clean this mess, don't leave the house and if anyone comes, you hide; got it?"

"Yes," I answered.

"You were checking her shoes out from under the bed, weren't you?" he asked, grinning.

"Maybe"

"And wishing they were on Reshi?"

"Yeah, I miss Reshi. I miss everyone."

"I know you do, Tim. Maybe that's why I'm helping you. You have a loyal heart. See you in two days," he said, before turning and walking out of the door.

CHAPTER XV

Just Wanna See His Face

Well, I'm the Crawlin' King Snake
And I rule my den
I'm the Crawlin' King Snake
And I rule my den

Crawling King Snake—The Doors

Kinsey,

Okay, so it's fairly clear that you're under the influence of Aswang. So what? I have nothing to offer you. It doesn't go away, I can tell you that much. The good news is that eventually you will get used to not getting used to it, if that makes any sense. Maybe reread it until it does. Here's how I look at it sometimes; like you, I used to waste a lot of time thinking about this too. Many famous folks, people brighter, more ambitious and better looking than us have probably been possessed by Aswang throughout history. I mean, the history books aren't going to explain it that way, but it is possible. All the gifted crazies and psychos, Elizabeth Bathory, Hitler, Lord Byron, Jack the Ripper, Jeffrey Dahmer, William Blake, Edgar Allan Poe, Rasputin and many others. In recent times even we have Pol Pot, Kim Jong II, Jim Morrison, Jack Kerouac, Richard Ramirez and lots more. Maybe not all of them had it and not all of them were *killers, but there's a chance that some of them might have. I mean, it's not inconceivable, right?*

I suppose everything is a trade-off. Imagine, and sometimes I do, how cool it is to be possessed by an ancient, evil spirit. We can now see dead people! We have dreams and visions! We can kill with impunity! It's kind of like Prince Hamlet telling his duplicitous friend Rosencrantz that, ". . . there is nothing either good or bad, but thinking makes it so." Our boy Hamlet lived in the royal castle and enjoyed all of the pomp and luxury available in his time; yet, he still felt like he was in a prison. It's your choice, Kinsey, having Aswang on board is either good or bad, depending on how you look at it. I choose to see it as a blessing. Whether it is or not is a whole different story.

I will give you a tip, though. I've learned a few things since Aswang has been with me, full-strength for a longer time than your newbie behind; there are two paths you can follow, love or death. You either learn to love having Aswang, or you can kill yourself. These are the only two options, which will become clearer the longer you have Aswang, the longer it festers through your blood. I sometimes wonder how many sad sacks have fired the barrel of a gun into their mouths because they were possessed by Aswang and couldn't learn to look at it right. They found a permanent solution to a problem that requires a permanent new way of looking at things. It's like a huge serpent that you can either dread, and be swallowed; or, you can learn to ride it and love it, love it to death.

It's your choice Kinsey, so choose wisely. Are you going to fight it and try to pretend like your mind can go back to the good old days of pre-Aswang innocence, or will you accept the change and embrace it? It's Aswang or you, and those are your two options. I choose Aswang and the exciting, unpredictable life that comes along with it. Sure, I'm not who I once was and there's lots of nightmares, but it's never dull and there's travel and adventure involved. If I tried to save my old-self, I would be dead. It's a paradox, Kinsey, like most things that are true. You will need to give your life over to Aswang so that you can save your life.

I'm glad you've come to your senses about not trying to find me. Your haphazard plan to go to Manila and find Lily, though; makes me wonder if you are retarded? She will kill you faster and more painfully than I would. It will involve torture and viciousness beyond your most depraved nightmares. Yes, she's smart. Yes, she's hot, all 100 pounds of her. The thing is; she is a wicked murderess. She kills with a nonchalance that would impress Pol Pot. And not just kill, but make you suffer. Take my advice and do not try to find her. She won't help you with Aswang and will not care about your feelings or problems. Her Aswang is the father of mine and the grandfather of yours. She will pretend to care and only deceive you.

I mean, by all means, travel to Manila. You'll enjoy the city and have a great time. It's a great place and I never would have left myself if Lily wasn't trying to kill me. Visit some of the places I wrote about, the Film Center, Balete Drive, The Giraffe, Mall of Asia and catch a sunset over the bay. Visit Burgos Street and get laid. Just keep a low profile. I will want you to get a little information for me. You'll be doing a little spy stuff. Nobody will know or care who you are, so it's perfect. I need to know a few things about the syndicate, so I'll send you directions once you are there. Don't mess it up or blow me off. Let's just say I know people there and it would not be in your best interest. Besides, you're curious to see Lily anyways, right? It's a win, win, Kinsey . . . win, win.

Sincerely,
Monkey Man

I looked around the house, realizing I had made one hell of a mess chasing the rat. I do not recall messing around with the bird, but the rat I know was real because the tip of my tongue was still pierced and bleeding from his sharp, long incisors. Furniture was toppled in the living room and the kitchen was a disaster zone, with blood and feathers smeared all over the white linoleum. Since I would be settling in for two days, I decided to clean up. The first job of major importance would be getting the refrigerator upright again. Hopefully, it still worked.

I tried to grip it at the bottom, wedging my fingers in between the floor and the top of the cumbersome appliance. It was tough to keep my grip, but using my leg power, I was able to bring the upper end off of the floor. The door swung open and I could hear things spilling out, but screw it, I had to get it upright. I could clean up the spills afterwards. I continued to hoist it up, and pushed it backwards, where it finally fell in place with a loud thud. I found the plug end and got it back into the socket, hearing the compressor hum to life.

I was soaked with sweat and thirsty. I quickly pulled the fridge door open, turning to look for a bottle of water. As I turned, my feet slipped on what appeared to be oily noodles that spilled onto the floor. My feet shot out from under my weight, suddenly, becoming airborne until the back of my skull cracked onto the hard floor. I was instantly knocked out, put down for the count by a slimy overturned bowl of noodles.

When I sat up, I had no idea how much time had passed. I felt around the throbbing knot on the back of my skull, checking my hand for blood. There was no indication of blood, but the size of the lump was impressive. I slowly and cautiously rose to my feet and walked to the living room, trying to fully regain my senses. I sat on the couch but the heat of the house was getting unbearable. If there was air conditioning it wasn't working. I opened two windows and also opened the front door, leaving it open to try to get a breeze to come through. I removed my t-shirt, using it to wipe the sweat from my forehead and neck. The open door helped a little, until a large snake slithered up to the threshold of the doorway. I froze in shock, not sure to chase it away and risk being bit or make some noise to scare it away. Before I could make up my mind, however, it was in the house, slithering authoritatively, in an S pattern, across the bare wood floor.

I was frozen in place, staring in disbelief. The snake was light brown and rather large and lifted its hooded head, like some kind of cobra. He didn't appear afraid, and even turned towards my direction. He acted as if it were his house, watching me and wondering why I was here. I moved to the couch, now standing on it, wondering how the hell I was going to get him back outside. There was plenty of scattered clutter and an overturned chair and coffee table for him to maneuver around, which he did, gracefully. He slid around the obstacle, head lifted, tongue occasionally flickering, then disappeared behind the overturned television stand.

It was now or never. I made a quick dash from the couch and grabbed the trusty umbrella that was in the kitchen, as I picked it up, I saw the brown, glistening scales quickly slithering out the opposite side of the television stand and turning towards the couch. I ran back to the couch before he cut me off, clutching the umbrella like a spear. The scales of the serpentine beast appeared to shine as metallic armor as it continued to slide towards the couch. It slithered, confidently, to the front of the couch, stopping to face me with elevated head. I stood, transfixed by the rhythmic movement and machine-like appearance. The snake did not belong in the house; it was difficult to balance the incongruity of such a primitive, ancient and wild creature being inside a domestic space. This vile representative of the origins of evil did not belong inside of a house. Yet, here he was, poised before me.

The beady eyes of his elevated, teetering to and fro head connected to my eyes. It was not a connection of friendship, or even acknowledgement of one another. No, it was a contest of wills. It was hunter and the hunted, only who was which was unclear yet, as if two strange dogs were about to fight and sizing each other up. The gaze evoked sheer burning wrath from both participants. The cobra hated me and I detested him. My mind was colored with red rage as the scaly shroud surrounding his head flared wider, making him appear larger and more threatening. The hatred I felt towards the scaly, slithering intruder increased as I stared into his eyes, as if it reflected from his menacing hooded shroud and rebounded back towards me. It became an ever increasing mutual exchange of hatred, the black energy flowing from and to one another through our eyes. His pink tongue flickered, as his body and head remained motionless. I was dimly aware that there was growling coming from my throat, a low, steady rumble, rising from deep in my chest, like that of a dog prior to sinking its teeth into an enemy. During our stand-off, stare-down, I forgot all about the umbrella I clutched in my hand. He was within striking distance, if I moved swiftly and struck with precision, the flamboyant little fuck didn't stand a chance. I tightened my grip on the wooden handle, continuing to stare steadily into his eyes, not wanting to give away the death strike that I was about to deliver. He read my mind, though, and leaned backwards to take his head further away. My opportunity to strike was slipping away if I waited a second longer.

Before I swung, the cobra quickly lurched forward with his head, spitting and propelling venom with the momentum. He spat poison into my face a second before my death strike, and I was instantly blind. It felt like the gentle sprinkle of someone dipping their hand in a bowl of water and flicking their finger towards my face, only this was not water, dear reader. This was like battery acid to the eyes. The burning increased with each second. I wildly and blindly swung the umbrella towards the vicinity of the snake, but made no contact. I needed to rinse my eyes and it now felt like molten lava had been poured directly into both. I had no idea where the little bastard was now and feared trying to navigate my way to the sink because I knew he still wanted to bite me. The burning sensation seeped further into my eyes, working its way back into the sockets. The pain became excruciating enough to consider gouging out my own eyes in hopes of relief. I screamed and buried my head into the corner of the couch.

"Tim, what the fuck are you doing here?" I heard her ask. It was Lily's voice. The unique, sultry voice of a diabolical angel; I was delighted and despaired simultaneously. The immense joy at hearing her say my name was soon clouded with the stark realization that she would kill me.

"Lily, be careful, there's a cobra in here. I shit you not! He spit venom in my eyes," I warned.

"Yeah, yeah, whatthefuckingever, Tim; you're so full of bullshit fantasies. What's your plan, distract me and run like a blinded bitch?" she asked, with a sarcastic chuckle.

"No, it's true; my eyes are on fire and it burns like hell," I replied earnestly.

"That's what she said," quipped Lily.

The fear and adrenalin of the situation, combined with the unexpected surprise of her words caused me to burst out laughing. Even though she would soon murder me, Lily could still make me laugh. It felt wonderful to laugh again, even though I could not see.

"Listen, I don't see a snake in here, so bring your sweet ass to the kitchen and we'll get those eyes rinsed out," she said, taking my hand and leading me. Her delicate fingers around mine, accompanied by the sexy click clacking of her heels on the floor, sent emotional electricity straight up my arm and directly through my heart. "Satan only knows what you got in your eyes. You must be having another psycho episode again, hot stuff," she said, before guiding my head to the sink. "Hold still and I'll pour water over your eyes. Try to open them a bit, to flush them." Her nimble fingers caressed my temple as she filled a glass and poured water with her other hand, a steady stream, over and over. As the water ran across my eyes, I opened them. The burning soothed a little and some blurred vision was returning. After opening and closing them countless times under the running water, I was partially able to distinguish the elegant beauty of Lily's face.

"Lily, are you going to kill me?" I asked, resolved to get matters of life and death out into the open.

She chuckled, "I was, especially since you called me a phony cunt the other day, but maybe I won't. Quit asking or I will," she said, now staring into my eyes. "Do you feel better now?"

"Yes, thanks," I replied.

"Good, because I want to fuck you now," she revealed, matter-of-factly.

"Well," I answered, slightly caught off guard, "I think I can work that into my schedule, sure," I answered, drying off my eyes with a dish towel. The irritation was minor now, though I could see okay.

"That's a good boy toy," she smiled, invitingly, tilting her head. I forgot all about my eyes, the burning, the cobra and even my love for Reshi in that moment. My entire being was focused upon Lily's radiant beauty and her smile that gave me the green light to touch her. I was horny and her Aswang was making mine aroused. I leaned towards her, gently cupping the back of her petite neck and guiding her lips to my own. When our lips touched, electricity coursed through my body and my hands moved to her hips where I clutched her slender frame and pulled her hips against my own. I began to kiss her under her ear as she arched her head back and whispered, "Fuck me, Tim."

I held her hip bones while grinding against the crotch of her denim skirt. I ran my tongue from the base of her neck, as she continued arching her head back, up to the underneath area of her chin. Her skin was as smooth as porcelain and she smelled of lilacs, cherry blossoms and pure sex. I could feel her pert nipples against my chest, one firm body against another lean, toned body. She moaned in a purring sound and my rod became as hard as steel. I felt like a lion again and she was my lioness.

I held her tightly against my crotch and lifted on her hips, all one-hundred and five pounds of her. I gently carried her into the living room and guided her slowly down to the hard wood floor. I knew she would kill me and dispose of my body without thinking twice after the sex, but I didn't care. What a way to go! I think Shakespeare once said it best as, 'tis better to have screwed her and be killed than to have not screwed her. I'd be the praying mantis because, well, she is a dirty, sexy bitch. Her body was flesh of pleasure, dear reader, and I was Kubla Khan, soon to taste of the honeydew and drink the milk of paradise.

She lay on the floor, her green eyes staring wantonly into mine. I slid my body down her body until my chest was near her knees. She raised both legs simultaneously, bending her knees with precision until they were all the way up against her chest. Her movement caused the skirt to ride up to her waist and her willowy, shapely legs exposed her black, lace, French cut panties. There was already a spot of moisture in the center. My brain began to reel with passion, there were flashes of red. I felt powerful as I pulled her tiny panties up to her knees and down over her heels. I felt as if I were about to kill someone, like a god. I became filled with Aswang, and I was horny. Something powerful held the reins to my brain. Only the kind of rage I felt wasn't a killing rage, it was a lustful rage, full-blown animalistic, carnal passion. It was the glowing, all encompassing horniness of puberty at its zenith, multiplied by a thousand.

"Fuck me," she said, softly but with a sense of urgency. It was the sensual sound of urgency that only Lily can utter. It wasn't expressed in the words but in the sound of her angelic voice, a voice that could be discerned from the chorus of a million lustful angels. Both of her legs remained elevated, folded back in perfect symmetry, with her knees positioned just below her perfectly pert breasts. The lust flowed through my veins like a river of blood coursing through Babylon. She was ripe for ravishing and I no longer knew where I was or even who I was. My identity was lost at sea and the demon of passion now steered the ship. I placed each of my hands on the underside of her thighs and pushed her legs downwards, gently but firm. They lowered easily to each side of her hourglass torso. She moaned, looking at me with her sparkling green eyes, cooing, "I want you, Daddy."

I wanted to fuck her forever. I wanted to fuck her to death.

I continued to press downwards on her thighs, feeling her toned hamstrings in the grip of my palms. It was as if the room began to hum, as the force of my thrusts increased in speed. The entire house, already warm, became thickly humid, like the inside of a terrarium. We were two bodies, locked in a pinnacle of pleasure. It was everything I wanted, but I was not there. My body became one with the most dangerous, vindictive bitch in all of Asia. I was Yin and she was Yang. She moaned, arching her neck and I could feel the vagina walls squeezing, again and again. The warm milk of paradise flowed in warm, thick abundance.

I released my grip on her thighs. The white handprint impressions of her flesh showed on each leg. "Roll over," I ordered. The cool air made it feel like ice. "I want to take you from behind, baby girl."

"Yes, Daddy," she said, compliantly, rolling on the bed to her stomach. She rose to her hands and knees, arching her back and slowly backing up her precious, firm Asian ass. Her tremendous beauty and the power of filling her with so much pleasure made me feel like god.

From the corner of my eye, I saw glistening motion quickly sliding under the nearby chair. It appeared metallic and scaly. I could not see under the chair from my vantage point, but I knew the cobra was still lurking in the house. I didn't quite care because I was with the most evil girl in the world. There was no fear. I was no longer myself. I was god and god wanted to continue with Lily until one of us could continue no longer, or died.

I guided her downwards, keeping inside of her, so she now lay on her stomach. Propping myself up, with my hands on her shoulder blades, I arched my back and continued to thrust. Her body was flattened against the floor, supporting nearly all of my weight, as I continued in and out of her, harder and faster. "Tim, I want you to cum," she moaned.

I began to drill harder and faster. I saw the snake again, from the corner of my left eye. He was sliding quickly along the base of the wall, heading towards the kitchen. He soon was out of my field of vision, and Lily was too caught up in the pleasure and ecstasy of the moment to notice, as was I. I noticed, but who cared? I had silky black hair and the perfect back with Chinese letters tattooed on the right shoulder, and was buried inside of her.

I was dripping with sweat, and beads fell from my forehead onto the smooth porcelain skin of Lily's back. Passionate, rage-filled lust consumed every fiber and cell of my being. I continued to raise my hips and plunge them downwards, over and over. She raised her hips up from the floor, while turning to meet my gaze with her green eyes. She pouted her lips, sensuously. I adjusted by leaning back, and looking back at her.

And I continued. Her eyes closed as I pounded with renewed fury. I could feel her body begin to spasm, tightening around me in a succession of tantalizing squeezes. The room began to shimmer. I could not last longer.

I drove into her as deep as possible, one final time. I could feel the backed-up intensity of the soon to be released magma welling up inside of me. I groaned in ecstasy as I felt like I was falling through the sky while looking into her eyes where Roman candles threw spider shaped sparks from the scintillating green orbs. My body locked up as I shouted, "I'm, I'm,"

A sharp pain struck during the orgasm, as if a dagger had been plunged into my scrotum. I now went from groaning to screaming in pain. The intensity of the affliction instantly overrode the joy. I pulled out, trying to find the source of the unbearable pain. I scrambled to my feet.

I felt weight and violent tugging, and upon looking down, noticed a trickle of blood running down my inner-right thigh. Suddenly, I saw the horrid source of my affliction. The serpent twirled as its jaw remained clamped on my nutsack, like a pit-bull from the depths of Hell. I screamed in horror as the cobra's beady eyes stared up into mine. He hung, twirling and dangling like a menacing dog playing tug-of-war. I instinctively raised a fist to pummel his head, but realized that hitting him while his teeth were in my flesh would only cause greater damage and pain.

I reached down and pinched the sides of his scaly, menacing face. I pinched his jaw as hard as possible, hoping for the mouth to open and extract the teeth. The pain grew more intense, as if my entire genital area was on fire from the inside out. His venom spread into my sack. I squeezed harder, hoping to crush his skull, but his mouth remained locked. I let go and gripped his body just below the head and pulled him downwards, hard. The pain became more excruciating as I felt some of the sack flesh being ripped apart. Blood began to trickle down the insides of both of my thighs. I dropped the snake to the ground and watched it slither towards the front door, leaving an "S" patterned trail of fresh blood. I then collapsed to the floor in painful agony.

"What the hell do you got going on now?" asked Jolen.

I looked up from my fetal position on the floor. I was naked, with blood and burning pain at my scrotum. "Where's Lily?" I asked.

"She's the reason I'm here. I have good news, but damn, you might bleed to death. What the fuck did you do to yourself?"

I winced in pain, just trying to examine my balls, "It hurts," I yelled.

"Looks like you got into Berto's fishing tackle. There's a lure stuck in your nutsack; what the hell?" asked Jolen, pointing and beginning to giggle.

I looked down and was shocked to see the source of my pain. There was a yellow fishing lure with red and black polka dots on it. The treble hook was caught up in the skin of my sack, where blood trickled out. I tried to remove the two hooks piercing the skin, but the barbs on the tips made an easy extraction impossible. "Ouch, motherfucker!" I screamed, still twisting on the lure.

"Well, at least you found something constructive to do with your time," laughed Jolen, "What's the saying; teach a man to fish, and he'll snag his sack?" I could not help but to also begin chuckling at the absurdity of my predicament, despite the pain.

"I swear I was with Lily and there was a snake in here; he bit me while I was screwing her!" I protested.

"It's all fun and games until the snake bites the sack," he quipped, adding, "I don't see any snake, and I've been with Lily the past two hours, my friend."

I gritted my teeth, pinched the skin near the hooks, and twisted the barbs until they came out, unwillingly. "Goddamn, that hurts!" I shouted, throwing the lure at the wall.

"Well nobody ever said the catch of the day would be easy," said Jolen, beginning to laugh, "Looks like your Moby Dick was a sperm whale," he said, now laughing harder, pointing at the shower of semen drops on the floor.

"Well, I swear it was real," I said, loudly, "It was just as real as you and I talking here right now; her voice, her hair and everything! I was banging her right here!"

Jolen continued chuckling, shaking his head, "Well, it looks like she's gone now, my friendly fisherman. But don't worry, there's plenty of fish in the sea," he said, beginning to laugh hard again.

Even with the pulsating pain in my sack, he was now making me laugh too. We began laughing very hard together, just like we used to.

Finally, he managed to stop and handed me some paper towels from the kitchen. "Use these to put direct pressure on the cuts and get the bleeding to stop."

I took the towels and crumpled one, holding it against my nuts. The damage wasn't bad and the blood was only trickles, but the sensitivity of the skin in that area made it extra painful.

"Damn, I wish I could be normal." I said, "Hey, you said you were coming back here in two days? I was out of my mind; has two days gone by?"

"No, just like two hours; I came back early because I have some good news for you."

"I could use some; and I hope this isn't another fishing joke. Did Lily say she doesn't want me killed?" I asked.

"No, but I have this," he said, pulling my passport out of his back pocket.

"Holy shit!" I exclaimed.

"Yeah, and we need to move fast. I have the syndicate credit card to buy you a plane ticket."

"Does Lily know?"

He chuckled, "My friend, I will deal with her later. I'm taking a big risk here, but I always follow my heart. You're my friend, and even though you're crazy as batshit, I've come to like you. If I like someone, that's that. I can't let you be killed. Lily will be pissed for awhile, but she loves me. It'll be okay."

"I don't think this spirit I carry, Aswang, will leave me even if I am far from here."

"Why do you say that?"

"Because I will never stop missing being in the syndicate; and when my brain begins churning over it, that's when Aswang steps in and takes control."

"Yes, I doubt you will ever forget Reshi either, my friend; but, at least where you're going there won't be a price on your head. You can do all the fishing you want and nobody will shoot at you."

"Yeah," I replied, now grinning again, "What a relief!"

Jolen chuckled, "Speaking of relief, that's quite a load you sprayed on the floor."

I took a shower and put some ointment on my sack. The bleeding finally stopped, though there was still some pain. I also rummaged through Berto's wardrobe to find some clean clothes that fit. Jolen was on the phone, apparently with the airline, while I got ready. "Hey," he called, covering the phone with his free hand, "What city do you want to get back to?"

"Orlando," I answered, suddenly realizing that I had been gone a long time, months. I had no job and no home to go back to. Maybe I could plead mercy with the college and spin them a heart wrenching tale of some sort. Maybe they would give me my teaching job back, maybe. I just didn't feel like a professor anymore. My whole life was different now. I had seen things and done things that changed me. It was like being a kid again and discovering Santa is not real and when the holiday rolls around, you want to believe Santa is real, like before, but no matter how much you try, you can't.

Jolen continued speaking in Tagalog into the phone before hanging up and looking at me, "We need to hurry. Just cram a paper towel in your undies in case your sack starts bleeding."

"What about the security x-ray machine?"

"Tell them you didn't want to leave your sack unattended," he said, before we both began laughing. "There's a flight to the U.S. leaving in ninety minutes, so we're already late."

"Well," I replied, patting my empty pockets, "I think I'm all packed."

As Jolen drove towards the airport, I looked around at the city of Manila for what might have been my last time. We were stuck in a traffic jam and I had an epiphany. I was in love with this city; the city that mirrored the versatility between extremes like Lily and Reshi; one being dangerous and cruel, the other beautiful and kind. It was a paradox of wealth and opulence mixed with poverty and crumbs; beauty and ugliness; coldness and kindness; energetic and lazy; busy and idle; loving and indifferent all crammed and condensed into a small area called Manila. The sounds, the colors, the food, the aromas and mostly the people all made it clear; there is no other city like Manila. It is the crown jewel beehive of Asia. It's not all pretty and it may never make the top tourist destination's lists, but once you are there awhile, the real beauty reveals itself. It is a city of beautiful people, the majority with hearts of gold.

I smiled, listening to all the horns blowing. Near the sidewalk, an elderly man pedaled past on a wobbly wheeled bicycle with baskets of strange looking produce. Near the corner, a rooster was chained to the pole of a street sign. A woman nearby sat on a crate, not a care in the world, smiling while eating a bowl of steaming noodles. Businessmen briskly walked by her in a hurry, with determined looks on their faces and wearing expensive suits while swinging leather brief cases. There were crowds of people pocketed around people selling things, bean curd, juice in a bag, candy, pastries and other unknown edibles and trinkets. Only in Manila can you see so much energy condensed into one corner of a block. Be it New York, Miami or Los Angeles; the energy is not as condensed, original and vivid as it is in Manila, not to mention safer. Manila is a delightful smorgasbord for the senses once you get used to it.

"This place is awesome," I blurted out, "Just so much energy everywhere."

"Because it's so crowded," replied Jolen, before giving the horn a few beeps.

"Maybe, but when the people are mostly kind, it all works out," I added.

"Works out to get laid; that's all most sex-pats are here for."

"Maybe," I chuckled, "I just love Manila. Give me a decent job and I will stay here forever."

"Yes, but powerful people want you dead here, don't forget."

"Well, maybe someday they will forget about me and I can come back to stay."

"Well, you could go away for awhile and maybe come back. I just worry you're going to mess up somehow with that Aswang spirit inside of you."

"Yes, maybe it'll go away if I am far away, then I can return."

"Okay, General Macarthur," said Jolen, chuckling, "Just know you always have a friend here. I am going to miss you, Tim."

"Yes, I'm going to miss you, too and the city of Manila. As messed up as things were here, I feel like I belong."

"Maybe you do; so go away for awhile, pull your head together, and then come back. You have my e-mail, so stay in touch," he said, parking the car at the international departure gate of Ninoy Aquino International Airport. "Let me deal with the people at the counter. Your tourist visa is expired, but I know some people here. Just sit in the crowd because I know Lily has given your bounty picture to people here. Once we get the ticket, you should be safe."

The Filipina girl behind the Delta counter was not only very pretty, but she also knew Jolen. Her eyes lit up and a smile appeared as she waved to him. Of course, one could never be sure with Jolen because he had an irresistible charm that people responded to even meeting him the first time. I went and found a place to sit as he approached the counter and talked to her. After about ten minutes, he waved me over to the counter. Jolen introduced me to Marie as she smiled and printed my boarding pass. "You can follow me, sir," she said, smiling. I turned to Jolen and he was giving me a beaming smile with his arms extended. We hugged and I patted him on the back.

"Thank you for all of your help, with everything. Thank you for your friendship."

"No problem, Tim; go back home and let the dust settle here, then come back home here. E-mail me, okay?"

"Will do; I'm going to miss you."

He smiled, "Yeah, that's what they all say. Go get your plane."

As I walked down the passenger boarding bridge, I thought about Jolen. Not only did he risk a lot to help me, but he also stuck with me through my most insane moments, eating a fortune teller's heart, digging up a corpse, eating rats and birds and snagging a fishing lure's treble hook on my own sack. He never judged me, just cracked some funnies and continued being my friend. He's also the only one who understood the depth of my loyalty to the syndicate and my love for beautiful Reshi. He recognized my passion towards both.

The flight to Japan was uneventful and I spent most of it drifting in and out of sleep. It was the long one, from Japan to Atlanta, where things got weird. I thought maybe the further we traveled over the ocean, further away from the Philippines, that the influence of Aswang might be less and less.

The 747 flight from Japan to Atlanta was crowded, every seat was occupied, but I really did not mind. I was happy to have a seat next to the aisle. The first hour in the air, most passengers passed the time with a variety of diversions, some read magazines or books, some tuned in to the movies from the mini-screens on the backs of the seats in front of them, business people pecked away at spreadsheets on their laptops with cocktails close at hand. I decided to follow protocol, attaching the complimentary ear plugs to the armrest and searching for a movie. It felt good to fit in, just another traveler on his way back to the U.S. I wasn't a killer; I wasn't possessed by a demon; I was just a regular Joe on a flight back to America.

I settled in and began to watch the comedy, or pretend to watch, since my mind couldn't focus. The stewardess came by with the cart and I got a cup of coffee (after an underwhelming meal) that was weak as hell, making it easier to fall asleep. The lights in the cabin were dimmed and I began to doze, falling in and out of the movie which I had no clue as to what was going on. Eventually, I opened one eye and saw most of the other passengers were dozing as well.

While checking down the darkened aisle to see if there was any vacancy in the bathroom, I noticed that a few rows of seats before the bathroom, there was one head turned back, staring right at me, grinning. It was a woman who looked vaguely familiar, but the cabin was dark, making it difficult to identify her. As I leaned forward, narrowing and focusing my eyes, she gave a friendly little wave. I waved back, but was shocked when I realized she looked just like Sheryl, the girl Lily killed in the iron maiden box and the one whose corpse I dug up.

"It can't be," I thought to myself, "It has to be some girl who looks just like her. Why would she wave to me, though?" As I continued to gaze down the aisle at her, the cabin seemed to get darker, and her face grew pale, the whiteness giving it an eerie glow in the surrounding darkness.

"Help me" she appeared to mouth with her lips, and then continued smiling at me. Her eyes became white, glowing orbs, like a zombie, as she grinned wider. All other passengers appeared to be sleeping, and just her head alone was turned back towards me, with its glowing white eyes. It became creepier than I could stand. I shielded my eyes with my hand as a visor, and just stared down at the floor.

I tried to relax, but my mind was racing and restless. It felt like the ominous quiet before a storm. I was having the familiar feeling again, the feeling of losing control of myself. I kept gazing at the aisle floor. As the stewardess pushed the beverage cart down the aisle, I saw something large and furry scurry away from the noise. I just caught the whiskers and beady red eyes, tiny, for a second as he rushed past my feet. I turned, looking back, and caught a glimpse of his fleshy, pink tail making an "S" pattern as he continued to run towards the back of the plane. Somehow, the rat that haunted me all through my time in Manila was going home with me on the same plane.

The squeaky wheels on the beverage cart matched the wobbly wheels that turned in my brain. The stewardess was taking drink orders from passengers in the row in front of me. Her cart was positioned right beside my seat, trapping me. As I stared at it, I realized how closely it resembled the iron maiden box that Sheryl was buried in. From somewhere inside the cart, I heard a feint plea for help, "God, help me," she cried. The stewardess pushed the cart further down, to my relief, and now stood beside me.

"Would you like something to drink, sir?" she asked, smiling. Even the stewardess looked somehow familiar. She was young, Filipina, and beautiful. She turned her body to face me and half of it appeared to be missing. I now realized it was Giselle, the girl Sonny and I had suspended upside-down and sawed completely in half. "Water, juice, blood?" she asked.

"Uh, no thank you," I replied, nervously and now sweating. I had to look away from her and was relieved to hear the wheels squeaking further down the aisle. The air in the cabin was becoming so thick, it felt like one could cut a slice of it and keep it in a plastic baggie for later. I knew the things I saw could not be real, but they were there before my eyes. When it's all you have, it's real.

I looked around the cabin to see if anyone else noticed the rat or the half of a stewardess. Everywhere I looked, I saw victims and villains from my time in Manila. Three rows ahead, to the right, sat Professor Coker, with a laptop on his serving tray. He was the first one I killed, and I recalled how liberating the slices felt. There was blood running out of his neck as he sat staring at the laptop. I looked at the screen and saw my dog on there, Blackie, sitting stoutly and letting out syncopated single barks.

A passenger on the other side got up to use the restroom and I could see the organs visible in his abdomen. It was Perillo, the one who we let the rat eat through. Further down the aisle, just past the bathroom, a tiny girl in a ballet tutu, Tik-Tik, performed pirouettes in the aisle, as a little boy, Seven, clapped his hands and counted her rotations. Directly in my row, but across the aisle, sat two men wearing bright wigs, looking like ghoulish drag queens. It was the two guards, Blondie and Red. They both had blood trickling from their mouths. When Blondie smiled at me, gun smoke rose from her mouth.

I was surrounded by living testimonies of my violent and insane experience in Manila. There was no escape. The flight was long and the cabin was small and crowded. I began to feel like god again. *Why should I be afraid or have any regrets? I will kill all these people again, and enjoy it twice. Maybe I will carve out their hearts and eat them.*

I felt a cold hand suddenly clasp my forearm on the armrest. I turned. It was Lucy, the Japanese mustache girl, sitting right beside me. She was the one who originally touched me and who I thought had transferred a spirit from way back at the Mirage. She now looked at me, holding my arm, smiling. Her eyes filmed over, completely going white. She began to chuckle and I could see and smell sulfur in her breath.

Oh no you don't, I shouted. *I'm going to twist your fucking head off!* I screamed, feeling the killing rage rise through the warm blood coursing through my mad brain. I grabbed her throat in both hands and began squeezing, hard. I rose from my seat for better leverage, shaking her violently while squeezing her windpipe harder. I felt a sharp pain in my side. There were wires stuck to my body. As I collapsed to the floor, the air marshal who fired the tazer was upon me.

CHAPTER XVI
Sweet Virginia

The answer is never the answer.
What's really interesting is the mystery.
If you seek the mystery instead of the answer, you'll always be seeking . . . .
The need for mystery is greater than the need for an answer.

—Ken Kesey

Kinsey, Kinsey, Kinsey; how does your mind garden grow? With rodent stain and psycho brain and all aboard the crazy train, or the crazy plane, the crazy plane to Manila. It sounds like you're surviving and adjusting there. Once you get used to the overpopulation, the poverty and the noise, you can begin to appreciate the underlying beauty. It's a bit like the thorns of a rose; you have to get past a few pricks and then you encounter the sublime beauty. What makes Manila most attractive, in my opinion, is the people. Pound for pound, the people of Manila are the kindest you can hope to find in such a large city.

Now that you've had your fill of getting drunk and getting laid and eating crispy pata (didn't I tell you that it was the bomb?), I have a friend there who I want you to meet. Her name (yes, it's a girl, you desperate fool) is Tessa and she is a very close friend. You can find her at the North Cemetery. Go there in the late afternoon on any given late afternoon. Stay near or in La Loma and stay until after dark. Either she or her friend, Flash will be there. He's a nice old guy, former boxing champ. Don't ask why or any stupid questions; just do it. And don't worry about how she'll recognize you. If you really have Aswang, she will find you. Write to me after you meet with her.

Just for the record, this is where you actually enter the story. If the journey happened as it's written, then maybe you will stop asking me if it's true or not. Crazy times and I don't regret them, though I do feel bad about choking Dan. Dr. Taylor, not so much remorse, since he has his rock and refuge. Something in me really abhors religious people. I mean, I kind of liked the guy and he meant well, but once I snapped into a blackout, well, it's a miracle he lived through it. Kinsey, for you getting possessed by Aswang is a blessing since no matter how cool you tried to act, you were a geek. Now you got a dark edge. You might not be happy, but at least you're less of a dork. That's something to be happy about now, isn't it?

It was hard to tell who was who during the interrogation at the airport. There were cops, TSA agents, FBI agents and anyone else with a uniform and a gun. I was handcuffed behind my back and roughly led to a chair at a table where I was asked an endless barrage of questions for hours. Things did not start off well and only got worse. They also lumped me up pretty good while transporting me from the plane to the terminal office.

Officer Kowder and Officer Blake did their good cop, bad cop routine on me. Kowder was the tough guy and Blake was my buddy, at least that's the roles they played. Mainly, they kept on wanting to know why I choked the lady sitting next to me on the plane, Heather Gortney, a middle aged, obese and ugly housewife from Minnesota. They would not buy the truth, which I told them again and again. The truth was that I did not recall or even know that I was choking anyone.

Blake leaned on the table in front of where I sat, smiling, "Timmy, your passport indicates that you overstayed your tourist visa limit there by a few months, what the hell were you doing there?"

"I was rat hunting, William." I answered, impatiently.

"The name's not William and I can't write poetry to save my life. I'm just curious why you were there so long, that's all, Tim."

Kowder stood beside him, glaring at me, "Listen, dickhead, your clever responses aren't going to win you any favors with the judge. Tell us why you decided to choke Mrs. Gortney? Your Filipina gal was fucking other expats so you took it out on an innocent housewife from Minnesota, am I close?"

"I thought she was someone else," I answered.

"Who did you think she was?" he demanded.

Your mother, Officer Chowder, I replied, grinning.

"Cute," he replied, his red skin showing signs of angry pressure, "Looks like your clever ass will rot in jail for a long time."

"He's right, Tim," interrupted the calmer, gentler voice of Blake, "Why don't you help us understand better; why did you think she was someone else?"

"Because, like I've been telling you guys again and again, I'm not always in control. Something takes over my brain."

"That's a crock of shit," bellowed Kowder, "You're just a pathetic coward who gets off on choking women. You were probably doing it so much in the Philippines you forgot you were on an airplane bound for the States."

Kowder was beginning to piss me off. I wanted to choke him but the cuffs were a problem. The endless same questions, the handcuffs, the lack of food and sleep were all taking their toll. My mind was seething, bubbling with rage and all I could see was the color red. I was beginning to lose myself.

"You better stop looking at me with that dumb-ass stare," warned Kowder.

I was suddenly outside of myself, watching the three of us as an observer. A strange voice erupted from my mouth, speaking in a language I did not know, but it sounded familiar, like Tagalog.

"Cute," returned Kowder, "Why don't you can the theatrical horseshit and answer the fucking question?"

Your uncle really messed you up, didn't he Kowder? came a voice now speaking English through me. *He made you do bad things to him.*

"Blake, go someplace," he resolved, "I need five minutes alone with this scumbag."

"Tim," reasoned Blake, "be smart about this. Your lack of cooperation is just bringing more jail time. Help us out here; help yourself out and we can all call it a day."

Here's the thing, I began, displaying a spirit of cooperation, *Chowder is still insecure because he used to enjoy his alone time with Uncle David.*

"Fuck you!" shouted Kowder, before leaning across the table and clubbing the side of my head with his hand, as Blake pulled him away.

I know it was hard to swallow, I continued, *But it's true, isn't it, Chowder?*

I felt the impact of his second blow, but remember little else. When I regained consciousness, I was restrained in a gurney in what looked like a hospital room. My left eye was swollen nearly shut and my entire head felt bruised. I tried to move but my arms were restrained and my torso and chest were also strapped down. An I.V. bag had tubes going to my arm. I drifted in and out of consciousness and though I wanted to yell for someone, anyone, just to loosen the restraints, the effort and ambition involved in the act of shouting was more than I could muster up. So I embraced the claustrophobic panic and endured the moments of being awake with determined stoicism and apathy. My trapped limbs reminded me of being buried alive back at the Manila Film Center, a memory I did not wish to revisit.

It could have been hours or days, but eventually a doctor appeared. He was smiling and holding a clipboard. "Hi Tim, I'm Dr. Jones, the intake counselor. I am wondering if it would be okay to ask you some questions?"

"Hi, I'm fine with questions, Doc, I have a few myself; like, how long will I have to stay strapped in like this?"

"Well," he began, motioning to the nurse, "We can get you out of them right now." He said, instructing the nurse to free the captive. It felt wonderful to be able to move my limbs and sit upright. "What other questions do you have, Tim?"

"Can I get some water? I'm thirsty as hell," I pleaded. The nurse returned with a plastic cup and a plastic pitcher of water. I gulped and refilled the glass.

"That's a side-effect of the sedative we had to give you. You came here pretty agitated and banged up."

"Excuse my language, but where the hell am I, Doc? Is this a jail?"

He laughed, "No, this is not a jail, but it is a maximum security health unit."

"Am I in the United States?"

"Yes, Tim, right now you are at the Hoffman Forensic Treatment Facility; they brought you here from the Orlando Airport two days ago. We are a mental health treatment facility for those patients who have been accused of felony crimes. Basically, we have about 150 patients, contained in eight different wings, who have possibly committed felonies and who have been determined incompetent to stand trial."

"So, I landed in the nut house?"

Dr. Jones chuckled, "That's not what we prefer to call it, Tim. Is it okay if I ask you a few questions?"

"Sure Doc, have at it."

"Why do you think you ended up here with us?"

"I don't know, Doc; I think I choked a lady on the airplane. The thing is I really didn't know I was doing it. I didn't even know the lady or anything. Is she okay?"

"I believe she will be okay, Tim. Does it happen frequently; that you act without knowing what you are doing?" he asked, showing sincere interest.

"Well, sort of; like if I start feeling angry, or if I'm trying to sleep but can't, or sometimes when the black dog barks."

"When you return to knowing who you are, is it usually after a violent act?"

"No, sometimes it's just sexually weird, or harming myself, or eating a rat or something involving my own death. Everything is okay, like right now, here, talking to you. But when my mind shifts and goes away, something else just does what it wants."

"I see," said Dr. Taylor, before scribbling on a clipboard he held. "You will be with Dr. Taylor; he's a specialist in cases of identity cognizance disorder like yours. He will evaluate you and after a certain period of time, a review of your status will be submitted. You appear rational and calm right now. I hope it continues."

"What happened to the cops who beat the crap out of me?"

"Well, the report says that you were violent, uncooperative and speaking in a foreign language before going into convulsions and that your eyeballs went white, apparently rising above the eyelids. Dr. Taylor will determine if you're suffering from a mental disorder, or possibly a physical ailment, or even some combination. He is one of the best, so I hope for your full cooperation here."

"And you will have it; I'm kind of tired of not being able to be normal," I said, though, somewhere, in the recesses of my head, a small voice not of my own design whispered, "No you won't have it."

I was moved to "D" Wing where there were 15 other male patients and a staff of nurses on rotating shifts. Some of the patients were either severely medicated or oblivious to their surroundings; there were three just sitting, comatose, eyes open, staring forward and appearing like statues. Another half-dozen were simply quiet or indifferent, keeping to themselves, but capable of movement. About six were actually willing to speak and appeared more interested in the world around them. I did not think I belonged here, but this is where I landed, fucking Hoffman Forensic Treatment Facility, home of the nuts.

"Hello Tim," said a young guy wearing a doctor's lab coat, shaking my hand and smiling. "I'm Dr. Taylor and I oversee things here on the D wing."

"It's nice to meet you, Doc," I replied, shaking his hand.

"Nurse Bortner will show you your bed area, clothes and locker. Once you're showered, changed and squared away, come to my office, over there," he said, pointing to a light wooden door across the room. "We'll talk then, okay?"

"Sure, doc," I replied before going with the husky, middle-aged nurse.

The nurses seemed nice enough, or tolerable, at least and Dr. Taylor was a reasonable guy. I had a bed and they were going to feed me. It seemed like it might not be a bad place to stay for awhile. I took my shower and changed into the light blue jumpsuit before going to Dr. Taylor's office.

"Come on in, Tim," he said, turning his gaze from the computer monitor.

"Sorry, Doc; hope I didn't interrupt your You-porn video or something."

He chuckled, "No, not quite, Tim. Tell me, how do you like it here so far?" he asked, while rising to close the door of his office. He returned to his desk and opened a folder and began reading a form.

"Seems like a pretty good place to be, Doc. I mean, it beats jail."

"Yes, Tim," he began, after bringing his eyes up to meet mine, "I don't really have a lot to go on here. Apparently, you were employed as a college English professor, is that correct?"

"Yes, Doc; but I never quite made it back in time for the fall semester this year. I got stuck in a Jacuzzi in Manila."

"Well, it's obvious that you're educated, so I will just tell you what concerns me most, and that is the propensity towards violence. What happened on the airplane, Tim?"

"Doc, I honestly don't remember. I remember more about the cops beating the crap out of me than anything I did on the plane."

"Let's stick with the plane, Tim; what do you remember?" he persisted.

"Honestly, Doc, I saw a bunch of weird shit and I was choking a lady, but it turned out to be some other lady than who I thought it was. Is the lady okay?"

"Mrs. Gortney is currently recovering from a crushed trachea. You nearly killed her, Tim. Why? What was the trigger that made you do it?"

"Doc, I'm going to be honest with you, even though it sounds ridiculous," I began, exhaling in resignation.

"Tim, what you tell me will just stay between us," he reassured, before leaning back in his chair.

"Okay, here's the deal, when I went to the Philippines, some weird shit happened. My first day there, I saw a huge rat. Instead of just running away, he stared at me from across a swimming pool with his beady eyes. I stared back at him and our eyes were kind of locked into each other's and his tiny eyes became red. Then I screwed some evil chick who was possessed but I didn't know it. Something changed, or, I mean, I felt different afterwards. Like my thinking wasn't the same. Then a few days later, there was this Japanese looking broad with a slight mustache and she was sitting at the table where I was staying. She like clutched my arm and her eyes kind of went white, like a zombie. Her breath was like sulfur and it entered my mouth. Something entered my head when I banged the evil chick. I still taste sulfur. A bad spirit lives inside of me, Doc. No shit; and when it takes over, I have no idea what I am doing." I confessed.

Dr. Taylor continued to sit, hands locked behind his head, silently considering what I had just told him. I said no more and it was an awkward minute of silence between us as I continued to wait for his response. Finally, he sat forward, bringing his arms on top of his desk and spoke, "Tim, I'm inclined to believe you. I mean, you have no previous criminal record and you've been steadily employed at the same job for years. Something dramatic must have occurred for you to be acting the way you are currently. It's my conviction that your problem might well be spiritual in nature, like a spiritual malady. We will have some work to do, but I think, if you are willing, that the darkness can and will be replaced by light. How long have you felt the presence of darkness?"

"I don't know, Doc. I'm not real good with time these days. I suppose it's been six or seven months since I saw the rat."

"Are you aware of hurting or attacking anyone besides Mrs. Gortney?"

"No, Doc; I'm tame as a kitten," I lied, "That was just a fluke."

"Tim, don't take this the wrong way, but I don't believe you. I'm not after a confession here, just trying to help you. You have to meet me halfway, though. You have to want to be helped in order for me to help you. Does that make sense?"

"Sure, Doc, and I am going to do my best to give you my full cooperation."

"Okay, starting tomorrow, you'll join us with the D Wing group at 8; it's an informal, interactive group discussion where we learn to care about and help each other, sort of like a family. After lunch tomorrow, at 1, we will meet again for some private spiritual based counseling."

"Sounds like a plan, Doc. I miss being part of a family."

"Very well, then," said Dr. Taylor, rising from his desk and extending his hand, "You can report to Nurse Rose for your medication schedule and she will show you the patient lounge. I'll see you in the morning," he said, still shaking my hand.

"You got it, Doc," I returned, smiling back at him.

After Nurse Rose dispensed a few pills for me to swallow, I was free to mix and mingle with the other patients. The first one I encountered was Jasper Fleckles, who somehow believed, earnestly, that he was a bona-fide Civil War general for the Union Army. He had an intense look on his face, shouting and barking orders while marching around in the hallway leading to the lounge area. His crazed eyes and serious expression hinted that nobody better interfere with his agenda, whatever it was. "Mount the Calvary, boys! The Union must be preserved!" He shouted, staring at me with such tenacity that I began acting like I was looking for a horse to gallop away on. "I have been authorized by President Lincoln himself! The woven fabric of humankind is an intricate tapestry each one of us must defend!" He screamed, from only three-feet away.

"Yes, it is," I replied. "My name is Tim; how are you?" I asked, offering my hand with a friendly smile.

His face remained unchanged. He stood straight, rigid. His eyes burned holes into mine with his unblinking stare. "Hand salute, Soldier!" He barked, snapping to attention and offering me a crisp salute. His intense glare made me think it best to follow protocol, so I brought my hand up in an uninspired salute, hoping nobody else was watching.

"Pssst, hey, new guy," whispered another patient, peering down the hallway from the door of the lounge.

"Me?" I asked, while retaining my feeble salute for the General.

"Yeah, you want to eat a turd?" he asked. I was hoping I misheard him when the General interrupted.

"General Jasper Fleckles of the Fighting Forty-Third Calvary; very good to meet you soldier," he shouted, finally retiring his salute.

"Just answer the question, newbie. Fleckles will be doing his stupid Civil War shit forever. You want to eat a turd?"

"Uhm, no, sorry buddy," I answered.

"Well, fuck you and the horse Fleckles thinks you rode in on," he replied.

"Okay," I said, approaching him slowly, with one eye on the disgruntled General, who continued staring at me intensely, without blinking. "My name's Tim. What's yours?" I asked, throwing caution to the wind and extending my hand.

"I am Dan," he answered, a bit friendlier, while shaking my hand. "I am king of the D Wing," he answered, proudly. He spoke slowly, with a Southern twang, like a bastard stepbrother of Elvis. "Most people here call me Dan the lion. That's what my friends call me."

"Okay Dandelion," I answered, wondering if he was a burnt out hillbilly hippy or something.

"No!" He bellowed, "Not fucking dandelion, Dan the lion. What the fuck, newbie?"

The confusion over his name made me chuckle, "Sorry, I guess I heard you wrong, Dan."

"It's Dan the lion!" He yelled, vehemently.

Another patient, youthful in appearance, came walking out of the lounge, "Dandelion, I can't even watch T.V.; how about shutting your mouth for awhile, buddy? It'll be good for all of us plus help to fight air pollution in the environment." He walked in front of me and put out his hand, "I'm Macmurphy, but I go by Mac."

"I'm Tim," I replied, shaking his hand.

"Well, Tim, welcome to the D Wing funny farm. Cinch up your seatbelt because you're in for a hell of a ride. I won't ask what grand event landed you here, but I do want to ask, how fucked up in the head are you?" he asked, grinning as if there were some joke being played on me that I was unaware of. His handshake also left a mysterious sticky residue on my palm.

"Well," I began, wiping my palm off on the side of my jumpsuit, "Most of the time I'm not too messed up, but I do have my moments."

Mac's grin grew wider, "Ah, those magic moments; what'd you do to end up here?"

"I thought you weren't going to ask about that?"

"Well, I wasn't, but the question serves two purposes; one, it's a test of your comprehension and memory skills. Two, you seem pretty normal, and the normal appearing ones are capable of the craziest shit," he reasoned.

"Well, I choked some lady on an airplane," I confessed.

"Were you boning her in the bathroom?"

"No," I began, before he interrupted again.

"Was she hot?"

"No, she was ugly," I replied.

"Good for you, then. So, you didn't know you were choking her until after the fact?"

"Exactly; you seem pretty sharp, Mac. What are you in here for?"

"Me? I'm what they call a sexual deviant. Outside of that, though, I'm a regular guy."

I chuckled, "Aren't the majority of guys sexual deviants? I mean, we think about it all the time."

"Yeah, but I'm extra, like a devious deviant. I get off on weird shit. I don't mess with friends, though."

"That's a relief," I replied, "So, what do we do around here all day?"

"Tim, the world is your oyster here. The food isn't so bad. Nurse Rose is hot as hell. The counseling sessions are funny as all get out. We get good dope. And if all that isn't enough, cable T.V. on plasma screen, ping-pong tables, and the clincher for me, two computer stations with high-speed internet. I have it better now than when I was a high school math teacher. We're living the dream here, my friend."

"You were a math teacher?"

"Don't judge me; what gave it away, my nerdy demeanor or the fact that I just told you?"

"The latter; and I'm not one to judge, I was once an English teacher."

"I feel your pain. Let me introduce you to some of the boys here. Half of them won't remember shit, but they're the unmemorable half."

We walked into the lounge and Mac began introducing me to some of the other patients. "Stablein and Cochran, this is Tim!" He announced, with a showbiz style arm flourish in my direction. The two men, both on the same couch, were unresponsive, eyes glued to the television screen.

"Hi guys," I said, smiling at Mac as they both ignored me.

"Isn't it awesome?" Asked Mac, "Watch this shit," he said, before going to the wall and unplugging the television. Both men continued staring at the blank screen, as Mac began laughing.

"Can they understand anything?" I asked.

"Not much, these two can barely talk. They can eat and shit, though. Hey, want to play some ping-pong?" He asked, walking towards the table.

"Sure," I replied.

"You any good?" He asked, "The only competition I can get around here is Jefferson and the night guard, Kinsey."

"Sure," I replied, "I got to play a lot when I was in the Philippines."

"In the Philippines? Is that where you can fuck fifteen-year olds for a quarter?" he asked, suddenly very excited.

I laughed, "Well, the girl I was with was older, but, sure, you might be able to find something like that there, maybe not for a quarter, though."

"Did you fuck your girl there?"

"Sure, she was hot."

What'd she look like?" he asked, moving his hand to his crotch and pinching a small lump in the jumpsuit. It was awkward, but I reminded myself we were in the nut house.

"Well," I began, "imagine a slender, shapely, lithe and log-legged, willowy Chinese girl with plump, perfectly shaped lips and elegant facial features, all framed in long, black silky hair."

"You had me at facial," replied Mac, continuing to pinch his protrusion with more vigor. "Did you give her a facial?" he asked.

"I showered her back and her stomach," I replied, his stimulated gaze hanging on my every word.

Mac was now stroking his tiny extension with his thumb and index finger. "Did you do some anal?"

"No," I answered, wanting to change the subject. "Are we going to play ping-pong or what?"

"Never mind all that," he replied, "Did she have nice tits?"

"Yes, she did, they were perfectly shaped, curving upwards with deliciously brown nipples." I answered, as I watched Mac's eyes roll slightly back in his head, with his face contorted, and a small wet spot appeared in his crotch. He finally released his tiny erection, the wet spot still pointing at three o'clock.

"Okay, let's play best out of five," he announced, not missing a beat after his orgasm. He went to the couch and, reaching underneath, extracted a tiny orange ping-pong ball. "I have to keep these hidden or one of these geniuses will swallow it whole."

"That's what she said," I replied, as we began laughing.

We began to play, which was a bit awkward against an opponent sporting a fresh semen stain. I won seven out of nine games, but Mac proved to be a formidable opponent, every game ending within a range of five points, mostly less.

A huge, three-hundred pound robust, black patient approached the table during the intense ending of our final game. He was very dark, very round but with evident muscle under the fat. He stood near the middle of the table, an intimidating presence, making it difficult to concentrate on the game.

Mac introduced us before his serve. "Jefferson, this is the new guy, Tim. Tim, meet Jefferson."

"Whooo! What you say, boss man?" asked Jefferson, loudly and smiling.

"Nice to meet you, Jefferson," I replied.

The game was close, 19 to 20 in my favor. If I scored the next point, I won. If Mac scored, we were in overtime. Mac served the ball with some hellacious topspin and I managed to return it. The volley continued back and forth at least eight times, before Jefferson, for reasons only he might or might not know, decided to sing, loud.

"You can tell the world, you never was my girl," he bellowed, so loud that even Langer broke his gaze from the blank television screen momentarily. He complemented the song with a bouncing dance move, bending his knees up and down while swirling both huge hands in small circles, as if washing a car. "You can burn my clothes when I'm gone"

"Mac continued returning the ball, but looked furious, "Jefferson, not now!" he shouted.

Jefferson, now with his eyes closed, was oblivious, "But don't break my hearts, my achy breaky hearts . . . "

Blocking out the garbled country crooning gorilla, I managed to spike an angled fastball that Mac couldn't touch. "Motherfucker!" he screamed, throwing his paddle across the room and missing Stablein's head by merely an inch.

Jefferson responded with a hearty, belly-deep laugh, "What you say, boss man?" he asked.

"Fuck you, Jefferson! If you weren't four times my size, I'd fuck you up right now!"

Jefferson continued laughing, "Whooooo!" he exclaimed, joyfully.

After losing at ping-pong, Mac turned the T.V. back on, where we joined Stablein and Cochran. "Scoot over Cochran," said Mac, "You know, I think you and Stablein must have quit smoking dope one joint too late." Both men stared ahead, vacant-eyed, oblivious to the verbal barb.

Dr. Phil was on and the guest was a woman who was dissatisfied with her stay-at-home husband, Greg. The husband justified his homemaker responsibilities by maintaining that he was studying for the bar exam. Surprisingly, most of the patients entered the lounge and were glued to the screen. Even Jefferson watched from behind the couch, while silently doing a raise-the-roof kind of dance.

A round, portly man with glasses entered the lounge and walked up next to the T.V. Even without the beard and with a jumpsuit (nearly bursting at the seams around his waist), he was a dead ringer for Santa.

He began talking while continuing to stare at the television, "Well, that just goes to show you who wears the skirt in this family," he began.

"If we are overcome, then farewell to our freedom gentlemen!" shouted Fleckles, from behind the couch, standing crisply at attention as Jefferson continued his silent dance beside him.

"Farewell to our freedom, indeed," began the annoying Santa clone, "The media is using a subversive ploy to undermine the traditional family structure of our Christian heritage. Now I'm not racist, but we need less blacks and Mexicans and more pilgrims. I believe John Bunyan wrote about it in a little book called *Pilgrim's Progress*, which was an allegory for our age."

"Shut up, Smith! You fat windbag, Socrates know-it-all; just shut the fuck up! Nobody wants to hear you ramble on about your stupid ideas!" shouted Mac, still seething from losing at ping-pong.

"Yes indeed," replied Smitty, now looking at Mac, "It's really no surprise that you, Mac, will vehemently defend your right to be brainwashed by the elitist media conglomerate. I believe Orwell spoke of your type in his futuristic, though I tend to disagree about the futuristic appellation for a variety of reasons, novel, *1984*."

"Smitty, what part of shut the fuck up don't you understand?" asked Mac.

"Well, I understand that the sleeper is now awake and, ironically, defending his right to go back to sleep. This reminds me of a little story from college, a story that I regret to tell with a straight face."

"Hey, what do you guys think one of Dr. Phil's turds looks like?" asked Dan, eyes never leaving the screen. "I'm guessing thick logs, 'cause he's kind of calm and husky."

"Gee, Dan, that's a profound insight. Thanks for sharing it," said Mac, facetiously rolling his eyes. Smitty continued to ramble on about how he learned in college that the family structure has been under attack since Roosevelt's New Deal.

"Hey, Newbie, how much money would you ask for to eat one of Dr. Phil's turds? I'm just curious," asked Dan.

"I don't think any amount would make that one a go, Dandelion," I answered.

"It's Dan the lion, dammit; what's with this dandelion crap?" he asked, with irritation, before collecting himself. "Now newbie,"

"It's Tim" I reminded.

"Right, now, Tim, if you could put it in a hotdog bun, with ketchup, some mustard, maybe a little relish; would it be more tempting?" I considered pointing out the absurdity, but reminded myself that we were in a mental hospital and these were patients, ambitious patients with felonies under their belts.

In the background, competing with Dr. Phil, Smitty continued his never ending monologue involving the media conspiracy to undermine the Christian heritage of our nation.

"That's just gross, Dandelion," said Fleckles.

"Whoa, are we having a brief escape from the Civil War battlefield, Fleckles?" asked Mac.

"What Civil War battlefield?" asked Fleckles, apparently unaware of his prior responsibilities as a General. "I just never understand why Dan never stops talking about poop related things, it's weird."

"Well, at least he's interesting sometimes. Smitty talks all day about nothing. I'd rather hear about shit than hear from shit for brains," said Mac, as Smitty droned on, oblivious.

"So, newbie, would you do a turd in a hotdog bun?" continued Dan, waiting on my answer as if the fate of all mankind depended upon it.

"No thanks," I stated, silently wondering what Dr. Phil might think if he were in the room with us.

A pleasant, smiling and attractive nurse showed up, "Dinner time, gentlemen," she announced.

"Thank you, Nurse Rose," answered Mac, gazing lustfully at her hips as she turned away and giving his wiener a few complimentary pinches through the jumpsuit. We formed a single-file line to walk to the cafeteria, which was down a long hallway after making a right turn. As I looked at an exit sign, the voice in my head spoke to me, "We gotta get outta here." It spoke in a hiss, and I tried to ignore it, as if it never said a word. I focused instead on Jefferson, at the rear of the line, who was now singing Al Green's "Let's Stay Together."

After dinner, we had more time to hang out in the lounge. While I still didn't feel like I fit in here, Fleckles and Mac seemed okay, when one was out of Civil War mode and the other wasn't masturbating in mid-conversation.

"Hey guys, what's up?" asked a lanky, tall guy wearing scrubs and some kind of official name tag badge. He walked limp-wristed, gangly and with a nerdesque demeanor. He approached Mac and they shook hands. It also looked like a rolled up plastic baggy was exchanged, but I pretended not to notice. Meddling in the drug deals of others was never smart, and doubly so in a mental institution for felons.

"Kinsey, my favorite guy on the nightshift, how's it going?" asked Mac, tucking the baggy into his jumpsuit pocket.

"Yeah, right; I'm also the only guy on the nightshift," replied Kinsey.

"Well played, Captain Obvious, well played. Never mind all that, this here's a new patient to D Wing. His name's Tim. And Tim, this is Kinsey, the gay guy they pay to watch us sleep."

"Hey Mac," said Kinsey, "You're a douche-bag."

"A well honed, scathing comeback, Kinsey. Its originality cuts to the core," replied Mac, as I shook Kinsey's hand and exchanged pleasantries. It was soon evident that Kinsey did not take his responsibilities at the hospital as seriously as the other staff members. He also seemed a bit immature.

"Mac, I have a date with a college girl tomorrow," he said, beaming with pride, "She's only 23!" he exclaimed, putting his hand up for a high-five. Mac ignored his gesture and Kinsey slowly lowered his hand, looking a bit offended.

"She just wants your money, retard. You're 38 years old, the wife dumped you and you're paying child support on 4 kids, and you're built like the Grinch," admonished Mac. "The coup de grace is that you live with your mom. If a young college girl is interested, it's only because a fool and his money, after paying support, are soon parted."

"Ugh, whatever," conceded Kinsey. "So, Tim, what brings you to the funny farm?" he asked.

I looked at Mac. "Yeah, you can tell Kinsey. He's a dork, but a trustworthy one," he assured.

"Well, I was on an airplane and I started choking some fat lady sitting next to me. That's about it," I revealed.

"I almost did that, too, when I was a Principal."

"Is that how you moved up the corporate ladder and landed the night gig here, Kinsey?" asked Mac.

"Screw you, Mac! Yeah, like I was saying, I've felt like choking a girl before and I probably would have done it, if she wouldn't have looked like she could kick my ass."

"Kinsey, it's a cool story, but if a girl can kick your ass, you probably shouldn't tell it," suggested Mac, as he somehow appeared to be snacking on bacon, which was odd because there was no bacon with our dinner in the cafeteria.

"I know, ugh!" exclaimed Kinsey, "It's taken me 38 years to finally realize what life is about. Don't worry about it."

"We won't, jackass," answered Fleckles, from the couch and now watching T.V.

"Okay, I see how it is. I've got lots of paperwork anyways and still have to make my rounds. You guys don't stay up too late. Nice to meet you, Tim; welcome aboard," he said, before walking out of the room and going into Dr. Taylor's office, which was next to the bunk room, where we soon made our way.

There were four rows with five bunks in each row. My small cot had Stablein on one side and a cement wall on the other. One the other side of Stablein was Fleckles's bunk. The lights were out for some time, and my eyes adjusted to see well in the room. Stablein appeared to have his eyes open, but was staring at the ceiling, comatose. Mac's bunk was at the opposite end of our row, closest to the door adjacent to Dr. Taylor's office, where the low drone of a baseball announcer could be heard. As the other patients began to drift off, my mind began to race. "Get back to Manila and your family," said the sneering voice inside my head, from out of nowhere.

The demonic voice in my head didn't really startle me as much as the memory of the syndicate did. I missed belonging badly, dear reader. I wondered what Reshi was doing right now. The more I thought about her, the stronger the urge came to want to get back to her. I needed her, to see her, to hear her, to touch her and to mount her.

So far, the nut house didn't seem so bad. Some of the guys were okay and the food was decent, but my heart ached, dear reader. I was only away from Manila for not even a week and my achy breaky heart could only think of getting back there. I had no idea who held my passport, I had no money and I was basically incarcerated for being a nutcase with a felony. How was I going to escape?

I continued to run the hamster wheel in my head, laying on my side and pretending to be asleep. What seemed like hours passed and I began to hear rumbling scratching noises from inside of the wall. I knew the sound well. It was the sound of an active rodent in the night. I continued to listen, as it progressed upwards within the wall and made its way into the ceiling, right above my bunk.

As I heard him digging and scratching directly above me, I worried the little critter was going to fall into bed with me at any moment. I then heard another sound, the pitter patter of light footsteps. Pretending to sleep, I turned with my pillow for a better view of the source of the footsteps. I could see the pale skin of Mac, glowing in the darkness. He crept between bunks of the sleeping patients, like an albino gnome on a covert mission. He stopped at the bunk where the mildly snoring Fleckles slept, and slowly eased himself under the blanket behind him. As they cuddled together, I pretended to be asleep. Don't ask, don't tell wasn't just for the military.

Sometime during the night, I felt something moving on my chest. As I opened my eyes, the weight upon my chest increased tremendously. There was a massive, muscular, black feathered creature perched upon me, looking down into my eyes. I could not move or scream due to the strength of it, and the sharp, pointed beak tip that was nearly penetrating my Adam's apple. Its eyes were milky white like death, at first, then as I looked into them, they transformed to glowing red. The beast's beak emitted a sulfurous, noxious breath, making me nauseous. The menace in the creature's eyes revealed that it did not just want me dead, but it wanted an agonizing death.

Get the fuck off me! I shouted.

The talons on each shoulder clamped harder, gripping the clavicles with supernatural strength. It twisted my upper-body right and left. I was powerless to escape, let alone move, suffocating in the sulfurous fumes. I managed to free one arm, and I swung with great fury, striking the terrorizing face of the beast. He squawked in pain and it allowed me to free my other arm. I clenched the bird's throat with both hands and squeezed.

"Hey man, you okay?" I faintly heard, before opening one eye in confusion and seeing Kinsey. He was shaking my shoulder, "Tim, you alright?"

I realized it was only a dream, albeit a terrorizing one. With this awareness came the added epiphany that to sleep was no longer an option. To sleep would mean to die. "Yeah, man, I'm alright," I mumbled, "Why?"

Kinsey looked incredulous, "Why? Because you just strangled Dan and almost killed him! You were screaming like you were on fire. I need to page a doctor for him, this sucks!"

"Nah, just a bad dream, sorry. I didn't even know Dan was there," I replied.

"Well, I think your screaming probably had him going to check on you when you attacked him. You can't do that! You're okay; I'll try to explain it was an accident, but you messed him up pretty bad. You'll probably get some solitary. Just go back to sleep," he said, before walking towards the office. He made it only a few steps before stopping and looking down at Mac and Fleckles spooning. Mac, in the role of big spoon, was wide awake, and brought a finger up to his own puckered lips, a signal for Kinsey to be quiet.

"Mac, that's just not right," Kinsey whispered under his breath while shaking his head.

"Don't worry about it," Mac whispered back, with a flapper hand gesture towards the doorway.

"Ugh!" exclaimed Kinsey, before walking away and back to the office.

Two medics arrived and carried Dan out on a stretcher. His windpipe was slightly crushed and he was wheezing when he breathed, but he seemed okay despite his pain. He also had a gash on his head from us falling to the floor as I choked him. I did not recall strangling him.

I spent the remainder of the night staring up at the ceiling tile, listening to the incessant scratching noise and hoping the rat would not fall through the drop ceiling.

At group counseling the following morning, Fleckles vented his anger to the group and Dr. Taylor. "The homosexual keeps sneaking into my bed during the night. I'm sick of this shit!"

Mac, sitting beside me in the circle of chairs, shielded his mouth with one hand, "That's what she said," he whispered, grinning like a lottery winner.

Dr. Taylor leaned back in his chair, considering how to respond to Fleckles, who was now looking at Mac with intense anger. "Okay, let's talk about this. Mr. Kinsey assured me weeks ago that he would put a stop to people moving from their beds at night therefore I'm surprised it is still an issue. Mac, maybe you can share why you continue to violate the other patient's personal space?"

"I sure can, Doc," began Mac, professionally, "Though I want to make it clear that I never violated Fleckles's personal space. He is either lying or delusional, but we do need to bring about a peaceful resolution to these charges, not just on the D wing but also on the battlefield of history, where Fleckles would think I was with the Confederacy."

"That's bullshit!" screamed Fleckles, instantly rising from his chair with clenched fists. The veins around his temples appeared to be pulsating near their bursting point. "I will loosen the lightening of his terrible, swift sword," he screamed, while moving towards Mac.

"No gentlemen," mediated Dr. Taylor, while motioning to the nurses to restrain Fleckles.

"In Dixie land, I'll take my stand to live and die in Dixie," sang Mac, adding more fuel to Fleckles's fire.

Suddenly Smith was now standing, "The concept of justification for war can be traced back to Christian Medieval theory."

"Smitty, shut the fuck up!" shouted Mac, as he covered his ears and now looked as angry as Fleckles.

From his seat nearest Dr. Taylor, Jefferson decided to burst into song, "War, huh, yeah; what is it good for? Absolutely nothing!" he bellowed, drowning out the voices of the others.

Stablein and Cochran both sat quietly, staring blankly at the wall behind Dr. Taylor's head.

"Okay, okay, enough guys; that's enough!" exclaimed Dr. Taylor, before everyone began to quiet down, the last being the portly windbag, Smitty. "I can see Mac does not wish to cooperate today. What's on your mind Mac?"

"I guess I'm just afraid, Doc."

"Well then, let's hear it. What are you afraid of?"

"Fleckles said he will kill me if I don't sleep with him. His anger issues trouble me, Doc."

"Bullshit!" screamed Fleckles, now standing with veins bulging in his neck.

"Okay, okay, stop! Mr. Fleckles, sit back down," chided Dr. Taylor. Fleckles remained standing, staring intensely at Mac, both fists tightly clenched. "You realize you are only proving his point about the anger issue?" Fleckles finally sat back down, begrudgingly. "I want to share some good news with you guys," said Dr. Taylor, before picking up a worn, hardbound Bible beside his chair. "This book can transform us. It can give us life," he claimed, while flipping through the worn pages. "This passage is about fear, from Matthew 10:28, 'Do not be afraid of those who kill the body but cannot kill the soul. Rather, be afraid of the one who can destroy both body and soul in Hell.'"

"Ah, that's not right," scoffed Mac.

"Nothing can destroy me," spoke a clear, demonic voice from inside of my head. It was not my voice, and it did not verbalize from my mouth, but in my head it was unmistakably startling.

"Mac, share with us, please," continued Dr. Taylor.

"Well, Doc, it's like Jesus is threatening us to either believe in him or he'll destroy us in hell. I mean, why?"

"Well, I don't think it's really a threat. It's more of a reminder to remember God's power," reasoned Dr. Taylor.

"And God be with the blue and gray!" shouted Fleckles.

"And God be with all of us," added Dr. Taylor.

"Okay, wait a minute," contested Mac, "The quote you read said to be afraid of the one who can destroy you in Hell. Why do I want God with me to destroy me in Hell?"

"Well, Mac, it's complicated."

"Try me, Doc, I'll do my best to keep up with the nuances and tangents."

"Keep up the good fight, brave Union soldiers!" shouted Fleckles, to nobody in particular, as his eyes drifted into space.

"Well, God allows people freedom. When people choose freely to do bad things, they can end up in Hell being punished by the devil, or Satan," reasoned Dr. Taylor.

"That's retarded," said Mac.

"His truth is marching on," sang Fleckles, now out of his chair and marching around the group. "Glory, glory hallelujah . . . . " Everyone ignored him as he marched and sang.

"Your language, Mac, please, why do you disagree?" probed Dr. Taylor.

"Well, disregarding other problems with it, if Satan is punishing bad guys, doesn't that make him a good guy?"

"Well," began Dr. Taylor, pausing to select his words carefully, "It's hard for us to understand how or why God does things, since our awareness is limited. It's safe to assume, I think, that Satan is the bad guy and Jesus is the good guy."

"Doc, I have a question," began Dan, back from medical with a neck brace fresh track of stitches running down his temple.

"Sure, Dan, maybe with the help of the group, we can answer it."

"Well, I'm wondering if Jesus's turds would taste good, like would they be better than Satan's turds?"

Dr. Taylor frowned, "I think we will disregard that question, Dan. Let's hear from the newest arrival to our group. How are you Tim?"

"I'm okay, Doc, just listening to the conversation here."

"And what do you think of it? It's safe to be honest here," he said, as Fleckles continued marching and singing the Battle Hymn of the Republic.

"Well, it's interesting," I replied.

"And what part is most interesting to you?" he pressed.

"I suppose it's a toss-up, Doc, between Satan being a good guy and wondering if Jesus's turds would taste good."

"See Doc," said Dan, excitedly, "It's a good question!"

"Now gentlemen, I hate to toot my own horn, but I've kept my peace and biting my tongue for the past hour. I have to kindly remind you all that goodness is a relative concept," began Smitty, as Mac rolled his eyes then buried his face into his hands. "Now back when I was in the army at Camp Pendleton, we used to have a saying. Wait, or was it Camp Schwab? I always have gotten those two mixed up. Sometimes when I was coming back to base after a night on the town, I would tell the cab driver to take me to the wrong camp by accident."

"Smitty, shut the fuck up!" screamed Mac.

"Yeah, for real," added Dan.

"Shut the light," began Jefferson, singing loud enough to drown out all other voices. "Shut the door. You don't have to be afraid anymore; I'll be be be be your baby tonight . . . "

Smitty, undaunted, continued to babble, "Yes, I believe it was John Stuart Mill, no relation to Eddie Mill who grew up two blocks away from me, who said something to the effect of one person having the power would be justified in silencing mankind,"

"I'm justified in giving you a tall glass of shut the fuck up!" screamed Mac.

Okay, okay," said Dr. Taylor, rising from his chair. "Mac, Smitty, we need to stop. Jefferson and Fleckles, we need you to join us so we can close in prayer. Let us all hold hands and bow heads."

"He's a Confederate, I refuse to hold his hand!" protested Fleckles, while moving away from Mac.

"Yeah, and he pinches his wiener," added Dan, giggling and also moving away from Mac.

"At least I don't put my fingers in my butt and smell them, like you do, Dandelion," said Mac.

Jefferson and I held hands with Mac as Dr. Taylor began, "Father above we thank you for this time together . . . . " I was suddenly aware of my hand being pulled by Mac, towards his crotch. I yanked it back. He tried the same with Jefferson until Jefferson squeezed and nearly broke the bones in his hand.

I was taken to solitary where I stayed for nearly two months. They needed the time to evaluate my violent tendencies. I was allowed out for counseling, but meals were delivered in isolation. The only thing that kept me sane through it all was that Kinsey brought me my journal and pen each day on the sly. It was a long, lonely two months. I got to know my demon well. I was never so happy to see a bunch of nuts watching television when Dr. Taylor finally decided that I could rejoin the boys on the D wing.

During our recreation time Mac was busy at one of the two computer stations in the lounge. He quickly shrunk the screen when I approached. I sat at the computer beside him and decided to read the Manila Bulletin news. "Hey, do you have Facebook?" asked Mac.

"I used to, but it's been so long since I've even been on there," I replied.

"How come you were screaming all crazy last night? You had a nightmare?"

"I have a lot of bad dreams. That's kind of why I'm here."

"Me too," agreed Mac, "Except mine are wet dreams. Hey, go into Facebook and I'll add you as a friend."

"Mac, I don't even remember my password or anything."

"No problem," he said, "Just use one of these and change it to your own name," he said, sliding me a business card with a list of 15 names, e-mail addresses and passwords for each name on the back.

"These are all Facebook accounts?"

"Yes"

"Why you have so many?"

"Don't worry about it," he replied, grinning.

I pulled up Facebook and used the first name on his list, John Ross. A complete profile opened up, including pictures and updates and 184 friends. "Mac, who is this guy?"

"It's just a guy I made up. John's an engineer living in New Jersey. He's 41 years old, recently divorced, one kid in college and he enjoys baseball and horror flicks."

"Damn, so you have a full profile for every name on that list?"

"Yes, and I have more cards too."

"Why so many?"

"I get off on fucking with people."

"Like tricking them?"

"Sure," replied Mac, grinning, "Not only is it great fun, but it helps me feel good about myself. You can change the name and information if you want to make that profile your own, or you can just be John and mess with people. The world is your oyster!" He exclaimed, rising from his chair and pocketing the list.

Kinsey arrived with a plastic hairdo that was combed back and apparently sandblasted with hairspray. He entered the lounge area. Mac approached him saying, "Welcome back, Kinsey! Here a little early today, aren't you? Can't get enough of this place?"

"Ugh!" he said, "They asked me to come in early and I can use the overtime," he added, before slipping into Mac's hand what appeared to be a rolled up plastic baggy.

"Yeah, well, at least you get paid for being here, right? The rest of us are just nuts for free."

"Oh yeahhhh!" said Kinsey, attempting to sound cool and failing miserably.

Mac returned back to the computer station. I was beginning to think maybe Mac didn't really belong here since he seemed to have his marbles together, but I had to keep in mind him pinching his ding dong before playing ping pong. Obviously there was a penchant for perversion just under the surface of his stability.

He began to open tab after tab on his browser. He was also running Windows Messenger, Yahoo Messenger and Skype and holding conversations in all three programs simultaneously. "So, are you going to change that profile or use it as John?" He asked me, his eyes never leaving the monitor as he continued to type frantically like a man possessed.

"Holy crap; how can you talk to four people at the same time?" I asked.

"I'm actually talking to six, well, seven if we include you."

"Hey, I see Kinsey as one of my friends on this profile," I said.

"Yeah, don't tell him shit, though. He's friends with a bunch of my profiles," he replied, pausing from typing to eat a piece of delicious looking bacon. Bacon envy was tearing me up inside.

"Where are you always getting bacon?" I demanded. "It looks incredible!"

"Shhh," he replied, putting his greasy index up to his lips as he continued chewing. After swallowing, he said, "Don't worry about it."

I then noticed the corner of the rolled up baggy poking out of his jumpsuit pocket. "How come Kinsey brings you bacon in a baggy?"

Mac stopped typing and looked at me, grinning. "You're pretty sharp. You've only been here a few days and you've already figured out some major things that I don't share with any of the loons. I'm impressed. Do me a favor, though."

"What's that?"

"Mind your own business," he quipped, before crunching into another piece of bacon. "Holy shit," he said, looking at his screen and grinning.

"What?"

"Kinsey just posted another gay status. Go to his page from your friends list."

I went to Kinsey's page and read, "I think I finally got it! Wow took 39 years . . . Maybe I'm a little dense. Lol, Oh well . . . better late than never!" Just when I finished reading it, a comment popped up below the status. The name was John Ross, the same profile Mac had given me.

"It took you 39 years to figure out that you were gay? What happened? You farted out a used condom?" commented John.

I looked at Mac, who was grinning like a Cheshire cat. We began to laugh.

"He doesn't even know it's you?"

"No," replied Mac, "That's the beauty of it."

"How come he doesn't just delete or block John from his friend's list?"

"Wouldn't matter; I have about 20 more in his friend's list."

"Damn"

"Yeah, and I also know his Facebook password. If he deletes anyone, I can just add them back."

Dan approached, "Hey, Newbie, I need to use the computer. You going to be on there long? It's kind of important."

"I'm pretty much through; have at it, Dandelion," I said.

"It's Dan the lion, but thanks Newbie. Hey, Mac, I need to renew my subscription because remember how my site is monthly?"

"Yeah?" responded Mac, "What's in it for me?"

"I can get another picture of Nurse Rose, upskirt crotch-shot, just the way you like."

"Alright, but if it's blurry, I'm yanking your subscription. The last one was fuzzy as hell. Great angle, poor quality; just remember if you get busted, my name stays out of it and the phone does not get confiscated. Got it?"

"Mac, come on; this is Dan the lion you're talking to."

"Alright, now what's the name of this lovely little website you need to renew?"

"Down for brown round dot com," said Dan, eagerly.

"Lovely, Dandelion, just lovely," said Mac, facetiously. He pulled up the site and clicked the age verification button. On his screen was a picture of a guy squatting and over a petite blonde. "Dandelion, I'm a pervert myself, but this is some messed up stuff."

"I know, his poop's really dark, isn't it? Looks like the shade of overcooked pumpkin pie."

"Yeah, sure," said Mac, sarcastically, "Never mind all of that, where is the membership area? You're a sick fuck, Dandelion," he said, while typing in the credit card information, which was under Kinsey's name. He clicked renew and a confirmation screen appeared. "Write down your password and don't lose it. I want Nurse Rose on my i-phone by Friday."

"No problem, Mac, thanks," he said, with eyes glued to a gallery of people defecating.

"Mac, you're good with computers, huh?"

"No, but I am skilled in the fine art of fuckery," he replied.

The next morning, Dr. Taylor began our group session by asking, "Okay, does anyone have a topic on their mind that we can discuss today?"

"He was in my bed again," said Fleckles, pointing at Mac with eyes that were seething with rage.

"Well, let's talk about," began Dr. Taylor, before Mac interrupted.

"I wasn't in your bed; what is this like your favorite fantasy or something?"

"Bullshit!" shouted Fleckles. "You're a liar!"

"Guys, put an end to it or we will cancel group," warned Dr. Taylor. "That means no lounge or recreational time."

"When the lights go down in the city," began Jefferson, bursting out in song that was louder than Dr. Taylor.

"Jefferson, please go to the lounge if you must sing!" shouted Dr. Taylor.

"He's lying, Doc; I tried to punch him this morning, but he ran back to his bed giggling like a little bitch!" shared Fleckles.

"Mac, were you in Fleckles's bed?"

"Doc, I honestly have no idea what he is talking about," insisted Mac.

"Bullshit!" screamed Fleckles.

"It's tearing you apart, every, every day yay yay, cause he's lovin', cause he's touchin', cause he's squeezin', another . . . " sang Jefferson, still at the top of his lungs and gyrating his gargantuan body to the point of sweat beads forming on his forehead.

"Mac," yelled Dr. Taylor, trying to be heard above the crooning giant, "Why would Fleckles make something like this up?"

"Uhm, because he's retarded?"

"Bullshit!" protested Fleckles.

"Cause he's lovin' and he's touchin' and he's squeeeeeeeeezin' . . . another . . . " continued Jefferson, now bellowing into an imaginary microphone.

"Has anyone noticed Mac walking around after lights out?" asked Dr. Taylor, slowly scanning the circle of patients. Stablein mumbled to himself, as drool hung down from the right corner of his mouth.

"I haven't noticed a thing, Doc," said Dan, "And I get up to shit a lot during the night. I always see Mac in his bed."

"Bullshit!" screamed Fleckles.

"Well, I can see we're not going to resolve this matter easily. Do you guys know the good news, though? Tim, do you know the good news?"

"Bacon at lunch today?" I asked, hearing Mac agree it would be good news.

"No, this is even better; this is the bread of life. Jesus died for our sins. He gave his life so that we could have new life, through him. According to the apostle, John, he died because of his love for us."

"Doc, did Jesus poop?" asked Dan.

"When the lights go down in the city . . . " crooned Jefferson, taking the song from the beginning again, much to Dr. Taylor's chagrin.

"He was just as human as you and me, Dan. He pooped, he cried and he probably laughed. The Bible says he was fully human and fully God.

"Does it say he fully took poops?" continued Dan.

"Dan, that's not the important part. The important part is that he died for our sins."

"Is pooping a sin?"

"Goddamn, can you forget about poop?" shouted Cochran. Since he was normally in a conscious coma, his outburst earned the attention of the entire circle. "Poop this, poop that . . . who gives a shit about poop?"

"Mr. Cochran," said Dr. Taylor, "Why does Dan's talk bother you?"

"Because it's weird! I mean it's a crazy people's place here, but shit this, shit that, is just weird!"

"Na na na na na na, na na na na na na . . . " continued Jefferson, now leaning back, eyes closed and singing towards the ceiling, his face straining to hit each soulful note.

"Okay," said Dr. Taylor, louder, "I think we covered enough ground for today. Let's close with prayer." He stood up and tried to get us to join hands, but it took another 10 minutes to get Cochran and Dan to quit bickering. Then there was another flare up between Fleckles and Mac that took some time to quell and, finally, we all had to wait for Jefferson to finish the final chorus and refrain of the song he was wailing out before he joined our circle.

This daily routine could get boring and monotonous sometimes, but the mix of personalities kept it somewhat entertaining. My main problem was not being able to sleep. I was physically tired, but the Aswang in my head, the dark demon, grew more furious with each passing day. It wanted to be back in Manila and I wanted to be back in Manila. If I did not get back soon, someone was going to die. I had to get back, somehow, some way. The voice in my head spoke more frequently and became unpredictable I used the time not sleeping to write this journal. Getting my pen and notebook from Kinsey wasn't a problem, since he was my loyal reader (yes you, Kinsey). I write to stay alive. It is my testimony. It is the black albatross that hangs around my neck. The voice seemed to detest Dr. Taylor, particularly during one on one counseling sessions.

"So, Tim, I'm curious. What do you think of being here? Do you feel your time here is worthwhile?"

"Well, Doc, I suppose. I mean the food is great. Some of the guys here are cool, most of them. It's just . . . "

"Just what Tim? Don't be afraid to talk openly. Anything you say here will only be between us. The incident with Dan, Kinsey and even Dan, rose to your defense and said you did not realize what you were doing at the time, that you were screaming and having nightmares and should not be responsible for the attack. Me, I'm not so sure, but for now I will take their word."

"Well, I don't always feel crazy."

"Isn't that a good thing, Tim?"

"Not when you're in the nuthouse, Doc."

"I see. Tim, do you know the parable of the sower and the seeds?"

"No Doc, but I sometimes like sunflower seeds."

He chuckled, "Well, Jesus said that there were three kinds of believers, comparing their faith to seeds that were planted in three kinds of soil. One soil is dry and barren, not allowing the seed to sprout. The other is rich soil, but shallow, so the seed sprouts quickly, but in time withers away. The last soil is fertile and deep and the seed grows and grows and bears much fruit. The question is, Tim, which seed are you?"

Before I could answer, Aswang spoke in my head, *The real question is when will you kill this sanctimonious prick and get back to Manila?* It was no longer even surprising to hear, though I had no control over it. I even agreed with it to a point. Hell, Reshi was in Manila. I wanted to be with her. It seemed my identity was slowly surrendering itself over to the demon that was Aswang.

"I guess I want to be the last soil, Doc."

"Great news," he beamed, slapping me on the shoulder, "Tim, let us pray together, that your faith might grow and continue to flourish."

The demonic voice echoed, *That my desire to spill your blood might increase, you self-righteous hypocrite.*

I soon learned that Dr. Taylor was attempting to convert each one of us during his one on one counseling sessions. "Did he explain the parable of the sower?" asked Mac, after I joined the boys in the lounge.

"Yeah, you too?"

"Oh yeah," replied Mac, "I told him I'm not interested in being a farmer, but I do want to fuck the farmer's daughter, or wife, if she's not too old."

"I told him I wanted to use my shit as the fertilizer," added Dan.

"Big surprise there, Dandelion," said Mac.

"It's Dan the lion!"

"Yeah, whatever; what'd you tell him, Tim?"

"Well, I told him I wanted to be the third soil. It was just what he wanted to hear," I answered.

"Yeah, that must have given him a raging hard-on," said Mac, prior to taking a bite of his seemingly endless supply of bacon.

"Yeah, and what he thinks is real and what is actually real are two different things."

"Dandelion, go get my phone from Kinsey. I need that picture or your beloved brown round subscription is going to end."

"Alright, alright," said Dan, reluctantly logging off the computer.

"Mac, how do you have an i-phone? I mean, I had to pretty much beg and bother everyone around here for weeks just to get an old fashioned pen and notebook, which I have to turn over to Kinsey every night. I thought we weren't allowed to have gadgets in here and you have an i-phone?"

"Phone?" interrupted Smitty, as he approached us, waddling like a know-it-all, busybody Santa, "Say, did I tell you guys about the time my buddy in college, Sam Leeds I believe his name was, though through the haze of the fraternity house barley and hops I could be wrong. But anyway, Sam had really tied one on, drinking beer after beer like an alcoholic jellyfish,"

"Smitty, shut the fuck up!" screamed Mac.

"Not shutting the fuck up is not an option, Smitty," shouted Fleckles, from out in the hallway.

Smitty continued, unperturbed, as if he did not even hear them, "Seems Sam got himself into a little pickle at the bar, a little fracas, as often happens when the young and indulgent over-imbibe,"

"Smitty, shut the fuck up!" screamed Mac, louder and with more fury, and inches from Smitty's ruddy, round face.

"Now gentlemen," said Nurse Rose, "We need to stop the loud outbursts. Control your anger and control your language."

Dan approached her from behind, in a creeper crouch, holding the phone camera just below the back of her skirt. His ninja skills were impressive and the angle of the shot was perfect, but leaving the flash on proved to be his downfall.

"What on earth?" said a startled Nurse Rose, as Dan, knowing he was busted, stopped, dropped and rolled sideways, then scrambled to his feet and sprinted out of the lounge. "Someone stop him!" Nurse Rose demanded, angrily in pursuit. "Stop Dan!" she yelled to another nurse, pointing down the hall.

Smitty ignored the commotion, "Now, Sam got himself arrested and as is the procedure under incarceration, the detainee is granted the privilege and liberty to make one, yes one, phone call,"

Mac stood in front of Smitty with both hands covering both ears. He lowered his head and began crying.

"Smitty, shut the fuck up!" yelled Fleckles, once more, from the hallway.

Undaunted, Smitty continued, "Yes, Sam made his phone call, hung up, went back to his cell, and thirty minutes later; do you know what happened?"

Mac brought his head up, wiped the tears from his eyes and asked, "You finally shut the fuck up?"

"No," replied Smitty, smiling, "But there was a pizza delivered to the jail for Sam Leeds, pepperoni and mushroom, I believe it was," he said, then laughed, while his eyes drifted into nostalgia, before waddling out of the lounge, continuing to laugh and shake his head.

"Thank god!" declared Mac.

"You think Dan is in trouble?" I asked.

"Nah, I'm sure he stashed my phone. He's probably just mumbling a bunch of stuff about poop to them. They'll soon grow bored and go back to realizing that he is crazy."

"Alright, you need to fill me in. I see you breaking the rules on the computers, having an i-phone that we are not allowed to have and eating bacon every day, how do you get away with so much?"

"Well," smiled Mac, "It's not an easy life, but someone has to do it."

"Yeah, but how? I mean, don't they ever bust you?"

"Alright, Tim, I'm going to include you in on my secret, but don't you ever betray me. I trust you. Dan knows bits and pieces, but only you will know the whole story. You want in?"

"Hell yeah, I won't tell anyone. You trust Dan?"

"Yeah, he's crazy as shit and fixated on shit, but once he's on your side, he's very loyal."

"So, how do you get away with breaking all the rules here?"

"Alright, look at this," said Mac, clicking the browser open to a website showing a number of files. "Dan doesn't even know about this, so I hope my hunch about trusting you is on target."

He clicked a video file and a clip began to play that showed a tall, pasty looking guy dancing around in front of a mirror to Gloria Gaynor's *I Will Survive*. He was only wearing high-heel shoes, panties and lipstick. It was very unsettling, especially when he began gyrating clumsily in front of a mirror and I saw his face.

"Hey, that's Kinsey!" I said.

"Oh yeahhh," replied Mac, grinning mischievously.

"How the did you get him to do that?"

"I didn't; he was doing it on his own. His mistake was to assume that all of us nuts would sleep through *I Will Survive*. I'm sorry, when a song sucks that bad, I have to turn it off. When I went to bang on the office door, that's when I saw him. It was like 3 in the morning. Luckily I was able to record part of the performance with my phone."

"Damn, he was doing this in Dr. Taylor's office?"

"Oh yeahhh, and drinking some brewskis too," he said, pointing to the screen where Kinsey could be seen trying to shimmy his hips while guzzling a beer.

"Wow!" I said, laughing.

"Yes sir, and now he has to do anything I ask," grinned Mac.

"So, you blackmailed him?"

"Well, blackmail is a strong word. I prefer to think of him as being in my pocket. I'm easy on him, just little things; keep my phone safe, bring me bacon, keep me out of trouble so I can do what I want. I'm not extorting him for money or anything."

"Is that why you still can get in Fleckles's bed even when he bitches to Dr. Taylor about it every day?"

"Yes sir"

"How come you keep doing it? Are you homosexual?"

"Nah, I just can't get enough of the look on his face when he wakes up with me curled up behind him; it's priceless!"

"He gets so pissed, how come he hasn't attacked you?"

Mac laughed, "I think it's because I subscribed him to some stupid Civil War Historical website. That's maybe why he doesn't get physical, or he's aware of the consequences of attacking someone. It is fun watching his tantrums though, isn't it?"

"Yeah, he gets furious. How do you subscribe to all these websites for everyone?"

"I have all Kinsey's credit card information. Oh yeahhh," he said, laughing.

From the hallway we heard Fleckles randomly yell, "Smitty, shut up."

"Listen, Mac, I might need your help soon."

"With what, you need a subscription to Anal Asians or something?"

"No, but I do need to get back to Asia. I'm getting out of here."

"You plan to escape? You do know this place is securely locked down with cameras and guards, right?"

"That's why I am going to need your help, Mac. Well, that and I need to get my passport back somehow."

Mac smiled, "Escaping, all the way to Asia? I love it!"

"So, you might be able to help me?"

"I got an idea, if I help you get your passport, a plane ticket and a plan of escape, in return will you send me pictures of smoking hot babes?"

"Like naked pictures?"

"Yeah, but real pictures, and I can tell the difference. With the pictures you can send me their names and a little information about them and about their lives."

"Sure, I can do that."

"Good, then get ready for your first stop, Amsterdam."

"No, I need to get to Manila."

"Oh, you will, but first you have to go to Amsterdam. It has always been a dream of mine to see the Swedish and Dutch hookers in the Redlight District. I've only heard about them my entire life, the tall, willowy brunettes and blondes with never ending legs, standing in windows nearly nude. You go there, get pics of hot hookers for me, tell me about each one and then from there I will get you a flight to Manila."

"Yeah, I can do that I suppose. But how long will I have to be in Amsterdam?"

"Just as long as it takes to get about twenty hot pictures with descriptions," replied Mac.

"Deal," I affirmed, shaking his hand. On the computer screen, Kinsey could be seen clumsily gyrating in panties to the closing refrain of *I Will Survive*.

"I will survive, too," said a shrill voice inside of my head.

"Yes, you, or we, will," I replied, audibly.

"Will what?" asked Mac.

"Uh, just talking to myself, don't worry about it. I'm going to go write for awhile."

I went to Dr. Taylor's office where Kinsey was busy text messaging a supposedly hot college girl. I feigned interest and retrieved my notebook and pen. I wasn't allowed to keep my notebook and pen with me after choking Dan.

"Hey, shut the door. I've been reading this notebook and it's wild. Is it all true?" asked Kinsey. "I'm just curious. Ugh! It's hard to believe, murders and stuff. Are you really possessed by a demon?"

"I just like to write. If you want to read it, please keep what you read to yourself."

"Okay, I can do that. High five!" he said, raising his hand like a dork. I did not raise mine and he stood for an awkward moment, looking hurt, before lowering his arm. "Well, I like reading it and I won't say anything to anyone. I keep it locked up in my private drawer. It beats listening to the radio all night!"

I wanted to ask what else he keeps locked up in his private drawer, but let it go. I took the notebook back to the writing desk and opened it to see where I had left off. The last page contained a poem that I did not remember writing at all, but it was my handwriting. An unsettling feeling came over me, like seeing a photograph from a place you don't recall but you are in the picture, or hearing your recorded voice played back and it does not sound like you but it is. The poem was centered on the page:

November Night

Gray sky at dusk, lifeless
A dark curtain shrouds the trees
Contorted by unseen torture
They've shed their tired leaves
Branches bent towards death
Clipped wings, wilted weeds, spilled blood
Mute rabbits and birds await their dismal, dark fate
A black duck floats belly-up, bloated
From the water's surface rises a thick mist
Coating the feet of a headless saint's statue
A girl smiles at the distant tolling bladed bell
Leaving the branch where the rope is tied
Tightly and taut, the jolted neck snaps
Her body sways in time
To the breezy blackness of night.

I read it and reread it, trying to recall when I had actually written it but there was no memory. Perhaps, I had written after I had hit attacked Dan during the night and they kept me alone for a few days on stronger meds. The current month was November, but who was I referring to as the suicidal girl? Was it Lily? Why would she be suicidal? I liked the poem, but it raised more questions than answers. Sometimes the questions are more interesting. Sometimes the questions are the answers.

Two days later, Mac slipped me my passport while we waited in line to go to lunch. I was shocked to suddenly have it in my hand and quickly tucked it into the blue jumpsuit.

"How the did you get it?" I asked, incredulously.

"Don't worry about it," he replied, with nonchalance, "Oh, there's a ticket with open dates for up to a year waiting for you. All you have to do is swipe your passport at the Delta gate in Orlando and you can catch the next flight to Amsterdam."

"Great!" I replied, my brain lurching into gear about when to escape.

"Once you're there and e-mail me my pics and short biographies, there will be a ticket to Manila from Amsterdam."

"Sweet," I replied, as the voice in my head giggled and said, *Time for us to get on down the line.*

CHAPTER XVII
Shine a Light

Has this world been so kind to you that you should leave with regret?

There are better things ahead than any we leave behind.

—C.S. Lewis

Kinsey, first, thank you for writing back to me in a timely manner. Some of the things, well, all of the shit you wrote is hard to believe. I'm pleased you met with Tessa, isn't she quite wonderful? As for not being able to locate Lily, this is troubling news. Perhaps she is traveling. And you also tell me that Tessa wants Lily dead, why? She already killed someone close to Lily, so it doesn't make much sense. Tread carefully, Kinsey, as Tessa is clever, smart and dangerous. I'm not sure how much she told you about herself, but she is a spirit, a ghost. When a person possessed with Aswang is near her, she has the ability to materialize and fit right in as a genuine person. Don't scoff or doubt me on this, Kinsey, it is information that you need to know.

Lily is also smart and dangerous, not to mention sexy. You know whose side I am on. Do not allow Tessa to sway you and do not go near Lily if Tessa is with you. Stay on the right side here and always remember, Tessa is just an angry ghost and a parasite off of anyone who is afflicted with Aswang. You do not have to avoid her, but never let her know that you and I communicate and try to communicate often. She is crafty, persuasive and deceptively filled with malice.

I'm going to be coming there soon. I can't give an exact date, but let's say within one month. I have to. Every idea and thought I have involves getting near the syndicate again. If you can keep Lily from harm's way by the time I arrive there, I will take care of you when I'm there. We will both be plugged in to the most powerful syndicate in Asia and we will live happily ever after. You've been a fuck up most of your life and now arrives the chance to redeem yourself and change all that. Don't fuck this up.

After lunch, it was time for my one-on-one, spiritual-based counseling with Dr. Taylor in his office. He closed the door after I entered and motioned towards one of the two chairs that were facing each other. "Well, Tim, how are you doing?"

"Just fine, Doc, just fine," I replied, as he came and sat across from me.

"So, no more bad dreams?"

"No, Doc, not since I choked Dan."

"You didn't know it was him that you were attacking, correct?"

"No, I had a huge demon bird on my chest, suffocating me, so I just swung at it and choked it."

"And since then, you've been sleeping okay?"

"Not a wink, Doc. That creature dream scared the living shit out of me. I'm afraid that if I sleep again, I might never wake up."

"Have you read the gospel of Matthew, Tim?"

"I've read it, but I suppose you want to refresh my memory, am I right, Doc?"

"Yes, let me share with you a relevant passage towards your particular situation," he said, retrieving his worn, hard-back Bible from his desk drawer and pulling his chair next to mine before sitting back down. He flipped through the bookmarked pages until locating the particular passage he was after.

"Here it is, Matthew 11:28. This is a verse I would like you to memorize. Jesus said, 'Come unto me all you who are weary and burdened and I will give you rest. Take my yoke upon you and learn from me, for I am gentle and humble in heart, and you will find rest for your souls.' What do you think of the passage, Tim?"

"Well, Doc, it sounds promising, but I'm not sure what it all means," I answered, as the demon in my head added, *It means to kill this fucker and get the fuckety fuck out of here!*

"I think you hit the nail on the proverbial head, Tim. It is promising because it's a promise. Jesus tells us to trust in him, and, in return, we can have peace. We can have a peace that passes all understanding, a peace that allows us to rest easy, in Him."

"How do we actually trust in him, Doc? I mean, most of the time I can't even trust in myself. What I say always seems different than what I actually do or believe."

"Do you believe in Jesus, Tim?"

"Yes," I replied, as the demon taunted, *Fuck Jesus, bastard son of a whore.*

"Then why don't you depend upon him. Take his yoke and rest easy in him?"

"It all sounds great Doc, but how?"

"Well, we can pray about it. You are right, though, I think. It is his will and his power that changes us. Our own efforts are limited at best. Do you want to pray with me, Tim?"

"Sure Doc; I would like that very much."

He pulled his chair close beside mine and closed his Bible, setting it on the floor. "Let us bow our heads," he began.

I clasped my hands together sanctimoniously and bowed my head.

"Dear heavenly father, we thank you for always being faithful and for using us as your tools to help one another, so that we may learn more about you and live better according to your plan for us. Father, today I come before you to ask your spirit to show us the way into your light and to ask that your love might flow through us. I come before you with my friend, Tim, who humbly desires to serve you and honor you . . . "

As he prayed, I opened my eyes and swiftly and silently picked the Bible up from the floor. I stood in front of his chair as he continued to pray, earnestly, with his eyes shut. I gripped the book tightly in both hands near the bottom and swung it like a baseball bat, a powerful roundhouse that struck him in the temple with the spine of the good book. The blow sent him sprawling to the floor, where I continued to rain blows down upon his head.

I'm not sure if I killed him or not, but he wasn't in too good of shape when I took his doctor clothes, credentials and keys. I left Hoffman in three minutes, driving to the airport in Dr. Taylor's new F-150 pickup.

True to his word, Mac had a boarding pass waiting for me in my name. All I needed to do was to scan my passport and I was good to go. I took the boarding pass to the gate and boarded the plane to Amsterdam with no luggage and 12 dollars in my pocket, plus the joy of knowing that I was one step closer to Manila.

There were some logistical concerns about arriving in Amsterdam. I would need a place to stay and I had to figure out a way to eat. There was also the problem of obtaining a camera and getting the cooperation of the girls to photograph. I knew Mac was clever enough that I would have to follow through on my end of the deal. I wasn't sure how, but he would know if I just tried to pass off any random pictures and make up biographies on them. And, well, a deal is a deal and he held true to his end so far.

Schiphol Airport was large, clean and busy with international travelers. There were plenty of signs in English and people speaking in English. I asked around and learned the train from Schiphol made trips to and from Amsterdam every 20 minutes. It was liberating to be free again, to mix right in with the other travelers. The voice in my head echoed, *Nobody here knows what a sick, crazy bastard you are.* I smiled and spoke out loud to myself, *Not a soul.*

I got a token and found the right train platform. Amsterdam was cold and the sky was gray. The train picked up and the doors closed before it started down the track. A woman wearing an official uniform made her rounds, checking everyone's token. I was sitting directly across from a tall, gorgeous girl with auburn hair, wearing a pleated skirt, black heels and a stylish leather jacket. I looked at her, silently wondering if maybe she was a worker in the Red-Light District. She met my stare while reaching into her designer purse and extracting a sandwich in a plastic baggie.

It fascinated me to see a woman so gorgeous just eating with such carefree abandon. She took huge bites, and chewed with her perfectly shaped mouth partly open. An announcement crackled through the train speaker in Dutch, apparently announcing the next stop, which ended with the word "Centraal". The train stopped and some passengers were exiting, so I followed them out into the windy, cool air. I hoped it was the right stop, but when you are not sure where you are going, any stop seems as good as any other.

It did not look like the right stop, since both sides of the tracks were just expansive farm land. The other passengers who got off made their way down the platform and left quickly. I watched the train fade on down the line, and could see my breath in the coolness as I exhaled. A brown rat scurried away from me on the inside rail of one of the tracks. I knew this was not the right stop for Amsterdam and that I should have stayed on the train for at least one more stop.

A pigeon was walking around on the platform, making a low growling noise. It bobbed around about 10 feet away from me. It was as if he was laughing, mocking me even. I reached down and, picking up a medium sized rock, threw it hard and accurate, striking him in the head. It squawked and fell sideways, kicking its legs. I ran towards it and snatched up the bird, staring at the beautiful brightness of the blood running from his head.

I twisted its neck, staring into its eyes as they grew wider. I licked the warm, crimson blood from the dirty white feathers. The irony taste was pleasing and the demon in my head said, *The pretty girl gets the sandwich but the early beast gets the bird.* I put the bird's head in my mouth and bit down hard, ripping it away from the body. I began to chew, and chew, through bone, beak and feather. The blood tasted divine. So far, Amsterdam seemed okay.

I was alone at the platform when the next train arrived. I caught it until the very next stop which was Central Station, the centerpiece of Amsterdam. Nearly all visitors to the city arrive and depart through Central Station. I walked down the stairs of the platform and into the station, continuing up a ramp until reaching the exit doors. I had no idea where I was going, but walked as if I did. Nobody questions you when you walk with a determined look of knowing where you are going.

The wind blew cold. People were whizzing by on bicycles and the trams were running in all directions. I simply decided to walk around, hoping to stumble across the Red-Light District sooner or later. There were small bridges and waterways nearly every block and historic architecture met the eye at every turn. I continued walking, seeing cheese shops, restaurants, coffee shops, clothing shops, art studios and more. Most buildings were straight and narrow, more than 3 stories high with long windows symmetrically appearing on each floor. Red ceramic tiles made synchronized geometric patterns on the rooftops, matching the geometric synchronicity of the cobblestone sidewalks.

After a few hours of walking, covering much of the same ground, I saw a tall, alluring girl coming out of a beauty salon called Body Spice. *Talk to this one,* said the demon in my head.

"Hey, excuse me," I began, "Could you tell me how to get to the Red-Light District?"

She turned to face me, tall, dark and very pretty. She wore a long black coat, with her hands jammed into the pockets, black jeans and black boots.

She looked at me with intimidating, fearless eyes. Her curly hair framed the exotic beauty of her face. This was a strong-willed, independent girl, or so said her authoritative demeanor.

"Yeah," she said, unsmiling, "I'm going that way."

"Okay, cool," I replied, grateful to find a cooperative, pretty, local to help me navigate the puzzling landscape. Her long legs took strides that were difficult for me to keep up with.

"So you live here?" I asked, trying to make small talk.

"Rotterdam," she answered, still looking forward at the ground. "It's a twenty minute train ride. Where are you from, the states?"

"Yes, I'm newly arrived a few hours ago from Florida."

"How long are you here for?"

"Long enough to just take care of a business thing, then I'm going to Manila."

"The Philippines?" she asked, showing a bit of interest. "I have a friend there, well, a business associate. I have not been there yet, but soon. She travels here frequently."

"No shit?" I asked. "It's a small world. I don't think I asked your name. I am Tim."

"I am Romina, Romina Lugosi."

"Kind of scary, but pretty, like you," I said.

"Turn here, Tim," she advised, walking into an alley that was on the side of an old church. The alley became narrower and narrower as we walked. It reached a point where we were forced to turn our bodies sideways and times when we had to slide sideways against strangers traveling in the opposite direction. Eventually, the narrow walkway opened up into a small courtyard.

"So what exactly is your business in Amsterdam, Tim?" she asked, now smiling, which made her less mysterious and threatening.

"You wouldn't believe me if I told you," I replied.

"Oh, I might; let's hear it. Try me."

"I appreciate your interest and all, but it's just a small task I have to do."

Romina smiled, instantly disarming her mysterious and threatening demeanor, "Well, what's the task?"

"I need to get some pictures of some hookers, some pictures and a little interview with each one, about twenty or so."

"Well, Tim, just so you know, they don't really like having their picture taken. After all, they're working girls. I've seen them run after people, shouting, demanding their cameras."

"Great," I replied, with sarcasm, "I like a challenge and I likes me a hooker with attitude."

"Why don't you just pay them to take some pictures? Look at her," she motioned with her head, her long curly hair gently lifted by the cool breeze, towards a shop. Inside the window stood a tall, voluptuous and hourglass shaped girl, with beautiful facial features and long blonde hair cascading down, covering the side of each ample breast. It was odd to see such a fine, young display of exotic beauty from the cold street in the middle of the afternoon, but there she was, dear reader, in all of her stunning glory.

"Damn," I said, in awe.

"I know, right?" added Romina.

"Should I show her all of my twelve bucks or hold back a few?"

Romina laughed, "You flew to Amsterdam with only ten dollars? What the hell?"

"Yeah, but I got a lot of potential."

"Where do you plan to stay? How're you going to survive?"

"I don't have all the logistics mapped out yet."

"Well, I'm pretty sure the girls working here are going to require more than 12 dollars."

"Yeah, so where can a guy find some work around here? Beings that I'm currently broke and homeless, I'll work my ass off."

"Actually, I might have something, but we need to go somewhere and talk a little more."

We walked to a small café called Bagels and Beans. The coffee was served in a bowl-sized cup, much to my liking. Romina ordered a bagel with sun-dried tomatoes.

"So, what kind of work might I be able to find?" I asked, before sipping from the steaming bowl of brew held in two hands.

She stopped eating and placed both of her hands under her chin, meeting my gaze from across the varnished table, her huge brown eyes nearly hypnotizing me. "Well, Tim, I can get your pictures and each of the twenty girls can write something about themselves, a few paragraphs. I can have it for you on paper or as computer files within two days."

"How?"

"I have ways. Don't worry about it. In addition, you can earn a quick thousand Euros.

"This sounds too good to be true," I said, skeptical.

She leaned forward, looking around the room before whispering, "I need you to get rid of somebody. If you can do it and leave the country, it's all the better for both of us."

"I'm in; I have some experience with this line of work." I replied, as the demon in my head agreed, saying, "Fuckin' a right you do. We're back in the saddle again!"

"Alright, tonight you'll stay at my place and we'll fine tune the details. Tomorrow, you do the deed. There's an attic apartment near where we first met today. You show me the head, I give you the pictures. In the morning, you will deliver the head to someone nearby and then go straight to the airport. Sound good?"

"Hacking a head and a surprise delivery; I like it. Can you bring a laptop tomorrow night? I will need to e-mail those files."

"That's not a problem. You're not kind of worried by this?"

"The deed doesn't bother me. I did this stuff for a syndicate. I just don't want to get caught. I have to get back to Manila. May I ask why this person deserves to lose their head?"

"Yes, this bitch calling herself Mistress Diamond is not respecting the ways the Dutch do business. She's just a smart hooker from the Ukraine who got herself plugged in with the Italians here. Fucking Italians; we let them open a few restaurants and pizza joints and they think they can take over Amsterdam. It doesn't work that way."

"So do you mean mistress as in the girlfriend of a husband or a dominatrix or what?"

"She's a wanna be domme, just a dyke with big tits who hates men. I can judge her because I'm a professional, Romina Domina. Well, actually, I have other girls working for me as dominatrixes, but I still keep a few pets of my own," she grinned. "I'm the businesswoman who organizes my girls with clients. I run the outfit. Call Diamond tomorrow and set an appointment. She works off a place at Vossiusstraat." She said, while sliding me a business card across the table with a diamond and whip emblem embossed on it above a phone number.

"I'll call her from a payphone," I said, "Standard protocol for killers."

"Alright, go make the call and tonight you can stay with me. Just so you know, I have a gun, but you seem like a nice guy, though."

"Yeah, and I have no problem killing a bitch for a beautiful new friend. I try to be loyal to friends."

I made the appointment with Mistress Diamond after a brief, customary interview. She wanted to know how old I was, where I was from, what my turn-ons were and how long of a session I wanted. Her rate was 500 U.S. dollars per hour, which I agreed to. She was called Mistress Diamond for a reason. She also stressed the importance of being well-groomed.

At Romina's place, I began to plan and prepare for the murder. There always seemed to be unexpected occurrences when going to kill someone, but it was good to at least have a plan to loosely follow. It had been quite some time before my last "hit" and it was getting me excited to be back in the game again. I was also pleased with my stroke of good luck in being able to get to Manila in short time, and, even better, to arrive with a few bucks in my pocket. I went back and forth on an idea of simply approaching Lily once I arrived in Manila, face to face, and offer her a dozen red roses. I would tell her that the syndicate is my only family and I need to be with them and her and Reshi, sweet, wonderful, beautiful Reshi. No matter how much I weighed all of the pros and cons of such an approach, it always brought me back to the realization that it would depend on Lily's mood at that particular point in time. Her moods were never predictable, never and her heart changed as the wind blew different directions.

Romina gave me all the necessities a killer would need; a backpack, latex gloves, a black leather purse with skulls etched into the leather, a hatchet and a dagger style knife. The leather purse was to keep the severed head in without the blood soaking through the backpack. I was beginning to get the old blood lust back again. My adrenalin was running higher than it had been for many months. I felt fully alive again, dear reader.

It was also familiar ground being with Romina because it felt a bit like the old days of making hits for Lily. I was seething with thirst to kill on the inside, a wild beast, but for Romina, I would gladly do anything. While in Amsterdam, I was her killing machine. Romina must have felt similarly, as she changed into a silky, black jumpsuit with elastic at the wrists and ankles. The loose material flowed breezily from her tall frame as she entered the living room. She walked to the couch with the elegance and poise of Vampirella. She laid back, propped against the armrest and lifted her long legs onto the couch and smiled at me. "The bottoms of my feet are dirty," she said, wiggling her perfect toes with black nail polish, "You want to wash them for me?"

"Sure," I answered, recalling similar, sensual power exchanges with Lily. It seemed the only boss that appealed to my demon was one that was a beautiful, confident and intelligent woman.

"Well, go get the bucket from under the sink and a clean washcloth from the bathroom and warm water and soap. First, bring me the computer," she pointed towards the table, "I'm suppose to Skype with Julio at eight, so just keep it down when I'm talking."

I returned with the warm water, washcloth and soap and kneeled on the floor at the bottom of her feet. They were long, longer than my own, and perfectly shaped and beautiful. I rubbed them with the cloth, gently and firmly, using soap and massaging the contours of her feet. I rinsed the cloth in the bucket and did it again and again as she talked through the computer with a deep male voice with a slight Latin accent coming from the other end. After twenty minutes of cleaning each foot thoroughly, I could no longer resist the urge to lick and kiss her feet. I licked upwards, slowly, on the bottom of her right foot. I was worried how she might react, but she looked over the top of her screen, one eyebrow slightly raised, then smiled and nodded a slight yes. Having the green light, I proceeded to lick and kiss her feet as she continued talking, for another joyful hour. I put away the bucket and cloth when she finished talking. It was time to try to get some rest, though the excitement of killing made it difficult. After she went to her room, I stayed on the couch, reading a book on her coffee table, *Presidential Liability* by Chris Taylor.

I rang the bell and waited at the address Mistress Diamond had given me. The Aswang in my head was active and driven. There was pent up fury. Each time I momentarily closed my eyes, there were splotches of bright red, wrathful red. There was only one concern and it was finding out if anyone else was in her house. My reading the night before had given me an idea right before she answered the door, wearing skin tight leather pants and a black corset. Her figure was voluptuous, but she was going to die regardless.

"Well, Joe (the name I had given her), you're very prompt. I like that. It's a good start. Come inside." I followed her into the small but amply furnished home. There was an area set up like a dungeon, with a St. Peter's cross and a variety of straps, furniture with manacles and whips, chains and paddles adorning the walls.

"Mistress Diamond, before we can begin, I must tell you that I am a high ranking politician back in the states, a congressman. Are you familiar with the United States Congress?"

"No, but if any others need whipped and humiliated, feel free to recommend my services to them," she said, placing her hands on her hips of the shiny leather.

"Well, here's the deal, I need to sweep for hidden cameras or microphones to ensure that I cannot be blackmailed. Is anyone else in the house?"

"Blackmail? Relax, pet, this is an insult. You can follow me through the house and look everything over, but I assure you that we are alone and nothing will be recorded, besides, that would cost extra."

I removed the dagger from the backpack as she was talking and, when she turned to face me, I brought it down from overhead, Altamont style, plunging the tip of the blade into the small concave area at the base of her neck. Her eyes widened in panic as the hard steel went through bone and cartilage. I yanked the blade out and drove it in again, higher up her neck, so that she could not scream. Blood erupted from the gaping wounds as I drove the blade into the middle of her throat a third time. My experience in killing taught me that the neck is the weakest link. Conquer one's neck and the deed is done.

She lay on the floor and I pulled the dagger from her neck, wiping the blood on her couch. I took the hatchet from the backpack and crouched over her nearly lifeless body. I felt like a god. A large pool of crimson blood continued to expand from her neck. I swung the hatchet from overhead, holding it firmly with both of my bloody hands. The impact went through the bones of her frail neck and the hatchet lodged itself into the hard wood floor. I pried it free and made a second blow, completely chopping her head off. It felt inspiring and rejuvenating to kill again. Like color came into the world again and everything was vibrant. I licked the warm blood from my hands and it tasted like life and victory. Picking up the head by her hair, I plunked it into the leather purse and put the purse inside of the backpack with the knife and the hatchet. I washed the remaining blood from my hands. My one hour session lasted a mere 5 minutes. It was time to go.

I secured the backpack and left the house. There appeared to be no witnesses but one could never tell who might be watching from a window. I needed to get to Korte Leidsedwarsstraat. There was an attic style apartment there and Romina had given me the key. It was where I had first met her, coming out of the beauty spa.

I must confess, dear reader, it's an odd feeling to walk through a bustling city with a freshly severed dominatrix's head in your backpack. It's stranger still when you hear the head speaking.

"You'll never get away with this, you stupid bastard, son-of-a-whore!" shouted the distinctive voice of Mistress Diamond. I told myself there was no way possible she could be speaking, and, yet, I could hear her with greater loudness and clarity than when I heard her in her house, while she was alive. Or, was she alive still? I told myself it had to be my imagination, maybe. I tried to focus on the sounds of traffic and the dinging of the tram bells.

"It's not your imagination, you filthy coward, stabbing a defenseless woman! Someone, please stop this man! He's a murderer! Help!" She continued shouting and ranting.

Pull her head out and cut her fucking tongue off, said the Aswang in my head, *That'll shut her up!*

"Help! Police! Murder!" she screamed.

"Just shut the up!" I said, loudly, suddenly aware of the startled people around me. It dawned on me that maybe they could only hear my voice. To make certain, I asked the man next to me waiting to cross the street.

"Excuse me, but do you hear a woman screaming?" I asked, as the head continued to wail from inside my backpack.

"Uhm, no," said the wary pedestrian, "Can't say I do." He turned away and began walking quickly.

While I was relieved others could not hear the head, it was disconcerting to figure out why I heard it. The confusion of her screams made me walk into a collision with an oncoming bicyclist, a sudden blow that knocked me to the pavement and brought me to my senses.

"Are you okay?" asked the gorgeous Dutch girl, after bringing her tank-like bike to a wobbly stop.

"Is he okay? He's a murdering coward!" shouted the head.

"I'm fine, and I must apologize," I said, getting back to my feet, "I wasn't paying attention."

I made it to the attic apartment and waited with the talking head. I wondered if Mac had sent me an e-mail yet. By now, I was probably featured on John Walsh's America's Most Wanted show. I also knew Mac would be suspicious that I could send pictures and bios of 20 girls in such a short time, so I hoped some of the girls provided their e-mail in order for him to verify they were legitimate.

"You are a coward! Killing girls, real tough guy you are!" came the endless loud bitching from my backpack. I considered stomping on the head, crushing it under foot. I knew Romina wanted it delivered and there must be a reason. Her face would need to be recognizable to send a message.

I saw a bathtub and began to run the water. My theory was that a submerged head can make no noise. As I waited for the tub to fill, I pulled the blood drenched head from the purse. "My hair still feels nice, doesn't it killer?" she asked, seductively. I felt the silky, smooth hair, damp with blood it still felt enticing. Inexplicably, I began to get aroused. "Mistress still makes you hard, doesn't she?" It was true, though I did not want to admit it. "Kiss me, killer. Nobody will ever know. My lips are warm for you."

I gave in and held her face to my own. Her lips came to life, puckering and nibbling on mine. Her tongue thrust into my mouth. We continued to kiss and I turned the bath water off. It had been a long time since I kissed a woman. I removed my clothes and entered the tub, holding her head above the water. Blood continued to drip into the water. We continued to kiss.

"Mistress wants you, Killer. Will you kiss her with passion?"

And I did, closing my eyes, our tongues circling one another, before tenderly nibbling on each other's lips. As I opened my eyes, I saw Romina standing in the doorway of the bathroom with a shocked expression on her face. The house of cards collapsed and the dark fantasy ended promptly. I suddenly felt like the perverted madman that I was.

"Well, that was certainly interesting," she said.

"Uhm, it's not really what it looks like," I said, dropping the head where it splashed into the blood stained bath water. I quickly put my clothes back on.

"Okay," she said, dragging the y out with hint of sarcasm. "Once you're done with your blood bath, come out here. I got the files you wanted."

I finished dressing, leaving the head to soak in the tub, and hurried out to the table. "I'm sorry about that. I really wasn't expecting company."

"Hey, whatever you're in to. Just so you get the head delivered to Peppinos in the morning."

"It's that restaurant around the corner? Do I personally hand it to the guy or what?"

"Yes, right around the corner; and you can just walk in and leave it on a table or even the counter, if you can. Make sure it is in the black skull purse so they will know who it's from; just a friendly reminder to the Italians not to play around with Dutch business in Amsterdam."

"Alright, so I drop the head off at Peppinos and that's that?"

"Yes, then we're done. Here," she said, handing me a stack of crisp Euros. "There's a thousand there. Also, the pics you wanted are on the laptop in a folder named girls. Each girl already had a professional bio used for potential clients, so those are included.

"They have contact information too, like e-mail?"

"E-mail and phone"

"Sweet!"

"Can I ask why you wanted this?"

"It's a long story, but, believe it or not, I was in the nuthouse for awhile back in the states," I began.

"Oh? After your little date in the bathroom, I can believe it."

"Yes, well, one of the other patients there was real smart with computers, but a real pervert."

"If you call someone a pervert, they must really be messed up. So this guy wanted pictures of girls?"

"Yeah, but not just girls, he always wanted to see girls in Amsterdam, like real girls, not models and stuff."

"Well, my girls are real, and they are all from the Netherlands. Most of them are pretty enough to be models."

"Okay, I just need about an hour with the laptop to write a few e-mails and send him the files."

"No problem, Tim; you can keep it tonight. Just leave it on the table, with the key, when you leave. Peppinos opens around 9, so you probably want to get there early and drop off the head."

"Okay, will I see you again?"

"I have your e-mail. I do business with some people in Manila, so chances are good I might see you there next month. I will e-mail you."

"Okay Romina; thank you for everything and I hope to see you again soon!"

"Good luck to you, Tim. Try not to get anymore head tonight," she said, laughing, "Bye!"

"I'll try," I said, hugging her.

The e-mail from Mac informed me that Dr. Taylor was alive, though still hospitalized. There were new staff members there in his and Kinsey's absence, but things weren't much different. Surprisingly, I also had an e-mail from Dandelion. It sounded like he had caught some Aswang too and was in the mood to travel. I would have to think that one over. I wrote to Mac and told him I needed the ticket to Manila by tomorrow, within 12 hours. I also sent him the files and told him they were legitimate, authentic Amsterdam girls. I asked him to write to me as soon as he bought the ticket. Within a mere 15 minutes, Mac forwarded me the receipt of my ticket to Manila. Deviant or not, Mac was a stand up guy.

In fished the head out of the bloody bath water and put it inside the black purse. I double-checked my pocket for my passport. In just nine hours I would be on my way to Schiphol. In nineteen hours, I would be back in Manila.

I tossed and turned on the couch. Sometime in the night, I heard someone in the apartment. "You're a sick one, Tim. Wake up! I know your name is Tim. You won't get away with this," chimed the voice of Mistress Diamond, from the black leather purse.

"Just shut the hell up!" I yelled, only half awake from the couch. It didn't bother me that a head without a body was talking, it bothered me that it's yammering on and on was interfering with my sleep.

"Lily is dead," she said.

"How do you know?" I demanded, "How do you even know who Lily is?"

"She killed herself."

"Shut the fuck up," I said, now fully awake and angry.

The voice continued, calm, rational, "The dead know the dead. Right now, all hundred and five pounds of her is swaying from a rope tied to a tree branch in North Cemetery."

"No!" I shouted, "You're a liar," I said, going and getting the leather bag and taking it to the refrigerator. The silence was relieving, but it was impossible to rest. I kept wondering if Lily really was hanging from a tree in North Cemetery. Anything was possible. *The dead do know the dead.*

In the morning, I left the key by the laptop and put the folded leather bag containing the refrigerated head under my arm and walked to Peppinos. The guy working watched me enter, so I ordered an espresso and sat near the door, placing the purse on the chair beside me. When the guy behind the counter had his back turned, I left 10 Euros on the table and made an exit, leaving the purse on the chair after pushing the chair all the way in. It would be found, but probably not until I was high in the air.

At Schiphol there was a flight to Manila already boarding when I arrived and scanned my passport to check-in. I was in the airport for a mere 20 minutes before finding myself in a seat on the plane. It was even more pleasing to learn that Mac had given me an upgrade to first-class seating. He must have liked the pictures Romina provided. It would be a long flight and I wasn't worried about anything going wrong. My demon was appeased since we were traveling towards Manila and not away from. I was even able to get a little sleep in during the flight.

The Manila airport was crowded as usual and the drab, off-yellow walls had little effect on dampening my enthusiasm at returning to the city I loved. Just seeing a throng of Filipino people again brought me joy. They were full of energy and optimism like no other people in the world. The Pinoy magic is contagious and I could see it and smell it in the air. Even the hour wait in the foreign passport line was joyful. I looked forward to seeing and talking and belonging to the syndicate once more. I wanted to reunite with the boss lady, to become her most loyal killing machine again.

As I walked into the throng of people and traffic outside of the airport, a sense of nostalgia washed over me. This was the same place that Lily had picked me up when I first arrived with Pete, with a suitcase full of dildos, more than a year ago. It was all lust, infatuation, hope and excitement then. Now, well, I wasn't sure what it was or would be, but I had hope and I had a strategy; find Lily or die trying.

I took a cab to the corner of Ayala and Makati Avenue and booked a room at the Shangri-La. It had been more than a year and I felt confident that the syndicate had moved on to more profitable and important ventures than having a hit on me. The speed of change in Manila was at a faster rate than most cities and hot topics today were long forgotten tomorrow. I decided the best way to test the climate of the syndicate was through the Giraffe, which was right around the corner.

Entering the Giraffe, I immediately recognized Raina. She was with a white gentleman, wearing an Armani suit, nearly twice her age at the bar. Her hair was longer, her dress was shorter and her boobs were bigger. She looked to be doing well and I wondered if it was the lovelorn expat she was currently with or another one who paid for her boob job. It looked like a valuable investment for some gullible sap. I approached the bar and her smile widened. She told the guy she was with to wait and not worry, then came and hugged me, her larger breasts mashing into my body. They felt worth every peso put into them. "Tim; I thought you were dead! How have you been?"

"Good, real good and as you can see, I'm still alive. I miss you. I missed everyone; how are things with everyone here?"

Raina ran her fingers through her silky black hair, pulling it outwards from the right side of her head. "My hair is longer; do you like it?"

"Love it, kiddo, you look fantastic. Listen, I know you have to do your thing here, but if you're free later, I'd love to see you."

"Sure, Tim; what do you have in mind?"

"Well, nothing too kinky. I just want to get caught up. I'm in 406 at the Shangri La."

"Okay, right next door; I'll be up around two in the morning."

I spent the next few hours shopping for some clothes and stocking up on some of my favorite Filipino food, spring rolls, lumpia, sugary bacon and crispy pata all packaged up to bring back to the room. I also used the business center to talk with Mac on Yahoo Messenger. He informed me that he hadn't heard from Kinsey in weeks and we were both concerned because it was out of character for Kinsey not to stay in touch. The dumbass must have gotten in over his head with something.

Raina arrived at 2:30, looking gorgeous in a skin tight black dress and sporting a Louis Vuitton handbag. She was pleased to see I had food and we ate together, using the microwave. "So, is this a date, Tim?" she asked, before taking a bite of lumpia.

I laughed, "No kiddo, don't flatter yourself. I can't afford a date with you anyways. You're beautiful, but young enough to be my daughter."

"Well, you would have gotten a discount, daddy, but I see how it is. Where did you go for so long?"

"I had to go back to the U.S. for awhile, when I killed the asshole German, Paul, things got real screwed up."

"I remember that; everyone was talking about it!"

"Yeah, well, I hope they've forgotten it. Paul will never hit you again though, will he?"

"So that's why you killed him?" She smiled, "I was young and naïve back then. I know my shit now; don't waste time on abusive assholes."

"So, let me get to the point, Raina, is Lily around?"

"Tim, I need to make a phone call. Just to be safe. She wanted you dead, remember?"

Raina used her phone and spoke in Tagalog. After ending the call, she said, "Tim, Juvi is going to pick you up out front at ten in the morning, okay?"

"Juvi; he's the best damn cabbie in Manila! So is she going to kill me? Was that her on the phone?"

"Just go with Juvi at ten; everything will be fine. I need to go now, love." She said, before we embraced and she walked out.

The next morning, Juvi was right on schedule. "Juvi; how are you?" I asked. He got out of the cab and walked around to hug me.

"Tim, we missed you here, my friend," he said, smiling. "I'm happy you made it back!"

"I feel the same," I said, as we both got into his cab. "So how are things with the best cab driver in Manila?"

He laughed, "Oh, I'm not the best, I just have the best friends," he said, before answering his ringing phone. He spoke in Tagalog while driving one-handed through a sea of vehicles, cutting the wheel, punching the horn, speeding up, slowing down. Juvi made driving in Manila look effortless. We arrived at the St. Francis Tower in Mandaluyong City just as Juvi ended his phone call. "Go up to suite 1009 and call me when you need a ride back, okay Tim?"

"Juvi, you don't think Lily still has a hit on me, do you? I mean, am I walking into her death trap here?"

"Everything will be fine my friend," he reassured.

"Famous last words," I smiled, "Okay, Juvi, great to see you and see you again soon!"

I nervously rode the elevator up to the tenth floor. Lily was always unpredictable, but she also was not one to let bygones be bygones. In business matters, she always followed through. It was a gamble I would have to take. I would either be back on board with the syndicate, part of the family, or I would be buried under the ground. I took a deep breath and knocked at 1009.

A short haired, muscular Filipino man in his 20's wearing a tight black designer t-shirt and sunglasses opened the door. I was pretty sure that he looked like one of the fake policemen that first hauled Pete and I out of the Mirage, way back during my first visit to Manila. He also wore a pistol in a holster.

"Hi, I'm here to see Lily," I said, trying to mask my fear.

"Just go through that door," he said, coldly, pointing to a door that was open at the end of a hallway. As I walked towards the hallway, he stepped outside and shut the door, probably to stand on watch. I was a little more worried. A female voice from behind another door, off to my left. I stopped to listen.

"Tim, in here," she said.

I opened the door and was startled to see Reshi, dressed in a sexy leather policewoman outfit, sitting on the long counter of the bathroom sink. From the police cap on her head, to her black shiny boots, her aura of sexuality made it difficult for me to think clearly or even speak. I began to get instantly aroused. "Reshi?"

"Hi Tim; you're not disappointed to see me, are you?"

"Uh, no, not at all," I said.

"It's about time you got your handsome ass back here."

"Where's Lily?"

"It's time you forget about her, Tim. I mean, she did have a hit on you, right? I will have you know that I was against it."

"Yeah, I remember the hit, but that was awhile ago. I was hoping to be with the syndicate again. I want to rejoin my family."

She moved her leg, bending the knee upwards, and her leg held a hypnotic effect on me. I gazed at the shiny boot as she spoke, "You will need to make a choice. The syndicate is divided right now and I know she is planning and plotting against me. I don't know where she is, but Jolen told me a few weeks ago that she was going to Bangkok with some big-shot banker named Mike. She's always going to Bangkok to Bangkok."

"You two are fighting, why?"

"It started when she put the hit on you and I made Jolen get you on a plane, alive. She found out and was furious, like unreasonably livid."

"So you were the one to have Jolen deliver my passport and airfare?"

"Yes"

"Where is Jolen?"

"That's a good question. His loyalty is torn, since he adores both of us. I think she will keep him, though. He likes her more. She also has Sonny with her."

"So the syndicate has fallen apart?"

"Not at all, it's just different. I'm running mine and she is running hers. Mine already is making more money than hers ever dreamed of. I have the political network and business contacts on my side. I need some soldiers, though. Someone loyal and fearless, someone who will do anything for me and that I can trust with my life. I want you, Tim."

"I'm in, Reshi; in my heart I have always been with you. It's just that, well, Lily was the boss and a control freak."

She smiled, "You talk a good game, but how do I know I can trust you and count on you? I mean, you once swore allegiance to Lily?"

"In time, my actions will prove my worth, Reshi. I will do anything for you and your syndicate. I will kill anyone at anytime that you wish."

"You have had fits of going crazy and doing unpredictable things, but I know why."

"I have a spirit in me, in my head," I said, "It's Aswang and sometimes it takes over, yes."

"How do you think you caught the spirit, Tim?"

"I've had nightmares and blackout spells since I got to Manila the first time. It all started with a rat I saw, or a Japanese broad named Lucy. I never felt right after seeing them."

"Tim, it's not a rat or Lucy," said Reshi, smiling. It was difficult to look into her beautiful eyes without succumbing to lustful thoughts.

"Then how did I get it?"

"From Lily, silly."

"How can you know that?"

"Just trust me on it. Have you noticed it's always worse when you are away from her? She uses it to control you."

"I'm confused, if she controlled it, then how come everything went to shit and she tried to have me killed?"

"Well, she's not just a bitch, but she's also something of a witch. She is capable of infecting people she chooses with Aswang, but she cannot control Aswang well. The spirit has a mind of its own. Plus, she drinks like a thirsty fish. Nobody can make very wise decisions when they're escaping reality all the time."

"You seem to know a lot about it," I said.

"I know the nightmares will end if you are with me. I just don't know if you are really with me or if your heart is still with Lily."

You've been barking up the wrong tree, Killer. Serve this one, said the demon inside my head.

"I have desired to serve you since I first saw you, Reshi. Hell, since the time you came to pick up those dildos at the Mirage. It's just that I was already with Lily by then and she was the leader."

"You can have a new leader, just as twisted, shrewd and kinky, but more loyal, rewarding and stable. I need a right-hand soldier, a personal bodyguard, a confidante and a 24/7 assistant who I can trust completely. I need a guy who has brains, brawn and balls, and is attractive. Business is booming. Can I trust you, Tim?"

"Yes, Reshi, I am yours. You know, I have even dreamed about you, dressed like you are now, a sexy policewoman. It must have been a sign or something."

"What happened in that dream, Tim?"

"I made love to you."

"So, it wasn't a nightmare?"

"No, well, the nightmare was when I woke up."

"Now, let me be clear, Tim. The situation with Lily, the division, there is no going back to her if you choose my side. It will be a permanent commitment. You can leave this office right now, and there will be no problems from me. How loyal will you be?"

"Reshi, I always had stronger feelings for you, but there was just no way to express them. You know how Lily is. I don't feel so screwed up when I'm with you. I've belonged with you from day one, Reshi."

"Can I put your loyalty to the test, Tim?"

"Anything," I said, confidently.

"Kiss my boot," she said, sliding the shiny toe forward. I leaned over it and slowly kissed the shiny surface. "Now tell me, when I was dressed just like this in your dream, what else happened?"

"I kissed and licked your boots."

"And then?"

"Then you wanted me to make love to you, so I did."

"And then?"

"Then we made love."

"Hmmm, I see, interesting," she said, turning on the counter so that both boots dangled over the edge. "I think we're going to make your dream become real. When you had the dream, you belonged to Lily. You belong to me now, right, Tim?"

"Yes, Reshi,"

"Good; come here then and kiss me,"

"Yes Reshi" I said, moving in closer towards her lips and enjoying the feel of her flesh against mine. We proceeded to kiss, fondle, rub and embrace, before ending up on the floor of the bathroom. I was as hard as a diamond as she removed her police uniform. I removed my clothes.

"Lay on the floor, pet. I want to ride that hard cock. That's for me, isn't it?"

"It's all yours," I said, lying on my back. She approached, wearing nothing but her shiny black boots and a police cap. She mounted me and my head felt as if it had pierced the clouds and hurled into the forbidden pleasures sequestered for Heaven. Her beauty, her body, her flesh and her form were more rewarding than I had dreamed. Her technique was also beyond what I could long endure. I screamed and gasped and drank of the milk of paradise.

After putting my pants back on, I said, "Reshi, you are amazing."

"Hmmm, call me Queen Reshi. I always wondered how that might sound."

"Queen Reshi, you are amazing."

"I like that, has a nice ring to it. Do you love me, Tim?"

"I love you Queen Reshi. I love you with all my heart."

I felt a sense of relief to belong, though it was different now, I belonged. I was a part of the family and I was Reshi's killing machine. I would spill the blood of the world, but I would obey her. She put my Aswang at peace with my head. With Reshi, I could have control over myself, by allowing her to control me. She called me from another room.

I went to where she was typing on a laptop. "Okay, Tim, your first job is going to be at the old warehouse in Caloocan. I took ownership of Lily's syndicate property there, but I need a killer watchdog there, someone who will guard the place fearlessly and ferociously; someone with the balls to move in there. I had a guard there, but he was a chickenshit. You're the only hardcore soldier I have right now, Tim. I need a few more like you. I got the moneymen and the lawmakers on my side, but to survive in Manila, I need a few warriors. You are a badass. I need a badass."

"Is the warehouse being used?"

"Just for storage; right now I have high-end electronics, arms and some other black-market goods all waiting to export to Vietnam, Canada and Holland. The next week is crucial to have someone there. Lily's people know the warehouse inside out. I know she has people in the area, scouting. All locks have been changed and an alarm system is in place, but we both know Lily. The good thing is, I know I can count on you. You have a reputation here; a ruthless killing machine and Lily's people will not be happy you're with the winning team. You got this, right?"

"Sure, as long as I have a gun with some ammo. I can't fend off Sonny and crew without hardware."

"Okay, I'm giving you the master key. The alarm code is on the keychain. You'll find a crate of various guns, silencers, scopes and ammunition all in the meeting room. Hell, your cot is still there too. Here's a cell phone with my personal number in the contacts, you can call me anytime for any reason, even if you're just lonely, got it?"

"Oh yeah; it's all good, Reshi. Thank you; I'm happy to be on board!" I said, as we hugged.

"Juvi's number is in your phone, call him," she said, before leaving the suite.

It was an odd feeling of déjà vu coming back to the Caloocan warehouse. Things were not much different. There were some new light fixtures installed and switches on the wall. The main warehouse held rows of good all on pallets, making it look like a genuine warehouse. There was no longer the open empty space or the ping-pong table that Jolen and I played hundreds of games on.

Down the hall, my cot was still there and there was also plenty of food in the kitchen area. The meeting room contained new computers, a large copy machine, printers and shelves and filing cabinets. It looked more like a business office now instead of just a room with a big table supporting empty beer cans. I sat down at one of the computers and logged in to check my e-mail.

There were two e-mails from Mac. One was forwarded from Kinsey:

Mac,

> *Please tell Tim to call me when he gets to Manila! Lily wants him back in the syndicate and said she misses him!! It's very urgent and important that he calls me: 905-874-4490. Or he can e-mail me at this address! Me and him are going to rock the Philippines together!!*
>
> *Hope things are good at the nut house; oh yeahhhh!!!*
> *Talk soon!*

Kinsey

Well, in addition to loving exclamation points, it also seems Kinsey loves betraying friends. The key lie was Lily missing me. I know Lily, she's just keeping Kinsey around long enough to lure me in, then we both would be killed. In his ignorance, Kinsey probably doesn't know any better, doesn't know he's a mere dispensable pawn in Lily's chess game. The naïve lout didn't stand a chance against the calculating shrewdness of Lily.

The other e-mail was from Mac. Apparently Dr. Taylor was back at the hospital and he claims that he forgives me for attacking him. He also wished that I hadn't run because he feels we were at a crossroads in bringing me to Jesus, but I took a wrong turn, or my demon possessed me to take a wrong turn. Mac also said that for as annoying as Taylor's preachy ways can be, he likes the guy for his heart of gold. I suppose I agree, though it's much easier to be rational now that I am with Reshi.

Mac also shared how Dandelion will not stop bothering him about coming to see me. Apparently he will be released soon and claims to have a passport. Outside of his fascination with talking about poop, Dandelion was a pretty trustworthy kind of guy. Reshi needed killers. I could train him. What the hell, I'll give Mac the green light to tell Dandelion to get on a plane. It's not too much of a leap from the nuthouse to the warehouse. There wasn't room in Manila for two powerful syndicates each led by an independent, beautiful woman. Soon, I knew, there would be war. A bloody, vicious and ugly war was on the horizon. I knew Lily was preparing for the battle. It was time to recruit some soldiers I could trust and count on. The shit storm was on the horizon.

I was able to sleep peacefully for the first time in a very long time, alone, with a loaded gun beside the cot. I belonged with Reshi. There were no rats, no voices, no nightmares and no black dogs. I slept for nearly a full six hours and only had one dream that I recalled with clarity. It was not a nightmare. I saw Lily, hanging from a tree by a rope and all one-hundred and five pounds of her gently swayed to and fro. I woke up with a smile.